Theaker's Quarterly Fiction #50

Edited by
Stephen Theaker
and John Greenwood

Theaker's Quarterly Fiction #50

Edited by
Stephen Theaker
and John Greenwood

Cover Artist

Howard Watts

Contributors

Jacob Edwards
Howard Watts
Walt Brunston
Rafe McGregor
Howard Phillips
David Tallerman
Douglas J. Ogurek
Mitchell Edgeworth
Matthew Amundsen
Antonella Coriander
Michael Wyndham Thomas

ISBN (print): 978-1-910387-05-4
ISBN (epub): 978-1-910387-06-1

ISSN (print): 1747-6083
ISSN (online): 1747-6075

Website: www.theakersquarterly.blogspot.com

Email: theakersquarterlyfiction@gmail.com

Lulu Store: www.lulu.com/silveragebooks

Feedbooks: www.feedbooks.com/userbooks/tag/tqf

Submissions: Submissions are very welcome! See website for guidelines and terms.

Advertising: We welcome ad swaps with small press publishers and other creative types, and we'll run ads for relevant new projects from former contributors.

Sending material for review: We are interested in reviewing almost anything that's fantasy-related. We prefer to receive books for review in epub or mobi format. Feel free to send ebooks without querying first. We have reviewed about 14% of items received, though many of those reviewed are things we've actively requested.

Mission statement: The primary goal of *Theaker's Quarterly Fiction* is to keep going. We need a new secondary goal, since we have not only caught up with *McSweeney's* but overtaken them (in issue numbers if not fame).

Published in Theaker's Paperback Library
on 31 January 2015.

Contents

CONTENTS

Interview

The Quarterly Review

Reviews by Stephen Theaker, Jacob Edwards, Douglas J. Ogurek, and Howard Watts

CONTENTS

Fifty Issues!

Stephen Theaker

Ten years and fifty issues! Our primary goal was to keep going, and we've done pretty well so far!

We put out a call for former contributors to return for this one, and we are so grateful to all those that did. Rafe McGregor and David Tallerman, Michael Wyndham Thomas and Matthew Amundsen, Douglas J. Ogurek and Mitchell Edgeworth, Howard Watts and Howard Phillips. I even managed to persuade my co-editor John Greenwood to drag a story from his trunk for us, not to mention the returns of Walt Brunston and Antonella Coriander, whose secret identities are at last revealed in our celebratory *Ask Theaker's* feature!

Of course this issue, bringing together so many former contributors, demonstrates one of our biggest weaknesses: a lack of female contributors. I don't think we received a single submission from a female writer last year. That's not to blame them; the terms we offer are terrible! If we offered better terms we'd receive submissions from a wider selection of writers, and you can't really reach out to authors to beg stories unless you know them well or have some money to offer.

I'll keep trying to make sure the work that female writers are doing in fantasy and science fiction is at least apparent from our review pages.

What's next? No big changes. Maybe fewer issues a year, maybe shorter issues – the last four issues have been a lot of work! The BFS took up quite a bit of my time last year, but I hope that won't be as true in 2014, giving me more time for you (and the little Theakers). In this issue's review section you can see my notes on books I've *Also Read*, an attempt to clear the backlog that had built up. I'd like to write more short reviews and post them to the blog more quickly, to stop a new backlog accumulating; *Also Read* may well become a regular feature. Assuming that submissions from the general public will continue to decline, I'm going to have to put more work into writing my own material for the zine, get into the habit of writing a new chapter of each serial especially for each issue rather than just writing fiction in November.

Was it worth it? That's the question that came to mind looking back over these fifty issues. People do sometimes ask why I don't put the effort instead into something more commercial, but that's what I do in the daytime. This is my weekend project hobby, and I'm finding it as rewarding as ever. It's a place to experiment, to be indulgent, to mess about, to do stupid stuff, to make friends, to put my daytime skills to fun use. Thank you to all the contributors from the last ten years who have made this so rewarding; to Howard Watts, whose experimental, playful approach to his covers is so much in tune with the spirit of the zine; to my co-editor John Greenwood, for keeping the magazine running during those years when I had no time to read submissions; and to you, our theoretical reader, for theoretically reading this.

A shout-out as well to the other zines, magazines, and small press publications from whom we drew so much inspiration and motivation and sometimes stole ideas: *Midnight Street*, *Morpheus Tales*, *Dark Horizons*, *Nemonymous*, *Jupiter*, *Postscripts*, *Estronomicon*, *Pantechnicon*, *The Third Alternative*, *Andromeda Spaceways Inflight Magazine*, *Apex*, *Murky Depths*, *Black Static*, *Interzone*, and of course *McSweeney's Quarterly Fiction*, without issue ten of which we would not be here. Some of those magazines have disappeared, some have transmogrified, a few are doing better than ever. Rivals, friends, enemies and unrequited crushes, we salute them all! Our zine wouldn't be the same without them.

Contributors

Antonella Coriander's story in this issue, "Crystal Castle Crashers", is the fourth consecutive episode of her ongoing Oulippean serial.

David Tallerman writes "The House That Cordone Built", which follows "Imaginary Prisons" (#29), "Friendly" (#31), "Glass Houses" (#34) and "Devilry at the Hanging Tree Inn" (#37). Angry Robot Books published his acclaimed Easie Damasco trilogy: *Giant Thief*, *Crown Thief* and *Prince Thief*.

Douglas J. Ogurek lives in a Chicago suburb with the woman whose husband he is and their five pets. This time he reviews the films *As Above, So Below*, *The Hunger Games: Mockinjay, Part 1* and *Tusk*, and supplies a story too: "Save the Dog", a sequel of sorts to "NON" (#33). See www.douglasjogurek.weebly.com.

Howard Phillips is a dissolute poet whose contributions to this zine have ranged from the mediocre to the abysmal. In this issue he begins a follow-up to the still unfinished Saturation Point Saga: "Love at First Sight" is the first episode of *A Dim Star Is Born*.

Howard Watts is a writer, artist and composer living in Seaford who provides the cover art for this issue, an article on his covers for us to date, a story ("Dodge Sidestep's Second Dastardly Plan"), and a review of *Borderlands the Pre-Sequel*.

Jacob Edwards reviews *Gatchman* and *Interstellar* in this issue. This writer, poet and recovering lexiphanicist's website is at www.jacobedwards.id.au, his Facebook page at https://www.facebook.com/JacobEdwardsWriter.

John Greenwood, co-editor and guiding ethical light, supplies this issue with the story "A Mare's Nest".

Matthew Amundsen follows up "House of Nowhere" (#35) with a new novella, "A Murder in Heaven". He has written extensive literary and music criticism for various alternative weeklies. He now lives in Minneapolis, Minnesota, with his wife and daughter.

Michael Wyndham Thomas writes "One Is One". We previously published his novels *The Mercury Annual* and *Pilgrims at the White Horizon*, extracts from both of which are sprinkled through our zine's history.

Mitchell Edgeworth writes "Heritage", sixth in the *Black Swan* series of stories, following "Homecoming" (#40), "Drydock" (#42), "Flight" (#43) and "Customs" (#46) and "Abandon" (#47). He keeps a blog at www.grubstreethack.wordpress.com.

Rafe McGregor provides this issue with "The Wrong Doctor", which follows "Murder in the Minster" (#25), "The Chapel on the Headland" (#34) and "The Last Testament" (#37).

Stephen Theaker lives with three slightly smaller Theakers. In this issue he reviews *Engines of War*, *Happy*, *In the Broken Birdcage of Kathleen Fair*, *Invincible, Vol. 17*, *Megalex* and *The X-Files: Season 10, Vol. 1*, and rounds up everything else he read this year.

Walt Brunston, follows his adaptation of a *Space University Trent* episode (#13) – we still miss that show! – with "The Morning of Seventeen Suns", the first astounding adventure of the Two Husbands.

Artful Theakering

Creating cover art for Theaker's Quarterly Fiction

Howard Watts

This winter marks my fifth anniversary of producing cover art for *Theaker's Quarterly Fiction*, some twenty covers, so I thought I'd tell you a little concerning how some of these images came about, and how they were produced.

Firstly, a few details about this issue's cover and what it represents. The robot at the bottom right is a version of Steven Gilligan's pencil-drawn robot from way back when. The UFOs preparing to land top right are versions of Stephen's UFO drawing. The dragon coming into land at the back of the chair is a nod to Stephen's extensive work for the British Fantasy Society. The astronaut in the centre is reading the first issue of TQF – again, a version of TQF's astronaut that holds a flag with the UFO on it, although sans waistcoat. The three other figures are simply generic SF: an alien, a hero and a heroine. To the left of the group in the distance is a rocket ship – something I added to give the cover a hint of retro, with the previous issues of TQF trailing either to the rocket, or from it.

The time has flown by working on TQF, I must admit – and to be honest, I cannot remember how I came to submit art to Stephen in the first instance. I'd

produced a couple of covers for the BSFA's *Focus* magazine, back in 1995/96, which were simple black and white drawings produced on my Acorn Archimedes. Then around 2004/2005 I stumbled across a free download of a 3D rendering programme called Bryce 5. This software, originally intended for fractal landscape rendering and animation, immediately seized my imagination with its potential.

My first rendered pieces were fairly basic, as Bryce proved (and still does today, to a degree) to be a very complex programme with a steep learning curve. On the face of it, Bryce's main render screen makes the software look fairly basic. It provides the user with a standard group of primitives such as cube, sphere, cone, pyramid, torus and cylinder. These can be instantly created with a single click of the mouse, and then edited through the X, Y, and Z planes, resized, grouped together and even subtracted from each other to create voids. Clicking the "Create" tab offers dozens of other shapes over various categories, and once I started clicking around, I found there were almost limitless options provided within the interface. It's when I delved into Bryce's materials section by clicking on the tiny "M" next to an object that the software's potential was understood. The materials are many and varied, ranging from metals, glass, waters, wood, stones, terrains, vegetation, flooring and crazy effects. All are all editable and can then be saved as user presets – but a word of warning, this can be highly addictive and time consuming until your edited preset renders exactly as you've imagined. I've had a dozen or so successes over the years creating my own materials, but the real beauty of Bryce is its ability to produce stunning landscapes from start-up.

The terrain editor allows you to "paint" mountains up into the sky, or erode them to produce river beds. Again, the options in the terrain editor are enormous. Coupled with the sky presets and editor (enabling you to place the sun exactly where you want it and define its colour, as well as alter cloud height, shape and density) acceptable landscapes are just a few clicks away.

As my fiddling with this software continued, I discovered (both by accident, and online research) hidden screens and keyboard shortcuts enabling me to tweak the standard settings, and I found myself tinkering with the software for great lengths of time, rather than actually concentrating on producing a finished piece. Following a year or so of laughable results, three of my "completed" pieces found their way onto the covers of the now sadly defunct *Fiction Magazine* during 2007. *Picture 1* is the best of the three. Today, it reminds me of the Chris Foss covers for Asimov novels from the 1980s.

Picture 1. Cover for Fiction Magazine.

I continued to experiment with the software, but soon found my Windows XP PC struggling with the millions of polygons I'd clicked into existence. It seemed for a while that the majestic cityscapes of alien worlds I'd imagined in my head would have to be not so majestic after all, as the software continued to crash, or refuse to remember all the shapes I required, giving me an "OUT OF MEMORY!" freeze message. One hugely complex cityscape piece in particular, entitled

Picture 2. Departure.

"Departure" (see *Picture 2*), refused to be brought to life, time and time again. I then had an idea. Within the Bryce File menu is an option to save the completed render as a JPEG. So, borrowing an idea from movie special effects, I rendered a quarter of the piece's completed city section and saved it as a JPEG. This can be done quite simply by using "Plop Render" option, and is achieved by highlighting an area of the render by clicking and dragging, then hitting a little button to render just that area then saving it as a JPEG. Going back to the piece in wireframe mode, I selected sections of the cityscape, dragged them into a new position, rotated them 45 degrees and rendered that area, again, saving it as a JPEG. This "compositing" jigsaw method gave me a collection of JPEG layers that, once knitted together in Photoshop, completed the piece. It took a great deal of concentration, time and care, as many times my jigsaw JPEGs were either incomplete or inconsistent with the background master file and/or with previous jigsaw pieces. I've since refined and employed this method of working, notably for the covers of TQF issues, 33, 36, 40, and the cover of this issue. Reflecting on *"Departure"* the ship looks a little silly; constructed of basic primitives it lacks thought.

At this stage I'd like to mention something a dear friend of mine once told me. He was a superb watercolour artist and illustrator – in fact the first artist to ever draw Doctor Who's K9 for a fanzine. We were discussing photography, and he told me it takes a split second to take a photograph, and, depending on the subject, perhaps a little longer to actually look at it. Art however, has time painted into it. It takes the artist time to complete a piece. Therefore, there's more information. It takes longer to look at than a photograph. I thought about this and agreed, and this belief pushed me toward building more complex scenes, more interesting pieces.

My first acceptable pieces came simply out of my imagination. Sometimes a shape coupled with another would then lead me down a certain track, my train of thought focused upon the destination of completion. Mostly they were SF landscapes, utilising Bryce's vast array of options to create a pleasing otherworldly picture – a particular mood I wanted to see. I'd then muck about trying to create buildings, ships, bridges and cities. Other times, I'd struggle to find inspiration – and decide to mimic images I'd seen before. Issue 35's cover being a case in point, the classic rocket ship – my take on Chesley Bonestell's illustration for Willy Ley's *Conquest of Space* from 1951. The rocket ship itself is essentially a combination of basic primitive shapes. The Union flag on the side of the ship was made possible by Bryce's ability to allow a JPEG to be placed upon a primitive, and if you have the issue you can just see a tiny vehicle making its way across the snowy landscape.

Issue 32, my second TQF cover, proved to be as difficult to realise as it was ultimately rewarding. I didn't know if Stephen would want to use my work again, following my fairly basic cover for issue 31, as I didn't know at that time my art had provided (as Stephen subsequently told me) TQF with a kind of corporate identity – a consistent style. I thought back then that perhaps Stephen wanted to keep TQF's look fresh, constantly moving forward and utilising other artists, as I'd noted that previous covers displayed a range of artists, ideas and methods. All I could do was submit again – I thought the worst Stephen could say would be a polite, "No thanks, but please continue to submit sometime in the future." With this in mind, I wanted to expand upon the landscape ability of Bryce, and set to work creating the surface landscape, water plane and mountains. Once I was happy with these components I remembered I'd built a small tracked exploration vehicle some time ago, and decided to use it in the scene. Once loaded, the angle of viewpoint prevented the vehicle from being seen correctly. It simply vanished into the page against the landscape. So, I deleted the tracks and wheels, a simple fix to transform it into a flying vehicle. Lifting it from the

planet's surface it provided a well-needed foreground component to the composition, so I copied the vehicle and placed it into the picture's mid ground above the water to establish the scale of the wreck it was exploring.

The three wrecked propulsion units were at first quite simple to create. Their bodies made from elongated tori, with a sphere to cap the middle unit off. Everything was taking shape quite nicely, with a planet in the top right corner hidden partially by streaks of cloud, providing a background focal point. Now I had my three elements, foreground, mid ground and background. But, the propulsion units were just as I've described – boring tori, one with a glass dome. Bryce came to the rescue. Once an object is created, it is possible to change it from a "neutral" state into either "positive" or "negative". An object with a negative state will subtract its shape from a positive object once they overlap (partially occupy the same space) and are grouped together. With this option, I was able to create a symmetrical lattice (in effect a mirrored mountain) and make it negative. I grouped it with the positive torus and when rendered they created the jagged wrecked propulsion unit seen on the left hand side of the cover. An identical method was used on the glass cap of the second unit to create the broken glass. This was all going quite well, but the scene still lacked movement.

The smoke escaping from the second unit took a couple of days to achieve the movement the scene needed. Made from a few elongated spheres, tweaking the material's luminosity and transparency were the keys to unlocking the look I was after, then a few hours of render time on my now long out of date Windows XP machine. I experimented with adding light sources to the engine cowlings of the foreground vehicle, but sometimes light behaves in a strange way when used in Bryce, and the light flooded onto the landscape ruining the scene. I decided to simply paint over the engines white in Photoshop when the piece was completed. It was then I had the idea to use a mesh material as the inner metal structure of the propulsion units. Each unit was copied, reduced very slightly in size and rendered with a mesh material. The only problem I had now was that these structures looked too perfect and undamaged, so Photoshop provided a solution. Saving these rendered areas as JPEGs and opening them in Photoshop enabled me to "bend" the metal mesh with Photoshop's "Smudge" tool. This took an absolute age, as a tiny slip of the mouse would ruin the effect as the landscape would smudge and I had to start again. Once this was completed, I turned my attention to the smoking

Picture 3. The Apoidroid.

propulsion unit. Masking off the unit in Photoshop, I applied streaks of soot to the broken edges. The shattered glass cap also needed a little tweaking as the reflections prevented the unit from appearing empty, so I just painted out the reflections to add depth. Finally, after a couple of weeks I was happy with the result and emailed the picture to Stephen. To my great pleasure he accepted the piece.

Roll on to mid spring, 2007. An email from Stephen asked if I could illustrate the story "Apoidroids" by Douglas Thompson. *"It's just right for you,"* (I'm paraphrasing) began Stephen, *"robot bees – I thought you could come up with something – if not, don't worry."* Now, I really didn't want to deflate Stephen's faith in me. Saying this, I had explained to Stephen previously to this email that I can't render figures. *"Robots and vehicles and cities – but not people – I haven't got the software needed and can't afford or justify the expense to be honest."* However, I could see where Stephen was coming from after reading the story – the menacing Y47p23x Apoidroid and its attack upon poor Gert, its creator. This had me thinking of the image I wanted to create, and it didn't involve Gert...

I googled my way through various images of bees until I found a couple that provided clear proportions to assist me build my own in Bryce. I began with the abdomen and worked forward – the most difficult aspect being the head, with the proportions for the eyes, mouth and antennae requiring precise placement and sizing. The material for the majority of the beast was an easy choice – a chrome metal with a high level of reflection. Although the Apoidroids in Doug's story featured wings, I went with a bladed arrangement, as I instantly thought this would look good from Stephen's initial email, so I googled radio controlled helicopters until I found the blade arrangement I was looking for. The legs took the longest to build and place in joints beneath the thorax, but once they were sized (the front pair are slightly foreshortened compared to the middle and rear pair) the whole metallic beast finally found a personality. I grouped the components and copied the bee a couple of times, placing these clones

in the background with slightly different poses, trying to establish the idea they were on the attack, toward the reader.

The landscape, an American desert setting, was quite simple to create, with only the rocks and cacti providing a few problems. Bryce has only one cactus as an object preset, and it can only be resized and rotated, so to populate the scene I had to resize and rotate the same cactus around 30 times in an attempt to make it look as though they were all individual. There are a few on the cover that are placed in identical poses unfortunately. The rocks suffer from the same problem, there are only six or so presets. I could have gone to the trouble of creating my own, but this would take a huge amount of time, eroding landscapes in the terrain editor to make a mound that looked like a rock. My solution was to build a group of eight or so rocks, group them and copy them, rotating them as a group and sometimes as individuals to form the scattering seen poking out of the sand. Thankfully, render time for this piece was quite swift, and within a couple of hours I'd finished my first "story illustration" for TQF. (*See Picture 3.*)

Issue 39 was a Christmas issue. The Christmas tree is a Bryce tree preset (the four tiny background figures are elongated spheres) and the planet Earth is represented as a fallen bauble sitting on the ground.

My concentration at this time however was on the upcoming issue 40 – a landmark by any standards in specialist magazine publication. I tinkered with various ideas – a huge decaying alien city in the shape of "40" – too Channel 4, I thought. Perhaps a "40" made up of the first 40 issues, placed upon each other – no, too render intensive and unoriginal – a "40" carved out of the landscape – oh no. Finally I settled for the ship dropping copies of TQF over a city. Bryce crashed a few times – the many previous cover JPEGS loaded into it caused it to choke, and it simply shut down, refusing to co-operate. I persevered, using the composite technique mentioned above.

Issue 41 provided me with the opportunity to render another story illustration in the shape of "The Big Burper", a huge tank. I added a middle track section just because I could – and the ladder protruding from the side between the two left side track arrangements establishes scale. Issue 42 saw another story illustration, followed by my favourite (at the time of writing, 11 August 2014) cover to date for issue 43…

My short story "Dodge Sidestep's Dastardly Plan" is my favourite of all the twelve or so I've written over the years – the sequel can be read in this issue. It was received well by one of the editors down at the Mitre Tavern in Brighton many years ago, during one of the many *Interzone* Friday night meetings I attended back

in the nineties. Sadly, not well enough to be included in the mag. It then many years later reached the final stage of the somewhat lengthy boarding pass sections of *Andromeda Spaceways Inflight Magazine*, only to be rejected at the final security barrier. Stephen decided it was good enough for TQF with a few editorial tweaks, and it was scheduled to appear in issue 43. In an act of shameless self-promotion, I took the dastardly step (at the time, not agreed or even mentioned to my editor!) to illustrate DSDP.

At that stage I'd not ventured into creating "real" or more accurately, "household" objects. But as the story featured a vast array of electronic musical equipment and speakers, I decided I needed to build a room (Dodge's) to house them. Bryce for the most part relies on its standard sunlight setting to illuminate objects with considerable clarity and realism. But once my two walled room was built, the interior fell into murky shade, with the sky seen through the window illuminated perfectly. Moving the sun's position darkened the exterior sky while illuminating the room, so I had to create a light source to show the objects I intended to populate the room with. This took a while to colour correctly and position, and then to establish the right brightness level and shadow position. Once this was completed, I set to work on the musical modules. Around this time I developed a new technique to aid the construction of detailed components. I would save the working Bryce page as a "master" file, then copy an attribute or object from the master file into a new document. I'd then work in this second file on whatever I'd copied into it, as I could change the viewpoint and zoom into areas to work on, without moving the positions of these objects. Bryce has a neat "Attributes" dialog box that can tell you the absolute coordinates of any object or group of objects. The function will also display the size of objects. It's an easy task to write all this down, enlarge an object, move it around to work upon it to get the detail right and then resize it back to its original size and position, copy it and paste it back into the master file. I built the stereo stacking system this way, in components – as if they were real world objects – using basic primitives for dials, switches and buttons. The speakers took a while to build, as in the story the tweeters double as eyes to watch the listener's position, thus adjusting their output for the best listening experience. I rotated the bottom pair of tweeters on each speaker so they appear to be looking out of the page toward the reader, with the rectangular bass hole appearing as a mouth.

The hatch and basement steps took a while to scale correctly, and I used a negative cube grouped with the positive floor to make the hatchway opening. The wallpaper is an old material I drew up a while ago with the window a Bryce preset object – saving me a lot of build time! There are a few little in jokes featured in this piece – two LPs (remember vinyl?) are mounted upon the walls. "The Theaker's Greatest Hits – 2112 – 2148" is a take on "The Seekers", while the year 2112 is the title of an album by my favourite band, Rush. Above the stereo rack is the CD cover enlarged to LP size of my album, "Ribbons", a classical ballet I wrote for the Brighton festival some years ago. On the floor are two CDs: "Driven Desire" the soundtrack to a play I scored for the Brighton Festival, and "The Urban Hiker", my third CD. But, without Bryce's superb wood and metal textures this piece would fall flat – I'm particularly pleased with the speakers, the sheen of the wood making them look as though they've just been polished, the satin black of the cones and metal sheen of their mounts complementing each other.

For issue 44 I used an old piece, rendered around the same time as "Departure". This is the first time I used Bryce's "Meatball" object primitive. A meatball is a sphere that morphs into a second meatball when placed next to it. The legs of these creatures emerging from their crater homes were created this way. The pleasing effect of meatballs is that if they are assigned different materials, they will merge these materials gradually into each other. Unfortunately there is not an option in Bryce to control the level of this, something I'd like to see in a later version of the software. The sky was a preset I tweaked to smooth the clouds into streaks and alter the ambient colour, and the craters are flattened and heavily eroded volcanos – another preset landscape object.

Just six months ago I bought Bryce 7 pro, having bought a new all in one desktop *Lenovo ideacentre*, as my old XP system died and my laptop refused to cooperate fearing the hands of my two children would end its pitiful life once and for all. Without Bryce on this new system – no more art! All my previous pieces are now locked away on the hard drives of these two once faithful machines – and one day I must rescue them. I found myself browsing the Daz 3D website as my latest version of Bryce downloaded. To my surprise and utter slack jawed salivating excitement I discovered Daz were offering a free download of Daz Studio 4.6. I couldn't move my mouse fast enough across the table, as this software would finally provide me with the ability to render figures! Daz Studio allows character creation and, most importantly, the posing of these characters. As you can expect from reading about Bryce above, Daz Studio 4.6 is just as impressive, allowing all kinds of manipulation of any created humanoid figure, and, again very importantly, the figures will, at a mouse click, port themselves into Bryce. This brings me close to the end of this story so far, and to TQF issue 47.

Antonella Coriander's "Bike Ride to Peril", found

Picture 4. Beatrice's flying bike in wireframe mode and fully rendered.

itself attached to an email from Stephen, as again he thought I could perhaps come up with something. I was excited beyond belief having read the story, as now I could introduce people into a scene.

The story involves jet bicycles being ridden over the cliffs of southern England, chalk cliffs I can partially see from my lounge window – so this story was close to home. At first I thought I'd create just that initial image, but the limits of the portrait orientation would mean the two figures and bikes would have to be dominant in the foreground – a test render proved this. Perhaps I could photograph the cliffs, then combine a render with the photo in Photoshop. The weather didn't allow such an option, so I decided to create a grassy cliff top in Bryce with the two characters resting before their ride. The bikes came first, and came together quickly using primitives. The handle bars, replete with brakes, took a while to build in a second document, and I gave the yellow bike a saddle similar to that of a seventies Raleigh Chopper bike – something I always wanted when I was a kid but could never afford. *Picture 4* shows the bike in wireframe mode and fully rendered. Now these two bikes were completed it was off to Studio 4.6 to create the two characters, Beatrice and Veronique. As the software was new to me, I didn't plan on experimenting too much, I simply created each figure separately, posing them, adding hair and clothes before sending them to Bryce and saving them as their own file for copying into the master file and resizing later. The background figure came first – the pose taking a while to achieve, as there are several ways to pose limbs within the interface's main screen. All aspects of the human body are poseable in Studio – each and every skeletal joint perfectly reproduced by the software – along with every muscle in the face. However, once figures are loaded into Bryce they become static objects, with only their surface materials, position and overall scale editable. I spent an age posing this first character until she appeared to be shading her eyes as she looked across the channel, whilst holding on to her bike with her other hand. The second figure was far more pleasing to create. I used a Studio pose preset and tweaked it so the character looked out of the page with a slight smile, whilst positioning her so she occupied as little space as possible upon the page. It took a while to scale her so as not to obscure her bike in the background, as well as the first figure and her bike. Once this was achieved I hit the render button and sat back. Unfortunately the sun's position in Bryce, perfect for the background figure shielding her eyes against it, didn't work with the foreground figure, as the light was insufficient to illuminate her face. I added a sphere light to the foreground, altering its brightness until the character was lit. Adding a flower next to her – perhaps the reason she sat where she's positioned – completed the scene.

As a side note, the majority of the covers I've spoken about here can be seen in their native res on my deviantart page: http://hswatts.deviantart.com/.

So now I find myself experimenting with Studio – watching YouTube instruction vids (as well as ones for Bryce as there's still so much to learn!), trying to

master the software. Producing artwork for TQF in Bryce and Studio is a wonderful hobby, but does take a lot of time, and can be frustrating as even my new PC crashes from time to time. However, the results are rewarding – even though I'm aware there are tens of thousands of better artists out there in this field. Stephen edits my art as equally well as he edits fiction, and for that I thank him. On several occasions he has suggested subtle changes or enhancements. These little nudges have always been for the best, improving the final piece. As for what's next – I have no idea. I may employ all three of my hobbies – a short story with a music soundtrack, illustrated by Bryce and Studio. Perhaps I'll experiment with photography / Bryce / Studio compositing again (as I did for the cover of issue 49), to be filtered in Photoshop to tie all layers together – I don't know. I do know I will continue to provide art for TQF for as long as Stephen is happy with my artful Theakering.

The Wrong Doctor

A literary adventure

Rafe McGregor

"When a doctor goes wrong he is the first of criminals. He has nerve and he has knowledge."

Sherlock Holmes, 1883

I

Baker Street, London

My dear Mr Langham – I am sure that you wish to forget the unfortunate circumstances of your meeting with Mr Holmes and I, but I nonetheless beg your indulgence. Holmes' intervention in the Windover Hill affair was motivated by the pursuit of justice and I suspect that your preference, as an agent of the law, was for the prevention of further offences. In this regard, I was pleased to discover that you have been living peacefully on the Yorkshire coast these last fifteen years. If you are able to accommodate a brief interruption of your retirement, I would esteem it a great kindness if you would favour me with your opinion on a criminal matter in which I am unable to consult Mr Holmes. I shall call upon you at 4pm on Thursday. I shall try again at the same time on Friday. In the event that neither is convenient, I shall await you

in the Royal Hotel, where I have reserved a room for the
duration of the weekend.

Yours sincerely
John H. Watson
March 25th 1902

I was surprised at the letter, but not at the skill with
which Watson piqued my curiosity. He was, of course,
something of a polymath – a doctor, a soldier, a
detective, and lately a man of letters – and in this
respect much more like Holmes than the self-
deprecating tone of his memoirs revealed. He
exemplified, in matter of fact, the ideal to which all
gentlemen in the British Empire should aspire even if
so many of us fall short of it.

My own fall had been administered by Holmes
when he had discovered my homicidal
somnambulism, an unfortunate symptom of a hitherto
unknown kind of dementia which resulted in me
investigating a crime I had myself committed. My
health and fortune had both taken several turns since
and I was now head of a modest household in Whitby.
I supported myself, my housekeeper (the aptly-named
Mrs Knaggs), and her young son with the anonymous
scribbling of the implausible adventures of *the other*
Baker Street detective, the fictional – and rather
ridiculous – Sexton Blake.

Watson's letter was part of a parcel that arrived in
the last post on Wednesday, the remainder of which
was a thick octavo volume entitled *The Hound of the*
Baskervilles. The latest of Holmes' adventures had
begun in the *Strand* the previous summer and the
penultimate instalment was still on my desk. I was
grateful for the gift, which would allow me to finish
the tale before the April issue of the magazine arrived,
but it was a strange choice. My identity as a Sexton
Blake author was known only to my editor and Watson

could not have guessed that I was an enthusiastic member of his reading public when all the evidence – my status as a victim of Holmes' scientific method – pointed in the opposite direction.

I set the letter aside, opened the novel, and flipped through the pages. The book contained full-page plates of all of Mr Paget's wonderful illustrations, but I ceased my perusal as I neared the end. I reached for the March *Strand*, numbered 135 in volume xxiii, where the instalment ended in high dramatic style, part-way through chapter fourteen, with the emergence of the hound "out of the wall of fog". I noted that on the previous page I had underlined Holmes comment to Watson on this meteorological phenomenon with a pencil: *Very serious indeed – the one thing upon earth which could have disarranged my plans.* By the time I finished Watson's novel, I knew precisely why he would be calling at No. 10 Flowergate the following afternoon.

II

Watson knocked while the clock was striking four and I opened the door promptly. He had changed very little since our one and only meeting and was an altogether fine specimen of a man our age – for we were both close upon our half-centuries. He was still athletic in build, maintained a military bearing, and continued to wear his handkerchief in his sleeve. The only difference I could discern were the streaks of grey in his moustache and I reflected that while I was but a shadow of my former self, Watson had remained the quintessential English gentleman. As host, the overture was mine to make.

"Good day, Dr Watson, how do you do?"

He smiled, removed his right glove, and took my

hand in a firm, honest grip. "Very well, thank you, Mr Langham. You too appear to be in excellent health."

"Pray come in. Allow me to take your stick and coat. The sideboard will support the weight of your hat and gloves admirably." I ushered him into my sitting-room, where the fire was keeping the cold at bay. "Do sit down and make yourself comfortable. I have asked Mrs Knaggs to make tea. May I offer you some?"

Watson's limp was slightly more pronounced than I remembered, though he walked quite steadily without his stick. "Yes, please, that's very kind of you." I rang the bell on the side-table, imagined rather than heard the corresponding grunt of disapproval in the kitchen, and sat down with less ease than Watson. He glanced at the copy of *The Hound*, which I had placed on a footstool. "May I also thank you for your kindness in receiving me today. I trust that my presence is not inconvenient."

"Not at all." Holmes impressed his clients by deducing facts about them from their appearance and mannerisms and I was determined to entertain Watson with an equivalent performance. I lifted the volume for effect. "Mr Holmes as represented in this gripping tale of yours is not quite the man I met in Sussex the previous year. He is, if I may say so, not at his best."

Watson betrayed no emotion, but asked, "What evidence leads you to that conclusion?"

"There are several points, but one is conclusive." I quoted without opening the book: "*The one thing upon earth which could have disarranged my plans.* What native Briton would be surprised by the sudden appearance of fog on Dartmoor? Common sense aside, Mr Holmes had both visited the moor during the Straker investigation and spent several days and nights on the tor. Furthermore, he had motive to exercise extra care in making his final plans given his earlier failure to safeguard his client's life – I refer, of course, to Selden's death. In sum, Dr Watson, Sherlock Holmes was wrong!"

I let the volume fall on the footstool, but the drama in my *dénouement* was ruined by Mrs Knaggs, who waddled in with a wide tray loaded with tea, biscuits, and custard tartlets. She greeted Watson with enthusiasm – he was still, of course, a handsome man much-beloved by the fair sex – placed the tray on the table with uncharacteristic care, and even uttered a gracious "thank you, sir" when I said I would serve my guest. Watson indicated his preferences for milk, no sugar, and biscuits, then waited for me to resume my seat.

"You are correct, Mr Langham. Holmes had not yet recovered from his physical breakdown in Lyon in eighty-seven and was on the verge of a mental one when I'm afraid to admit that I abandoned him for my late wife." Watson's face contorted with pain for a moment. "Eighty-eight was also the first occasion on which he crossed swords with Professor Moriarty, and whatever other work he was engaged upon, he was always also unravelling Moriarty's web."

I seized on the mention of Moriarty for my second *dénouement*: "It is no coincidence that you decided to consult me when I happen to reside some fifty miles from an assassin with whom I myself crossed swords during my police career." I leaned forward and picked up *The Hound* again. "Moriarty was the man behind the attacks on the Baskerville family and Moran was his agent. Colonel Sebastian Moran, lately retired to the Grange in the Yorkshire Dales, is the real killer of the Baskervilles!"

Watson shook his head. "No, not Moriarty or Moran, Mortimer."

My shock rapidly gave way to horror and I opened the novel to the first page of the final chapter: *Sir*

Henry and Dr Mortimer were, however, in London, on
their way to that long voyage which had been
recommended for the restoration of his shattered
nerves. "Sir Henry's voyage with Dr Mortimer!"

Watson continued to shake his head. "A sabbatical
from which he never returned."

III

Now that I'd been told, it seemed not only the obvious,
but the inevitable, conclusion to the narrative. "You
left clues, didn't you? The adversarial nature of
Mortimer's first meeting with Holmes, Holmes'
recognition of his scientific acumen, Mortimer's
position as executor of Sir Charles' estate, his
defensiveness when questioned about the will, his
apparent willingness to believe the legend..."

"I wrote some drivel about an unseen force
entangling us in an imperceptible net, but it was true.
It was Mortimer. He was always *there*. Everywhere! It
began with the ruse with the stick to put us off guard
and finished with him dragging Sir Henry off to sea.
Mortimer introduced us to first the legend and then
Sir Henry, he never left Sir Henry's side in London, and
he visited Sir Henry and I every day at Baskerville Hall.
He shepherded the young baronet to his death and
stage-managed Holmes, Stapleton, the whole damned
case. I told Holmes of my suspicions, but he wouldn't
believe it."

"The missing page from your letters!" I cried.

"Yes."

I knew I was caught up in the thrill of it all, so I
forced myself to adopt an analytic approach, probing
for weaknesses. "But what about Stapleton – and his
wife's statement?"

"Rodger Baskerville was a bloody fool. Holmes

couldn't account for his plan because he didn't have one. He disgraced himself as Baskerville in Costa Rica and Vandeleur in Pickering and I think his arrival in Dartmoor was a sign of desperation. He was the perfect foil for Mortimer."

"I thought it was odd that Holmes' description of *a foil as quick and supple as my own* ended up referring to such a bungler. Why did his wife implicate him if he wasn't guilty – good God, Mortimer was having an affair with her, wasn't he!"

"You are most perceptive, Mr Langham. Mortimer told us that his wife was an invalid, but he was in fact a widower. Mrs Beryl Baskerville was tired of being dragged around the world by her petty criminal of a husband and appears to have been easy prey for Mortimer. It's not enough to cover one's tracks, one needs to offer an alternative suspect to the authorities and who better than Stapleton? I don't know exactly what transpired at Merripit House after Sir Henry left, but I do know that Mortimer was waiting for Stapleton on the moor."

I wasn't convinced yet. "But the Baskerville case was about securing the fortune. Surely Sir Henry wasn't foolish enough to leave it to a gentleman he had just met?"

"I am not presenting my conjecture clearly. Mortimer was in league with Mr James Desmond, Sir Henry's cousin."

"Ah, I thought he was dismissed rather too quickly by Holmes. An elderly clergyman or some such?"

"The *late* Mr Desmond was retired from the pulpit, infirm and reclusive. Holmes eliminated him as a suspect on the basis of a telegram from the Westmoreland constabulary and nothing else. He was, as you have said, far from his best."

"Mortimer killed Desmond?"

Watson enumerated Mortimer's crimes on his

fingers. "Mortimer murdered Sir Charles, Stapleton, Sir Henry, and then Desmond. The first and last death were attributed to natural causes and the second and third involved disappearances in circumstances where it was impossible to recover the corpses. Mortimer was Desmond's sole beneficiary. He committed four perfect crimes and secured a fortune of close to three quarters of a million pounds."

A man with less charisma than Watson could have persuaded me to accept his theory: the re-solution concealed in the text of the novel was a great deal more plausible than the purported solution. "How may I be of assistance?" I asked.

"I am shortly to abandon Holmes for a second time and I should like to bring the matter to a close beforehand by way of compensation. I intend to confront Mortimer tomorrow morning and would very much appreciate your company."

"Then I'd better pack." I reached for the bell.

"There's no need. Mortimer used his ill-gotten gains to build himself a manor house on the North York Moors. Would you believe he lives on the edge of *Howl* Moor? If I put that in a memoir I'd be accused of writing fiction."

"What brought him here, the archaeology?"

"Possibly, but more likely his wife's bidding. The ghost of Mrs Vandeleur has returned to her old haunt disguised as Mrs Mortimer."

IV

Watson and I boarded the first train for York on Friday morning and arrived in the little village of Goathland fifteen minutes later. The station-master directed us to the inn-keeper, who offered us a sturdy wagonette, for although our destination was only a few

miles hence, the road was poor. Watson declined the
offer of a driver, took the reins himself, and moved
over so that I could join him. He seemed to know
where he was going and we set off into a bright but
chilly morning, the surrounding mist gradually
yielding to the combination of sunshine and a stiff
breeze from the west. The track upon which we
travelled traversed the gentle slope of the moorland,
rising to our right and subsiding to our left. Both sides
were dominated by the bright purple of the heather
rather than the darker greens and browns of the grass
and shrubs. Aside from the distant ridge from which
the wind fell and a small forest a mile or more away,
the horizontal expanse was punctuated only by a few
black-faced sheep and the occasional dry-stone wall.

I had spent Thursday evening consulting the records
of the Whitby Literary and Philosophical Society, of
which I was a member, and committed a large-scale
map of the north-eastern quarter of the moors to
memory. Hunters Hall was located between Hazel
Wood and Grey Earths Wood to the north and Wade's
Causeway and Howl Moor to the south. Mortimer had
already made his mark on the moors by clearing the
causeway of vegetation and had published papers to
the effect that the landmark was a Roman road. He
was no doubt in search of skulls – skulls which he had
apparently been depositing in, as well as removing
from, the earth. Watson kept his own counsel
throughout our journey and I was not altogether
certain of the reason for my presence. My guess was
that I was a deterrent in the event that Mortimer
decided to add a fresh corpse to the Neolithic and
Bronze Age skeletons beneath the causeway, but
maybe there was more to it.

Shortly after passing Grey Earths Wood, we turned
south onto a narrower track that curved around a
rock-strewn rise before ending in a line of rowans,

twisted and bent by centuries of storm and wind. A
tall, narrow tower rose above the trees. Watson
pointed with the whip. "Hunters Hall."

We approached an ugly ironstone lodge, squatting
next to a pair of shiny wrought-iron gates. The gates
were open and there was no sign of life in the lodge.
The avenue beyond was deep in shadow, bending
sharply out of sight after a few dozen yards. In the
shade, hard and clear like an equestrian statue upon
its pedestal, was a mounted man. He was sombre and
stern, a penang-lawyer poised over his forearm as he
watched the path of our approach.

"Watson," I whispered, but he was already halting
the horses.

The rider emerged from the gloom. "Well, if it isn't
Mr Sherlock Holmes and Dr Watson."

I recognised James Mortimer M.R.C.S. from
Watson's thumb-nail sketch in *The Hound*. His height,
emaciation, protruding nose, and bowed back
combined to give the impression of a human sickle
perched precariously on a horse's back. He was
wearing an expensive broad-brimmed hat, gold-
rimmed spectacles, and a smart silk cravat, but his
attire deteriorated as it descended: a shabby frock-
coat, creased trousers, and muddy riding boots. He
had not lost the air of peering benevolence with which
Watson had characterised him and indeed he thrust
his head at us as if to bring his close-set eyes nearer to
their target.

"I've been expecting you gentlemen for a very long
time. I thought I'd been granted a reprieve when Mr
Holmes' demise was reported, but when I heard you'd
survived I was sure you'd find your way here. When
Beryl told me about the publication in the *Strand* in
August, I awaited you each evening. Now, I must –
hallo, you're not Mr Holmes! Who's this, Dr Watson?"

"My associate, Mr Roderick Langham. Mr Langham,

Dr James Mortimer. Why were you expecting Holmes and I?"

"Because sooner or later it must have dawned on Mr Holmes that he was wrong. If Sir Henry's disappearance at sea wasn't obvious enough, the brevity of the period Mr Desmond's god granted him to enjoy his fortune must have made my position plain." Mortimer was neither fearful nor contemptuous as he all but admitted his guilt.

"You murdered both Baskervilles, Stapleton, and Desmond." There was ice in Watson's voice.

"Morally, I am responsible. Legally... I'm not going to insult your intelligence by pointing out the public facts of two deaths by natural causes, one by misadventure, and one by suicide."

"You gloat, sir."

"I am a man of science, Doctor, I deal solely in facts and leave others to pass judgement."

"I assure you I am here for that very purpose. I am well-acquainted with the facts and I intend to share every last detail of my judgement with you. I may not have proof that will stand in a court of law, but you will not sleep soundly from this day forward."

"No, sir, no, you are in error. Hiring Mr Holmes gave me a credibility with Sir Henry which I could never have gained otherwise, but it was always a calculated risk. The reappearance of Mr Holmes at some later date was a part of that risk so I have been prepared for this day for many years. To be perfectly frank, I am relieved that the moment has arrived at last and I feel that you have done me a service, even if that was not your intention. I should like to repay that service. You are seeking some sense of an ending, something akin to that with which you complete the stories my wife admires so? As long as this gentleman," he rotated his head towards me, "has no official standing, I shall be glad to receive you both tomorrow evening and answer any questions that lie between us. Say five o'clock? Very good. Now that's settled, would you be so kind as to remove your conveyance from my gateway. There is just enough room for you to manoeuvre without having to enter."

V

Watson asked if I would mind postponing discussion until we had returned to Whitby, so I spent the journey back by wagonette, train, and foot smoking my pipe in silent contemplation. I could not fathom Mortimer, who seemed as cool a customer as any criminal I had ever faced in my day. My main concern was Watson. What would he do? He had maintained a steely calm throughout the interview and an immobility and impenetrability of countenance worthy of Holmes since, but what could he hope to achieve? Mortimer had committed the most perfect series of murders imaginable. Even the circumstantial evidence was severely limited and if Mortimer was able to prove prior acquaintance with Desmond, then that too would evaporate like the mist. If Watson wasn't careful, he might find himself embroiled in a libel battle with an extremely wealthy man, in the process of which Holmes' reputation would be torn to shreds by the press. A glance at my acquaintance's fine, noble features nonetheless gave me confidence in his ability to find a solution to the problem.

Midday found us back in my sitting-room, drinking tea while Mrs Knaggs prepared luncheon upstairs.

"Now that we have both had sufficient time to mull this conundrum over, may I enquire as to your thoughts?"

I cleared my throat. "I must disappoint you, for I see only danger ahead."

"So do I. Holmes once said *when a doctor goes wrong he is the first of criminals; he has nerve and he has knowledge.* Mortimer's nerve enabled him to do away with the two younger gentlemen with the utmost efficacy; his knowledge enabled him to take advantage of the older gentlemen's respective medical conditions. I have seen many cases with a great deal more evidence fail to reach the courtroom."

"Were I still a detective, I would not embarrass myself by presenting the case to the Director of Public Prosecutions as-is. The only way I can see that changing is if Mortimer's wife can be persuaded to testify against him and now that we're discussing the matter, I wonder if we placed her in danger this morning."

Watson's brow furrowed and he scratched his head. "I think that you're right about Mrs Mortimer being the only witness, but then again, how much has she actually witnessed? She will have known something of Mortimer's machinations on the moor, but I doubt she was privy to much more. He would only have confided in her completely if his trust was total, in which case she will not stand witness. If, on the other hand, she knows as little as I suspect, she would be no good on the witness stand. Either way, I think Mrs Mortimer safe."

I nodded. "And we mustn't let chivalry or prejudice against the weaker sex blind us to the fact that Beryl Garcia has chosen to spend all of her adult life with criminal husbands. Furthermore, the performance you describe at the end of *The Hound* was quite obviously just that, a performance. What do you intend to do?"

"I am afraid that I cannot answer that question, but I would be very grateful for your company tomorrow evening."

"You may count on it."

"I am indebted, sir, thank you."

"If Mrs Mortimer doesn't join us, perhaps you could slip away and seek a private interview with her. I could always distract Mortimer with talk of Bertillon or Lombroso."

Watson fixed me with a grave stare, the meaning of which was far from clear. Eventually, he said, "I think Lombroso would be more to his taste."

"I don't read Italian, but I have several of his papers from *The Monist* in my library. I shall spend tomorrow brushing up on them!"

Once again, I had predicted Watson's intentions. He was going to turn that gentlemanly charm which had so impressed ladies on three continents to a lady from a fourth. I wondered if he had perhaps been more intimate with the then Beryl Stapleton than he had revealed in the memoir. It mattered little. I was convinced that Watson would succeed and determined to assist him in any way possible.

VI

Watson and I crossed the threshold of Hunters Hall at a few minutes after five on Saturday evening. He had opted to hire a driver this time, so we were both sitting comfortably in the back as the wagonette clattered along the avenue. Though the sun was far from setting, the day was overcast and the canopy formed by the trees clutching at each other low over our heads contributed to the gloom. The dark tunnel soon opened onto a broad turf lawn and we saw the hall for the first time. The building was a huge basalt block, with a porch projecting to the front and a single steeple rising high above us. The steeple was surrounded by four great chimneys, three of which puffed grey smoke into a greyer sky. The antique style, augmented with mullioned windows and copious amounts of ivy, was at odds with the pristine stone, but the cheerful freshness made a welcome change from the sinister gateway. We were met by a smartly-dressed footman, who led us up the stairs into a modern entrance hall raftered with baulks of timber and decorated with innocuous paintings of rural and pastoral scenes. Watson appeared to pay the hall careful attention as the butler took our hats, coats, sticks, and gloves. I suspected he was familiarising himself with the floor-plan in the event that he found himself alone. We were directed from the hall to a parlour with cream and blue décor, a high vault, and fashionable clutter.

Mortimer was warming his hands by the fire, dressed much the same as the previous day. He turned to us. "Good evening, gentlemen. May I offer you some refreshment... tea, coffee, something a little stronger?"

"Just privacy, Dr Mortimer – unless Mrs Mortimer is joining us, of course."

"No, Doctor, Mrs Mortimer has no desire to renew your acquaintance. That will be all, Soames, please make sure I am not disturbed."

The butler left, closing the door behind him.

"Now, you must excuse my attire, but I've only just returned from the moors. I'm rather busy at present, with two excavations in addition to the work on what I can safely call Wheeldale Road. Please make yourselves at home."

There were four armchairs and a settle arranged around a long, low table atop which sat a large silver tray and cloche, a battered old cigarette case, and a leather tobacco pouch. Mortimer favoured the settle and Watson and I sat facing him. There was a second door behind Mortimer, which would be useful if Watson had to slip out undetected.

Mortimer peered over the table at us. "I hope you don't mind, but I've invited Stapleton to join us."

Watson kept his cool, but I couldn't help myself. "*Stapleton*?"

"Well, no, 'Stapleton' was one of his many aliases; Rodger Baskerville is his real name."

I turned to Watson, then back to Mortimer. "If Baskerville is alive, then your marriage to his wife is null and void."

Mortimer smiled. "I didn't say he was alive." He leaned forward, removed the cloche, and revealed a perfectly preserved skull.

I gasped. Not because of the skull or the surgical implications of its presence on the tray, but because of the legal use to which it could be put. It was all we needed. If Watson had brought his service revolver along we could simply seize it at gunpoint and make good our escape. I turned to him again, but he was staring at Mortimer.

Mortimer laughed. "Do forgive my little jest, but I admit it was worth it. If you could have seen your faces! This is the skull of the man you knew as Jack Stapleton, Dr Watson. You may note that it bears a remarkably similar supra-orbital development to that of Mr Holmes. Unfortunately in Baskerville's case it was not an indication of intellect, for the man blundered from one disaster to the next like one of his hapless butterflies. There were two scandals in South America, not one, then the school in Pickering and finally the fiasco on Dartmoor. I allowed him to flit about in my net until Mr Holmes skewered him with the blame and then I with something more substantial. Let me remove my *memento mori* so we are not distracted." Mortimer returned the cloche to its place, stood, picked up the tray, and stepped over to the sideboard. "As I am acquainted with the nature of your quest let me say that I shall be telling you that which I have not and will not confide to anyone else."

Watson flashed a glance at the windows flanking

the sideboard, then at both doors, and then at me. He raised his left hand, indicating I should stay seated.

I nodded.

Watson rose, and moved in behind Mortimer.

I knew he was capable of dealing with our host, so I decided to grab the skull and make for the wagonette if a struggle ensued.

Mortimer set down the tray. "But where is Mr Holmes?" The low clang of metal on wood was muffled by a sharp click, a sound that I hadn't heard in a while, but recognised instantly. Mortimer turned as Watson raised his right hand from his pocket.

Mortimer's mouth dropped open and Watson shot him through the forehead; flesh, blood, and brain matter spattering sideboard, curtains, and window.

Watson turned, clutching the smoking revolver in his fist, and I jumped up, grabbing hold of my chair.

He marched towards me, kicked his chair over, reached down to edge of the table, and flung it on its side. Then he faced me, cocked the revolver again, and lifted it.

He was going to kill me too, blame Mortimer's murder on me.

In the fraction of a second I hesitated, Watson pressed the barrel to his left thigh and fired.

There was more smoke and more blood.

He cried out, dropped the weapon, and fell to the floor.

"I'm sorry, Langham, but this has always been my intention. I couldn't let Mortimer escape unpunished any more than I could let Holmes' good name be destroyed. We are all in your hands now."

VII

I do not know if my decision to bear false witness for

Watson has redeemed my past or damned my future,
but I do know that I could not let him throw his life
away for the likes of Mortimer. Watson committed
murder to defend his friend's reputation and I
committed perjury to defend his, and the reputation of
the English gentleman which he epitomised for me
and so many others. He had nerve and he had
knowledge.

The House That Cordone Built

David Tallerman

"Damn it, Lovett, I've got a clear shot."

For six months now, agents Lovett and Sykes of the Anti-Sedition Squad had been in constant pursuit of Edwyn Cordone, the galaxies' most flagrant and eccentric criminal. And for all those months of effort, they had precisely nothing to show: they'd rarely been more than a day behind Cordone, but whenever the distance narrowed he would shake them off spectacularly. The craft they pursued him in had been designed for speed rather than comfort, for one person not two, and so, inevitably, tempers were wearing thin.

"Sykes, it's stolen," Lovett protested. "Do you really want to foot the bill?"

Now the hunt had brought them to the farthest inhabited regions of the galaxy. The rapidly expanding dot before them was Earth 199, and Cordone's course suggested that it was to be his next target. Within the cramped space of the cruiser, this alone had been enough to trigger another argument.

"But, it's our *job* to shoot him."

Lovett only glowered at his partner – who after an awkward silence responded, "All right. Have you tried contacting the authorities on 199?"

"Authorities? It only went up last month. There *are*

no authorities. There's no nothing. The place is a builder's yard."

"There must be somebody."

"A few matter-engineers," Lovett said. "Maybe five thousand settlers. That's it."

"So it's just us then?"

"Just us. Isn't it always?"

They spiralled through the newly manufactured atmosphere, following the lock on Cordone's purloined cruiser. He had come down near to one of the tiny encampments clustered around the Matter-makers. Sykes claimed he could make out a figure walking leisurely across the intervening distance, but Cordone was less sure.

There was no disguising the smell of a newly terraformed planet. It reminded Lovett of freshly mown grass – the turf was, after all, only a few days old – but the comparison didn't begin to do it justice. In a couple of months this place would be another clone of Earth Zero, perfect in every detail. Right now, it was something altogether more electrifying: a blank slate. Lovett stood stretching his cramped legs and inhaling deeply.

Sykes, meanwhile, bounded gleefully up the slope to examine Cordone's craft. He was soon back. "He's not been gone for long, the seat's still warm." He held out one hand, displaying a metal rod the size and shape of a fountain pen, and added, "He won't get much further. I took out the control pin."

Lovett pointed towards the distant Matter-maker, which towered over the hamlet beside it. "That must be what he's after. It's the only thing big enough and powerful enough to cause any trouble. Although what he thinks he can do with it is anybody's guess."

The partners started in the direction of the nearby village. It could never have been mistaken for anything other than a temporary measure: there were two dozen colono-domes (which despite the extravagant claims made by their manufacturer were little more than old-fashioned tents), a couple of shapeless industrial spacecraft and cabins for the workmen. The settlers sat about eating, smoking long-stemmed pipes or chatting half-heartedly; a mob of children were throwing a ball about without enthusiasm. Even the matter-engineers were doing next to nothing.

Behind them all towered the Matter-maker. The design was deceptively simple: a long pylon raised above the ground by two moveable sets of legs and resting upon tracked, rectangular feet. The unfathomably complex technology was mostly packed within the vertical struts. This one was gigantic, close to a quarter mile in height and about twice that in length.

Of Cordone, however, there was no sign. Lovett drew the attention of one of the engineers, who regarded the partners with grave disinterest. "Have you seen any strangers?" he asked.

"Other than you two?"

"Of course."

The Engineer grunted thoughtfully. "Bloke came by a few minutes ago I didn't recognise. Tall, skinny, in a big coat and hat. He said hello, and that his name was Winstanley."

"We don't know what he's wearing, or what he's calling himself." Lovett paused, struggling for the right words. "How did he *look*?"

"What do you mean? Wearing a coat and hat in this weather? He looked bloody ridiculous."

"Then that's him. It's very important we find him."

"Why's that then?" asked the Engineer, rubbing at the mess of stubble covering the lower half of his face.

Sykes, clearly frustrated by this display of

nonchalance, cried, "Damn it, he's the most dangerous anarchist in the galaxy!"

"You must mean Edwyn Cordone. Isn't he the *only* anarchist in the galaxy?"

"Well, yes. And the most dangerous."

"Maybe you saw where he went?" interrupted Lovett, with icy calm.

"Right." The engineer pointed to a cabin protruding from the side of the Matter-maker. "He went in there."

Lovett paused just long enough to sigh deeply, before setting off at a sprint with Sykes close behind.

Matter-makers were the workhorses of the colonisation program. Landed after the initial terraforming, their function was to erect the dwellings, administrative centres and other structures that the settlers would inevitably need. They didn't, of course, actually *make* matter; rather, they subatomically reconfigured raw materials to meet a given requirement. The actual effect, however, remained more than impressive.

From the look of the sedentary settlers, this 'Maker had probably been programmed with the generic template for residential building, a block of identical apartments two miles in length. As the members of the Anti-Sedition Squad drew nearer, they could hear a dense whirring, and feel the earth shivering beneath their feet: unmistakeable signs that the machine was nearly ready to begin. They were almost at the control cabin, fitted into the nearest strut a few feet above the ground. Sykes had his Incapacitor drawn and aimed at the figure visible within, but was panting so much he could barely aim. Lovett, too, had slowed to a jog.

Which proved fortunate – for had they been in better shape they would surely have been incinerated when the Matter-maker's engines shrieked into life. As it happened, they were only hurled flat by the wave of heated air that billowed from beneath its mammoth feet.

Lovett wrenched his head around to look at Sykes, shouted over the howl of straining machinery, "We should really move before..."

But even if Sykes could have heard, it was too late. The noise crescendoed to agonising volumes, accompanied by a blistering wave of radiance.

For some minutes, Lovett was too dazed to open his eyes, let alone to speak. Finally the din ebbed, and there was no longer the sensation of light trying to sear through his eyelids. It was a while, even then, before he felt able to move. He sat up with a pained grunt, surveyed the scene before him – and immediately regretted it. "Good Gaia," he whispered, "he's done it again."

The Matter-maker had come to rest about two miles away – meaning the building Cordone had engineered was the same length as the intended block of flats.

That was probably the only meaningful similarity.

The edifice was basically rectangular; though balconies, patios, statuary and window boxes jutted at every conceivable angle. It was arranged around a colossal central tower, and there were also various turrets and brightly coloured minarets, giving the distant impression of a ramshackle fairytale castle. The inside – much of which was visible due to whole sections constructed without exterior walls – appeared to consist of endless rooms supported by columns, stairs, walkways and occasionally even by ladders.

Up to that point, the structure was merely peculiar, archaic and impractical. What marked it beyond question as Cordone's handiwork was its defiance of the laws of physics. It should have been impossible; Lovett felt sure that it *was* impossible. It was there nonetheless, and seemed perfectly solid. Only, the angles were all wrong.

Staircases ran up and down, but also in every other direction. A flight of steps climbing upward and only upward around the outside somehow managed to meet itself at its lowest point. Walkways and corridors were inverted, or on a side, just as there were doors and windows at right angles to the ground. Huge rooms were supported by tapering columns, which in turn protruded from what would normally be supporting walls. Whole wings hung suspended only by the passages joining them to other parts of the building.

Lovett could have dismissed the whole thing as a clever illusion, even with all that evidence, were it not for one final detail: Cordone himself stood grinning at them from a platform near the top of the structure, and he was upside-down.

"We can catch him!" exclaimed Sykes, scrambling to his feet.

Lovett was less convinced. "That place is a maze. If we go in we might never come out."

But by then Sykes was already through the nearest entrance. Lovett hurried after, a curse on his lips. The fact that they were this close to Cordone could only be a bad sign.

He easily caught up with his partner, who'd come to a halt near the top of an inward-leading flight of stairs. The stairs themselves were perfectly normal – it was just that the landing they joined to rose vertically before them. The landing itself led to other steps, perpendicular to those they were standing on.

"It's a dead end," said Sykes.

Lovett was less certain. Cordone was certainly iconoclastic and probably insane, but in the past there had always been a baffling pragmatism to his eccentricities. It wasn't like him to build a house that couldn't be navigated.

Lovett climbed to the top of the stairs and then,

with infinite care, leaned backward – until he was looking towards the roof. The landing was now at the correct angle, and he stepped gingerly onto it, expecting at every moment to tumble backwards. It didn't happen. Yet the wall through which they'd entered was now, disturbingly, above his head. "It seems safe," he called to Sykes.

Once Sykes had been through the same reorientation, the partners hurried up the steps to their left, trying to ignore the fact that they were horizontal and moving towards the wall. Reaching the top, they entered a short corridor – at which point the exterior wall became a ceiling. Apartments broke off to either side, above and below them, filled with elegant furnishings that should theoretically have been plummeting towards the ground.

At the end of the corridor, a left turn and another lurch through ninety degrees – undertaken with less hesitation this time – returned them to their original alignment, with the earth again beneath their feet. They stepped onto a trellised bridge, which led to a tower that rose from the base of the structure. From there they could just make out Cordone, supine against a wall some feet above. When he saw the partners he disappeared into a doorway.

"We need to get higher," yelled Sykes, hurrying into the edifice before them. A ladder within led in the right direction. They hastened to the next floor and out into a tubular corridor, which at first seemed relatively normal. It was only as Lovett continued, and glimpsed the exterior through windows to either side, that he realised the floor formed a gentle spiral. They were climbing steadily up what had been the left-hand wall towards what was, from their original perspective, the ceiling. But a glimpse of Cordone was enough to make him ignore their vertiginous circumstances, and he plunged on.

The tunnel opened onto a ramp, which appeared to slope downward and in fact led skyward. Now they were upside-down again. Cordone was visible once more and noticeably closer, though travelling in a different direction and at a different angle. He set off briskly, ducking behind a fountain that spewed water towards the ground. Sykes still ahead, the partners jogged upwards down the slope, through an arch, out into a magnificent garden of reversed trees and shrubs. They chose a door in the floor, which led towards the roof.

Lovett was breathing heavily by then, and clutching his side. Even Sykes, despite his enthusiasm, was beginning to flag. Halfway up the vertical walkway Lovett came to a halt and collapsed with a long gasp. Sykes staggered on for a short distance and then swayed to face his partner. Bent over, hands on knees, he panted, "We've got to... got to... we've nearly caught..."

Lovett, propped on his elbows, gasped back, "We'll never..." Then he broke off, startled, and instead began to nod frantically.

"Lovett, are you..." But Sykes, too, was arrested in mid-sentence, as his eyes followed his partner's excited movements.

Behind them was another walkway, parallel to theirs – and there stood Edwyn Cordone, perhaps a dozen feet away and gazing over at them. He was disguised by a tattered overcoat, an archaic trilby hat pulled low over his eyes, and an obviously fake beard. Sykes went with renewed energy for the Incapacitor holstered within his jacket.

"Sykes, I wouldn't..."

Sykes fired before Lovett could finish his warning. There was no chance he could miss from such a distance. The shimmering, flamingo-pink beam glided straight towards the peak of Cordone's hat.

It never reached him. A moment before impact it recoiled, to skim in the direction of a nearby minaret. The beam disappeared for an instant and then, having curved round the spire, came back in their direction, zummed over their heads and zigzagged down a staircase, before rebounding again and this time shooting out of the building, to impact harmlessly against a sandbank in the distance.

Sykes, evidently surprised, nevertheless began aiming for a second attempt.

"Damn it," Lovett cried, "put that thing down! The gravity, the physics, it's all relative. You could hit just about anything from here."

"What?"

"Look, why aren't we falling towards the ground right now? The gravity is relative to whatever angle the ground is at."

Sykes looked crest-fallen. "Lovett, he's broken every law in the book. And now gravity? We have to stop him."

"All right." Lovett clambered to his feet. "It just means we'll have to take him alive."

Presumably Cordone had overheard this exchange, because he dashed off again up his walkway. Once more, the partners of the Anti-Sedition Squad gave chase.

This time, though, the pursuit was a brief one. At the end of the bridge were a half-dozen shallow stairs, which apparently led nowhere. Sykes, reaching them first and familiar by now with the building's peculiarities, barely broke his stride.

Lovett was alarmed to see his partner reach the top of the flight and, apparently, disappear. He tried to stop before the edge, but by then it was too late. Stumbling forward with a yelp of alarm, he flailed at the air, with his right foot on the last step and his left extending into the void. He flapped his arms in a hopeless attempt to steady himself, as the world spiralled horribly about him. Then momentum took hold and he found himself lurching forward, until finally there was solid surface beneath his outstretched foot. He staggered onward, into Sykes.

When eventually Lovett managed to steady himself and look about, it revealed three findings of note: they were the right way up again; they had somehow reached the top of a pedestal, with what appeared to be a sheer drop to the ground beneath them; and above them was Edwyn Cordone, once more upside-down and watching them curiously.

Lovett shrugged, and sat on the cold stone, better to look up at Cordone. Sykes went for his Incapacitor and then, no doubt remembering the earlier attempt, reluctantly joined his partner.

Once Cordone had their mutual attention, he gave a slight bow, doffed his outdated hat to reveal an equally ridiculous ginger wig, and exclaimed, "Hills! Mountains! Cedars! Might Men! Your breath is in your nostrils!"

"Did that make any sense to you?" Sykes whispered.

Lovett ignored him. "You've done it this time!" he roared at Cordone. "Where are these people going to live now? Your insane games have cost them their home!"

Cordone merely smiled through his preposterous false beard, gave another quick bow, and disappeared through a nearby doorway.

Sykes stared despondently for a long while at the point Cordone had vacated, while Lovett gazed at nothing in particular. Finally, Sykes abandoned his futile vigil and said, "Lovett?"

"Yes?"

"I think we've lost him again."

Sykes's observation was confirmed a few minutes later,

when they saw their cruiser hover into the purpling late-afternoon sky. It drifted towards the cloud layer, and the last they saw of it was a silver speck moving rapidly away from Earth 199.

Another hour passed before their despondent silence was broken. This time, the voice came from a window to one side and a little above them, and belonged to the Engineer they'd spoken to earlier. "Are you two stuck?"

Lovett was too taken aback for the sarcasm he knew the question deserved. "Yes," he said. "We are."

"How did you get up there?"

"We ran," replied Lovett, and Sykes added, "chasing Cordone."

"Oh. He left."

"Yes," Lovett agreed.

"Looks like he stole your cruiser."

"We noticed that."

"Yeah? Well. Good luck then." The Engineer ducked back inside his window.

Lovett called after, "Hey! Wait a minute."

The unshaven face re-emerged. "What's up?"

"I was wondering... what are you going to do with this place?"

"*Do* with it?"

"Well... demolish it and re-make it? What?"

The Engineer ran a palm through greasy black hair and cleared his throat. "Yeah. Well. We thought we'd leave it alone for the moment. Folks seem happy enough." He made an expansive motion with his other arm, which took in much of the structure beneath them. Lovett, on hands and knees, shifted to the edge of the pedestal to glance anxiously downward.

Only then did he realise that the settlers, who they had last seen lounging about the makeshift camp, were well into the process of moving into their labyrinthine new home. The children's ball game had developed new and convoluted rules to accommodate their unique surroundings, while the adults were shifting furniture or stood about conversing at improbable angles. The place was a hive of life – and the colonists seemed distinctly more cheerful.

"But... surely there isn't room for everyone?"

"Well, that's the funny thing. What with this place breaking the laws of physics and everything, there's actually quite a bit of living space. Mostly in the fourth and fifth dimensions, the Gaffer says."

Lovett lay back and groaned. The Engineer frowned for a moment and asked, "Will you two be all right? We could lower a rope or something."

Sykes, probably remembering again his disastrous attempt to shoot Cordone, replied, "I don't think that would work."

"Right. Well, if you're sure, I'd better leave you to it. We've another one of these to get up before nightfall."

"Another...?" Lovett stammered.

But by then the head had vanished again.

Moments passed. Moments became minutes. Then Sykes turned to Lovett, who by then was reclining with his eyes half-closed, and said, "Lovett? Lovett, perhaps we should be making a move after Cordone?"

In the end, however, it was late in the evening when the partners worked up the courage to crawl, with extraordinary caution, over the edge of the pillar.

And by then, Edwyn Cordone was long gone.

Dodge Sidestep's Second Dastardly Plan

Howard Watts

"He's out."

Philippe turned from his perch next to the hob, his servo's high-pitched whine preceding similar exasperated vocalisations from myself. I could see the little veg prep was scared, as the wooden spoon he held hung motionless in the air, save for a slight nervous quiver. I considered a soft reset with a two minute RAM wipe to erase this revelation, given by the Warden. Then I realised the risotto would be ruined if I did so, as he would forget he'd forgotten the dry white vermouth – which I'd just impatiently (and a little early in the method, but that's how I like it) reminded him to include. He'd then add it again, if he remembered, convinced (and quite rightly so if the wipe took place) that I hadn't reminded him.

"Carry on, Philippe," I said bluntly – resigned to the fact that whatever he came up with would have to suffice as dinner. Untying my apron I nodded to the Warden to head for the lounge. We adjourned there, and I closed and locked the door behind us, as Philippe had developed a little habit of turning up his ear, following him overhearing a conversation I had about him some weeks ago with the fridge freezer concerning his over-use of garlic.

The Warden sat straight-backed at the far end of the sofa, black trouser suit, white blouse, straight blonde hair bobbed half way down her neck. "We believe Mr Sidestep used the VV (Virtual Visitor TM) system to enable his consciousness to walk straight out of maximum security in an adopted host."

I sat down in my armchair, shaking my head. She started to deflect, managing a half smile which didn't suit her. "It must've taken him months to attune the projectors, thoroughly clean the system to hold the data without corruption, speed up the bandwidth so the transfer took place during visiting hour."

"Was he still using me as his primary Virtual Visitor?"

She looked uneasy, clasping her hands together upon the black leather satchel that sat upon her lap, and shuffled two seats up to be closer to me.

"I'm sorry, Martin, but..."

I leant forward, "But, I was *assured* my Bilateral Buddy's rights would be upheld? He told the judge and prison service, in holograph and writing, he would *only* be prepared to visit Dodge once a month."

"His rights *were* upheld, to the letter," she cleared her throat, "as I was just about to say, but it looks as though Mr Sidestep was not only visited by your Bilateral Buddy more frequently than originally agreed, more importantly evidence suggests your old system assisted in Mr Sidestep's escape, as Mr Sidestep's consciousness piggy-backed your BB's cache. As soon as he was out, Mr Sidestep's consciousness vacated, storing itself in a hired E-lock-up for a day or so."

I stood up and took a deep breath, placing my hands on my hips as I stared out of the lounge window into the summer's early evening. The TV read this posture and turned its screen on, selecting The Exercise Channel from the Altostratus Cloud Box, assuming I wanted a workout. I was about to speak as my smartwatch began shouting at me, complaining my side stretches simply weren't up to scratch, and I should start again. I told my watch to shut up and gave the TV a frown. The watch did so and the appliance got the message, blinking off without even the courage to show a standby light, and I relaxed, relieved my rapid movements hadn't triggered a far more embarrassing channel selection – not that *that* kind of stuff was shown at this time of day.

"He'd never help voluntarily," I said, turning on the spot, "his evidence was key to convicting Dodge of my attempted murder. His own appliances, abused and neglected, gave further evidence, resulting in his incarceration following the judges' verdict that he was (and probably still is) completely stark raving slack-jawed, mad as a bucket of frogs."

I could see she was thinking about what I'd said, turning things over in her mind – either that or she was just, well, looking at me? "You're not aware of all the details, Martin," she said opening her satchel. She passed me a grey folder and I sat back down to read, my glasses unfolding from behind my ears as they detected the text in front of me. It was all laid out in plain English – which was a relief as English is my first and only language. I did dabble with the odd poem written in binary during college, but unfortunately

01001001 0110110001101110111011001100101
0110110101110101011100110110100101100011

didn't really cut it as a catchy opener according to my English lit tutor – although he admitted with some enthusiasm that the rhythmic quality showed a certain unique, innovative prose, even though the intonation needed work, especially the zeros. Anyway, I scanned the page, blinking thrice so my glasses saved it all to their drive and handed her back the folder. Strange I thought – a folder, quaint and oddly tactile for someone her age, and I began to admire this woman's liking of the old traditions as my glasses folded away.

"So he could be anywhere," I said. "What about his physical form, the report doesn't mention if he's managed to find his corporeal body?"

She edged forward as she replaced the folder, clasping her hands together once more.

"It was released due to a court order obtained by his solicitor. Before that, it looks as though he floated around for a few days – getting to know the newness of the outside world, living for a while in the Gleampipe network, listening to traveller's conversations, adding a harmony vocal track to several commuters' music as they listened to their Strollpersons." Her smile became genuine as her eyes wandered to the carpet at my feet. "You must realise, he does have quite a unique insight regarding melodic function, his conjunct and disjunct motions, pleasing to the majority of listeners. Musicologists say his take on the chorus for..."

"I'm not interested," I said quickly, and her eyes shot back to mine as I continued. "What now, where is he, what is he up to, what does he want?"

"To answer your questions in order, I don't know, we don't know, probably singing, and royalties, perhaps. His remixes of several ancient recordings – well past their copyright and part of public domain – have generated considerable favour for him. He's become quite the sensation, and the public are eager to see him perform live."

From her expression I could see where this was going. I'll give her her due, she didn't have to hear my concerns as my face said it all.

"I'm afraid, Martin, Mr Sidestep's music has generated such a huge following, and don't forget he was up for parole next year – his fellow inmates can't speak highly enough of his Friday night punk rock sing-alongs – that my superiors have decided to ignore his escape and bring forward his parole date – public opinion demands such. The four judges are looking forward to seeing him live, too."

I knew it. Through the exposure of our case the Bleep Thump Bleep band had not only achieved sales from the re-issue of "Dance Detritus" enabling each member to purchase a private island, but Dodge was now heading for an appearance on The Ex-Con Factor. At this stage I was assuming his musical talent was somehow gained following a reversal of the "Full Rinse" cycle I had given him with his Build-a-Band Boogie Box, saving my life during his attempt to take it, and that some of the musical skill and awareness contained in that machine had bled into his head. So unfair.

"How the bloody hell can all this be *fair*?!" I asked. "What about me – still living in the same place – how come these people, Dodge especially, can profit from criminality and crap music?"

She looked bemused and shot me a disappointed frown. "No one said life was *fair*, Martin."

"Humph," I said, throwing my arms about, remembering to glare at the TV as its standby light flickered, "you haven't read the news – from next Tuesday, the Equal Opportunities World Authority are issuing 'Fairness Guaranteed' certificates along with all birth certificates. Any unfair treatment during life will be addressed and levelled out by a specially commissioned oversight committee."

There was an uncomfortable pause before she finally spoke. "Martin, listen. We've deciphered a key, a little clue he's left behind in every vocal performance he's released."

"They're not performances; they're plagiarism, just

adding a harmony to an already established recording – or changing the tempo. Oh, and they're not released, they escape, just like him."

She frowned at me. "Have you actually *heard* any of his music?"

Heard? Yes. Listened to? No. There's a *big* difference. From the kitchen I could smell Philippe had burnt the risotto, and I was eager to help – he was only a veg prep after all – perhaps I'd pushed him too hard too quickly, but on my money I couldn't afford the chef prep upgrade ROM board for him. "No, and I have neither the time, nor the intention of..."

She held up her palms for me to remain silent. "Please allow me to continue. Once Mr Sidestep's performances were analysed in order, start and end keywords were found embedded in the lyrics. They're way up in the range, only audible to cats – between 55 to 70 kilohertz. The words sung between these keywords in the normal range can be strung together, forming a message. You should hear it."

Reaching into her pocket she produced a microflec. I took it reluctantly, placing it into my system, thumbing "Play Once and Copy". A cacophonous mess invaded the lounge; it was so terrible even the speakers were looking at each other in confusion, wondering if I'd finally taken that last small step into frenzied musical lunacy.

> *"I get hysteria, hysteria*
> *I will survive, I will survive,*
> *Working my way back to you,*
> *I'm gonna find ya,*
> *In the summer of '69,*
> *I'm gonna finish what he started ..."*

I shrugged, thumbed Eject then Delete and passed the recording back to her as the lounge door burst open, splintering the wood at the lock.

Philippe stood there clutching my battery operated high speed roux whisk and my favourite paring knife. He lunged forward with the knife as the whisk's blades rotated, and I leapt for the floor, realising I couldn't miss, although with my recent luck there was no actual guarantee – even from gravity. The blade cut into the armchair's upholstery as his little legs moved quickly, kicking the splintered pine into the air, pointing the whisk at the Warden. A tune filled the room – identical to the brief edited clip that had just invaded the lounge, and I realised Philippe was *singing* Dodge's message. The Warden instinctively reached for the fruit bowl in the centre of the coffee table and threw it to my maniac Veg Prep. The bowl shrieked with a sorrowful loss of purpose as her fruit fell from her embrace, just as Philippe's primary protocol took hold. All those Braeburns and Valencias were a temptation too much and the paring knife angled down, intercepting the first of the bowl's windfall, and he dropped the whisk to begin peeling. Before he'd managed to quarter the first apple, the Warden had produced a weapon from her jacket pocket, and within seconds Philippe was a smouldering pile of broken components, whirring and clicking in his death throes.

She replaced the weapon as rapidly as it had appeared, her expression one as though nothing had happened.

"As I was about to say, Mr Sidestep's consciousness could be anywhere," she nodded to poor Philippe's remains, "proof, you'll no doubt agree?"

At that stage I wasn't convinced – perhaps it had been the garlic criticism he'd overheard that had pushed him over the edge. I wanted to believe that, but common sense (which, from experience is about as common as artificial intelligence) told me she was right, as he had been warbling Dodge's song. I swore at the smoke detector, telling it to switch itself off and not worry – upon reflection I realised with some embarrassment I was a little harsh, as it had been sitting quietly on the ceiling for three years without a single utterance.

"I was your veg prep's target, Martin. Not you."

"And what convinces you of that, Warden?"

"The lyrics Mr Sidestep arranged. It's almost the middle of June, 2069. That's when he intends to end your life."

Living alone is a psychologically expensive, emotionally dislocating experience. Modern life doesn't cater for singularities, even though the universe insists upon them and supermarkets still sell microwaveable "Romantic Meals for One". Every aspect of life today is geared toward sharing. Share buttons festoon everything. Even my coffee cup has one, so if I press it, my coffee cup's contents are immediately analysed and shared with my friends on VisageVolume, the recipe then downloaded to my cloud profile. Then, when I take a trip *anywhere* in the world, the bloody hotel knows exactly how I like my coffee.

Everyone wants to know the trend, where you are, what you're doing, what restaurant you're eating in, what pub you're drinking in, what you're drinking and with whom. Some people believe someone, somewhere's collecting all this info so they can replicate everything everyone has / likes / is used to, should it all go suddenly wrong and the info lost in a kind of return to reality reboot. Others know it already *has* gone wrong, and just wish someone *had* started to collect all this info to reboot life to the simplicity it once was, decades ago – sadly, before the technology existed to actually do so. Others think it's all a PS16 gaming master plan, to create a duplicate virtual world so real everyone would be online playing and the world's economy would collapse before tomorrow lunchtime.

Quite a few people say it (life in general) is all getting out of hand. On the odd occasion I drive the car, the driver's seat informs me how much weight I've gained since my last drive. "*Not very fuel efficient, are you Martin,*" or lost, "*Weight loss can point toward serious health issues, Martin.*" Wine bottles "*tut, tut,*" sealing their necks if they detect their wares being poured into a single glass, their labels scrolling warning text concerning alcohol abuse. Smart plates' rims scroll with the exact calorie, salt, sugar, fat and saturated fat content of your meal, once you've dished it up – and if that wasn't enough, as you fork up a mouthful the plate will blink with exactly what's on the fork, warning you of what you're putting in your mouth – "*A balanced diet's best, don't forget to eat your 5.8 a day,*" it reads, the vegetables surrounded by little red flashing arrows. Couple this with a smart loo and once your daily visits are complete, you'll get a printed percentage breakdown on the toilet roll of how efficient your digestive system's been in processing everything the plate told you about. At least the readout can be put to good use.

I remember a time when I was a little kid, a time when life was fact. Nowadays, every social update has to have some kind of importance, a revelation – everyone's sensationalising triviality. Sociality has taken hold of the human condition by the throat and will not relinquish its suffocating grip. Info updates have transported us into the realm of compulsive liars – and of that I'm ashamed to admit I'm guilty myself, and would like 9,738.7 online offences taken into account since I was born. Saying this, I realise I was conditioned at a very early age by my entire family, my schooling, my church – hell, the *very fabric of this reality*, to lie and accept such. Why should I trust them? Sorry you lot, there ain't no such thing as Father Christmas – you all lied about that and broke my heart, furthermore, what else haven't you been honest about?

Okay, back on track and up to date. I once postboasted I was sitting in a rather large and expensive restaurant in London on a Saturday night – only to be messaged by a friend saying he was there too and where was I sitting? In my armchair at home, actually. That night cost me more money in private express Gleampipe fares and a waiter bribe than the meal itself, as I hurried to get there and not be found out by my friend as a fraud.

Enough of my social commentary, but I would like to say one more thing before I continue my tale. There was an old form of punishment called solitary confinement – cut off from human contact. Alone, in the dark, with only your thoughts of guilt, your self-belief spiralling away as inwardly you stared at the circumstances responsible for delivering you there. Dodge delivered me to that place, manoeuvred me into my present situation. I'm now cocooned, cut off from the outside world, the essential exterior skin of reality erased through necessity. Freedom, my lover so taken for granted, she so unaware of her benevolence, myself, so aware of her unconditional love.

The Warden insisted upon it, just when I bloody well thought I was getting somewhere (wherever that was) with her.

"Martin, it's for the best," she said. "Cut yourself off," she said, "absolutely no contact with the outside world whatsoever – Dodge could infiltrate any mechanism which contains a memory cache. What's next, suffocated by your Big Cuddles Dream A Dream TM Duvet in your sleep, is that what you want?"

All that, just after I asked her to share a take-away with me, just after she shot poor Philippe, and just before an invite to The Ex-Con Factor arrived on my screen.

"Why on earth – or any other uninhabitable planet for that matter, would Dodge invite me along to this rubbish?" I mumbled, as the Warden studied the details on the screen.

"Perhaps to murder you live, during his performance?"

"Doesn't make sense," I argued. "He'd be too busy perfecting his act, always too determined to come out on top – that's one aspect of Dodge that's never changed." I squinted at the invite's fine print. "Ah, and this," I said pointing. The last line of the rather lengthy terms and conditions read, *I bet you don't make it, Martin – half the prize money says so.* I sat back and folded my arms. He had me, he knew I couldn't turn down a bet.

"You can't attend," said the Warden, standing and brushing a few metallic flakes from her trousers which the carpet thanked her for and began to recycle. "It's suicide."

"No," I said, my eyes fixed upon the screen, "it's the only way." I looked up at her with a wide cocksure smile. "Security will be tighter than ever if I attend, and if Dodge does try something, he'll go away again for attempted murder and be out of my hair for good. The life sentence was guaranteed if he tries again."

"Martin, I don't want him going away for murder."

"?" I thought.

Perhaps she did care.

She reached into her inside breast pocket and unfolded her phone. She contacted the Bleep Thump Bleep band's agent, to see if any member had been convicted and therefore eligible to appear on the Ex-Con Factor, briefly holding her fingers over the mouthpiece to whisper. "Imagine if you compete against him, with the band – the public will be behind you all the way and you'll have a very good chance of winning. Just think, the prize money will be enough for you to vanish somewhere where Dodge will never find you."

Fortunately, they declined, citing, "Previous commitments".

For me, I came *close* to being convicted for, and I quote the actual law: *It is illegal to avoid telling the tax man anything you do not want him to know, but legal not to tell him information you do not mind him knowing.* As I had avoided telling my taxman absolutely everything I wanted him to know, on the basis that either I wouldn't live long enough to recite everything I know – or he long enough to hear it if I did, I found myself in a spot of bother. But, as I didn't know what he didn't want to know, and he admitted he didn't know either, I was saved prosecution. I *was* however convicted in Brighton, some years ago under the following law: *It is illegal to have sex under the pier while Morris Dancing.* My defence concentrated on the fact I'd stubbed my toe on a rather large pebble, and was actually hopping around in pain, chasing my hanky as it blew around in a wind vortex that had been conjured up by the pier's supporting structures. Okay, my swimming trunks had taken a dive to my ankles, due to a faulty waistband cord, and with one foot free of them it may have appeared from a distance I was dancing. As for having sex at the same time – impossible – I hadn't had a girlfriend in years, well, not a real one. Brighton Magistrates' Court wouldn't have it, and I was fined and escorted to the city limits, banished never to return. Portslade was nice, though.

The Warden sighed as she put her phone away, "Without musicians to support you, there's no way you can perform."

"Then I'll sit in the audience," I said, "It's probably for the best – to end this." With that I hit print and waited for the invitation to appear from beneath the screen. At the bottom of the document were two tear-off Gleampipe express tickets.

"You're allowed to bring a guest," she said scanning the invitation before tearing off a ticket for herself. "I'll arrive early at the venue, check in with security and we'll meet up in the V.I.P. bar as indicated on the invite, before the show begins."

The 02.3 arena is a fine building. Plenty of Gleampipe exits, toilets, restaurants and bars, superfluous architectural adornments and colour schemes. I eventually found my way to the V.I.P. bar to find the Warden had changed into a posh green evening gown and matching high heels. She smiled and waved as she caught sight of me.

"You're looking very un-warden like," I said as I joined her side, unable to hide my attraction to her, even though she now towered above me in those heels. She smiled down to me briefly. "Is that in a good way, or bad?"

"Oh, good," I said under my breath, ignoring her gaze, attempting to catch the Beverageprep's attention. The machine finally slid over on its rail to face me.

"Lager?"

"No thank you."

"Are you sure?" it said, its monobrow creasing into a V above its single eye. "You look as though you're the kind of person that enjoys chemically enhanced long shelf life alcoholic beverages."

"Looks can be deceiving," I muttered, glancing at the Warden. "Do you have any real ale?"

"Only fake," said the machine, folding four of its eight arms in defence. "Our fake ales are so realistic, you couldn't tell them apart from the authentic."

"I'll have half an Imperial pint of anything light and hoppy," I said, producing my wallet.

"Phone payment only," said the machine as it reluctantly filled an old and out of date glass with liquid.

I pulled out my phone and placed it on the bar next to the Warden's then took the drink as the two phones began chatting. As they started to argue about operating systems and upgrades we both turned their volumes down once they'd paid.

"Here's to an uneventful evening," said the Warden, holding out her flute of what appeared to be champagne. I clinked my glass to hers, unsure if she referred to Dodge's possible antics, or those mounting in my head.

I nodded, then frowned a little after taking a sip of ale.

"Not good?" she asked.

"Yes, no – I mean yes, it's fine. I was just thinking, throughout all this, I don't know your name. I really can't keep calling you Warden for the remainder of the evening, can I?" My last two words sounded almost pleading, as though I was afraid she'd say yes.

"It's Astrea," she said, looking toward the door.

"What, they're on now?"

"No, that's my name." She turned to face me. "I'm happy for you to call me Astrea, Martin."

The bar filled with a brief overblown fanfare, trailing off as a brash gravelly voice asked the audience to take their seats. We finished our drinks and filed out of the bar to the auditorium.

I must say the seats provided for us were top-notch, affording us a superb view of the expansive stage. The lights dimmed and the gravelly voice returned, as a single spotlight shone upon the centre of the stage.

"Ladies, gentlemen and children, please welcome tonight's judges. Lord Chief Justice, Sir William, Vane-Tempest-Hightree." As the scarlet, black and white robed figure appeared from beneath the stage the

arena erupted with cheers, whistles and applause. The sound was deafening, but I couldn't stop myself from being caught up in the moment and found myself applauding too as the disembodied announcer continued as the three remaining judges joined the first. *"Chancellor of the High Court, Dame Barnstable-Tableberry-Ward, Senior Presiding Judge, Sir Rinstone-Harvey, and Deputy Senior Presiding Judge, Dame, Quella-Foxbottom."* Their expressions remained impassive, weathered alabaster, fissures of age, topped with their traditional pale wigs of tight curls. They moved in unison to their chairs and the arena fell silent. I noticed Astrea glance at me, but my eyes remained ahead, an uneasy feeling in my stomach that wasn't caused by the fake ale.

As the acts performed there was a distinct feeling of impatience, as though they were simply warm ups. For the most part, and as I'd expected, the acts were far below par, and I found my mind wandering as the night continued, wondering what Dodge had planned as I watched various ex-con artists try to out-perform each other. As the announcer spoke Dodge's name, the arena erupted once more. He walked on with his usual over-confident grin and swagger, arms held wide above his shaven head, hands waving, dressed in orange prison overalls. From the opposite side of the stage a group appeared. "That's the Bleep Thump Bleep band," I said, craning my head towards Astrea's right ear.

She nodded. "Previous commitments indeed," she said loudly, trying to compete with the surrounding cheers.

At once silence fell as the band stood behind their instruments, one behind a bass drum and high-hat, one holding a mobile device, the other standing in front of a microphone. "Martin – this is for you!" shouted Dodge into his mic, as the band played the intro to "Dance Detritus". Pandemonium exploded. There were people dancing on their chairs, dancing down the aisles, and I was certain I saw a judge's head bob side to side at one point during the first chorus.

"This is great," said Astrea, turning to me with a smile, "those harmony lines are superb!"

I instantly felt alone amid this sea of revellers, a human tide of unadulterated (and quite childish) abandon, lacking any composure whatsoever. My eyes darted about, expecting an imminent attack. But it never came, and before I knew it the performance was over.

The voice appeared once more. *"Ladies, gentlemen and children. Please welcome his Royal Highness."* A giant screen at the back of the stage leapt to life, there, the boyish grin of the king. Baseball cap worn back to front, straggly blonde hair protruding from the sides. *"The judges have passed sentence."* The king squinted, pushing his earpiece further into his ear with a thumb, nodding. Everyone sat and composed themselves as the other acts joined Dodge upon the stage as the king finally spoke. "The royal pardon goes to..." Then there followed that excruciatingly annoying pause, or in this case, a lengthy recess as members of the audience shouted for their favourite act. The king smiled, "The royal pardon goes to... Dodge Sidestep!"

"Let's go," said Astrea quickly.

I nodded, stood and pushed my way to the aisle, hurrying to the exit. We'd taken around five or so steps before a spotlight fell upon us. Instinctively we froze as Dodge's voice filled the arena.

"Martin – I owe you, please join me upon the stage." We turned slowly to see him holding out a welcoming hand as the audience turned to face us, applauding. "All this has been made possible by you, old friend."

I watched the audience as we walked slowly to the stage. Some had absolutely no idea who we were, the looks of bewilderment upon their faces similar to those of people who had realised they hadn't received a royal flush following the first five cards dealt in a game of poker – which I found a little strange, as I knew from my early betting days the odds were 649,740 to 1. Others knew exactly who I was, and were muttering behind cupped hands.

I looked at Astrea and she shrugged. "Don't worry," she whispered as we walked slowly up the stage steps, "security have taser snipers trained on him. One move out of place and they'll drop him."

I nodded and we joined Dodge as the band and other acts exited stage left.

"I always keep my word, Martin. I placed a bet with you that you wouldn't make it tonight."

From his breast pocket he produced an envelope and pulled out two small cards. "You did, so here's your half of the prize money." He handed me one of the small laminated E-cheques, which smiled up at me and winked as I took it. So cocky and confident, he knew he'd win and had already prepared two E-Cheques of equal amounts from his previous royalties, just to show the audience how fair he was. My eyes widened, half a million euros – just enough to pay off the balance of the mortgage on my one-bedroomed flat. Astrea took it from me and examined it, the cheque giving her a rather cheeky and somewhat inappropriate grin.

"Dodge," I said, not knowing what to say, "I don't know what to say."

He shook his head, "You need say nothing, old friend. Consider this repayment for all the considerable trouble I've put you and your appliances through over the years."

All three of us turned and walked down the steps, Astrea positioning herself between us. The audience began to applaud again and I looked over to the judges who stood, their expressions remaining impassive. Then shrieks filled the air and I turned to see Astrea topple down the steps in those ill-fitting heels, taking Dodge with her in a jumble of orange and green. I hurried down the steps and helped Astrea to her feet.

"I'm okay," she said, passing the E-cheque to me as Dodge stood, picking up his own. "Terribly sorry Mr Sidestep," said Astrea, "I'm not used to these high heels. I take it you're alright?" Dodge nodded back and we headed for the Gleampipe exit.

Security had cordoned off a Gleampipe booth for us. They allowed all three of us to pass and we stood there for a minute or so as the paparazzi took their pictures.

"So, what for you now, Dodge?" I found myself saying.

He shrugged as he smiled and waved, bathed in the flashlights. "An album, perhaps a soundtrack, perhaps a book. I don't know." Finally he looked at me. "Good luck, Martin, and thank you for this opportunity to finish what I started."

He keyed in his destination then stepped into the Gleampipe booth, turning to face his fans. Then his expression changed as the booth buzzed with uncertainty – you know, that tell-tale noise they give off when your area destination code doesn't match that of your ticket. He pulled out his E-cheque, and I was certain I heard it laugh as I watched his body become slowly disassociated. A distant scream came from the booth as Dodge's mouth opened wide, his fists clenched above his head, his expression one of utter contempt and hatred as the cheque arced to the floor. Then he was gone.

Astrea raised an eyebrow and shook her head. "I thought so."

"What on earth's going on?" I said.

She pointed to my E-cheque. "This is Mr Sidestep's. I swapped them during my faked tumble down the steps. I knew he had to be up to something, and the cheque was the only contact he had with you." She opened her clutch bag and took out a small security scanner, pushing the E-check into the slot at the top. The machine made a few offensive gurgles before spitting out the cheque. "Invalid," she said, "just a prop. The prize money is no doubt already sitting in Mr Sidestep's account."

I didn't understand. "So, why was he so angry when he left?"

"Realisation." She walked to the booth's keypad and thumbed in an administrator's code. "There, see?"

Upon the screen above the keypad was a wireframe representation of the last trip the machine had executed. It was a torus, a closed loop, without departure or destination icons or names.

"The cheque he gave you had an override built into it that would detour your ticket's destination – that's my guess, anyway."

I looked at her with an expression of "?"

"A tiny instruction to keep the traveller in an infinite loop. I'm betting Dodge intended your body to be stored indefinitely in the travel system until it died from dehydration and starvation, your consciousness trapped forever. He realised I'd swapped the E-cheques as it laughed at him. He's travelling in a circle, without an exit."

I nodded. "Just like the Wolverhampton ring road. He's alone, watching the same scenery passing by – no doubt listening to an infinite loop of his winning performance. He really did intend to repeat his original method of causing my demise."

She nodded. "Martin. Go get a drink, I'll meet you in the bar after I've confirmed this with the Gleampipe system admins and passed the info to the judges."

I took a pint of fake ale this time, taking the top off the pint as it sat upon the bar, knowing I'd spill it if I tried to pick it up as my hands were shaking with Astrea's revelations, just like poor Philippe's. The Beverageprep managed another disapproving stare as it watched me, even with one eye. Astrea joined me as I was halfway through my second pint.

"I was right," she said, pulling off her high heels and ordering champagne. "The judges have met in appeal and passed sentence, they're going to leave him there in the loop – punishment fitting the proposed crime."

I shook my head and took a gulp of ale as she sipped from her flute.

"So, what now for you, Astrea – back to work I bet?"

She shook her head. "You'd lose your money. I have a few days' leave left to take, so I think I'll take them now."

"Any plans?"

She sipped her champagne and thought for a few moments, then shot me a sideways grin as she clinked her glass to mine. "I hear there's a rather lovely pier down in Eastbourne. Would you care to join me for a weekend of Morris dancing?"

Martin, Dodge, and perhaps Astrea will hopefully return for one final plan...

One Is One

Michael Wyndham Thomas

The bird, there, right in the middle of the field. It didn't move – well, it did a bit, enough to show that it was alive. Its wings fanned a little, its head twitched. I looked away a minute and when I looked back it was over the trees. So it could fly. I couldn't believe it: was tempted not to but that was to be expected. It happens: you think you see what you want to see. I've played myself false that way before now, with other things. But it was there all right. They hadn't all gone, then, the birds.

It's the quiet, really. That took some getting used to. When I was a boy and we'd be on holiday, some remote place, one of the family would say *Isn't it quiet?* And it would be. None of that engine rumble at the edge of the day. *Isn't it dark?* was another one. You'd see a few lights at night, scattered, minding their own, but it wasn't town-night, not that sodium mist all across the horizon like bombs frozen just as they go off. Now it's all quiet and dark like that. Now everywhere is remote.

The animals are doing all right. To begin with you'd have thought they'd go berserk, be at each other's throats, driven by the sudden need to reconfigure the food chain. Bulls and dogs, I thought: bulls and dogs would be the ones to stake their claim at the top, along with anything that managed to quit the zoos. And sometimes, in the distance, you hear a flare-up of barks and growls, but then it stops again. Either they're quick killers or defending their territory or just greeting each other after their kind. But I don't think it's the first: I haven't seen any blood or mangling on my travels. As for territory, you don't see the same animals in the same places, either. This can make for surprises – nearly made my heart stop at first, to turn a corner, come face to face: "Shouldn't you be behind bars?" I'd think, or "Shouldn't you be on a TV screen, cantering around places with unpronounceable names?" Conditioning: I'll never be rid of it, I suppose, but it doesn't bother me. Since I see so few physical reminders of back then, memories have become almost physical themselves. It's almost as if, while they're floating through my head, I could pluck them out, set them in my hand like little music-boxes. My souvenirs. Well, lighter to carry than a lot of bits and bobs.

They don't bother me, the animals, don't bother with me. They just look – not quite through you but with the merest brush of awareness that you exist. "Oh, one of you," they seem to say. A bit like what you used to see in people's eyes, town centre, home time, buses and jams. You'd be caught in their vision for a flickery second, then dropped because, well, they have a place to go and a thing to do, just as you did, looking back at them the same way. Buses and jams, lights, sirens, home-time. More bits and bobs in the head.

Cars are funny. They're the exotic animals now. You see them in the oddest places. One was in the middle of a field. That's partly why I did a double-take when I saw that bird. I'll look away, I thought, and when I look back it'll be another sad little car gone as far as it can go and now at peace among the green. Back before, you might have called it art, someone's idea about dumping technology in Mother Nature's lap. And sometimes it is plain comical. One car I saw at the top of a ridge: a sporty job, flash and filigree, like you'd have seen barrelling down a hair-pin pass in an advert, open-top, pretty people, freedom and sex, always on open road, nothing in front or behind, nothing coming the other way. When did this country ever have such roads? Well, it does now, of course, everywhere. But this car on the ridge, it was perched on its underside, that's how narrow the ridge was. I was down below a bit and I worked my way over from side to side. Front and back, its wheels were touching nothing. You'd have thought a giant car-stork had let go its sling overhead, dropped the poor baby smack on the spine of the ridge. Nobody in there. Nobody in any cars I've come across, but that's how it was. The cars knew first. They came thundering out of garages, in conga-lines down multi-storey levels, out of supermarket car parks. They knew, and they tried to get as far as they could while they could. But then... perhaps that car on the ridge was driving at the sky. Beyond the blue horizon, eh? Isn't that how the song goes? Beyond the blue horizon waits a beautiful day.

I was in a place much like this when the cars tried to escape. An evening road, I recall, lush verges – just walking along. A car came screaming towards me. I might not have noticed anything – well, you know, country roads, hotheads making the most of a bit of space, pretending to be in one of those adverts. But there was a sharpish left bend where I'd got to so I could see right into the car and it was empty. I didn't think about the logistics of it all: a car driving itself, getting faster though the road was starting to climb, so nothing to do with momentum. Life, that's all I thought of, and whether I could throw myself deep enough into the hedge to hang onto it. But the car swung with the bend and raced past, still screaming. I mean, screaming. Not over-revving, not the whine of going flat out in low gear. Screaming with fear, human fear. Later, when I thought back on it, when I had a second to think with everything else going on, I actually wasn't that surprised. Humans made cars; hand-crafted or born by the hour on assembly lines, cars got to know their creators. Small wonder, then, that they became human themselves in some way: all that exposure to banter, anxieties, frustrations. Like they used to say about old churches, how the stones absorbed all the millions of prayers and something of those who prayed them. You can't blame the cars – if I'd been one, I'd have tried to get out sharpish and I wouldn't have waited for humans to leap in me. I'd have known that what was happening was all about them. Why give a ride to a problem when you can leave it in the dust?

I'm no omega man. You see the odd person here and there. To begin with it was like you'd expect: eyes shining suspicion in the dusk, movement of hands into pockets for something to attack or defend with. But it was just gestures, and anyway, it's always one to one. There are no packs of feral survivalists. Maybe there were, and maybe some of the heftier animals set aside their new unconcern and dealt with them. I can just imagine it, the beasts of the field walking away afterwards, turning once to look back, thinking, that'll learn you, shoe on other foot and all that. Feral survivalists. Films about the future were full of them. Always that scenario, dystopias every which way. Well, it made for good box-office: what's to come is what's to fear. Just think of all the films pumping out that message in a trillion cinemas, deep into all those heads. Abuse, really, an imposed disablement. Shake in your boots and carry on. Trust those who lead. They know how to sound like they know. Dystopias. One of the many cons back then.

When I meet someone, we keep things to a minimum. If one of us looks in a bad way, sure, the other will help. But no-one really does. Whoever I meet just looks a little woozily surprised, as though they've just woken up and the first thing they see is me. No doubt I look the same. We keep things light: how are you doing? Shoes holding out? Good berrying round here, good leaves? But there are unspoken rules. We never say "Have you seen anyone else?" It's a kind of fancy that – telepathically, you might say – we remind each other to stick to: the notion that we're the only two and when we've spoken we'll be on our separate ways and we'll make out however we make out and good luck to you, all the best. Things feel safer that way.

One thing we always swap, though, is where we were when it happened. One jolly lad was in the back of a car with a woman who wasn't his girlfriend. Naturally, the car came to life, handbrake-turned, flung them out and gunned it. They just lay there all crumpled and stunned. That is, he did:

"Not the foggiest idea where she went. Just me face down with my pants all askew. I got up, looked about, called. Thought she might have clung onto the car but she'd have needed to be a proper Houdini doing that. No, really – she'd been with me, I swear it, wrapped all round me when we got the bullet."

I was out for one of my walks, like I said, when that empty car came haring past. Alone when it happened. A sad feeling for a while, gut-pinching. But, as it turned out, the best preparation.

I like to keep my voice in trim. Nothing better than strolling along, orating to the day. I say, orating but I keep it low: still early days, after all, and despite what I've seen, how things are turning out, you still have to be careful. I have a bit of fun, putting on different accents, reeling through all the phrases that meant nothing and led nowhere: *systemic failure, lessons have been learned, we shall instigate a full review, the good of the nation, the good of the community, the*

good of the people, people, people... You could say I'm a
custodian. I have a care for the words, I pity them their
maltreatment, chained in phrases like that. I try to give
them the meaning they were always denied. If I say, *at
the end of the day*, it always is at the end of the day,
when the light's tiring and I'm looking for a place to
turn in. I found a bunch of stationery at the roadside
once, no doubt from a fleeing van. Between a wad of
paper was an envelope. I gripped it hard at either end
and said what I was doing out loud as I did it. Not too
hard, though; it was a nice one, cream, good quality, a
bit like they used to use for deeds and wills. I've still
got it. It might come in useful.

What that man said about his disappearing girl. It
made me think about the Bible, the rapture, that
prediction that all the good folk would be scooped up
from the earth before the end of days did for the rest.
I'm no scholar, no expert on anything: big pictures in a
primary school *Life of Jesus,* a vicar who always ended
his phrases with "um" – "Our Fatherum, Which art in
Heavenum" – that's all I remember on the faith side.
But I'm just wondering if it hasn't happened arse-
about. That things are trying to get back to what they
were, so all the *systemic failure* merchants have been...
what? Sucked into a fiery pit? De-moleculed? It's just a
theory – hardly that. And it seems hard lines on
someone like that girl flung from the car. Perhaps I'll
meet a theologian, a vicar, and they can fill me in, slip
me the word. Unless they too have been... well, like I
say, I'm just puttering round the edges of it right now.

Towns and cities I keep clear of. I suppose that
much in the dystopian films was right. Not that I have
any hard reason to – it's nothing I've seen,
experienced. The odd few people I've met, they weren't
country-folk. When we trade tales of where we were
when it happened, they weren't sitting pretty on a
hayrick or worrying about a fallow field. Then again,

they weren't all sagging and breathless, hotfoot from some metropolitan hell-hole. When it all happened, I expected to see streams of maddened townies at large upon the land, kitchen-knives aloft, laying hold of everything from squirrels to Herefords. But no. I did wonder if they'd all stayed put and were troughing on each other, or maybe the reverse-rapture had exploded them along with all the spokesmen and advisors and what-have-you. I went to the edge of a town one day. Silent. I went back the same night. Silent and dark. Streets empty, curtains still, nothing whizzing past my ear, or worse. There was one sound, like a saucepan lid sliding off. An open window somewhere, maybe, a kitchen where someone was just in the act of checking the veg when it happened and didn't have time to replace the lid. Didn't have time to remember lid, kitchen, street, world. Or maybe a gazelle was ambling about, knocking against something with its... flank, is it? If I'm honest, I never bothered with those nature programmes on TV. I'm making up for it now, of course, for real.

So the towns and cities might be ok. It's just one to watch, for now.

One fear I have. It woke me a few nights back, got me out of someone's abandoned bed and up at their abandoned window. A parakeet, I thought, a cockatiel floating about across the moon. I think that must have planted in my mind the hope that the birds hadn't all gone, which was why I was so happy to see the one in the middle of the field. A parakeet, I told myself, a cockatiel. A peacock? That kind of hard, air-tearing sound. I prayed it wasn't a klaxon, a trumpet: the announcement that, even now, there was someone out there with, God help us, a plan, an advisor who had, say, dodged the rapture-cull and was set on rounding up anyone who was left so that they – he – could lay new footings, place the foundation stone for cementing in, start on the new... the old... the same old...

That's the one thing that troubles my journeying: that the blue sky, the quiet water, the lazing clouds, the own-business-minding dogs and cheetahs will instantly be megaphoned out of existence by some hand-me-down Caesar. Who begat Charlemagne. Who begat Napoleon. Who begat...

Save the Dog

An Unsplatterpunk Primer

Douglas J. Ogurek

The renowned designer – an angioma covered a quarter of his face – petted a three-legged dog, then pivorted his client a profile of a severe burn victim amputee. She wore lingerie.

The client pivorted back his archive of digital prostitutes of both genders. He already had a burn victim amputee in his collection.

The designer pivorted his latest creation: a morbidly obese, wheelchair-bound man. He was naked, except for a colostomy bag.

Light and achievements radiated from the client's clothes. He made himself pass out to show his acceptance.

Loud applause preceded the next man, the designer's boss. The sound came from the boss's shoes. He pivorted the designer. "President of Waveroids is coming in two weeks. I want a challenge like Mommy Lard."

"But she was beautiful."

"She turned her babies into lard. That's not beautiful."

"Beautiful's boring."

"And I have to upgrade Righty. I'm sorry."

The designer, touching his angioma, limped to the dog. "He's fine."

"He's old. It's humane."

"He's in perfect health."

"I know, but image."

"Righty's healthy."

"The Waveroids client likes symmetry. Perfectionist.
Go with Mommy Lard."

Subject: Re: Unsplatterpunk
Mike Castro
mcastro@warpfissure.com
To: Douglas J. Ogurek

Hi Douglas,

This pivorting is an intriguing concept. It seems to
be a kind of 22nd century version of Twitter that
replaces vocal conversation and enables instant
absorption of vast quantities of data.

However, your work still needs more polishing to
achieve *WF* standards. I always espouse taut prose, but
you're taking it too far. I'm afraid my readers are going
to want more depth than what can be achieved with
the near-scenic POV that you've employed. I prefer
your more literary work with deeper POV penetration.
Comparatively, this story seems a bit juvenile.

Then there's the setting: a futuristic brothel whose
products are digital manifestations of staggeringly
unappealing prostitutes? I understand the thought
process behind this, but I think you'll have to tone it
down. I know it picks up on your recurring theme of
using controversial containers to convey a positive
message – I believe you call the sub-subgenre
"unsplatterpunk" – but my audience isn't as receptive
to this material as your typical reader.

You've also taken a risk in making your protagonist
a "renowned artist". I'm willing to accept that.
However, does the struggle that your artist faces have

to be in a brothel? Does his art have to be physically, mentally, and/or morally scarred prostitutes? "Hot Burn Victims"? "Homeless and Feckless"? "Death Row Discards"? Too much. Then there's the courtyard scene. What kind of harpist lights his instrument on fire and introduces Pachelbel's *Canon in D* with "Are you f—king c—ts ready for this sh-t?" You're taking it too far.

Could your protagonist have a similar goal in an atmosphere that's perhaps a bit less distasteful? Think about music, dance, or other art forms. Your story "NON" in *Theaker's Quarterly Fiction* #33 did this tastefully, if protractedly and in a lexicologically overindulgent manner. (I note with relief that you've really cut down the neologisms.)

And what about the three-legged dog slated for the chopping block? It encapsulates your unnamed protagonist's dilemma and mirrors his own disability, but it's rather melodramatic and obvious, don't you think? Dickens's Tiny Tim comes to mind. Perhaps you can make the source of your protagonist's conflict less external.

I remain open to publishing an edited version of this story. My advice for the next round: don't sacrifice clarity for economy, tone down the controversy, and eliminate the dog.

Respectfully,
Mike Castro, Editor
WarpFissure magazine

Subject: Re: Unsplatterpunk
Douglas J. Ogurek
To: mcastro@warpfissure.com

Thanks for your comments, Mike.
The precision of prose relates to the future. With

this pivorting thing, people don't need to talk. Everything is controlled through technology embedded in the brain. My characters communicate through a kind of mental messaging. The POV with minimal thought intrusion reflects this world. I want the reader to feel removed, but still interested in what's going on. Admit it: there's something damn compelling about a colostomy bag. It's a symbol for all the shit that's floating around the infosphere and competing for attention.

I've got ten pages of notes on the protagonist's backstory. His attention-seeking mother could have easily fixed his facial blemish and his limp, but she chose to use those imperfections to get pity from the husbands that she repeatedly upgraded.

The protagonist's existence is defined by his desire to exact vengeance on his mother and the wealthy men she lured. The "staggeringly unappealing" prostitutes that he creates as challenges for the more daring of his society are inversions of his quite attractive mother. So it jars with the protagonist's MO when the boss asks him to design a physically attractive prostitute.

I don't need to say anything about that bitch mother; all I need to do is keep the story going. Still, I really like *WF*, so I'll dip into the protagonist's head a little more in the next draft.

Regarding the controversial aspects of this story... yes, I like to hide a Christian message in gore, violence, and other taboo subject matter. The brothel and its products take to the next level society's obsession with conquering fear and repulsion. Today it's skydiving and horror films and roller coasters and reality shows. Tomorrow it's trying to screw someone that you find physically unattractive.

I want to write stories that would get me kicked out of church in the first paragraph, but hide a positive message within those stories. That's what unsplatterpunk is all about. Otherwise I'm just preaching to the choir. However, if this subject matter prohibits the story from publication in *WF*, I will gladly take it down a notch.

Regarding the dog, the protagonist does see it as a form of himself. So he has a dilemma: he wants to save the dog, but he also wants to get back at his mother by making the prostitutes as undesirable as possible (including that for the Waveroids president). Still, I get what you're saying about that dog being like something out of a Dickens novel. So I'll get rid of it.

Mike, I respect what you're doing at *WarpFissure* and I appreciate your willingness to work with me. I'll get you a revised draft soon.

Yours,
Douglas

Vile. That's what The Martyr would have said had she seen the bruised and bloody doll head floating on the reflecting pool. The head had provoked many since Peel arrived at Introspection Plaza to meet Focal Mezzo Rifter, who had yet to show.

Lip lights shone green and red through the artificial fog that clutched the plaza. Occasionally, the fog offered glimpses of the sculptures that contorted above the pool and, even less frequently, of a female painter staring at a canvas stained with a reddish-brown glob.

A giggle intermittently filled the plaza, but the shoe sounds that would likely precede Focal Rifter had not come. So Peel chewed a nebula and contemplated the piece that the Waveroids president had commissioned, but that doll head, now the focus of a foursome, kept disrupting him. Although The Martyr would surely express repulsion toward the head, she was never one to overlook the opportunities that came with physical imperfection.

The giggling again. Its source was a man hopping and pointing at the canvas. He spoke in falsetto. "She's painting! She's painting!" The painter started to hop too.

Something fluttered by Peel's head, then there was laughter. A gap in the fog revealed a woman on the ground beside the pool. She convulsed and shrieked with laughter. Even stranger, she didn't have a lip light.

From the fog emerged a man whose clothing carousel showed images of Genrelation Tower's "Sorceresses and Witches" gallery. Peel pivorted him. "Focal Rifter? I'm Peel Straits."

The lip light turned green and the carousel showed a piece from the "Teacher Teacher" gallery on the 53rd floor. "I know you. How can you design that uncleused filth?"

It wasn't Rifter. Peel held out a nebula. "These are good."

"Your work's deplorable. I don't care if you're disabled. A disgrace to Genrelation."

A scan of the man's collection revealed that he had repeatedly visited the tower, but never the 132nd floor, where Peel designed its most extreme pieces.

The lip light turned red and the man retreated. Each day as Peel ascended and descended Genrelation, he observed the many weaker galleries. If he designed for Rifter a piece like his boss Ceofix wanted, Peel might as well display it in one of those galleries.

The fog surrendered a view to one of the sculptures that twisted into a shape resembling Peel's inferior leg.

He popped a nebula about his boss's next potential spouse. Ceofix had passed out the nebulae to employees to celebrate the termination of his latest marriage contract. Then he had given Peel only two weeks to design a challenge for Focal Rifter.

The doll head drifted toward the painter, who continued to stare at her glob. Ugly, like Peel's angioma.

The giggler – he hefted a thick book – stepped out of the fog and waved at Peel. "Hi!" He sounded like a cartoon character, and he did not have a lip light either. The second person without a pivort system. He talked slowly. "I... understand... that... you..."

The woman, still on the ground, grabbed her stomach and chortled.

Peel pivorted "Point" out of habit. Then he spoke. "Get to the point."

The giggler giggled. People peeked through the fog. Unhurriedly the giggler licked his fingertips, then opened the book to the first page. "I... wanted... to share... this... story..."

"I don't have time for this."

The laugher crawled to Peel. "I see you are rushed," she said. "What's a *cinnamon* for 'rushed'?"

"What?"

"Another word that means 'rush'. You know... a *cinnamon*." Laughter. Giggling.

"I'm meeting someone." Peel stepped into a heavy patch of fog. Focal Rifter, founder of the Waveroids synthetic steroids baseball league, had very exacting standards. It was a major commission and Peel had to get it right.

The painter swayed her brush as if it was a conductor's baton. Despite all Peel's protestations, The Martyr never had his angioma removed or his leg repaired. So Peel kept the flaws as reminders.

The fog revealed a man staring at the doll head. His lip light was blue. Peel switched his system to hear the public pivort. "...outblur," the man complained. "I want the name and divicity of whoever did this." The profile revealed the speaker: Focal Mezzo Rifter. Rifter swiped

at the air, then something – it looked like a leaf –
tumbled into the pool.

The giggler and the laugher sat and watched Rifter.
They held hands and each had a voluminous book.
What kind of people still read?

A sound seized the plaza. It was Focal Rifter's shoes.
He pivorted, "I created this sound. It combines
trumpets and the sound of glaciers calving."

The painter watched the doll head – was nobody
immune to its lure? – while one of the sculptures grew
and then, as if curious about her dark glob, leaned
over her.

How easy it would have been for The Martyr to have
Peel's defects fixed. Instead, she used them to elicit
pity from the husbands that she upgraded twelve
times.

The painter reached into the water near the doll
head. She extracted her hand, flattened, palm up. The
thing on it looked like a piece of paper.

Focal Rifter, continuing his diatribe against the doll
head, emerged from the fog. His clothing carousel
displayed his collection of extreme works available at
competing towers.

The thing in the painter's hand moved slightly.

Fog covered Focal Rifter.

The giggler and the laugher stood. Since they didn't
have pivort systems, it was impossible to tell when
their contract expired, or if they were even married.

The painter, continuing to hold the white object,
reached into her pants with her other hand, then
pulled out a soiled maxi pad. The object took flight. It
was a moth.

The giggler and the laugher – they looked surprised
– clapped.

The painter used her pad to rub a red streak across
the canvas.

Perhaps the couple was married, and had been so for many years.

Subject: Re: Unsplatterpunk rev
Mike Castro
mcastro@warpfissure.com
To: Douglas J. Ogurek

Douglas,

You nixed the dog, you delved deeper into the protagonist's head, and you made the story more palatable for our readers. Your decision to mask Peel's art with vagueness wasn't without risk, but it's a risk that pays off. Moreover, the new conclusion subtly wraps up the story.

There's one area where I'm still not comfortable: the painter. Though she's certainly an improvement from the vulgar harpist in the first draft, she doesn't need to use menstrual blood to get your point across. Consider replacing the blood with something a little cleaner, something that's more... harmonious.

Other than that, I'm impressed with this, and I look forward to your final draft.

Respectfully,
Mike Castro, Editor
WarpFissure magazine

Subject: Re: Unsplatterpunk rev
Douglas J. Ogurek
To: mcastro@warpfissure.com

Thank you, Mike.

Based on your suggestion, I changed the painter's medium to watercolour. I also changed the conclusion as follows. I'm afraid that I'm not willing to make any further edits.

Yours,
Douglas

She was staggeringly appealing, and diarrhoea ran down her taut thighs as she laughed and cried and stabbed a baby. "...thousand five, one thousand six..." Through the filthy kitchen ran a waist-high transparent tube.

Trumpets and rumbles sounded from the shoes of the man who entered. A blue light glowed on his lip. The video on his shirt showed an obese man wearing a bra and sitting on a toilet while slurping cocoa that dribbled down his chin.

Vagueness permeated the kitchen. So did the smells of vomit, mildew, and other unpalatable things.

The woman – she had clean hair and lips that shimmered intriguingly – threw the dead infant into a pot of boiling water, then dumped a vat full of glop over her head. "Rooooaaaarrrr!"

The man removed his shoes. "You must be Mommy Lard."

The woman's eyes beckoned subtly, and glop dripped from her. She defecated on the floor, then mashed the faeces into a hot dog bun. A dog trotted through the tube.

"I see you turned your babies into lard." He took off his shirt, which now showed a limbless man sucking a straw inserted in a massive, faeces-smeared buttocks.

Mommy Lard pulled out a maxi pad, then scraped the blood from it onto the bun. Another dog stopped in the tunnel. Mommy Lard got down and squeaked, "Hi."

"Yes. You're a dog lover too."

She depressed one nostril – her nails gleamed a harmonious shade of pink – then shot snot onto the bun. "Ehhhhhhh."

The man took off his pants. His lip light turned red.

Mommy Lard ate the bun and its contents. Glop splashed on the floor.

The man's erection protruded in a more literary way. "Miiiiiiiiiine."

A three-legged dog limped unmelodramatically through the tunnel.

Heritage

Black Swan #6

Mitchell Edgeworth

"Your bile analysis indicates a high level of alcohol," the toilet said pleasantly. "You are suffering from... *Mild* Alcohol Poisoning."

"Shut *up*," Chase snarled, gripping the toilet seat. Strands of vomit clung to his lips. He jerked an unsteady hand out to fumble for the flush, and watched the purely liquid contents of his stomach swirl away down the s-bend.

"Not feeling so well?" A woman's voice at the doorway.

Chase remained on his knees, pressing his forehead against the toilet seat. "The toilet is talking to me. Why is the toilet talking to me?"

"It's a Europan hotel chain," she said. "You've never seen that before? I think it's a German thing. They like to analyse it."

Chase clambered to his feet. He was naked, and felt like he was about to die, and wherever he was it wasn't his cabin on the *Black Swan*. He stumbled over to the door and propped himself up against the frame.

A nice hotel room. A suite, in fact. The woman – Indian, around his age, wearing a dressing gown – had her arms folded and was raising an eyebrow at him. Fragments of the previous night crumbled down from the decaying plaster ceiling of his brain. What was her name? Started with N...

"Nisha," she said.

"I know," Chase said defensively. "I just... had a lot to drink, that's all. Don't worry, I'll be out of your hair in a minute." He began searching the tangled bedsheets for his underwear.

"I'm going to get some breakfast," Nisha said. "If you want to come."

Chase paused. He'd found his underwear and had one leg in his jeans. "Really?"

"Why not?"

Jupiter Junction – officially Leopold Cuvier Station – was the Jovian system's most important flight interchange and waystation. It hugged close to Jupiter, a tight orbit inside Io, switching passengers from interplanetary flights onto smaller ships and shuttles to take them to their final destinations: the floating ocean cities of Ganymede, the undersea cities of Europa, the forests and tundra of Callisto, and the dozens of smaller moons and stations in between.

By any measure Jupiter Junction was the solar system's largest spaceport, seeing over ten million passengers a year. It had a permanent population of three thousand but ten times that amount passing through at any given time: spacers, tourists, businessmen, backpackers, pilgrims, preachers, traders, smugglers, bounty hunters, immigrants, refugees, and a thousand others who rode the spiderweb of shipping lines across humanity's great diaspora. It had been expanded and developed and built upon for more than a hundred years, decade after decade, creating a vast labyrinth of docking stations, concourses, hotels, restaurants, bars, nightclubs, casinos, warehouses and freight yards. It was, in short, a flying city.

Chase sat at an al fresco cafe on Wells Boulevard with Nisha, wondering if he'd be able to make it to the bathroom to throw up in time without spilling it on an innocent diner just trying to cram down scrambled eggs and a latte between flights. He was trying to recall the previous night, without much success. The beginning was easy enough: leaving the *Black Swan*, going to one of the casinos with Keiji and Kingsford, a bar, another bar, maybe a nightclub... he only vaguely remembered meeting Nisha, and was surprised that she'd considered him worth taking home when he was clearly blitzed. "So, uh, sorry about the vomiting," he managed.

Nisha didn't look up from her menu. "We've all been there," she said.

"Totally," Chase replied. "Um, excuse me."

He made it in time, hurling up in the closest stall. On his way out the bathroom attendant gave him a disapproving look and muttered something in French. Chase returned to his seat with the pleasant feeling that comes after vomiting while hungover, the nausea abated, knowing that he wouldn't have to vomit again for at least twenty minutes. He was somewhat surprised to find Nisha still there.

"Uh, I should warn you," he said, after they ordered. "I'm first mate on a cargo ship. So... I'm not from around here. We move around a lot, I mean..."

"Just because I invited you to breakfast doesn't mean we're going shopping for wedding rings," Nisha said. She glanced up at him. "First mate? Aren't you a bit young for that?"

"I'm fourteen," Chase said defensively, then thought again. "I mean... twenty-eight. I still keep thinking in Martian years. And it's just a tramp freighter. Me and two other guys. Captain's the same age as me, actually."

"And how is the tramp freighting business?"

"Oh, okay," Chase said. "Not as good as it used to be.

Or as good as people say it used to be. We only got it off the ground this year."

"What were you doing before that?"

"Oh, this and that," Chase said. "Crewed on a canal ship on Mars, and an airship in Valles Marineris. I was a bouncer in Aaru, for a while. And I was in the army, on Callisto. What do you do, anyway?"

"I'm in the arts world," Nisha said, as her breakfast arrived. "Buyer and seller. I'm from Io, originally, but most of it's on Ganymede and Europa. What do you trade?"

She seemed genuinely interested, and it was the first time Chase had found a woman impressed by the cavalier life of a tramp freighter – not traditionally an irresistible vocation. "Oh... lots of stuff," Chase said, trying to gauge whether she was the type to be thrilled or repulsed by a man living at the edge of the law. "Sort of in a grey area, legally. Not drugs or anything, but you know. Bit of bioware. Earthware."

"Really?" Nisha said. "So you're smugglers?"

Chase leaned back slightly, suddenly suspicious. "You're not a cop, are you?"

She laughed. "No. "

"We're not smugglers," Chase said. "I mean... not first and foremost. We shift plenty of legit cargo. It just doesn't pay as well, you know? You do what you have to, to get by."

"Hmmm," Nisha said. "Do you have a cargo at the moment?"

"Nah. Just brought in a load of earthware from a dealer on Lucia." It had actually been a cargo of ball bearings from a tiny industrial shithole called Reikofen, but he was leaning once more towards Nisha being impressed.

"I might have need of a private ship," she said. "If your captain would be interested..."

"He's always interested in cargo," Chase said. He'd

finished his coffee, and his stomach was starting to churn again. "We're at Dock 228 at the moment, if you want to come talk to him. The *Black Swan*."

"Tell him to get in touch with me," she said, and slid a business card across the table.

NISHA RUPANI

Art, Antiques & Earthware

Chase pocketed it. "Very fancy. So, you want to write this breakfast off as a business expense?"

She grinned. "I think you can be the gentleman. I'll see you around."

Chase swiped his wrist across the paypad, watching Nisha's ass as she walked off down the boulevard, past the throngs of travellers, disappearing behind the manicured birch trees that divided the curving orbital street. He pushed his chair up and slouched out of the cafe, feeling fairly certain he wouldn't make it back to the ship before he needed to throw up again.

Keiji, the *Black Swan's* captain, was lying on the couch in the mess room reading an old paperback when Chase burst in and ran down the corridor towards the head. Keiji listened to him vomit noisily in the toilet before he returned to the mess and flopped down on the opposite couch.

"You look like shit," he said.

"Oh, really," Chase said with his eyes closed. "Because I feel fantastic."

"Spend the night in the drunk tank?"

"In a beautiful woman's hotel suite, actually," Chase said.

"Chase, if you need a raise, just ask," Keiji said, going back to his book. "You don't need to sell your body."

"You're just jealous that I got lucky while you came

back to the ship at a reasonable hour and played
backgammon with Kingsford, or whatever."

"No, he's still at the casino as far as I know. Anyway,
I hope for her sake you didn't throw up all over her in
the morning."

"For your information, we had breakfast together,"
Chase said. "Well, I mean, she had breakfast. I wasn't
really hungry." He pulled her card out of his pocket
and flicked it across to Keiji. "And she wants to meet
you."

"I hope she doesn't think we're running some kind
of travelling space brothel."

"She needs a ship for something," Chase said.
"Something to do with cargo."

"What, exactly?"

"Christ, I don't know," Chase said. "I was trying not
to throw up in my coffee. Anyway, I'm going to bed.
Give her a call. Or don't. Whatever."

Keiji arranged to meet Nisha that evening at a cocktail
bar called the Cabaret Voltaire on the Uber den Riese,
one of the fancier thoroughfares of Jupiter Junction,
near a cluster of high-end hotels and tax-break
penthouses for Europan billionaires. Chase was still
languishing in his cabin with his hangover, and
Kingsford had wandered back to the ship around
midday in the foul mood he was usually in after a long
losing streak, so Keiji went alone. He arrived slightly
early and sat on a plush leather sofa drinking an
overpriced negroni, looking out the Cabaret Voltaire's
wall-to-wall window. Nearly half the view was
comprised of the great planet alone, an enormous vista
of brown and beige bands, the station so close that the
planetary curve was more like a straight line. The sun
was a mere pinprick, a particularly bright star. The
frozen, glittering ball of Europa hung beside it like a
Christmas ornament. The bar had a genuine Steinway

piano and a decent player, and wafts of Mozart's 16th sonata drifted amongst the clink of highballs and chatter of conversation.

Keiji wondered why he'd picked such an expensive venue; it had been his suggestion, not Nisha's. They'd had a good run of cargo recently, but the *Black Swan* was never more than a few contracts from tumbling down a slope of fiscal catastrophe. It had been years since he'd burnt his bridges in Zutphen, but he still found it hard to tamp down on his subconscious expectations of high living.

It was the stupid piano, that was it. How many Steinways could there be left in existence? A hundred, maybe. Keiji's parents had owned one – a 2034 model, certified and authenticated – but he'd never once seen either of them play it.

Nisha, when she arrived, was more than he had expected. Beautiful, and dressed in what he surmised was a fairly expensive outfit, with a few rings that were either diamonds or convincing counterfeits. "Well," he said. "I guess I owe Chase a coke."

"Captain DuVal." She shook his hand. "I didn't really believe him when he said you were his age."

"I'm half a year older, actually," Keiji said, and regretted sounding like an indignant schoolboy. But something in his mind was ticking. Despite his good-natured ribbing, he had no problem believing Chase could bed somebody as attractive as Nisha. What he had trouble believing was that he could do so while wearing the sneakers, faded jeans and the bleach-stained t-shirt that he'd pulled on that night, when the woman across from him seemed to be wearing about twice the *Black Swan*'s monthly net profit on her fingers alone.

Or maybe he'd spent too much of his life in the snobby upper strata of Mars' wealthiest families. Still, aside from the clothes, Chase had already drunk enough liquor to leave him a shambling mess by the time he'd wandered away from the bar he'd been at with Keiji. "When you met last night, did he mention to you that he was first officer on a freelance vessel?" he asked.

"He did," she said, flagging down a passing waiter and ordering a glass of wine.

So there was that. "Did he mention what type of freelance trading we tend to engage in?"

"He did," she smiled.

Keiji tilted his head and looked at her with suspicion. "You're not a cop, are you?"

Nisha laughed. "You know, he said the exact thing! You two haven't been doing this very long, have you?"

"I've owned the *Black Swan* for nearly five years," Keiji said, which was not untrue, although it had spent four and a half of those in a junkyard on Mars.

"You're a young entrepreneur," Nisha said. "Nothing wrong with that."

"Your card says you're an arts and antiques dealer."

"Yes. Earthware, mostly. To high-end clients."

"And how large is the earthware you'll be needing transported?"

"Small enough," she said. "It'll be in a package, perhaps one metres by twenty centimetres. It will be part of the agreement that you leave that package unopened."

"I'm not transporting something unless I know what it is."

"It's earthware," she said. "And you won't need to get it through customs. It will be left in orbit around Jupiter, in a cargo pod, with a beacon that I'll give you the co-ordinates for. You deliver it to me on Ganymede, I pay you, the end."

Keiji leaned back in his chair. "So it's that kind of deal," he said. "Well. That sort of thing isn't cheap."

She tapped a number into her computer and flashed it over to him. "$50,000!" he said.

"No. Gannish francs."

"Oh," Keiji said. "So that's..."

"About 40,000 Martian dollars, at the moment."

"That's still an awful lot of money for a jaunt from outer orbit to Ganymede."

Nisha shrugged. "There aren't a lot of independent vessels around these days. I need somebody discreet."

Keiji stared at her inscrutable smile. The pianist had switched to "Doll's Funeral", by Tchaikovsky, one of the first songs Keiji had ever learned to play. It made him feel eight years old again, in the musty smell of his tutor's sitting room, earning a rap on the knuckles from a straight edge ruler whenever he lost concentration and looked out the ivy-fringed window at the canals of Zutphen, wishing he was anywhere else. Stefan Langeveld had been a rickety, decrepit ninety-something, Earthborn, from Roermond, who claimed to have once played for the Residence Orchestra in The Hague. As a child Keiji had hated that man. Now, as an adult, he looked back and wondered what that would have felt like – your best days trapped behind glass inside picture frames, adorning the room where you lived out your last days teaching piano to uninterested children.

Keiji didn't trust this woman. But then, when did he ever do business with people he trusted?

He drained the last of his negroni. "You've got a deal."

When Keiji returned to the *Black Swan*, Chase was sitting on the couch in his underwear eating a bowl of cereal, probably his first meal of the day. Chase's infrequent hangovers were about the only time Keiji saw him without an alcoholic drink of some kind in his hand. "Oh, good, I thought you might have died," Keiji said.

"So did you meet her?" Chase asked. "She's a looker, right?"

The captain sighed, sat down on the couch and pulled his shoes off. The TV was blaring a subtitled Europan cop show about a German shepherd that was apparently also a homicide detective. "She slept with you because you told her you were the first mate on a private ship. You were probably drunk enough to tell her you were a smuggler, too. She used you."

"Somehow my broken heart will get over it," Chase said through a mouthful of cereal.

"In any case. She has a job for us. We're picking something up from Jovian orbit and delivering it to her on Ganymede."

"From where in Jovian orbit?"

"Just... in orbit. A cargo pod, or capsule, or something. She's sending us the co-ordinates later."

"Uh-huh," Chase said. "I know that we're not the law-abiding types, but I'd generally prefer to know what it is that we're becoming accessories to."

"Yeah, well. Beggars and choosers. Keep it in your pants next time."

Jupiter's orbit was one of the busiest sectors in the system. The Galilean moons alone had a population of over two hundred million people; tally up the remaining fifty-nine moons, stations, drifters and caravans and it was closer to two hundred and fifty million. The flight corridors between the inner moons and stations were tightly controlled by the ISA, routing tens of thousands of ships every day, from tiny independent traders like the *Black Swan* to enormous container vessels hauling thousands of tonnes of iron ore.

Further out, beyond the realm of the Himalian

moons, space was quieter. The *Black Swan* was out past
Elara, in a slow parked orbit around Jupiter, as close to
being motionless as it was possible to come in the
vicinity of such a huge planet.

"So what are we thinking it is?" Chase said. "Drugs?
It's drugs, right?"

"It's not drugs," Keiji said. "She's an earthware
dealer."

"So we're out here surreptitiously picking up a 20th
century armoire, or something," Chase said. "Probably
cheaper to go with Solar Express."

"Well, I mean, obviously it's going to be stolen,"
Keiji said.

They were sitting on the flight deck. Chase was
slouched in the co-pilot's chair with his feet up on the
console. Kingsford was sitting at the pilot's controls,
while Keiji had the navigator's desk. They'd been
sitting there for several hours, awaiting Nisha's beacon
code, which was late. Chase's empty beer bottles were
starting to stack up on the console, and Kingsford was
playing online poker, a waft of his cigarette smoke
coiling up towards the air vents.

"Well," Chase said, "I reckon she's been caught." He
stood up. "I'm going to the fridge, anyone want a
beer?"

"We're on a job here, you know."

"Get me one," Kingsford said, without looking up.

Keiji sucked his teeth in irritation, and turned to the
nav panel. To take his mind off things he scrolled
through the registered vessels coming through the
Jovian system, their trails lighting up the screen like a
cat's cradle as they weaved their various paths through
the moons and stations. He could see those coming
close to the planet itself, angling past it on an
interplanetary route, upsystem to Saturn or
downsystem to Mars and Venus. Gigantic mineral
freighters, some dragging trains of cargo pods a

hundred kilometres long, still dwarfed by the bulk of
the planet. They were all registered to the mining
companies, tagged with nothing but serial numbers. It
was the smaller vessels that were named. He picked
out two cruise ships, the *Spirit of Adventure* and the
Celestial Queen, one departing from Jupiter Junction
en route to Mars and the other curving in from Venus
to return to Ganymede. There were private vessels with
private itineraries, ranging from a tiny pleasure yacht
registered in Europa called the *California Condor*, to
an enormous, stately cruiser called the *Lince*, which
Keiji checked and confirmed as the Adrastean royal
family's private ship. There was a Romani caravan
heading out to the Trojan trading posts, a Europan
navy vessel on routine patrol, a few rag-tag traders like
the *Black Swan*...

And then there was something else. An insistent
beeping on his computer. A message, from an
unknown sender, with a single string of code attached
to it. The beacon. "Kingsford," he said, and flashed the
data over.

The pilot cracked his knuckles, closed his poker
game and fired up the *Swan*'s engines. "Three
minutes," he said. Keiji went down to the airlock to
suit up, and in the corridor he met Chase coming back
from the galley with a bottle of Green Dragon in either
hand.

"You want me to go?" he said.

Keiji snorted. "What have you had now? Four
beers?"

"Oh, please. This is me we're talking about."

"I'll go," Keiji said.

"Seriously. I'm fine."

"Not because I think you've had too much to drink,"
Keiji said, pulling his spacesuit out of a locker.
"Because I think you'll probably crack it open to see
what's inside as soon as you get it back in the airlock."

Chase chuckled. "Well, I mean… yeah." Keiji grinned as the airlock door slid shut behind him.

"OK, I'm getting you close as I can," Kingsford said over the suit radio. *"Looks like it's about a metre long. Very thin. Confirm tether?"*

"Confirming tether," Keiji said, buckling himself to the safety cable. "Opening airlock."

Keiji had done maintenance spacewalks half a dozen times since they'd left Mars, but the thrilling feeling of stepping out into space never quite left him. This was it – as close as you could get to the void. Nothing between you and sudden death but the skin-hugging membrane of the second-hand spacesuit you bought on sale at an army surplus store.

At this distance, Jupiter was merely a bead of light; only the digital tracery on his spacesuit visor marked out the positions and orbits of the other moons ringing it, revealing it to be a planet. That was one of the great myths everyone carried in their subconscious – the idea that the moons of gas giants were all bunched up and close together. They were, compared to the distance between planets, but that was not a useful comparison. The *Black Swan* was now more than ten thousand kilometres away from the restaurants and cocktail bars of Jupiter Junction.

Keiji floated in space for a few moments, the tether unspooling behind him, hunting the star-studded blackness in front of him for the package. *"I see it,"* he said, and pushed forward from the airlock, drifting towards it. Kingsford had been right: it was a small white cylinder, one metre long, maybe twenty centimetres wide. A tube, really, vacuum-sealed and featureless, with a tiny green light flicking on and off at one end. As he loomed towards it Keiji reached out and grabbed it with both arms, hugged it tightly, and flicked the command for the tether to reel him back into the airlock. *"All good,"* he said to Kingsford as soon as the airlock doors slid shut. *"Set a course for Ganymede."* He felt the *Swan*'s engines purr slightly louder as the pilot locked in a course.

Chase was waiting for him in the mess. "Soooo," he said. "What is it?"

"I don't know and we're not going to look," Keiji said. It had seemed pointless to go put such a small package in the hold, so he'd stored it in an empty spacesuit locker.

"She'd never know."

Keiji snorted. "You don't know that. She could have anything rigged on there. Besides, we probably don't want to know. Plausible deniability."

"I bet on your deathbed you'll wish you looked," Chase said. "How long to Ganymede?"

"Two hours, depending on traffic."

Ganymede had once been an icy wasteland, a rocky moon enveloped by a frozen ocean hundreds of kilometres thick. Rather than the Europans, much closer to Jupiter, who had sheltered in undersea cities in the liquid ocean beneath their ice cap to be protected from the great planet's radiation, or the Callistans, whose ice and rock mix had been developed into an equatorial band of tundra environment, the settlers of Ganymede had warmed and melted their ice cover almost entirely and created a single enormous ocean covering the moon's surface. Orbital reflectors which had once melted the ice now provided heat and light, and the world-wrapping ocean was dotted with great floating cities, roaming ship-towns and artificial islands.

Keiji had assumed Nisha would want to rendezvous in New Rheims, the largest and greatest of the Gannish cities. Instead she'd provided them with the address of a pleasure resort near the equator on an island called Nouveau Taravai. It was a strip of rainforest mountain, a spine of green jungle fringed with sandy beaches and coral reefs, maybe ten kilometres long. Macaws screeched through the treetops and dolphins swam in the lagoons. It was all artificial, of course, gengineered and gene-spliced and carefully modelled. Even the island wasn't real, it was floating, because Ganymede's seabed was a hundred kilometres below the surface. But as they bounced along a gravel track switchbacking down a slope stinking of rotting, florid vegetation, all Chase could think was how nice it was to be back on a solid world again, a place where the horizon stretched away, where you could look up and see blue sky instead of the other side of an asteroid's sculpted interior. His shirt was slick with tropical sweat and he could feel the warmth of the sun on his arms – the real sun, even if it had to be magnified.

Keiji was driving. The package was inside a duffel bag in the back seat. Kingsford had stayed aboard the *Black Swan* in the island's small harbour, which had been built on the other side of the ridge to shield the holiday villas and beachside bungalows from the sound of ship engines or aircraft.

Chase glanced into the back seat to look at the duffel bag. "Last chance," he said. "Sure you don't want to know?"

"You're fucking hopeless," Keiji said, shifting the gearstick awkwardly as he negotiated the jeep down another bouncing side-track. For somebody who had successfully turned the *Black Swan* from a decaying heap into a spaceworthy vessel, he had a shockingly bad feeling for machinery. Chase winced every time he changed gears. He could feel the gearbox grinding in distress.

Keiji didn't care. The jeep was a fifth-hand Martian Army vehicle which had survived worse trauma than its current owner's indifference. They passed a hand-

scrawled wooden sign which read: PLAGE DE LA
PERLE. Nouveau Taravai was irritating him. The
quality of the jungle road, in particular, was irritating
him. He wanted to get the package to Nisha and leave,
not least because Chase's relentless curiosity was
contagious.

The road eventually opened out onto the eastern
beach, a crescent-shaped curve of powder-white sand
dotted with thatched-roof bungalows. Plage de la
Perle – Pearl Beach. Wooden jetties ran in a rickety,
maze-like fashion out into the lagoon, villas perched
above crystal-blue water. Bikini-clad holidaymakers
from New Rheims, Laguna and Osiris were tanning
themselves on beach beds, strolling in the gently
lapping water, and drinking cocktails in the shade of
palm fronds.

"Jesus," Chase said. "Can we stay a while?"

Keiji snorted. "It's all fake. If you want a beach
holiday we can go back to Mars and go to Chryse or
Haven."

"How is that any less fake?"

Keiji considered that for a moment, as they
crunched across the sand, the strap of the duffel bag
rubbing across his sweat-chafed back. "Well... they
don't pretend. They know they're Martian, that they're
terraformed. This is all... I don't know. That shitty road,
right, that nearly took out the jeep's suspension?
Bouncing up and down all over the island? Why
couldn't they have just paved it when they built the
place? Because they want to pretend they're in
Indochina in 1925. That's why."

That argument lost a little weight as they
approached the resort, which was less Cambodia and
more Polynesia. Jet skis buzzed between yachts riding
at anchor in the bay, and French pop songs came
floating over a thatch fence concealing a private pool
party – Keiji caught glimpses through the gaps of

tanned bodies and drunken antics, girls wrestling with each other on boys' shoulders. They followed the directions Nisha had given them, walking deeper out onto the labyrinth of jetties. They gave the appearance of being rustic, ill-shaped planks warped by the salt and the sun, but Keiji suspected they had a carbon-polymer underlay. Even as the water became metres deep, the sandy bottom was clear. A salty breeze brought some relief from the heat. It stirred sudden feelings of nostalgia in Keiji, the way that only a smell can, of family holidays on private beaches in the Haven Islands, a long time ago.

"I don't see what the road has to do with anything," Chase said, watching a bunch of kids running off the jetty and cannonballing into the water. "I like it, anyway. Nice place. Why don't we stay a bit and go swimming?"

"Not here," Keiji said. "Not a place where she is. You want to have a holiday, we'll get the 50,000 francs and go. But not here."

They found Nisha in a private villa at the edge of the lagoon. A security bot buzzed angrily at them, like a disturbed wasps' nest, before she called it away. There was a glass-walled infinity pool at the edge of the ocean itself – Keiji thought that a tad ostentatious – a four-poster bed, a small bar. The entire ocean-facing side of the villa had no wall, and opened up onto the deep blue sea and the cerulean sky, Jupiter's mass just beginning to peek over the horizon. Keiji thought it looked quite pretty but wondered what happened come monsoon season, before remembering the entire island was probably surrounded by an invisible protection field. The outer worlds were much more reliant on technology than Mars was.

Nisha herself was reclining by the pool, wearing a bikini and sarong and drinking a French martini. She stood up to greet them as they entered.

"I hope you're just renting this place," Keiji said. "If you live here, I'm going to have to ask for more money."

It was a weak joke, but he was feeling uneasy about the whole deal. It had fallen into their laps too easily and they'd pulled it off too easily. Easy money was always suspicious. As an unlicensed trader and occasional smuggler Keiji was often, in the back of his mind, expecting men wearing sunglasses and flak jackets to pop out from around a corner screaming something like "Federal agent, hands in the air!" This was one of those times.

But then, they hadn't really done anything wrong. Just picked up an innocuous cargo pod. From random coordinates in Jupiter's outer orbit. And then brought it to a lavish beachside villa. For 50,000 francs.

Nisha smiled. "This is one of my business partner's timeshares. I'm of, shall we say, no fixed address. I take it everything went well?"

Keiji unzipped the duffel bag and handed her the pod. "Can we please ask what it is?" Chase said. "Please? It's killing me."

"It's something very, very old, and very, very expensive," Nisha said. "Literally priceless, if you ask me, but my clients think otherwise, and what would I know?"

"I thought you were a dealer," Keiji said.

"Oh, I am. But my talents lie towards the procurement side."

"A thief, then."

"An ugly word. I wouldn't use it." Nisha flashed her computer open and signed off on a transfer to Keiji's Lucian bank account. "Let's just say I get things from where they are, to where they should be. I'm just a courier, really. Like you. Can I offer you a drink to celebrate?"

"Thank you, but we have a schedule to keep," Keiji said, before Chase could jump on the offer.

She shrugged. "As you like it. I have to say, I had my doubts, but I'm pleased with your professionalism. Perhaps we can do business again sometime." She offered him a business card.

"I already have one," Keiji said.

"Maybe you, then," she said, handing it to Chase. "I'll be here for a few more days, if you're around," she added lightly.

"See that?" Chase said, after they'd said goodbye and were walking back down the wooden jetty towards the coast. "Did you *see* that? I told you she was into me!"

"I forbid you to see that woman again," Keiji said.

"You're not my dad!"

"I am your captain," Keiji reminded him, "and something feels wrong about all this."

Chase sighed. "You know, sometimes I wonder why you got into the shady space cargo business at all. Kingsford does too. I mean, God, for all we know this was one of the more ethically sound deals we've done. It might have been a pod full of sawdust for all we know."

"Yes, I'm sure it was a pod full of sawdust," Keiji said. "Anyway, I'm not bringing the *Swan* down through low orbit again, all the way out here, so you can have a booty call."

"I'll take the shuttle then," Chase said sulkily.

A few hours later they'd left Ganymede's atmosphere and were on the slow, quiet cruise back to Jupiter Junction. Keiji had been lying; the *Black Swan* never had any particular schedule to keep, and they'd kick around the space station for however long it took to secure another cargo contract. He was feeling good, despite his misgivings on Nouveau Taravai. Nisha's job had been quick and easy and no harm had come from it and now, even after running the gauntlet of his bank's exchange rate, there was another $39,422 MAD in his bank account. He even found himself whistling in the steam-filled galley while he cooked stir fry for the crew's dinner. Life as owner and operator of a tramp freighter was a financial rollercoaster, but that was no reason not to enjoy the highs while they lasted.

The three of them ate in the mess, leaving the ship on autopilot and gathering around the TV. It was just past 6pm in New Rheims, and the evening news bulletin was on some local channel – French, but subtitled in English. Chase and Kingsford were talking about the casino back on Jupiter Junction. Keiji was half-listening to them, half-watching the subtitles.

Something caught his eye. He paused with chopsticks clutching beef and capsicum halfway to his mouth, halfway through a subtitle.

taken in the past 12 hours and reported missing this afternoon.

"...supposed to tip them if you've lost all your money?" Chase was saying. "I mean, yeah, you should at least try to..."

"Shut up!" Keiji hissed. "Look!"

Carpo's Shinto priests have requested assistance from Interpol in dealing with the investigation, as Carpo has no local police authority. Investigators from the Gannish Gendarmerie and Europan Federal Police have been dispatched. Kusanagi has featured in Japanese folklore for over two millennia and archaeological records indicate it could date back to at least 200 AD, which would make it the oldest human artefact in existence. Experts say it is literally priceless.

"Oh, fuck," Kingsford said.

The TV news had long since moved on to a government sex scandal in New Rheims, but Keiji had his computer scanning all the news channels now, flashing images and sound bytes out across the walls of the mess. Carpo looked like a pleasant place – a tiny little asteroid moon, green trees and Zen gardens, Japanese tile rooftops and Shinto monks walking around koi ponds. That was the stock footage. The live footage had stern-eyed detectives and sanitised forensic bots crawling all over the place.

"This is fucked," Keiji said. "This is so fucked. What the fuck are we going to do?"

"It's probably not a big deal," Chase said, although he looked worried. "All we did was move it. She's the one who stole it."

"I cannot believe," Keiji hissed, "I cannot *believe* that your dick has got us into this! That you getting drunk and falling into bed with some floozy has led to this... fucking... a fucking heist and manhunt!"

"Don't blame me!" Chase said. "You're the captain, you're the one that went and made the deal! What does it matter how we met her in the first place?"

"If you could keep it in your pants..."

"You know what?" Kingsford said, over their shouting. "I don't remember seeing any package or any news story or hearing you talk about this. All I know is that I fly the ship. Yep. I just fly the ship." He headed for the flight deck, before sticking his head back around the doorframe and adding, "And if you want me to fly the ship the fuck away from Jupiter, just say the word."

"No!" Keiji said. It was louder and bolder than he'd meant – he was standing up, sticking a finger out at the pilot's worried face in the doorway. His eyes were locked on one of the screens he had open. A Europan newsfeed, running with exclusive security footage. A barely noticeable shape in the shadows of a traditional

Japanese interior, wooden floorboards and paper screens. The TV graphics helpfully highlighted it, pointed out the camouflaged shape at the edge of the camera's field of view. A person wearing a camosuit, a silhouette of colour and shadow. A lithe, female figure.

"We're going back to Ganymede," Keiji said.

"Hang on," Chase said uncertainly. "What are..."

"Set a course for Ganymede," Keiji said. "We're stealing it back."

Ganymede's day lasted for something like 170 hours, or a week, as far as Martians were concerned. It was quite disconcerting to return to Nouvea Taravai eight hours after they'd left it and find the sun – concentrated and amplified by orbital solettas, so that it was almost as bright as on Mars – still in the middle of the sky. "Why don't they just turn the solettas off at night?" Chase muttered as they walked back up the beach.

"It's not like flipping a light switch."

"Yeah, well, I tell you what, this'd be a lot easier if it was night-time."

"Wishes and fishes, Chase. Anyway, go do your thing. I'll wait here."

Chase sighed. "I'm not happy about this."

"Me neither, so let's get it over and done with."

"Is this, like, a Japanese thing?"

"Oh, for fuck's sake."

"Well? Is it?"

"You don't need to be Japanese to appreciate something like this," Keiji snapped. "It's the oldest fucking... *thing*, object, in existence. That's part of all of us. You don't have to have a shred of Japanese heritage to think that maybe it belongs in a shrine instead of the private collection of some business magnate in Agassiz." He glanced down the jetty. "So go and get it back before it ends up there."

Chase walked down the jetty, hands in the pockets

of his jeans, tropical sweat gathering in his armpits. He was tempted to go back and tell Keiji to try to get the sword back himself if he wanted it so bad. He wished he'd never met the woman.

The security bot was more aggressive upon his arrival this time; it locked onto him and let out some shrieks. Nisha silenced it, but didn't look particularly happy to see him. "You're back quick," she said.

"How could I stay away?" Chase grinned, doing his best to look like a cocky teenager, and being surprised that he succeeded; although if anybody had experience living a lie it was him.

"Right," she said. "I'm afraid it's not a good time."

"Oh?" Chase said, stepping inside the villa. The sea breeze rippled the infinity pool, and fluttered the flowers on the dining table. "Are there other suitors?"

"Not in the way that you think," Nisha said. "I'm sorry, but you'll have to come back later. You could have called first, anyway. Come back tomorrow."

Chase frowned. Now he was going to have to be pushy, and that wasn't something he was used to acting. "What, you're expecting people? It can't be that urgent, can it?"

Nisha narrowed her eyes. "Yes, it is. Now piss off."

Chase sighed. "Oh, jeez. Alright." Nisha had already told the security bot to recognise him as a guest, so it made no objection when Chase flipped open its control panel and powered it off entirely.

"What the hell are you doing?" Nisha said, but Chase had reached into the back of his jeans and pulled out his Webley. Nisha's eyes went wide. "I'm sorry about this," he said. "I really am." Into his computer, he said, "Keiji? Yeah, she wasn't having a bar of it. You better get up here."

"Jesus Christ," the captain's voice came back. *"Coming."*

"What the hell are you doing?" Nisha said, suddenly alarmed. "Did Belevsky send you?"

"Huh?" Chase said. "What? No. Look, I can see you're confused, so, I'll sum it up for you: my captain has a really inconsistent moral code. You just never know what's going to set him off. And the whole oldest object in the world thing, you know, heritage of humanity, et cetera..."

"You're joking," Nisha said.

"I know!" Chase said. "*I know.* Tell me about it. But I gotta live with him. And keep your hands where I can see them, if you don't mind."

Keiji arrived a moment later, and glanced at the deactivated security bot and the gun in Chase's hands. "Way to go, Romeo."

"She wasn't happy to see me," Chase said. "Says she's expecting someone."

Keiji looked at Nisha. "The sword. If you don't mind."

"I'm expecting the *buyers*," Nisha said. A note of panic had crept into her voice. "You can't take it. If they show up and it's not here..."

"Where is it?" Keiji said.

Nisha shook her head. "No. No way. You can't have it."

Keiji sighed, and started searching the villa. There was a safe under the bed, but it was too big to fit in there. He went through the cupboards and wardrobes, and eventually found the pod underneath the bar, shoved between bottles of rum and vermouth. He supposed Nisha hadn't been expecting to hold onto it for too long.

He glanced at Chase, and then popped the seal open. There was a hiss of air. The canister opened down the middle to reveal its contents, nestled in cushioning gel.

He'd been expecting a katana, a samurai sword. But

Kusanagi was older than that – Bronze Age, Iron Age, somewhere back in the day when a sword had been a straightforward weapon for killing rather than an elegant piece of art. It was long and thin, double-edged, a dull black. The blade was terribly chipped, and the metal was tarnished all over. Keiji felt a sudden moment of vertigo, as though he was looking down a telescope two thousand years into the past, when this sword had been smelted in some nameless and forgotten village on Honshu.

"Well," he said. "Isn't that something."

"What are you going to do?" Nisha said, increasingly distraught. "You think you can just find a buyer yourself? You're an idiot. That's the hottest cargo you'll ever carry. This was a commission job, it's *literally* priceless! Who the hell else do you think you'll find to take it off your hands?"

"The people it belongs to," Keiji said, sealing the pod again and zipping it up in his duffel bag.

"I told you," Chase said. "He's got this really selective moral code."

"You can't be serious," Nisha said. "No. No. You can't have it. I need it! They've already paid for it, if they show up and it's not here, they'll kill me!"

"Then I suggest you leave," Keiji said. "As we're about to. Goodbye."

"They're here," Nisha said faintly.

Keiji glanced up. Out beyond the infinity pool, a sleek white hydrofoil was cutting across the waves. As it passed the barrier, the protective field around the island shimmered with rainbow colours, like oil spilt on water. A moment later it was cruising into the private wharf at the edge of Nisha's villa jetty.

"Yep, definitely time to go," Keiji said, slinging the bag over his shoulder.

"You have to take me with you!" Nisha said, following them out of the villa. They reached the jetty and moved quickly – not running, not trying to draw attention, but moving back to the beach as quickly as possible. Chase had hidden his gun beneath his shirt again. "You can't *leave* me here!" she hissed.

"I don't see why not," Keiji said, although he also didn't see how he could stop her, not without drawing attention to themselves. The active atmosphere early in the day had eased now, and the resort was mostly quiet; it was almost midnight local time, even though the sun still blared high overhead. Looking behind his shoulder, Keiji could see a group of men coming down the gangplank from the hydrofoil.

"To be fair..." Chase said hesitantly. "Well... come on. We've kind of put her in a bind."

They'd reached the beach now, where the jeep was parked on the sand. Keiji tossed the duffel bag in the back seat, and looked down at the tangle of jetties leading out to the villas. The men from the hydrofoil had entered Nisha's villa; it wouldn't be long before they emerged again. A trickle of sweat ran down from Keiji's forehead. He'd been awake for nearly twenty-four hours now and the Gannish sun was playing havoc with his circadian rhythm.

"Fine," he sighed. "Get in." He looked over at his first mate, already jumping over the passenger door into his seat. "But she's *your* problem."

Private vessels were not permitted to dock at Carpo, which was one of Jupiter's smallest moons, really just a captured asteroid. Keiji caught the daily shuttle from Jupiter Junction, a two-hour flight full of tourists abuzz with the news of the stolen imperial regalia. It sat in its duffel bag in the overhead compartment, while Keiji's seat neighbours talked about conspiracy theories and the Mangala Tong. When the shuttle docked at Carpo the tourists were funnelled through a number of corridors and safety locks before emerging into sudden, surprising sunshine.

Carpo was a world flipped outside-in, like so many asteroids, but smaller than most. It had an interior O'Neill radius of only about a kilometre, and if you turned your head too quickly you felt dizzy as your inner ear tried to keep up with the centrifugal force. For a Martian like Keiji every asteroid always seemed small, but Carpo in particular felt like a fragile little snowglobe, a bubble of green lawns and cherry trees floating in the void. The population hovered around fifty, all of them acolytes at the temple. Light came from a false sun hovering at the world's centre, but if you squinted past it you could see the same panorama of Japanese landscaping on the other side. The tourists dispersed amongst the grounds, posing for photos, consulting their pamphlets, listening to the audio guide. Keiji made his way across the gardens to the main temple.

A pair of Interpol officers blocked his way at the torii. "No admittance for tourists to the building today, sir," one of them said. "Ongoing investigation."

"I have a personal appointment with the guji," Keiji said. "Keiji DuVal."

The officers radioed, checked, and one of them escorted him through the courtyard. "Any leads?" Keiji asked conversationally as they passed clusters of forensics detectives and robots, sweeping for DNA fragments or fingerprints.

"Can't discuss an ongoing investigation, I'm afraid," the officer said. "You'll have to take your shoes off here, before you go inside. It's a Japanese thing."

"I know," Keiji said, placing his boots on a rack and padding inside in his socks.

The temple smelt of sandalwood incense, a smell which immediately took him back to his childhood, trips to the Zutphen shrine on Blankenstraat with his mother. His father, of Dutch blood, was an atheist; his mother, a fifth-generation Japanese Martian, kept to the old ways. His older brothers never went, and as he grew older Keiji had also ceased his visits. If his mother had been disappointed she hadn't shown it. Maybe she'd been through the same thing with his brothers. He'd never really understood it, not even the blurry line where Buddhism ended and Shintoism began. All it was to him now was an aesthetic sense of bittersweet memories – the torii gateway, the suzu bells, and the smell of sandalwood.

The guji was waiting, kneeling, on a rush mat in a room shielded by paper screens. Keiji could see the shadows of detectives moving on the other side, could hear conversations in English and French. The guji spoke to him in Japanese. "You are fortunate that you are your mother's son."

"In this instance, maybe," Keiji said.

He kneeled down, placed the duffel bag on the table, unzipped it, and removed the pod. The guji cracked it open carefully, and closed it again. The expression on his face was unreadable. "A wiser man might have mailed it back to us."

"My crew wanted me to."

"Why didn't you?"

Keiji hesitated. "I wanted to apologise. I was involved in this... burglary. I didn't know what it was at the time. It was a minor role. But it was wrong."

"I am a shinshoku," the guji said, "not a Catholic priest. I cannot grant you absolution."

"I did that myself, by returning it," Keiji said. "I thought I owed you the courtesy of doing it personally." He hoped none of the detectives outside could speak Japanese.

"So you think yourself an honest man," the guji said.

"As much as anyone can be."

"Would you like to know a secret?"

Keiji said nothing.

"This particular sword is old, as swords go. It was manufactured by an artisan in 2100. Its predecessor was destroyed in the fires of Earth the previous year, in the 72-hour War. The tale of Yosuke Ishikawa and his band of devout followers sweeping it to safety – I am sure your mother told you that story, yes? – that is a lie.

"Its predecessor, in turn, was smelted in the 1940s, after the sword before it was destroyed by an American bomb in the Second World War. That one in turn was only two hundred years old; its own predecessor went missing in the 18th century. And so on, and so forth, back to the beginning of time."

Keiji stared at him. "So you would have made another one."

"Yes. It would have been no great loss to us if this version was never returned."

"Then why all this fuss? Why the police? Why let anyone know it had been stolen?"

"Thievery is thievery regardless of what the thief believes he has stolen," the guji said. "And while it may not be the same physical sword, be comprised of the same molecular components, this piece of metal is still Kusanagi. It is still the Grass Cutting Sword of our people's legend, and it is still a valuable part of our heritage."

"What, like the Ship of Theseus?"

The guji looked irritated. "Typical. Typical a hafu would think that. Do not bring your European myths into this. What I am telling you, young man, is that Kusanagi transcends physicality. It does not matter that this sword was smelted in 2100. It *is* Kusanagi."

Keiji remembered the feeling of awe he'd had, when he first opened the pod and looked at it. He'd thought he was holding in his hands something that was two millennia old; a tangible link to the ruined Earth.

"Others might disagree," he said. "You're lying to people."

"Is a myth a lie? A legend? Is a story a lie? The truth of a myth lies not in what we believe, but what we want to believe. The myth of an object has as much value as the object itself. More, possibly." The guji tested his thumb on the blade's edge. "What am I to make of a man, half-Japanese, who returns a priceless artefact to us, after playing a part in looting it? What do I want to believe about him?"

Keiji looked around at the rush mats, the woodblock prints, the paper screens. He was beginning to remember why, as a child, he had found his mother's shrine stifling. "I'm not half-Japanese," he said. "I'm not half anything. I'm Martian."

"You will find that no matter how much you wish to relinquish the past, it will always be with you."

"Why'd you tell me that?" Keiji asked. "About the sword?"

"Because whatever honour you think you have displayed by returning Kusanagi to us, you are still a thief," the guji said. "If the Europans or the Gannish had a better notion of justice than a comfortable prison cell and three meals a day, I might turn you in. Instead, I will have to be satisfied with letting you know that you have endangered yourself in the criminal underworld for a cause which is not as important or righteous as you thought it was."

Keiji suddenly felt very irritated. Even if it had been real, he thought, so what? How would it have been any worse off in a private collection than in the hands of an order of priests for a mostly-dead religion, who kept it just as secret and hidden as it would have been elsewhere?

"You're not as smart as you think you are," Keiji said, and left. He wished he could have thought of something better to say.

Carpo had a faster day-night cycle than he'd thought; either that or his audience had taken longer then he expected. The sun had dimmed, and the tiny world was dark. Insects ticked and whirred in the bushes, yellow squares of light lit up the temple, and red paper lanterns hung in the branches of the trees.

He stopped by the shoe rack, listening to the trilling insects and the distant murmur of conversation. Tying up his bootlaces gave him a moment to think. He was at a loss as to whether he'd done the right thing or not, and he was surprised that a venerable Shinto priest had turned out to be as vindictive and human and wrong as anyone else. Keiji had vaguely imagined a scenario in his head in which his honesty was welcomed by the guji, and they had a long talk about spirituality which reminded him of his mother, and maybe green tea was involved. That had been stupid. Oh well. At least he hadn't been arrested.

He sat for a moment longer at the edge of the temple, looking out on Carpo's darkened little world, a difficult and expensive feat of engineering which had turned a distant moon of Jupiter into a tiny little pocket of long-lost Japan. An idealised Japan, at that – shrines and temples and zen gardens and koi ponds. All that money and effort on something old instead of something new.

After a while he went back across the temple grounds to the shuttle.

Chase had been uncertain of what to do with Nisha. She'd wanted to come with them, wanted to get off Ganymede. So she wasn't a prisoner, strictly speaking. But he didn't want to give her the run of the ship, either; she was pissed off, and who knew what kind of revenge she might take? He opted for sitting in the mess with her, gun in its holster at his side, drinking coffee and smoking and waiting for Keiji to come back

– if he came back. They were watching an old black and white Western on TV. An American cowboy with a chiselled jaw and his band of outlaws had fled from the cavalry after a bank robbery, chased out into the desert to die.

Chase was watching it, anyway. Nisha was sitting in the armchair fuming. "Sorry this place is such a pig sty," Chase said, considering for the first time how the *Black Swan*'s mess must look like to a visitor. Bulkheads with streaks of rust, an antique television, a couple of ratty sofas and an armchair. The coffee table was covered in empty beer cans, overflowing ashtrays and bowls with tidemarks of microwave soup and reheated noodles.

"If you think I'm concerned about the state of your living room – which is, yes, a pig sty – then you haven't been paying attention to the last twelve hours," Nisha said.

"Look, you know you can just get off here if you want."

Nisha laughed bitterly. "Jupiter Junction? They'd find me in half an hour." She was still barefoot, wearing the bikini and sarong she'd had on when they'd come to the beach villa, suddenly looking very out of place in the *Black Swan*'s grungy corridors. Chase genuinely felt sorry for her, even if he didn't trust her.

"Well..." Chase said. "I don't know where we're going to be going from here."

"To a prison cell," she said sourly. "Thanks to your Boy Scout captain. Police are probably coming down the dock right now."

Chase sighed. He couldn't really argue with that. On the TV, the cowboy and his gang had stumbled into a clapboard settlement, only to find it a ghost town. Hope collapsed, and so did they, dropping down on the sandy street before being found by a shotgun-toting woman. *And now your troubles begin*, Chase thought.

The airlock buzzed open. Chase half-expected it was going to be the police, and force of habit sent his hand towards his gun – but it was Keiji. The captain stooped through the airlock, tossed his empty duffel bag on the floor, and sank down on the couch. "They didn't arrest you?" Chase said incredulously. He'd already been wondering precisely which moon they'd be tried on and which prison they'd be sent to.

"No," Keiji said. "Go tell Kingsford to get us out of here."

"Where to?"

"Anywhere. Celestial Harbour. Mars. Saturn. Wherever."

Chase disappeared up the hallway, and Keiji turned to Nisha. "You're still here."

"Where am I supposed to go?"

Keiji nodded his head at the airlock – down the boarding corridor, onto the clamour and bustle of Dock 135, out into the great freewheeling city that was Jupiter Junction.

"You have no idea what you've done to me," Nisha said. "Do you? You think I can just walk out of here, but I can't. They'll find me and kill me. I can't touch my bank accounts, I can't go to my apartment, I certainly can't risk talking to any of my contacts for a long time. You've ruined me."

"I could have turned you over to the police," Keiji said.

"No, you couldn't have," she said. "Because then you would have been finished too. Which I thought you would have been, on Carpo. You're lucky. Luckier than someone as stupid as you deserves to be."

Keiji sighed, leaned back into the depths of the couch, closed his eyes. Kingsford had fired up the engines, and he felt the familiar trembling through the bulkheads as the *Black Swan* shifted away from the space station and started curving towards Jupiter, dropping into the gravity well to be slingshotted out the other side. An empty beer can rolled off the coffee table. "Look," he said. "It's been a long day and I'm not in the mood for a lecture. We'll drop you off at the next asteroid where you aren't scared you're going to be murdered. There's plenty of spare rooms on the lower deck. There's food in the galley. Make yourself at home. Just… stop asking me why I did it, because I don't know myself."

"You owe me fifty thousand francs," she said. "For starters."

"I owe you fifty thousand francs," Keiji agreed. "Anything more than that, no. Consider it an occupational hazard."

"*Boka chele*," Nisha muttered, and stalked out of the mess. Keiji didn't need to look up what language that was to get the gist of it. Richard Parker, the ship's cat, was purring insistently at his feet. He picked the cat up, walked over to the porthole holding him, and stroked his head as he watched the clouds and storms of Jupiter swim past underneath.

"I'm not an idiot," he said to the cat. "Am I? Just trying to run an honest business here."

On the television behind him, the cowboys had begun to bicker over the hidden gold in the ghost town. Gunplay and violence were not far behind. Keiji switched it off.

A Murder in Heaven

Matthew Amundsen

Detective Bishop didn't know what the kid was doing in the alley or how he had gotten a gun. Looking no older than five, Bishop wasn't even sure if the kid could pull the trigger. Still, the stakes were too high to take chances. An errant gunshot would alert Lesandro and ruin months of planning. Where the boy had gotten the weapon was impossible to say. How he had slipped past Chicago's Finest was another issue, one that Bishop was happy to leave for Diaz to figure out later. Bullets were about to fly, and in his experience the strays found the innocent more often than the guilty.

Bishop knelt, holstering his own gun and raising his hands to show that he meant the child no harm. "Let's get you out of here, buddy. The police have work to do."

At Bishop's words, the boy's forehead creased and his arms trembled, the gun unsteady though his eyes looked more vacant than confused. Too far away to grab the pistol outright, Bishop knew he had to hurry if he wanted to get the kid out of the alley unharmed. Soon Diaz and his team would flush Lesandro into the alley like a drowned rat.

"I'm not going to hurt you. I just need to get you somewhere safe because there are a lot of bad guys around here."

Like with most children, Bishop got nowhere. Wearing a faded Bulls t-shirt, the kid blinked but said nothing, his scrawny arms shaking as he tried to hold the gun straight. Bishop didn't want to hurt the child and had to give diplomacy one more chance.

Bishop cocked his head and smiled, beckoning to the boy on a bended knee. "Let's get out of here. I'm sure your Mom's looking for you."

Something in the kid's eyes changed then, some recognition or spark that caused them to refocus, and Bishop thought he'd reached him at last. Standing to reach for the boy's hand was how Detective Martin Bishop – one of Chicago's most beloved local heroes – fell into blackness as a bullet entered his skull through the bottom of his jaw and lodged in his brain.

The sound stuck with him, that ear-rupturing blast he'd heard so many times before, ricocheting off the brick walls and exploding into the sky, hissing in slow motion and gasping like a final breath before it melted into the automated huff and wheeze of life support. Bishop knew that sound as well, from his father's last days. It was the sound of helplessness, of waiting and goodbyes.

Bishop wanted to open his eyes but couldn't. Nor could he move his limbs or extremities or even turn his head. With horror, he realised he was trapped inside his own body with only the blips of machinery and forced air for company. Luck might speed recovery, but even in this state he knew that death might be the only escape. Swallowed by a claustrophobic darkness, the faces of those who deserved goodbyes comforted him as his thoughts turned into light.

Two men stood over his bed when at last Bishop opened his eyes. Neither looked familiar. The man on the right was sinewy and tall, dressed in clothing of an alien cut and colour. Fair-skinned and clean-shaven, his golden hair draped over his shoulders while his demeanour suggested that he had never lifted a finger in his life. His companion dressed similarly but had thick braids of brown down his back and a beard half so long. Shorter and broader than his partner, the steel in his eyes made him more dangerous by far.

The blonde one smiled. "How are you feeling?"

Bishop was surprised he could open his eyes, let alone speak. The tubes in his nostrils didn't irritate him, nor did the needles connecting him to the IV drip hanging beside the bed. He felt no pain at all. The morphine must be working.

"Surprisingly good." Even his throat lacked dryness or stiffness from disuse.

"Wonderful." The blonde man's smile held fast. "I am Erotami. My colleague is Strefon. We regret the tragic circumstances bringing us together, though it does present us with a splendid opportunity for mutual satisfaction."

These men and their unusual names were unknown to Bishop, as were Erotami's strange inflections and intonations when he stretched his mouth around syllables. Bishop was no stranger to foreign accents, but this one he couldn't place at all. It certainly wasn't South Side. "Do the nurses know you're in here?"

Erotami shared an anxious look with Strefon before turning back to Bishop. "Where do you think you are?"

"Am I not at Stroger? We were off Randolph Street, and it's closest."

Strefon glared at Erotami and folded his arms. "I told you it was too realistic. He still thinks he's alive."

Erotami shrugged. "I thought it would be comforting."

Bishop hated how they talked about him as if he weren't there. "Wait a minute. I'm not dead."

"No, but you're not alive either. That's you down there." Erotami pointed to the floor.

With a sudden lurch and a burst of light, Bishop plummeted from the sky headfirst, barrelling toward

Stroger's roof in the middle of the city but in little position to appreciate the view. The wide rooftop filled his vision with frightening speed, and he clenched shut his eyes and lifted his hands to shield his head from imminent impact. When the moment passed and nothing happened, he opened his eyes again only to find himself hovering on the ceiling of one of the hospital rooms. The broken body below, languishing under a horde of tubes, hoses, and bandages clustered underneath the jaw, was unmistakably his. Shrinking back in surprise, Bishop looked over the wall to see the hallway beyond. The officer posted outside his door looked like Peretti. A mere heartbeat from the monitor later and Bishop found himself back in the first room, sitting on the edge of what he had thought was his hospital bed but must be something else entirely.

The confusion on Bishop's face clearly amused Erotami and Strefon. "If that was really me, then where are we now?"

Erotami started to bend over but halted when he noticed that Strefon wasn't following his lead. "Aren't you going to join me? It's what we discussed."

Strefon shook his head. "You discussed it. I always said it was stupid."

"Only when I do it alone." Erotami bowed to Bishop with extravagance, as if his disagreement with Strefon had never happened. "Welcome to Heaven."

Strefon rolled his eyes. "Don't make it harder than it has to be. Everyone knows there is no Heaven. This is Bardopolis."

Erotami raised an eyebrow. "Don't you think that's rushing it a bit?"

He was about to say more, but Strefon stopped him. "We don't have much time."

Erotami gave up. "Let's get to it then."

He waved the scene away until the three of them

stood in an abandoned warehouse. Dying afternoon sun streamed through grids of broken panes to illuminate motes of dust dangling in vast emptiness. A fleet of trucks could have fit under the roof, though the place bore no indication of its former use. From beyond its walls came the sounds of gulls and gentle waves. Bishop guessed they were somewhere in Cal-Sag harbour.

A drab jacket clung to Bishop. Strange and constrictive, it felt only a little more dignified than the hospital gown.

"As Strefon mentioned, there is no Heaven. No harps, no clouds, no gates or white linens. All that stuff is wrong, which I'm sure you guessed long ago. I hope you're not a religious man." He made the statement sound like a question.

Bishop shook his head. He hadn't spent any significant time in a church since his mother had died when he was a teenager, almost twenty years ago. His father had thought it would be good for them, some salve for the injustice wreaked by a drunk driver, but after a year of attending services and mouthing the words like wolves among the faithful, neither had felt relief, still endless sorrow. Since then, Bishop only went to churches for funerals.

"Good. All of your plane's religions are wrong, and this will go easier without having to contend with preconceived notions about where we are. What the religious institutions on your plane picture as Heaven is actually something else, a place called Bardopolis. The only true Heaven in the ecstatic sense is sublimation into the One, at the cost of your personality. Only the pure achieve that state, but how could they be expected to know that's really just another form of death?"

Bishop had no idea what the man was describing. "I

don't know where we are, how this is possible, or if this is merely a dream."

Erotami cocked his head. "It is a dream, but it's also real."

"I don't understand."

"Let me try," Strefon said. "Consider Bardopolis an amalgamation of every civilization's memories and hallucinations. People dream here while alive but live here after they die. You're here because you're in a coma, trapping you between life and death."

"And why are you here? Are you dead or dreaming?"

"We're Enforcers, basically the guardians of Bardopolis. Crime is not uncommon here, nor is it always punished. But this is a special case."

"We're here to solve a murder," said Erotami.

Bishop thought he understood. "A murder in a dream?"

"Sort of. You see, dreamers come and go at will, but the dead live here as citizens until they reincarnate back on your plane. For them, that's the only way out of Bardopolis."

"That's what makes this a special case," Erotami said. "One of our own, an Enforcer, disappeared a while back and we're stuck here until we can figure out what happened to him. You're our last shot."

Strefon nodded gravely. "We thought you would understand our predicament and loss."

"What makes you think I can help?"

"We know you're a good cop, and that's exactly what we need."

"I just do my job."

"And he's humble too," Erotami said, with a smile that Bishop thought masked irritation.

"The fact you're here could be our lucky break. In return, we can give you information that will help you back on your plane," Strefon said.

"Like what?"

"Like the identity and whereabouts of Lesandro's boss."

Bishop shook his head. "Lesandro doesn't take orders from anybody."

Erotami shrugged. "Maybe we can find the child who shot you."

That detail puzzled Bishop. "How do you know about the kid?"

"From here, we can see everything on your plane. Interacting with it is another matter."

"Look, Bishop, we're not expecting miracles," said Strefon. "Our hope is that your instincts and diligence might uncover something we've missed. At the very least, another pair of eyes to look things over won't hurt. And who knows, maybe people will talk to a fresh face? Keep in mind that we're stuck here forever until we solve this. Enforcers don't get reassigned."

Everything about this was peculiar, including the hard sell. Nor could he dismiss the thought that this might be a bizarre dream induced by the sedatives coursing through his body. No matter the source, any new information about Lesandro or his shooter would be useful, and he saw no reason not to help them.

"All right."

"Fantastic."

The pair looked pleased and relieved. From within the folds of his clothing, Erotami removed a metallic emblem the size of his hand and gave it to Bishop. "This is our only evidence. Maybe you can tell us what it does."

The metal was like nothing Bishop had ever seen, green and shiny. Concave with rounded edges, it fit easily into Bishop's palm. The insignia in its centre was inscrutable, the nature of its design changing whenever Bishop rotated the piece in the light. Although heavy, it didn't seem like an effective weapon. He wasn't sure what to make of it and slipped it inside the jacket.

"Where did it happen?"

"Here," Strefon said. "But time is an ephemeral notion."

Erotami tapped his wrist where a watch would be. "Speaking of..."

Both he and Strefon grew transparent in the dying light of the warehouse.

"Our energy is spent," Strefon said. "And one last thing, don't take off the jacket. If you need us in the future, we can use it to find you."

"Wait, how can I tell the difference between the dreamers and the dead?"

"You can't," Strefon said, disappearing.

They were gone before Bishop could ask about the victim. Charged with the task of investigating a murder in an unfamiliar location with neither witnesses nor leads, the similarities between this state and his normal life weren't lost on him. Even while languishing in a coma, he was expected to report for duty.

The warehouse itself offered no clues, its only exit a huge rolling door of corrugated metal and its concrete floor empty. Nothing differentiated this place from hundreds of others in cities around the world. On the other end of the building, an open door led into an office also barren but for another closed door at the back of the room. Once white, the same grime permeating the rest of the warehouse had stained it the colour of rotten teeth.

Bishop opened the door. What little light filtered in from the deserted office revealed a dank, disgusting bathroom. The sink had lost its spigots and its plumbing while the toilet had been reduced to a bowl leaning upon its base, the tank and its cover lying in pieces upon the floor. The worst, however, was the brackish mould creeping over every surface from floor to ceiling like a carpet of fine hair. Fighting revulsion, Bishop covered his nose and mouth as everything went black.

The wheezes and bleeps of the equipment, along with the smell of plastic and the stark fumes of antiseptic cleanliness, told him he was back in the hospital. Like before, he couldn't move a muscle nor open his eyes. Although the other senses remained mute, the clarity of his hearing and his sense of smell made him question whether or not meeting Erotami and Strefon had been a dream. How much time had passed in this place, he couldn't say.

Muffled voices grew louder as two people entered the room. By the faint smell of cigarettes, Bishop guessed that one of the visitors was Diaz. The stale smoke clouded a more refined scent, delicate and all too familiar.

"Oh, Martin." Bishop hadn't heard Viv's voice in over a year, and never had it sounded so hesitant and small. Their break-up hadn't been a falling out so much as an acknowledgement of divergent goals. He'd made it clear that his desire to scrub the filth from the streets of Chicago made marriage and a family a liability. She had moved to Milwaukee shortly thereafter, telling him in their last conversation that even a city like Chicago seemed small when crowded with the ghosts of happier memories. At the time he had been so certain of his decision but now, hearing her sobs, he realised he never should have let her go.

More than anything, he hated that she had to see him like this and wished he could sit up and hold her, tell her everything was going to be okay. He wanted to see her but couldn't penetrate the void no matter how hard he visualized floating on the ceiling like he had earlier. Apparently it took more to leave his body than mere thoughts and wishes.

Viv's tears gradually ceased. "How did this happen?"

The answering voice confirmed it was Diaz who accompanied her. "On a raid. Martin was waiting in the alley for us to flush out a scumbag, and we found him like this."

"I hope the bastard's behind bars."

Bishop hoped so too but knew immediately what Diaz's hesitation meant. "Unfortunately, he went to the roof instead of the alley and got away. We don't know who pulled the trigger."

"You've got to be kidding."

"I wish I was."

Bishop felt sorry for his friend. He'd been in that position himself countless times, delivering bad news to distraught loved ones with no silver lining to cushion the blow. That the victim was his own partner made it worse.

"So how is he?"

"His vitals are good, but the surgeon wants to wait a little longer before trying to remove the bullet. Apparently it's lodged in there pretty deep. And Viv, in all honesty, even if he gets the bullet out, there's no telling how much brain damage he may have suffered. He may never awaken out of the coma."

Viv renewed her sobs. Bishop hated this and wanted out of his body so badly he wanted to scream, seething in rage at his own helplessness. With a slight shock, he found himself on the ceiling as before, watching from overhead.

They huddled together, Viv's head on Diaz's shoulder while he tried in vain to comfort her. Even as she pressed a wad of tissues to her nose, seeing Viv made Bishop ache. If he ever came out of this, he needed to make some changes in his life. At last the pair stood apart.

"I wish I had better news, but I don't want to give you a false sense of hope either."

She nodded. "You've always been a good friend to both of us."

"If there's anything else you need, a place to stay—"

"Thanks, but I still have a key to our – Martin's place. The only thing I need from you is to find the bastard who shot him." Viv glanced at the bed one last time.

"Don't worry, we will."

Bishop wanted to tell them about the kid who had pulled the trigger, but he couldn't form the words or make any sound in this state. He tried following them down the hallway, but they walked faster than he could drift and were soon beyond his reach, their footsteps and conversation dimming into silence. Watching Viv walk away hurt more than the bullet had.

The familiar slap of water told Bishop his location before his eyes could even focus. Louder than the first visit, he guessed he was outside the Bardopolis warehouse. One look confirmed it. Rust blossomed through patches of paint peeling like the memory of another skin. The glittering eyes of broken panes were still beyond reach, with neither fire escapes nor climbable crates or vehicles for further access. A quick walk around the perimeter of the building revealed no more entrances than the interior had. The rolling bay door was the only way in or out. Whether from an unseen lock or other device, it wouldn't budge.

The docks had seen better days, warped, stripped of their hardware, rippling with regret. No gulls floated overhead, and the lack of dung to indicate their presence was conspicuous in its absence. Dampening fog obscured the view beyond the inlet. From inside, he had assumed the warehouse was in Cal-Sag. Now he wasn't so sure.

In the other direction, all he found were dilapidated buildings, empty and menacing in their vastness.

Crumbling structures of brick, wood, and stone
crowded upon the road while discreet alleys and
narrow passageways led deeper into labyrinthine
desolation. Sometimes power poles bisected the road,
effectively blocking any vehicular traffic and perhaps
explaining the lack of cars or trucks. Although his skin
prickled with the feeling of being watched, there were
no signs of life, not even scavengers. Beyond the dock,
his footsteps made the only sound. The lack of activity
amid this bleak cityscape unsettled him. Solving a
murder under these circumstances seemed ludicrous.

Bishop looked back the way he had come. Nothing
seemed familiar despite that he had just come from
that direction. No obvious landmarks or associations
presented themselves, while the road itself vanished
into the last remaining wall of a collapsed storehouse.
None of this made any sense, and he admitted he was
lost.

He wondered how to best retrace his steps when he
heard the keening. Both roar and lament, the howl
came from no animal Bishop recognised. Although
not particularly worried since it had come from so far
away, he scanned his surroundings for a weapon
anyway. He had hoped for a board with a nail sticking
out of it, but all he spotted were stray bricks and loose
rocks. He didn't bother picking up either. Bishop
missed his gun and felt naked without it.

The chorus answering the first cry confirmed that
feeling. They were closer than that one had been,
much closer, and seemed to come from every
direction. Their voices intertwined in haunted
harmony made sinister by the echoes leaping through
the abandoned structures in this otherwise deserted
neighbourhood. They easily numbered more than a
dozen, and the hunger in their moan made Bishop
grab a brick in each hand just in case. He quickened

his pace, hoping to escape this maddening architecture, but the road only grew more serpentine.

An offensive odour overtook him, reaching his nostrils stealthily at first but soon erupting into a noxious cloud that strangled him with mould and iron. Turning, he spotted shapes amassing behind him. They appeared wolf-like, albeit of a more robust species than he had ever seen, with pelts of whirling shadow. Their spines flexed when they caught sight of Bishop. Their great slavering mouths, jutting with shards of broken glass, grunted in anticipation. What concerned Bishop most, however, was that the creatures had human eyes.

With a yelp from somewhere within the pack, the creatures gave chase. Bishop ran, unsure if he'd be fast enough to get away. Thunder drowned his own footfalls as the creatures charged him, their paws like cascading rocks. A furtive glance over his shoulder showed them gaining quickly. He'd never outrun them. Bishop saw no way to gain higher ground. Another pack of the same creatures gathered on the road up ahead, blocking his way. He'd never be able to fend off this many, not with mere bricks. Bishop had to abandon his plan to stay on the main road and darted down the first alley he found, dropping the bricks as dead weight.

The strange wolves followed him, heads low to the ground and growling. Their number swelled as the two packs merged like a writhing snake with a hundred eyes. The first door he came to had the thickness of a wall and complex iron locks. Breaking it down would take too long. Bishop found the next door and the next to be immovable as well and didn't bother trying any others. Gambling with time would be lethal.

The putrid stench of his pursuers outpaced the pack, strengthening its miasmic grip on Bishop. He pushed himself to run faster. Heat flashed from the

metallic emblem Erotami had given him. Removing it
from his jacket, he found its surface warm to the
touch. As he did so, a door to his left that otherwise
looked exactly like the others shimmered with a
golden haze. With the swarm of creatures closing the
gap, Bishop had to take a chance.

Opening into another unfamiliar alley, Bishop
hurried through and whipped the door shut behind
him. A snort of the creatures' fetid odour trailed him
but soon dissipated in a breeze. Unlike where he'd left,
ordinary city sounds came from the street beyond.
Overhead the skies were sunny, and he was no worse
for wear. Awed by how the emblem had saved him, he
straightened his jacket and stepped out onto the
street.

The city seemed surprisingly normal, full of people
and activity. Pedestrians covered the sidewalks as they
went about their daily routines, vehicles proceeded
calmly, and the streets were straight and orderly. Gone
were the abandoned buildings, the nonsensical roads,
and the creatures with their maniacal teeth and rotten
odour. Somehow Bishop felt that this must be
Bardopolis proper.

Emerging from the alley, he crossed the street to the
far sidewalk. No one appeared to notice, and he found
it easy to blend in, like in any city. He planned to walk
around and get a feel for the place, hoping the context
might help him find a murderer. Assuming the task
doomed to failure, he didn't expect much. Erotami
and Strefon hadn't given him much of a choice, nor
had they pledged anything of tangible value in return
since any new information would only help him if he
awoke from his coma. That, apparently, wasn't
something within their power to grant. If nothing else,
he'd keep his eyes open. For now, he knew he still had
a lot to learn.

That the city felt like Chicago, if but vaguely,

surprised him. He couldn't pinpoint exactly where he was, but the vibe was familiar. The thought crossed his mind that maybe it wasn't Chicago at all. Maybe this was some other city he had visited in a dream long ago but didn't remember. Or maybe this assignment to hunt down a murderer was merely a dream within a dream, a way for his mind to occupy itself while his body lay in stasis.

The city certainly felt real. Clothes and hairstyles of the people around him were of contemporary fashion, with occasional lapses into old-fashioned or futuristic styles. The makes and models of the automobiles passing in the street seemed relatively familiar but for a few exotics he couldn't identify. Likewise, he browsed a neighbourhood market stocking mostly conventional produce mixed with some strange types that no one seemed to find unusual. The words Bishop read on street signs, at bus stops, in shop windows, or on t-shirts were in a gibberish language, though it was easy enough to guess their meaning.

Reaching a prominent intersection, Bishop could finally see beyond his immediately surroundings. In the distance, looming over this neighbourhood and several beyond, stood a hazy collection of familiar skyscrapers: the Prudential, the Aon, Trump Tower, the Sears Tower – or the Willis Tower, as it was called now, though he doubted he would ever get used to that name – and what had been the Hancock building. None looked quite the same as its counterpart, and some absent buildings had new ones in their places, but those he recognised were similar enough to provide his only comfort since coming here. Although this version of Chicago strayed from reality, the similarity was enough to boost his spirits.

As much as Bishop hated a cold line of questioning, he didn't know what he could do besides ask passers-by, store clerks, cab drivers and bike messengers alike if they'd heard about this case. The few who bothered to answer shook their heads or shrugged, clueless and of no help. None of them knew about any murder or what Enforcers were. Clearly there was nothing to be learned here. Although he wasn't crazy about the idea, he needed to go back to the warehouse to find what he'd missed the first time. There had to be a way inside he'd been too impatient to see.

Finding the alley from which he'd emerged wasn't difficult. He'd committed its details to memory – the overflowing dumpster, the particular staggered pattern of air conditioners jutting overhead, the serviceable fire escape. But something had changed in his absence: the door through which he'd arrived had vanished. Without that door, he couldn't return. He needed help.

Bishop clutched the jacket, closing his eyes and picturing Erotami and Strefon in his mind, repeating their names like a mantra. Sure enough, before long they shimmered into being before him, coalescing out of the shadows like something from one of those old science fiction shows he used to watch with his father as a child. Bishop had a hard time reading their expressions, which seemed to linger somewhere between admonition and apprehension. He didn't know if they were upset to find him here, so far from the warehouse. It struck him then how little he knew about them.

Strefon spoke first. "Is everything okay?"

Bishop tried to lessen his failure with a smile. "All I can say is that I'm stuck." He explained what had happened to him back at the warehouse, from his investigation of the interior up until he reached this part of Bardopolis, only leaving out how the emblem had saved him. If it had any other properties, he wanted to discover them first. Erotami and Strefon shared a look when he mentioned being chased by those creatures, but otherwise they betrayed little reaction.

Strefon nodded in understanding when Bishop finished. "I know what we've asked you to do is difficult. We can try to get you back inside the warehouse, if that would help."

"I don't know that it would. You never told me the victim's name."

Strefon uttered a few guttural syllables unrecognisable in any language Bishop had ever heard. "That's his name. I wish there was an English equivalent, but there isn't one."

"Where's the body now?"

They looked embarrassed at the question.

Erotami finally answered. "The body is no longer with us."

Bishop wasn't surprised. "How was he killed? Was it with this piece of metal you gave me?"

"We weren't given that information."

This investigation was beyond ridiculous. "Let me ask you this. Who do you work for?"

Erotami gave Strefon a worried look. "It's complicated."

"The One," Strefon said. "The One commands all Enforcers."

"Who is the One, exactly? Can I talk to him?"

Strefon chuckled. "I'm afraid not. The divine vibrate on a different plane."

"Divine? You mean like God?"

"In a manner of speaking, though not a god as interpreted by your world's religions. The One is a sentient force, a conglomeration of transcendent souls that some would call love." At that, Erotami snickered but Strefon silenced him with a stern look before continuing. "We didn't want to make this too complicated when we first met you, but not everyone who dies on your world remains in Bardopolis or is reincarnated. There are rare beings who join the One in transcendence. The One dispatches avatars of itself as Enforcers that watch over Bardopolis and ensure that its laws remain."

"Like cops."

"Yes, but unlike a cop, Enforcers uphold the laws of metaphysical reality."

Bishop shook his head. "This is beyond me. I don't think I can help you."

Erotami smiled, a stab at reassurance that was anything but. "Not so fast. Why don't we put you in touch with someone who can assist you?"

"Who were you thinking?"

"Why not Detective Diaz? Maybe he can help while he's dreaming."

By Strefon's look, he didn't like that idea.

Erotami cocked his head. "What?"

"I'd hate to pair him with someone who may not want him to return."

Erotami's face brightened then fell. "You don't think he planted that child, do you?"

"That's impossible," said Bishop.

"I'm sure it is." Strefon's tone implied the opposite.

"Let me talk to him myself."

"Fine," Erotami said, looking pleased. "We called on him earlier at the station to corroborate some details about Lesandro but were told he had the day off and was attending a baseball game. Maybe he's still there. Shall we try?"

"All right." A familiar face would be welcome.

Unlike when Erotami had sent him flying through the sky to the hospital, there was no rushed blur of activity or any sensation that he had travelled at all. He merely blinked and found himself somewhere new, a ballpark that felt familiar but not entirely. Both the stadium and the rooftops facing it had a third tier of seating, the ivy wall in the outfield had grown to twice its normal size, and the scoreboard's lettering had changed to yellow from white, yet he knew the place. Wrigley couldn't be mistaken for anywhere else, but that Diaz might have come here instead of Comiskey didn't make any sense.

Bishop found Diaz before long, though his partner wasn't exactly conspicuous in a Cubs cap and dark sunglasses. Thankfully Bishop's skills hadn't dulled to the point that he couldn't locate somebody he'd known more than ten years despite the disguise. Bishop took the empty seat next to Diaz without announcing himself and waited for his friend to notice him. To Bishop's surprise, it took a minute for the realisation to set in. Back in the waking world, Diaz would have spotted him as soon as Bishop had entered this section of the stadium.

"Bishop, man, shit! What are you doing here?" Diaz stood to shake Bishop's hand and give him a one-armed hug.

"Looking for you. A little bird told me where to find you, though I have to admit I'm a little surprised to see you here." Bishop indicated the field as they sat down. The Cubs had different uniforms but their colours remained the same. He didn't know the other team.

Diaz shrugged it off. "Yeah, well, sometimes you need a day off, you know?"

That wasn't what Bishop meant, but he didn't press it further. As a diehard Sox fan, Diaz had more than one rant aimed at their Crosstown rival under his belt. Some of the guys back at the precinct would pay good money to see Diaz in a Cubs cap. In the waking world, Diaz would be embarrassed at this turn of events, if not offended, but in Bardopolis it didn't seem to matter. Did Diaz realise this was a dream? Bishop didn't want to ask him outright.

"What a day," Bishop said, smiling.

Diaz leaned back in his seat. The crack of a bat

briefly drew his attention, but the ball went foul, deflating the fans' rising voices to a sigh. Diaz looked back at Bishop. "Unreal, right?"

Bishop had never seen his partner so relaxed. "I hate to bother you on your day off, but I was wondering if you knew what this was."

He pulled out the emblem, careful to keep it out of sight from their neighbours. Its reflection played about Diaz's face, its insignia still impossible to pin down. His partner's eyes widened.

"Can I hold it?"

"Maybe later." Bishop put it away. "Ring any bells?"

"Not really. What is it?"

"Found it on a victim, law enforcement but not local. Happened in a warehouse near water. I need whatever details you can dig up."

Diaz pulled out a small notebook and a half-worn pencil and wrote a few lines. "Sounds like one for the feds."

Bishop looked grave. "Might be big."

"Let me make some calls. I'll let you know what I find." Diaz slipped the notebook and pencil into his shirt pocket. "By the way, we found the kid who shot you."

"No kidding? Where?"

"At a playground down the street. Some kids pointed him out to one of our patrol cars and said he'd been telling them about it for days but nobody had listened to him. He was so young, they figured he was making it up until they saw it on the news. We haven't been able to track down the parents yet."

"Did you find the gun?"

Diaz looked sheepish. "No, but he still had powder burn because he hadn't washed his hands in a couple of weeks. Kids these days, huh?"

"Go figure." Bishop got up to leave.

"Sure you can't stick around for the rest of the game?"

"Wish I could."

"Your loss. It's a good one."

Bishop left Diaz there, watching the game, torn between laughter and concern, confused as to what constituted truth in Bardopolis or if such a thing even existed here. Walking through the concourse, Bishop wondered if there existed a Bardopolis version of the hospital where his body rested in the waking world. If he went to the same room on this plane, would he find another version of himself in a coma or was he now that version but walking around? The implications boggled his mind to the point of paralysis, and he decided to look for a different place altogether. He wanted to find his own house.

Making his way toward the exit, he had the queer feeling he was being followed. He knew better than to turn around and instead stopped at a souvenir stand, feigning interest in the memorabilia. He scanned the array of ball caps and kept the concourse in his peripheral vision. With most of the crowd dressed in street clothes and combinations of team colours, nobody stuck out. Seeing nothing, Bishop stepped away from the booth and continued toward the exit.

On the way, Bishop stopped abruptly and leaned against an iron support beam as if waiting for somebody. Counting to five, he doubled back behind another beam, trying to remain inconspicuous. Not ten seconds later, a middle-aged man wearing an unremarkable t-shirt and ordinary jeans stopped before reaching the turnstiles, looking for excuses not to leave. The man was so average that Bishop couldn't tell what had triggered suspicion but trusted his intuition enough to avoid him. Bishop turned away to head in the opposite direction when a fan in a cap and jersey stepped from behind a pillar to block his way and shot him three times.

After the reverberation of the shots and the spectators' screams died, Bishop knew only darkness. Out of the numbing silence grew a quiet voice at his side, talking, drawing him to the surface. He wasn't in an ambulance, nor could he feel the ground at his back. Nor would his eyes open. Disoriented, it took him a moment to realise that the voice was Viv's and that she was reading to him. When the rush of tenderness at that thought slowed to a mere throb, he realised she was reading him a Sherlock Holmes story just like his mom used to those days he stayed home sick from school as a child. He had told her about that years ago, back when they had started dating. How Viv had remembered, he had no idea. He wanted to embrace her but had to settle for her voice, his mind following its nuances and the happier memories it triggered far more than the story itself. Although he wasn't surprised when the door opened abruptly and interrupted the story, Bishop couldn't help but resent the intrusion.

"It's time, Viv," Diaz said from the doorway

"Okay." Viv didn't move right away. Her next words came to Bishop in a whisper, as if she were leaning close. "I'm praying for you, as silly that sounds. But I am. I love you and always will."

This confession from a professed atheist highlighted the bleakness of his condition. Bishop didn't know she'd left his side until he heard her sobs erupt from the hallway as the door closed. This time he was glad he couldn't see the grief his condition caused. It was better this way.

When the door opened again, Bishop heard a couple of nurses talking in low tones over the sound of rolling wheels, fussing with the equipment, and coordinating their efforts to hoist his body onto the gurney. By their urgency and fastidiousness, he realised they were preparing him for surgery. As they wheeled him down the hall, he retreated, trying to fade under layers of attention.

Bishop knew right away when he opened his eyes again that he was back in Bardopolis, though he couldn't tell what part. Not Wrigley, anyway. His clothes were the same yet the shirt and jacket bore no ragged holes from the bullets. His lack of a weapon made him feel exposed and vulnerable after what had happened at Wrigley. Even now, his unknown enemies could be following him. He needed a gun and thought he knew where to find one but had no idea how to get there.

This neighbourhood looked like one of many without any landmarks to guide him. He pulled the emblem out of his pocket, hoping it would illuminate another hidden portal, but no such luck. Bishop wished he were home rather than navigating the tedium of transportation and the thing warmed in his hands, delivering him there at the speed of thought. The result startled him with a new respect for this polished slab of metal and its tricks. He tucked it away, anxious to keep it close.

Bishop's place in Bardopolis wasn't exactly the same as in the waking world, though it was close enough to ring true. The lights were off, and he realised that he didn't have a key to get inside. The emblem might help him with that. Like Bishop had hoped, the metal delivered him inside with a thought. He slipped it into his back pocket, noting its warmth whenever he used it.

The den in this version of his home was no different than that in the waking world. His father's rolltop desk crowded out any other furniture, its cover masking a scrambled mess of papers and its drawers similarly disorganized. The only difference was that the locked drawer on the bottom had been wrenched open and its contents eviscerated. The handgun he kept there was missing, as were his and his father's shotguns he kept in the closet. He had been cleaned out.

He knew a place where he might be able to find help, but going there entailed a different kind of risk altogether, one he wasn't sure he could handle. Yet urgency made it necessary. Before leaving, he stripped the jacket from his body like a second skin and dumped it, rumpled and useless, behind a shrub in the front yard where no one would think to look for it. This next visit was personal and private. He palmed the metal from his pocket before he lost his nerve.

Pulaski's looked like it did in the old photographs he had seen as a kid, the entrance back in its original spot on the far end with the long front window intact. The neon beer signs hanging against the glass advertised unfamiliar brands in odd colour combinations, but the place felt right nonetheless. Known as a hangout for retired cops, Bishop hoped its clientele remained unchanged.

No doorman meant the joint wasn't busy yet, or at least it did in the waking world. That should make it easier to find somebody. The bar itself was of the same rich mahogany as in the waking world, with stools to match. Standing opposite the bar was the same Philco cabinet playing the same crooners and big bands while, untouched by daylight, the black leather of the back booths glistened in the murk.

Bishop ordered a beer from a bartender wearing suspenders, an unfamiliar guy half the age of the usual staff.

"Put it on my tab," said a grizzled veteran drinking alone at the end of the bar.

Bishop knew the voice immediately. "Dad."

Grinning, his old man left his stool and embraced him, slapping him on the back. He stood back and took stock of his son. "Marty, I can't tell you how happy I am to see you. Have a beer with your old man."

His father returned to the stool most Pulaski's patrons in the waking world still referred to as Randall Bishop's. Bishop took one beside it, and the bartender brought him the beer he'd ordered. Bishop took a sip. Tasteless and viscous, it was more like motor oil than beer. He did his best to hide his revulsion and nudged the glass away.

"To be honest, I wasn't sure you were going to show up," his father said.

"Were you expecting me?"

His father shrugged. "We had a real conversation here once before, so I always hoped you'd come back."

"Really?" None of Bishop's past dreams sprang to mind. "How long have you been waiting?"

His father's smile faded as he stared Bishop dead in the eyes. "The longest years you could imagine." Emptying his beer, his father flagged down the barman for another. "I want to make it up to you for how I behaved after your mother died."

"Dad—"

His father waved him aside. "You deserved better. I've always loved you, you know."

The words touched Bishop. Expressing emotions had never been easy for them. "I know. You too."

Bishop wanted to say more, but his father interrupted, which maybe was best. "Listen, I'm here because you're in deep shit. A really nasty crew has their eyes on you, and they won't give up until you're gone."

The news didn't surprise Bishop. "Who are these people?"

"I'd tell you more if I could, but that's not how Bardopolis works. I'd break the rules if I knew how."

"Maybe you can tell me about this." Bishop pulled out the metallic emblem and set it on the bar.

His father's features darkened, and Bishop realised it was the first time he'd seen fear upon his father's face. "Put that away."

Bishop did so while his father peered at the other patrons to see if they'd noticed the exchange, but what few others inhabited the place had their own concerns. Once he was satisfied that it was safe, his father leaned closer, his voice deep and urgent. "What are you doing with an Enforcer's badge?"

Bishop felt stupid for not guessing it sooner. "Some Enforcers gave it to me as evidence in a murder investigation."

His father looked puzzled. "That doesn't make any sense. Enforcers are mute and work alone."

That surprised Bishop. "What else can you tell me about them?"

"Not much, just that they're made of light and come and go as they please. Their badges are the embodiment of their power. Without it, they don't exist." His father pointed at Bishop's pocket. "The only way to get that thing from an Enforcer is to rip it out of its chest. Whoever did that has some serious balls."

Bishop thought of Erotami and Strefon. "Do Enforcers ever go bad?"

His father shook his head. "Impossible. They're pure manifestations of the One."

"What is the One, exactly?"

"I hate to sound like a damned hippie, but the One is love. That's all." His father looked vaguely embarrassed at the admission.

While interesting, that information wasn't particularly helpful. "Tell me about this place. Bardopolis, I mean. I heard it's a city of the dreamers and the dead."

His father nodded as the bartender brought him another beer. "That's more or less it. When we die, we gravitate toward lives that are like the ones we left behind. It makes the transition easier. Dreamers, on the other hand, come up like tourists, get their kicks, and go back to their lives none the wiser. Sometimes the dreamers realise what's going on, but most of the time they don't. The rest of us, we're stuck here until we figure out how to reincarnate or choose not to. Not everyone does."

"Bardopolis seems pretty normal to me. I've had a lot of dreams far weirder than anything I've seen here."

His father smiled the same way he had when Bishop had made some naïve mistake as a child, like when he had innocently put dish soap in the old dishwater and turned the kitchen into a stage of bubbles that would have made Lawrence Welk envious. "Dreams only seem that way because the human brain is too primitive to make sense of this place, and so it compensates with imaginary substitutes."

"What about dreams that happen in the woods or the desert or on another planet?"

His father shrugged. "Bardopolis is all cities interconnected, with everything in between. The logic unravels sometimes, but that's why the One has Enforcers."

"You mean, like cops?"

His father's face grew forlorn. "There are no cops in Bardopolis. People can get away with anything here. If bad things happen to dreamers, they wake up. When bad things happen to residents, like me, they return home and wake up not knowing any better, like blacking out."

"And that keeps things in check?"

"It used to. Now whole sections of the city have gone dark, and people are disappearing. At first, I thought it was a bunch of reincarnations, but the numbers don't add up. And the murder of an Enforcer is bad news. There's a storm headed this way." His father took another drink. "Sometimes I even hear wolves at night. In the city, can you believe it?"

Bishop froze. "What can I do about it?"

His father laughed, free from the wheezing that had plagued his last days. "You always thought big, even when you were a kid. I admired that, still do, and wish I had better advice. All I can say is watch your back and trust your intuition. You remember what I used to say?"

Bishop rolled his eyes because forgetting his father's lesson had never been an option. "'A good cop trusts his gut. A great one knows when to listen to it.'" His father beamed at Bishop's recitation, his good mood giving Bishop an opening to lean closer. "Those are fine words to live by, but what about a gun?"

His father pushed himself back from the bar and looked at Bishop with mock incredulity. "You know Pulaski's doesn't let us bring guns inside, especially not us retired coots."

"Yeah, and I also know that you've never come here without one. Can I borrow it?"

His old man chuckled. "You know me too well, Marty. Here, don't let anyone see."

With practised discretion, his father removed a revolver from within his jacket and passed it to Bishop under the table, grip first. Without looking at it, Bishop knew the gun was a snub-nose .357, his father's favourite, and stuck it into his belt, underneath his shirt.

"I hope things work out, Marty. Just be careful." His father reached over to put a reassuring hand on Bishop's shoulder. "Either way, I'll wait here for you. Don't forget that."

The bar had filled up during their conversation. Other voices had grown louder, and the music had been turned off in favour of a college basketball game on the television. His father turned to the bartender to ask the score, and Bishop realised that their conversation was coming to an end, at least whatever part of it had been real.

Before Bishop left, he had one more question. He had to tap his father on the shoulder to tear his attention away from the television. "Does Diaz ever come around here?"

His father turned to him as if he'd forgotten he was there. "Oh sure. He stops in from time to time to chat with us old timers when he's not down in Florida."

Diaz loved big sea fishing and had once dragged Bishop down there with him, laughing when Bishop had been too queasy to even stand up in the boat because of the choppy waters, let alone reel in a catch. They had stayed with one of Diaz's aunts somewhere near Miami in a modest bungalow. Diaz still spoke of it often.

By now Bishop's father's attention was completely invested in the game. Not anxious to leave his old man just yet, Bishop thought about making small talk with him about anything, the Bulls or the Bears or the weather, but he could see it would be futile and left his father at the end of the bar. To avoid a sense of finality, Bishop didn't look back. One way or another, however many days or years in the future, he wanted to return.

A thousand questions Bishop could have asked instead followed him out the door like white noise, clouding his mind. He wanted to know more about the nature of this place and his father's life here, if it could be called that, about the afterlife and the One and reincarnation, and especially about his mother. Her accident had been decades ago but Bishop was curious if his father had seen her or lived with her or had forgotten about her altogether. Perhaps these questions were better left unasked. Their conversation had been heartbreaking enough.

There were other things he needed to know that his

father couldn't tell him, particularly when it came to Erotami and Strefon. They were neither mute nor loners like his father had described Enforcers, so who were they really and why had they lied? Someone wanted him dead and he needed to know why. Yet even if they knew, could he trust their answer? Before confronting them, he wanted to see if the thieves who had stolen his guns had left any clues.

Touching the badge, Bishop pictured his den and found himself there before he could finish the thought, its metal flush with heat. He found no signs of forced entry near the closet where he had stashed the shotguns, simply an open door. So much for clues. On the other hand, on the bottom desk drawer where he kept his handgun, he found gouges in the wood surrounding the hole where the lock had been. Sharp tools could have made such gashes, but their even spacing suggested something more like claws. He wondered if one of those mournful creatures could have followed him here. Although the floor didn't bear their marks, thinking of them creeping through his house made him uncomfortable.

Faint sounds reached him from downstairs. He withdrew his father's revolver and stood at the top of the steps, leaning for a look. The entry and living room were dark and empty. The rolling of drawers, shifting of plates, and clattering of utensils told him that someone or something was in the kitchen, going through his things. What they expected to find, Bishop couldn't guess. Down the stairs and through the living room, Bishop used the sounds to mask his approach. Just beyond the counter that linked the dining room and kitchen, he tensed, preparing to lay the intruder out. After all the things that had happened to him in Bardopolis, he wasn't expecting the figure standing before him.

"Viv."

Bishop stuck the gun in his waistband before she spun around from where she dug in a drawer, her hand on her chest. Only when she saw who it was did she exhale.

"I didn't hear you come in," she said, chuckling as if feeling foolish. "Have you seen the corkscrew?"

Caught off guard by seeing her, even if it was only in Bardopolis, Bishop paused before responding. "No. "

Her face softened when she registered his haggard expression, and she drew closer, touching his face. "You've had a bad day."

Bishop wrapped his arms around Viv as he'd wanted to for longer than he could admit, glad to feel her body pressed against his. He longed for the scent of her skin but came up empty. Not everything translated to Bardopolis. Still, holding her felt good. Only when she released him did he let her go.

"Dinner's almost ready, and you can tell me all about it." She opened the oven to check on the meal.

Bishop couldn't catch a waft of its contents. "What did you make?"

Viv, flustered, smiled absentmindedly. "Your favourite, of course."

This was a rare surprise. Of the two of them, Bishop usually did the cooking. He saw that the dining room table had already been set with their finest place settings and candles. The scene felt so real that Bishop wondered if he'd forgotten an anniversary or a birthday before remembering that he was in Bardopolis and none of this had any true meaning. As nice as it would be to pretend like their last year apart hadn't happened, indulging this fantasy wouldn't solve anything. If nothing else, it would only make his heartache worse.

"Listen, I hate to do this, but I can't stay."

"You just got here, and I went to all this trouble. At least eat something."

"I'm not hungry."

Viv folded her arms. "What's so important that you can't stay?"

"I have to see Diaz about an important case."

She brightened. "Oh, he said he might stop by. You can just wait."

"When did you talk to him?"

"He called for you earlier. I forgot to tell you."

"What phone did you answer?" Bishop hadn't owned a functioning landline since getting a cell years ago.

"That one."

She pointed to a tan phone hanging on the kitchen wall, dangling a curly tail. Bishop had never seen it before.

"This is too important to wait."

Viv frowned briefly but perked up. "Can I at least get a kiss first?"

"Of course."

Her kiss felt alien and lacked the sparks Bishop had hoped for. At first he had thought that any version of Viv was better than none, but now he wasn't so sure. None of the details he cherished about her – like her self-deprecating sense of humour, her admitted lack of culinary skills, the scent of her skin or the way she constantly blew one strand of hair out of her eyes rather than tying it back – had translated to Bardopolis. She looked the same but acted more like a construct than the flesh and blood version he knew. Before he left, he wanted to see how well the two corresponded.

Facing her, he held her hands. "Listen, Viv, I want to apologise for how things ended before."

"That's not necessary. The fact we're together now is all that matters."

He shook his head. "I need to say this." Struggling with the delivery, he looked her in the eyes. "The worst mistake I ever made was making you get that abortion."

Sombre, Viv nodded, her eyes welling with tears. She hugged him and sobbed into his chest. Bishop held her tight, stroking her hair.

"Things will be right again, you'll see," she said, and Bishop wanted to believe her.

"I'm sure they will," he said, and left her with as hopeful of a smile as he could muster.

Outside, Bishop retrieved the jacket he'd thrown behind the shrub. As he brushed off the dead leaves, Viv knocked on the screen door, from where she watched him leave. She smiled and waved. Bishop lifted a hand to wave back, and gunfire erupted behind him. The last thing he heard was Viv screaming.

The antiseptic odour and the medical devices' enigmatic noises struck him first. He felt stronger and tried opening his eyes but nothing happened. All he wanted was to wake up and end this nightmare. With a sense of urgency, he tried again. This time he felt a flurry in his gut. Instead of finding himself back in his body, however, he floated above it. The operation hadn't killed him anyway. His body had fewer machines hooked up to it, though he still needed a respirator and an IV.

Familiar voices carried from far away. Like a cloud, Bishop drifted along the ceiling toward them. Using the ceiling for ballast, movement was easier this time. Viv and Diaz stood near the nurses' station. An officer whose name Bishop couldn't remember stood nearby, looking down the hall and pretending not to listen. Their words grew intelligible as he drew closer.

"The operation went as well as we could hope. Now all he has to do is wake up."

"What are his odds?"

Diaz raised his eyebrows. "Better, now that the bullet is out."

"Do you think he'll come back?"

"Are you kidding me? He's too ornery to give up." Diaz smiled, trying to give Viv the reassurance she needed. Bishop didn't know if Diaz himself believed it. One of the hardest parts of their job was providing comfort when there was none to give.

Viv looked like she wanted to believe him, but she had always been a pragmatist. "How long does he have?"

Diaz lost his smile. "As long as it takes. Anyone who says different will have to come through me."

A twitchy blur burst past the officer on duty, skirted Diaz and Viv, and ran down the hall toward Bishop's room. Diaz pulled his gun and motioned Viv to the side while his fellow officer fell into position. Before Diaz and the officer could reach him, the intruder darted around a corner. Two gunshots blasted from the hallway, sending the nurses and onlookers to their knees with screams and then a brief, frightened silence.

Diaz called from the end of the hall. "Peretti!"

Over grunts and scuffling came the slap of handcuffs, and Peretti dragged the gunman into the hall. Diaz whistled at the sight of them, and two more officers came from each branch of the hallway. Wearing a hooded sweatshirt and a denim vest, Bishop didn't recognise the man they'd captured. To have been that fast, he had to be young.

"Nice trick switching rooms," said Peretti.

Diaz waved at Viv, and she threaded through the crime scene to join him. He led her to a room opposite from where Peretti had captured the assailant. Viv went inside, and Bishop followed her. He recognised his healing body as he'd left it moments ago.

Viv gasped with relief. "He's okay."

"And don't worry, this punk's going to give us some answers."

Viv nodded as if not really listening, lost in thought as she gazed upon Bishop's comatose body. She kissed Bishop on the forehead.

Bishop didn't follow them when they left, seeing no reason to torment himself further. But the success of Diaz's trick buoyed him, his partner's resourcefulness a welcome flood of affirmation. No matter what it took, Bishop was going to find a way back.

The waking world drained him, and he couldn't fight the pull of Bardopolis any longer. He felt cast adrift, insubstantial, somewhere between awake and asleep. Images of the hospital flashed upon his mind as made his slow ascent, alternating with street scenes of Bardopolis as he made his transition like a form of dreaming.

Bishop recognised the neighbourhood when he materialised in Bardopolis this time. The heritage museum, the alcohol crisis centre, a Polish deli and even the lousy pizza joint at the end of the street told him he was in Ukrainian Village. Altered from the waking world, certainly, but the personality of the neighbourhood still shone through whatever changes it had undergone. That meant he had only drifted a few blocks from home since his last visit, but he had another stop to make before going back to confront whomever had shot him. Remarkably, he still had his father's pistol tucked into his belt and wore the wrinkled jacket. There wasn't much time before someone discovered that he'd returned, and he had to move quickly.

Removing the badge from his front pocket, he envisioned Diaz's apartment and found himself there in less than a heartbeat. Dark and cluttered, little had changed relative to the waking world other than some insignificant details. Diaz himself, however, was nowhere to be found. And if the dust was any indication, he hadn't been home in a while. Even if

Diaz happened to be asleep and dreaming back in the waking world, there was no guarantee he would dream of his apartment.

Bishop wondered how far the badge would allow him to travel. He held it, recalling all the details he could of the bungalow Diaz had brought him to in Florida. Diaz's aunt had decorated the place with doilies underneath plastic gladioli on every surface, generic paintings of the beach, and a makeshift altar to Diaz's deceased uncle on the mantle, adorned with coloured paper, candles, and crosses. Bishop focused on these details, hoping they were enough to take him where he wanted to go. Without blinking, he stood in the living room of a familiar home and found that they were.

The dimensions of the place had grown, but the plastic flowers and their accompanying doilies, the bad art and the altar, not to mention the wall of family photographs Bishop had forgotten, confirmed the location. There were no immediate signs of occupancy other than a folded newspaper and some dishes in the sink. Palm fronds brushing against the bay windows brought Bishop's attention to the marina that led to the ocean. After Diaz's uncle had passed, his aunt had kept his boat though Diaz was the only one who used it. The dock was empty, and Bishop hoped that was a good sign. He took a slip of pastel stationery and a cheap ballpoint pen with a gibberish slogan from the kitchen table and scrawled a message, careful not to let haste compromise clarity. When he finished, he draped the jacket on the back of a chair and set the badge on the note as a paperweight. This was a risky plan, but he had no choice. He covered the badge with a hand and thought of home.

Bishop reappeared in front of his house. Clear and free of stains, the sidewalk bore no indication that a murder had taken place. Maybe more time had passed than he'd thought. A light in the window told him someone might be home, and the unlocked door all but proved it. That was encouraging. What he had in mind would do no good if he were alone.

"Viv?"

There was a pause before he heard Viv's voice coming from the kitchen. "Martin? Is that you?"

Grateful, Bishop went inside. Hampered by her apron, Viv ran from the kitchen to hug him, the wooden spoon in her hand dragging red sauce across his back. She kissed him, her lipstick matching the sauce. Bishop had never seen such a vision of domesticity when they lived together. He felt better seeing her like this.

"You don't know how happy I am you're okay," she said.

"I'm lucky to be here." Bishop nodded toward the kitchen. "Dinner smells great." In truth, he could smell nothing.

"Hope you like it." Viv put her arm through his and led him toward the kitchen at the back of the house. "They'll be glad to see you."

Bishop tensed knowing there were others in the house and resisted the urge to draw his gun. When he and Viv entered the dining room, he noticed that the table had settings for four, one of which had a booster chair and a plastic cup with a monkey on it. Voices approached from the backyard, and the door opened.

"Which is why they say an elephant never forgets," said Diaz, looking over his shoulder into the backyard. That he still wore a Cubs cap amused Bishop.

A child ran past Diaz into the house, his eyes fixed on Bishop. "Daddy!"

The tyke wrapped his little arms around Bishop's legs. Sandy-haired and with a ready smile, the child couldn't have been older than three or four. He wore a faded Bulls t-shirt.

With care, Bishop pried the boy off and chuckled. "I think you got the wrong guy, buddy."

Viv rolled her eyes and went to the stove. "Very funny, wise guy."

"What do you mean?"

"Daddy." The kid tugged on Bishop's leg to get his attention.

Diaz nodded at Viv. "See? Like I told you. He was acting this way when I ran into him at the game, like he has partial amnesia."

Viv looked up from dishing food from the pan. "Carlos, he's joking. He knows who Daniel is. Don't you, Marty?"

Maybe there was a slight resemblance to someone he knew, but Bishop couldn't make a clear connection. The boy smiled at him with no hint of shyness.

"Our son?" Now Viv looked worried. Her spoon froze. "Are you serious?"

"We don't have a son," Bishop said.

Viv fought tears. "Here we do."

Diaz stepped closer to Bishop, whispering over the child's head. "Whatever happened to him down there is irrelevant."

This was something Bishop hadn't considered. He knelt to meet Daniel at his own level. Still smiling, the kid wrapped his little arms around him, and Bishop awkwardly returned the embrace. He released the kid and held him at arm's length, putting a hand on either side of the child's head to look him over. All he could tell for sure about Daniel was that the boy was missing a few teeth and had the same freckles as Viv. Bishop twisted the boy's neck before he could scream.

Viv shrieked as Bishop pulled out his father's gun and fired it twice at Diaz, who fell against the back door and slumped. From the gun came a little smoke but no smell.

Viv collapsed to the floor, cradling Daniel's limp

body and weeping. Her wails were convincing in their wretched despair. "How could you do that? You murdered our son!"

Bishop faced her. "Viv was never pregnant, nor would I make her get an abortion. And Diaz hates the Cubs."

He pointed the gun at the back door and saw that the floor was empty. Before he could turn back to Viv, something heavy struck him on the back of the head. Lights like diamonds flashed in his field of vision as he spun to the ground. A cast-iron pan fell from Viv's hand as she and Diaz towered over him, watching him. Their forms dissipated before his eyes, and the last thing he saw before everything faded was Erotami and Strefon in their place.

Bishop became aware of bouncing as he returned to consciousness. Too groggy to open his eyes, the vibration soothed him. He became aware of voices, though he heard them long before he understood them. The meaning of the words solidified as his awareness grew, and it didn't take him long to realise that he was listening to Erotami and Strefon. His last, brief glimpses of them came back to him, as did what had happened in his house in Bardopolis. His instincts had been right all along, but they hadn't done him any good.

Keeping his eyes closed, he tried to move without his captors noticing only to find that his ankles and wrists were bound, his arms behind his back. Tape covered his mouth like an overgrown moustache. By the softness of the surface underneath him and the nearness of their conversation, he figured he was in the back seat of a vehicle. The roads were bad even in Bardopolis, and all the turns and backtracking made him queasy.

"The important thing is that we got him."

Erotami was obviously pleased with himself, but

Strefon couldn't share in his conviction. "That was too close. We were sloppy and unconvincing. He saw right through us from the beginning."

"Speak for yourself. I had him wrapped around my finger."

"Almost. You screwed up the first night."

Erotami grew irritated. "How was I supposed to know his favourite meal? You're the one who thought his partner was a Cubs fan."

"He should be a Cubs fan. Who doesn't like the Cubs?"

"You're just jealous because you think I liked kissing him."

Strefon slammed a fist on the steering wheel. "Just admit it."

"Not this again."

Silence followed for a few moments before Strefon resumed. "I wish I didn't have to beg for respect like a dog. It wasn't easy being the other cop and the kid at the same time, you know."

"I know, Strife." Erotami's voice grew tender. "You do all the heavy lifting around here."

Strefon finally heard what he needed. Nothing further came from the two, but Bishop's skin prickled as though from static electricity. He fought the urge to open his eyes until he heard Erotami's voice inches from his own.

"I think he's awake."

Erotami's face loomed from the darkness as he reached for Bishop. "Don't worry. This is for your own good."

Then, not for the first time, Bishop was aware of nothing.

Bishop couldn't feel the vehicle moving when he came to. The surface he lay upon was uncomfortable, and his legs were tucked up behind him. Opening his eyes, he found himself swaddled in darkness. No longer in the back seat, he must be in the trunk. Around him, through the metal, he sensed other bodies stirring. Faint bristles brushed along the chassis like an impatient school of fish, interrupted by sniffs and snorts. Something slammed into the exterior of the trunk, startling him. When it howled its piercing cry like a declaration of war, he realised what was happening. Despite the relative safety of the trunk, the sound chilled him. Those strange, wolf-like creatures surrounded the car, blocking its passage.

"They're restless tonight." Even muffled by layers of cloth and metal, Erotami sounded nervous.

Strefon didn't sound so alarmed. "They're just hungry. The smell of him torments them." The horn blared, and Strefon's shouting matched its intensity. "Get the fuck out of the way!"

Erotami laughed. "Poor pups. We've been neglecting them."

Strefon wasn't concerned. "They'll be fed soon enough."

The horn started up again in impatient staccato bursts. Even Bishop could tell that the sound was impotent.

"Fuck it," Strefon said, lurching the car forward.

A couple of pitiful squeals and rolling bumps later, and the vehicle moved again, albeit slowly, like wading through a sea of grass. Strefon laid on the horn a few more times, but Bishop didn't feel the vehicle roll over any more bumps. Exhaust chugged underneath Bishop like foul judgment throughout the length of their languid but labyrinthine route. The horn and the voices eventually stopped, as did the car itself. Neither of his captors said anything for several minutes until Strefon finally broke the silence.

"Well?" He was annoyed.

"Well, what?" Erotami mirrored his annoyance.

"You know damn well. Aren't you going to open the door?"

Erotami sighed. "I see that I have to do everything around here."

Bishop heard Erotami slam the passenger door and take a few steps across concrete before reciting some words in a language Bishop didn't recognise. A moment later came a deep boom as if some heavy piece of machinery had disengaged after a lifetime of tension. The bay door slid up, rattling in its frame.

Strefon pulled the car inside, and Erotami said a few more strange words. The door fell with an ominous boom, the vastness of its echoing shockwave telling Bishop they were back in the warehouse. Strefon killed the engine as Erotami walked toward the back of the vehicle.

"Help me get him out."

The trunk popped open, and his captors met him with eager smiles.

"Welcome home," Erotami said. "Ready to have some fun?"

The pair hauled Bishop roughly from the trunk, each grabbing an arm as he sagged between them. Hoisted upright, Bishop's feet hit the ground, sending shivers that barely registered up his dormant legs, his ankles still bound.

Erotami ripped the duct tape from Bishop's face with a grin. "Scream all you want. The sound delights us."

The skin around Bishop's mouth smarted from removal of the tape, but he tried to smile anyway. "So now that you've dragged me back to your secret lair, are you going to rough me up and leave me for dead or just kill me quickly and toss my body in the river?"

Neither of his captors said a word, their silence unnerving, until Strefon said, "We're going to flush you down the toilet."

Remembering the nauseating bathroom in the back of the building, Bishop twisted in their grasp. His bonds did him no favours, and his captors were stronger than they looked. Bishop soon gave up and went limp, his feet trailing a path in the dust. Like dead weight, they dragged him to the other end of the warehouse.

Stopping before the far brick wall near the office, Erotami turned to Strefon. "Since we're all friends here, can we let our hair down? I'm worn out from keeping up appearances."

Strefon nodded. "I could use a breather too."

They dropped Bishop unceremoniously. His bonds snagged when he hit the ground, burning his wrists and ankles. After both captors sighed, they picked Bishop up again. The hands that clutched him felt rougher, if not stronger, digging into his flesh more sharply. They deposited him against a brick wall like a prop. Feeling drugged and unable to control his own body, Bishop slumped on his side, staring up at them.

The overhead lighting stabbed his eyes, making circles of colours, sharpening his captors into new lines and shapes. Expecting to recognise them, those standing before him were something else entirely. Taller by several feet, covered in oily scales, and with horns both broken and intact scattershot across both sides of their torsos, Erotami and Strefon revelled in Bishop's stunned reaction. He could still tell them apart because Erotami had tufts of coarse blonde hair sprouting in patches from his hide while Strefon's was thick and black. Erotami wore a patch over his left eye, while Strefon had no right hand. The sight confounded Bishop.

"I don't think he recognises us like this." Erotami's voice hummed with razor teeth surrounding a muscular and inquisitive tongue. He crouched and stepped closer, his tongue encircling Bishop's face without touching it. Erotami cocked his head so his one good eye could wash over Bishop before he stood up again, folding his arms. "I can't tell."

"Maybe he's faking." Although Strefon's voice had deepened, the limitations of his slavering mouth, protruding with tusks, lent his pronunciation rough edges. "He's fooled us before."

"No matter. Our experiment's almost over anyway."

Bishop had a hard time wrapping his head around their conversation. "What experiment?"

Erotami smirked. "The one where we kill an Enforcer and see if he can solve his own murder."

"I'm not an Enforcer."

"You were until we fed you to the Beast. For some reason, you reincarnated instead of returning to the One. We can only guess that the badge brought you back, which is why we're going to toss it in with you this time. Shame we couldn't unlock its power for ourselves, but apparently it doesn't work the same for our kind."

"What kind is that?"

"The kind from which nightmares are born," Strefon said, and Bishop believed him.

Erotami shuffled forward and rifled through Bishop's pockets, the probing of his meaty fingers and pointed claws intrusive and unforgiving. Finding nothing of value, he shrieked and smacked Bishop's head against the wall. "It's not here."

Bishop's vision flickered upon impact. The blow sent his body to the floor, and it was all he could do to avert his face before contact. He struggled to push himself upright despite his bonds and the weakness in his limbs.

"Enough," Strefon said, pulling Erotami back to his feet with his good hand. His claws were nubs compared to his partner's, though his fingers were thicker and looked stronger.

"Do you want him to keep coming back for us?"

"Of course not, but we need him to talk. Beating him unconscious will only delay us."

Erotami crossed his arms. "Fine. What did you have in mind?"

Strefon pointed his stump at Bishop. "The nightwolves will gladly help us convince him."

As if in response to Strefon's suggestion, a nightwolf howled outside, a lone distant cry that spread as others took it up and passed it like a warning. Soon the keening surrounded the warehouse, stark and foreboding. One of the creatures slammed into the door, spreading shudders through the corrugated metal.

Strefon followed Bishop's worried gaze and smiled. "See how eager?"

The nightwolves bayed again, unanimous and impatient. They threw their bodies at the door, pockets of dents blooming under the battery. A growl from nearby drowned their syncopation, heavier than an earthquake and shaking the floor. Bishop thought it had come from the bathroom.

Erotami leered at his partner. "The Beast is impatient tonight."

"The Beast is always impatient."

Their conversation made Bishop uneasy. "What's this Beast you're talking about?"

A raspy laugh erupted from Erotami's reptilian throat. "He's not faking, Strife. Memory alone should have him begging for mercy."

Strefon saw the truth of it and nodded. "Then remind him."

Erotami grabbed Bishop's scalp, the points of his claws scraping his skin. Erotami looked into Bishop's eyes with depthless voids, his breath iron vapour. "We are talking about the Beast that Will Devour Eternity. The One's greed for sacrifice has made it too fat to protect its realm. There are cracks in the shell of Bardopolis, and the Beast found a way inside from Beyond. It gorges on the laws of existence and excretes despair. We hide in its shadow, fattening it with forgotten dreams. As it grows, that living blasphemy will swallow the One and all it holds dear." He shoved Bishop backward.

Bishop recovered before striking the wall. "I don't see what you two get out of all this."

"Emptiness nourishes us," said Strefon. "Through the Beast, we water the dark heart of humanity to watch its evil flowers bloom. We've made your city a marvellous garden from which we harvest at will."

Bishop couldn't let that statement pass. "Not entirely."

"He has you there, Strife." Erotami raised an eyebrow, looking amused.

"True," said Strefon. "He has been a nuisance even reincarnated, but tonight he vanishes for good. Maybe if he screams loud enough, the Beast will take pity and bring him back as a nightwolf."

Bishop shuddered at that fate more repugnant than death. "How about, instead, I wake up and forget you two ever existed?" He knew they wouldn't go for it but had to stall for time.

Erotami chuckled. "It's too late for that. You're already dead. Now tell us what you did with the badge before we feed your fingers to the nightwolves."

Bishop knew Erotami lied and couldn't resist bluffing. "How do you know Enforcers aren't surrounding this place as we speak?"

Strefon didn't blink. "Impossible. The Beast cloaks itself in confusion to mask its trail. Besides, Enforcers aren't known for their hesitation." He grunted, impatient. "This is your last chance. Where is the badge?"

Bishop had nothing left. "What can I say? I lost it. Sorry."

Strefon's eyes narrowed, his temper rising. "You picked the wrong time to test us, human."

Bishop would have held up his hands if he could. "The problem is that you're asking the wrong guy. I'm not the real Bishop."

By their stares and stunned silence, Bishop could tell that his words had the intended effect. How long they would believe him was another story.

Erotami glowered, confused. "Then who are you?"

"A decoy. The real Bishop is outside with the badge, watching for an opening. He used me as bait to bring you here."

"I doubt the Beast will be able to taste the difference."

Erotami wrapped an arm around Bishop's neck and dragged him toward the office, his scales digging into Bishop's skin. Choking, Bishop struggled in vain to free himself. His bonds did him no favours. A stench clouded the air the closer they drew to the office. Halfway there, Strefon halted them.

"Stop, Era. He might be telling the truth. The beacon is back in range and acting strangely. Don't you feel it?"

Erotami's tongue ran along the side of Bishop's face. "I thought the tingling was anticipation."

Strefon sounded perturbed. "The signal keeps circling the building, back and forth. It doesn't make sense."

"How did we miss it?" Erotami's grip loosened, air rushing into Bishop's lungs.

"He must have come back stronger than we knew." Strefon howled in mockery of the nightwolves. "This experiment annoys me. Let's hunt."

Erotami gestured toward Bishop, still squirming under his arm. "What about this maggot?"

Bishop felt the slow burn of Strefon's lingering gaze. "Let the nightwolves have him."

Erotami dropped him where they stood. Bishop grunted when his body slapped the ground, his head knocking the floor. His captors strode past the car toward the metal door at the far end of the warehouse with surprising swiftness. Strefon shouted an incomprehensible phrase that wrenched the door upwards with careless vigour, birthing a metallic thunder that dispersed both the nightwolves that had been sniffing at its edges as well as those that had been testing its resilience with their skulls. The door rebounded at its zenith, creeping its way back toward the ground after Strefon and Erotami passed below and stopping several feet short. Several nightwolves slipped underneath and trotted toward Bishop while Strefon and Erotami bellowed outside.

Bishop could neither run nor defend himself. His bonds were of no ordinary material and too tight to escape. All he could manage was to roll onto his back with his head away from the door. The nightwolves who dared enter padded toward him in leisurely arrogance, knowing full well he couldn't escape. Bishop drew his knees to his chest, prepared to kick. He braced for the worst as they advanced, snarling. Shots rang out from behind him before the nightwolves could close the gap, felling two, then a third, and sending the fourth running to join its mates outside. Deep and angry, a roar from the bathroom filled the vast warehouse, rattling the foundation like a minor earthquake.

Before Bishop could turn around, someone cut the ropes that bound him. Stiff and sore, he sat up to find a hand waiting to help him stand. Like he had hoped, it belonged to Diaz. His partner wore a fisherman's vest, replete with tackle, over a Hawaiian shirt and swimming trunks, sunglasses, and his familiar Sox cap. At his feet was a large bag.

Bishop chuckled. "Man, am I glad to see you."

"Strange crowd you run with," Diaz said, smiling. "I thought those creeps would never leave."

"How much did you hear?"

Diaz shrugged. "Most of it. I followed the car here using this thing." He handed over the badge with reluctance. "Sure is a nice toy you have there. Where can I get one?"

The badge felt good back in Bishop's hands. "I'll let you know if I hear anything."

"So which of those bastards tried to pass me off as a Cubs fan?"

"The one missing a hand."

"What a dick." The indignity of any association with the Cubs visibly irked Diaz. "So what's the plan?"

"You brought me presents, right?"

"Of course. You think I can't read?" Diaz unzipped the bag at his feet and removed a couple of shotguns, passing the first to Bishop and keeping the second one for himself. He passed Bishop a handful of shells. From outside came an angry shout, followed by a pitiful wail.

Bishop stuck out his hand. "You better give me your pistol too. I'll need it to distract them until they reach me."

Diaz handed it over. "Is this going to be enough to get rid of them?"

Bishop tucked the pistol into his belt. "Are you kidding? I'm just trying to slow them down." More shouts and a yelp came from outside. "We better get into that office before they come back."

Diaz's eyebrows creased. "Isn't that where the tremors came from?"

"Yeah."

"What the hell are you getting me into?"

"Don't worry about it. You're just having a bad dream."

The office was as Bishop remembered it, empty but for a metal desk and a folding chair. A miasmic fog billowed from the bathroom, staining the air in expanding circles. Covering their mouths, Bishop and Diaz wedged the desk behind the door, allowing just enough room for Bishop to slip outside.

Bishop cracked the bathroom door and propped his shotgun inside, just beyond the entry. He closed the door behind him to keep the nauseating odour from invading the office. On the other side of the door, Bishop heard a muted gurgling. What the Beast truly looked like, he didn't want to know.

Diaz looked queasy. "That thing can't reach us in here, can it?"

"I don't think so."

"Is that supposed to be reassuring?"

"Don't worry, I'll shoot you before it eats you. You'll thank me later." Bishop gave the badge back to Diaz. "Don't leave me hanging."

Eyes wide, Diaz took the badge and disappeared.

Bishop squeezed past the desk and back into the warehouse just before Strefon sent the metal door slamming against the limits of its rails as he and Erotami returned. Strefon dragged a limp nightwolf by the neck with the jacket Erotami had given Bishop stuck in its hide with fishing hooks. He tossed it aside as he and Erotami lumbered past the parked car with enough force to rattle its windows. Bishop drew Diaz's pistol and fired. The first shot veered wide but the next two his Strefon squarely in the chest. Strefon hissed but didn't slow down. A wide legion of nightwolves followed in their wake, the pack's numbers vast and unknowable.

Bishop ducked back into the office and shoved the desk against the door. He didn't know where Diaz had gone but trusted his partner would know when to return. Strefon kicked the door, the feet of the desk wailing against the floor as it skittered backwards. His pursuers burst into the room angrier than he had ever seen them, their faces distorted with hunger, their eyes without mercy. Through the office window, Bishop saw nightwolves filling the warehouse, lining up as if awaiting orders.

Squeezing the trigger a few more times, Bishop gave up when he saw that the calibre was too small to do much harm even at close range. One of the bullets clipped Erotami's ear, but the missing piece grew back so quickly as to make the damage inconsequential. Bishop dropped the pistol and walked backwards until he registered the bathroom door at his back. He opened the door behind him without looking, unleashing another blast of the fetid odour into the abandoned office. Keeping an eye on his reptilian adversaries, Bishop reached for the shotgun. His hand came up empty. Reaching to feel if it had fallen aside, he brushed the corner in futility. The shotgun wasn't there.

Over Strefon's shoulder, Erotami ran his monstrous tongue along his razor teeth. "Time to feed our pet."

Diaz appeared beside Erotami, visibly startling them. He raised his shotgun. "Here's an appetiser."

Erotami only had time to turn his head before Diaz blasted him in the face, pumped, and blasted again, obliterating the creature's skull. Erotami's headless body teetered and collapsed backward against the wall, crashing to the ground with a meaty thud. Strefon lurched toward Diaz with surprising speed, grabbing him by the fishing vest.

Bishop dove into the bathroom to find his own weapon, knowing he had no time to spare. When he didn't hear another blast, he expected Diaz had escaped with the badge. Instead Bishop heard a crash and a scream – a human scream. Without his help, Diaz wasn't going to last much longer. Bishop didn't know what would happen to a dreamer fed to the Beast and didn't want to find out. If he didn't locate his shotgun, they were both doomed.

The noxious smell did little to prepare him for what he found. The bathroom had been illusory, he saw now. Where the broken toilet had been lay a vast, gaping maw lined with concentric circles of spiky teeth the colour of granite, descending into a throat that knew no end. Encircling the mouth was a forest of dark green tentacles as slick as sewage. They filled the room, writhing independently along the floor, walls, and ceiling. Bishop ducked and dodged a few that snaked toward him seemingly at random. Noticing only a mouth and tentacles on the creature, Bishop realised that the Beast was blind.

A metallic glint opposite the doorway revealed his weapon to be entangled in a mesh of wet appendages, rising precariously in the air and swinging wildly in every direction. As Bishop stretched a hand toward it, a tentacle slithered along the trigger, pulling the weapon taut and pointing it, if vaguely, at Bishop. Bishop tried to wrench the shotgun free but found it was like wrestling with the stubborn branches of a tree. En masse they lifted him in the air and banged his head on the ceiling, his feet flailing beneath him. Bishop clung to the shotgun, jamming a finger alongside the tentacle in an attempt to gain control of the trigger. Their struggle fired a shell, its blast slamming Bishop against a wall. The Beast screeched shrilly, sending shudders throughout its limbs and shaking the room.

A shadow fell across Bishop's face as he struggled to keep the tentacles from overwhelming him. Strefon ducked and turned sideways to squeeze himself through the doorway, the Enforcer's badge clutched in one hand. Undaunted by the appendages stretching in supplication, Strefon made straight for Bishop.

Fighting the urge to panic, Bishop used the wall as leverage to push himself toward Strefon with all the strength left in his legs and pulled the trigger. The blast was only partially successful. Although the right side of Strefon's reptilian skull vanished, in his remaining left eye swirled all of his fury and hatred. Growling, Strefon raised his stump to beat Bishop as if with a club when the remaining portion of his head exploded, splattering Bishop with gore. Strefon's headless body stumbled forward as if in disbelief at its own fate. Diaz stood bruised and battered in the doorway, lowering his gun to reload it.

"I was afraid you had woken up," Bishop said.

"From this nightmare? I'm not that lucky." Diaz's eyes widened as he registered the full extent of the Beast for the first time. "What the fuck is that thing?"

"No time. Behind you."

Diaz spun to find a phalanx of nightwolves pushing through the office doorway. He blasted the first wave of the marauders, scattering them back into the warehouse for now. Diaz disappeared briefly and Bishop heard him push the screeching desk back up against the door. Judging by the number of nightwolves, it wouldn't hold them back for long.

Bishop let go of the shotgun and dropped to the floor. The shotgun itself vanished as the tentacles drew it into their depths. On his knees, Bishop scrambled to pry the badge out of Strefon's claws before the Beast could claim it.

Diaz came back and helped him to his feet, pulling him into the office and shutting the door.

"Are you going to tell me what that thing is in there?"

"Sure you want to know?"

Diaz considered. "Point taken. Now what?"

"Now we feed it."

"You kidding me?"

"I wish." Bishop nodded toward Erotami's body. "These things aren't dead."

Standing over Erotami, Bishop was right. The creature's body quivered in its struggle to regain its form. The base of Erotami's skull had already grown back and, as they watched, a mouth materialised as if from an illustrator's hand, beginning with the bottom lip and growing into teeth and a snarl. The process transfixed them momentarily until the mouth began to speak.

"It's over, Bishop. You and your friend are about to disappear forever. The Beast will gnaw—"

Diaz muted Erotami's tirade by shoving his shotgun into the demon's mouth. "Can I pull the trigger? Pretty please?"

Something about this creature brought out the worst in Bishop. "Wait until his good eye reforms. I want to be the last thing this bastard ever sees."

Erotami screamed unintelligibly around the barrel, but his pleas and curses had no effect on Bishop and his partner. The right side of Erotami's face filled in first, the leathery skin and random white hairs appearing first, then a couple of slits for the creature's nose, and finally his eye appeared like a hot wax injection into a prefabricated mould. When it moved back and forth to take in both Diaz and Bishop, Bishop nodded. Both men turned their heads to avoid the mess, and Diaz pulled the trigger.

Bishop and Diaz each threw one of Erotami's limp arms over their shoulders and dragged the body toward the bathroom. Bishop kicked the door open, and together they hauled Erotami inside. A few of the tentacles had wrapped themselves around Strefon's body though they lacked the strength for much beyond constraint. The creature's head already half returned, Strefon watched Bishop and Diaz with a smouldering burn as they dragged Erotami's body across the dirty floor toward the room's foul orifice. Reaching the Beast's mouth, they counted to three and heaved Erotami's headless body into the treacherous maw.

The Beast collapsed like a Venus flytrap around the offering. Rows of teeth gyrated in alternating concentric circles, pulping Erotami's body as efficiently as a woodchipper as it swallowed him. Neither Bishop nor Diaz could look away. The process was brutal and primal and without sentiment, an inevitable cosmic force of blind nature. The detectives looked at each other once the body vanished as if seeking affirmation of what they had witnessed. A rumbling roar from the unseen belly of the Beast startled them. Once fed, the Beast was awakening.

They moved on to Strefon. His body had moved little despite the resurgence of the Beast, and when Bishop and Diaz tried to lift him, they could see why. Thicker and heavier than Erotami had been, not even the Beast's tentacles could move him alone. Strefon glared at them with hatred as they shoved and dragged him closer to the Beast's cavernous orifice. Bishop and Diaz realised pretty quickly that they wouldn't be able to heave Strefon into the Beast's mouth and instead dropped him on the outer circle of the Beast's teeth. Its jaw rippled like a conveyor belt, drawing Strefon deeper inch by inch.

When Bishop tried to step back, however, Strefon grabbed Bishop's arm to prevent him from escaping. Bishop beat at Strefon's hand, but the creature's claws dug into Bishop's skin without forgiveness. The deeper Strefon went into the Beast, the tighter his grip, pulling Bishop with him. Bishop fired several shots at Strefon to no effect. Diaz grabbed Bishop around the waist to keep him from succumbing to Strefon's inexorable pull, but it was only when the Beast's jagged teeth crushed Strefon's skull beyond repair that the creature finally let go. The last expression on Strefon's face had been a grin so defiant that Bishop took little solace from his victory. Diaz yanked him away from the Beast and out of the room.

Beyond the office, the nightwolves filled the warehouse. With eerie silence and unnerving calm, their eyes followed Bishop when he passed the window. Through them was no exit, and only one person could use the badge to escape. A growl from the Beast shook the walls of the office, sending ripples of restlessness through the ranks of nightwolves.

Diaz followed Bishop's anxious gaze. "I have a feeling we're not done here."

Bishop shook his head. "We just killed that thing's caretakers, but it still has these nightwolves to serve as its eyes and legs. If we don't do something about them, it will destroy everything we care about."

"Just tell me what to do."

Another shuddering scream from the Beast agitated the nightwolves, many of which bared their teeth or howled. Their baying filled the warehouse with an atonal melody both alien and lonesome.

"We woke it up," Bishop said, "but now we need to piss it off."

"What are you thinking?"

"Depends. How do you feel about getting a little dirty at the risk of eternal annihilation?"

Diaz grinned. "That's why I'm here, buddy."

They burst into the bathroom firing their guns. The Beast had grown since feeding, its tentacles perceptibly thicker and stronger while its angry orifice seemed wider and deeper, its teeth elongated into tusks and razor sharp. The stench was fouler than ever, a putrid earthiness now mixing with the effluvium of rank sewage. Bishop used his handgun to keep himself and Diaz free from the tentacles and their attempts at entanglement while Diaz concentrated on the mouth itself, his shells shattering teeth and removing chunks of flesh. The Beast bellowed and flailed wildly when each shot struck, yet whatever damage they inflicted seemed only temporary as the wounds healed and the missing parts regenerated more quickly than had those of Erotami and Strefon. Not until there was a lull in the gunfire did Bishop realise they were having an effect on the creature. Despite the ringing in his ears, one thing was clear. Incensed, the nightwolves howled. From the office came heavy blows against the outer door, not to mention some hollow thuds that could have been against the windows. The nightwolves were coming after them.

Diaz noticed it also, and for the first time alarm registered on his face. "They sound mad."

"Good." Bishop closed the door separating this room from the office and made sure to turn the flimsy lock on the handle. "You'll need to wake up soon."

Diaz inclined his head toward the Beast. "Then let's make the most of this."

They renewed their attack while the Beast did its best to answer them, either crashing its tentacles into them to knock them off their feet or entwining itself around their limbs, yet Bishop's volley of bullets kept them clear while Diaz did his best to pummel the Beast's maw with enunciations from his shotgun. The blasts slowed the Beast somewhat, but the activity coming from the room beyond proved that the creature wasn't taking their punishment lightly. Even over the gunshots, Bishop heard glass shattering as the nightwolves burst into the office. Moments later, they threw themselves at the bathroom door.

Bishop knew Diaz was out of shells when his partner swung his shotgun like a baseball bat at the reaching tentacles. He didn't want to get any closer to the Beast's mouth, and Bishop couldn't blame him. Now that it didn't suffer the continuous blasts from Diaz, the Beast devoted more energy to ridding itself of the intruders in its lair. Not only did the tentacles reach for them with an emboldened sense of purpose, the nightwolves also attacked the barrier with increasing vigour. Bishop couldn't imagine how many nightwolves filled the office, not to mention the warehouse. The bathroom was the last refuge, and its door rattled in its frame. Another couple of blows and the nightwolves would overflow them like rats.

His own supply of ammunition dwindling, Bishop could no longer keep the tentacles at bay. The creeping appendages swarmed Diaz, entangling his limbs and dragging him toward to the Beast's immense valley of teeth. Although it was necessary, Bishop hated what he had to do next.

"Look away."

Diaz looked up at Bishop's words, bewildered and terrified but trusting, and turned away. Quick and precise, Bishop shot him in the head. To his relief, Diaz vanished immediately, the tentacles collapsing upon emptiness. Bishop hoped Diaz wouldn't remember any of this when he woke up.

As tough as that had been, what Bishop had to do next gave him even more trepidation. He pulled out the Enforcer's badge, reassured by its presence. The nightwolves broke through the door at last, their sheer numbers pummelling the wood into non-existence as they filled the room like water through a broken dam. When they gave chase, Bishop dove into the centre of the Beast's throat.

The badge spared him from the gnashing of the Beast's jaw. In the backseat of the car at the rear of the pack, there was little time to appreciate his strange victory as the nightwolves funnelled into the Beast's hungry mouth by the dozens. The Beast, blind to everything but its own hunger, greedily swallowed them as they swarmed into the room after their nonexistent prey. Like an unwitting Ouroboros, the Beast fed upon itself.

Although the remaining nightwolves halted their headlong rush and milled around nervously, the damage had already been done. Everything built upon the Beast began to fall apart as the warehouse shook. The walls rumbled, shattering the windows, while chunks of the ceiling collapsed, denting the car with a thud or sending up clouds of dust where they struck the floor. Slabs of the warehouse crashed around him as the walls toppled like mere building blocks. Support beams curled like wilted flowers, and darkness blossomed all around him as Bishop inhaled sharply, deeply, opened his eyes and gasped for air.

A Mare's Nest

John Greenwood

There are two books I associate with my grandfather. The first was a little black, leather-bound notebook tied shut with garden twine. He kept it on him at all times, every day of his life that I knew him, and I was nearly a grown man when he died. Nobody knew what he kept in there, but he was forever adding to it, minutely, with the stub of a pencil. If he could not find his own pencil he would tell one of his grandchildren to run and fetch him one from our pencil case or school bag, this in tones of the greatest urgency, as though history were in danger of losing a momentous aphorism for want of the means to record it.

As a young boy I found his haste infectious, and would race to the little desk in my room to fetch a pencil for him to preserve, so I imagined, the fruits of his intellectual labour. But with my grandfather's ingratitude, his refusal to share the contents, his senility and my cynicism advancing at an equal pace, I began to resent his requests, and like my older brothers and sisters would feign ignorance of whether there were any pens or pencils to be found about the house. Those he did borrow he never returned. I would discover them in a parlous condition, ends chewed and still damp with his spittle, points hacked into use by his penknife, the shafts greasy from resting between the few remaining tufts of hair and the groove of his ear. There was no question of asking for them back. My grandfather was capable of fits of spectacular viciousness when the mood took him, and my father, a phlegmatic authority on Middle English poetry, preferred not to intervene. The volumes covering the walls of my father's library provided excellent sound insulation. He suffered my grandfather's presence as a sceptic lives in a haunted house. Reports of grisly phenomena were discouraged by silence or a change of subject. My mother was a martyr to migraines, which kept her in bed, or Bath, or one of the more fashionable spa towns, taking the waters and whatever rest cures she could lay her hands on.

Speculation about the contents of Grandfather's notebook waxed and waned with the ambient level of boredom. A private diary was the obvious candidate, notwithstanding the paucity of material. From his late rising through his afternoon nap to his early retiring, my grandfather's activities were limited to eating, smoking and cleaning his pipe, chastising and beating children and servants, and taking pot-shots from a favoured window at trespassing crows and other vermin. Far more likely that he used the notebook to record the comings and goings of the rest of the family, my father's shortcomings, my mother's outgoings, the many fallings-short of his grandchildren.

In addition to my grandfather and the domestic staff, we were oppressed by a series of tutors. For a stifling summer we were convinced that Grandfather's notebook contained love poems to Mrs Hooper, the widowed martinet my father had employed in a doomed scheme to turn my eldest sister into a pianist. For close to twelve months my grandfather's attitude towards Mrs Hooper, openly avowed, bordered on civility. Our suspicions were apparently ill-founded. When Mrs Hooper broke her neck in a riding accident, my grandfather's grief did not exceed that he had shown when a stag gored his second-best pointer.

Turf notes? Poetry? The observations of an amateur naturalist? My grandfather had never shown the smallest interest in these subjects. Seduced by accounts of solitary scientific geniuses, I hoped that Grandfather was of the same mould. I conjectured proofs of other dimensions, the practical possibilities of time travel, rogue particles hitherto strangers to physics. This would have explained why the notebook had to be always at hand, rather than simply secreted away – the house was not short of loose bricks and floorboards, abandoned outhouses and unfrequented attics which even the older children feared to penetrate. In my mind, my grandfather's grand unified theory was incomplete, and he needed a few more proofs to clinch the argument. Hence the secrecy, hence the constant annotation, hence (even) the absent-mindedness. But as my eldest brother pointed out, a man so incompetent at chess as to be regularly beaten by the dullest of his grandchildren (referring to me), and sufficiently venal to improvise spurious rules to avoid losing, was unlikely to possess a brain capable of quantum physics.

Daily my grandfather would fly into panic at the thought that he had mislaid his notebook, or that one of us had stolen it. It would turn up in his waistcoat pocket, trapped between the sofa cushions, behind the mantelpiece clock, or in one or other of the hiding places around the house he had laid claim to. Invariably my grandfather would accuse the finder of having sneaked a look inside. Even if his temper were not an adequate deterrent (it was certainly enough to deter me), the mare's nest of knots would have made this no simple matter.

My grandfather had chosen to settle his family in a county to which he owed no allegiance, but which tolerated our presence. The house shared no family resemblance with any of the seats of gentry in the area. It was odd, and its lack of a name was one of its oddities. In the villages which hemmed us in (and none claimed our house as its own) it was known as the French house, though our name was not French nor were we, as far back as living memory could recall, of French stock. Perhaps at some point in the house's history, France was as far away as any of the villagers could plausibly imagine. I liked to think it had been shipped over, stone by stone, and hauled through the cobbled streets, the greens and commons and meadows, and into the midge-ruled gloom where it had been reassembled. It may only have been that the house had a resemblance to a French *manoir* of a certain kind: massive, dour, ivy-choked and oppressively symmetrical but for the x's of cast-iron anchor plates holding the walls together. The identical white shutters on the windows were redundant: rampant cypresses ensured our protection from sunlight, and there were no prying passers-by to guard against. People stayed away. Guests, invited by obligation or misunderstanding, usually found that pressing business called them back within a day or two. Only those bound by blood or marriage repeated the mistake of intruding on our privacy.

I never knew the age of the house, but it was older than my grandfather, who never built anything that I knew of, but who had had, in my father's words, a good war, and taken the house at around the same time as he had taken a wife from one of the better families in the neighbourhood. What Grandfather had done before the war, my father claimed perfect ignorance, and professed no interest, less than that, "a negative quantity of curiosity". Here and there, this and that, import and export: such was the extent of my grandfather's autobiography. The darker hints he did let drop were usually connected in some sideways fashion to a certain forbidden and eternally obscure book.

It was never named. If it had a name, it was never to be spoken aloud. My grandfather called it "that wicked old book", "the book of shame", "an execrable volume which I shall not mention". Catching me at my studies, he would ask me what I was reading. Saint Augustine, Pascal's *Pensées*, Bulldog Drummond – the answer hardly mattered. A bellow of incredulity would follow. "What would you have me believe now?" Snatching the book from my hands, he would rifle through the pages, hunting down the lie. But as the quarry evaporated, so would his zeal. "Well then, well then. The *Confessions*, so you say. You put me in mind of another book of confessions, confessions of quite another sort. We both know which disgraceful book I am talking about."

"Grandfather?"

"No need to play the innocent with me, boy. Do you think I don't know what you and your insolent brothers talk about? You know, some of the more unscrupulous booksellers have been known to bind it into the covers of another title. Put the authorities off the scent. There are, if you'd believe it, respectable private libraries the length and breadth of England whose Venerable Bedes contain something far from venerable. Something very different."

But different in which particulars, my grandfather could never be induced to say. Had he seen the book himself? It was not our place to ask about such barbarities. Merely to speculate, to wonder about the book's contents was irredeemably shaming, and I would know the back of his hand (we were already acquainted) if I breathed a word of such abominations. From hints dropped here and there I gathered that the book contained descriptions of the worst acts that human beings were capable of performing, on themselves, on one another, and on the world at large. Illustrations too, possibly. Over time my imagination proved capable of ever-deeper atrocities, and this compulsive groping towards the utmost depravity probably had a negative influence on the development of my psychology. I took it for granted that whatever unnatural acts I could stand to picture to myself, my grandfather must have seen worse. How else could he be explained?

Determined though he was to warn us away from temptation, my grandfather could not stop himself from turning the topic of conversation in that direction. More than once he announced, during the summer break, his intention of driving me back to school next term, so that he could have the opportunity of "straightening a few things out" with the school librarian. "Make sure there are no restricted volumes left lying around that ought to be under lock and key."

I lived in dread of my grandfather carrying out these threats, but as far as I know he never did. It was often our saving grace that grandfather's intentions, to punish or interfere, generally expired overnight.

A stack of library books on the kitchen table would elicit comments as to the moral character of the librarian. Grey head inclined to the horizontal, he would scan the spines mistrustfully. "I trust these contain nothing unwholesome."

"It is a school library after all." (My father from behind his newspaper.)

"One ought never be complacent. Librarians seldom know just what they harbour in their own collections. All those unpolluted young minds – it takes but one mishap and dozens are gathering round, greedily drinking in the poison. The damage is done! Corruption spreads from child to child. And there are some very pestilential books in the world – one in particular, which decency prevents me from naming, the product of a mind unrivalled in degeneracy, I may have mentioned it once before."

"Yes, we know all about it." (Somebody, possibly me, possibly an older brother.)

"I pray to our Lord and Saviour that you do *not* know all about it! That is one book about which there cannot be too much ignorance. If you had any idea of the mortal sins that book has driven men to – and boys too, boys your own age and younger, you needn't feign surprise with me, you know exactly what I am referring to. Those acts, the sight of which is blasphemy, the very thought of which is to spit in the face of the Infant Jesus. Do you think I don't know what goes on at that school, how the whispers go around? I was young too once, don't forget that!"

But it was all too easy to forget that grandfather had ever been other than decrepit and bilious and the terror of children.

Generations of my family's sons had been educated at the same slightly disreputable school, and while I witnessed many acts of cruelty and lust (and even love) in those dormitories and playing fields, I never heard mention of any such notorious book. It was not a topic I ever raised with my peers – bookishness was not encouraged in the circles in which I moved, and my own intellectual curiosity was something I soon learned to stifle for the sake of my reputation.

There was another reason too, a queer superstition, acquired I don't know when, that to speak of Grandfather's ghastly book was to invite the same obsession to which the old man had fallen victim. My grandfather was unable to sit through any conversation without covertly nudging the discussion towards the topic of forbidden books, and the sullied consciences of adolescent boys exposed to them. It was as though he was willing the unnameable book to return to him, and all his moralising cant an incantation to this sole end.

Sometimes it seemed as though he would never die. When he did, I had already left the French house, and had not seen or spoken to my grandfather in over a year. When the call came, I was alone in my room, struggling against a suffocating hangover. There was just one telephone in the college, and a porter had to bang on my door pretty hard to get me to come to the phone. This, I remember saying to myself, is all I need.

"It is my sad duty to inform you that your grandfather passed away this morning at five thirty," said my father's voice. "He died peacefully in his sleep."

I wondered whether my father had that "sad duty" stuff written down on the jotter. He often did that when he had to use the telephone. And what did it matter that I know the exact time? I didn't, of course, ask him either of these questions. What I asked was, "Could you send some flowers to the funeral and say they're from me?" I explained my budgetary constraints and the importance of my studies. My father refused but agreed to reimburse me for the train fare home, as long as I set off the same day.

As I'd feared, they had waited to move him out of bed until I arrived. Everyone else was already home. We all squeezed into my grandfather's little room, which was in rather a state.

My mother hugged me. "We wanted you to see him one last time," she said. "At home, the way we remember him."

I did not remember my grandfather ever lying on top of his bedclothes with his suit and shoes on. I had, in fact, rarely seen inside this room, and now that he could no longer bar our entry, it was clear that there was no mystery to it. It wasn't as though I had expected to see the infamous nameless volume sitting there on his bedside table. But something, more than his white face beneath the patchy beard, and my brothers and sisters trying to look sufficiently solemn. No books that I could see (nor any discovered later, when they cleared out the room). The bookcases were instead littered with old tools, shotgun cartridges, dressing gowns, sticky brown medicine bottles, cold bedpans. There had been a series of strokes, I learned, of increasing severity. I could see little alteration. A little paler, maybe. I cannot have been the only one wondering about Grandfather's little black notebook. Who would dare reach into his jacket pocket to claim it? I was too frightened that a hairy white hand would shoot up and clamp around my wrist. In the event, nobody mentioned the notebook. My mother said some charitable words that she cannot have meant, and we all sloped off for a drink to allow the professionals to do whatever it was that needed doing to Grandfather. After the funeral I forgot about the notebook and went back to my hall of residence. It was only recently that I was reminded of it.

I don't sleep well, and when I do sleep, I am disturbed by dreams. They started after my wife left. My doctor says it could be a side effect of the pills, but he doesn't know I'm drinking again. The dreams are very straightforward. I am a vole, a shrew, a tiny mammal of some kind quivering in a hedgerow. There is a rush of air above and behind me, the overwhelming certainty of a predator readying claws and teeth. I scamper for the shadows, knowing full well the futility of scampering: its jaws are already about me. I wake in a sweat, or on the floor, roaring to the empty house, adrenal glands disgorged, heart hammering at my ribs like an enraged prisoner.

This dream ended differently. I was still vole-like, but this time I happened upon my grandfather, asleep on the back lawn in his deckchair. My twitching nose could smell the familiar tobacco on yellowed fingers that trailed in the uncut grass. The black notebook was by his hand, unguarded. My incisors made short work of the knots, and by wriggling my soft body between the pages, I flipped open the cover. The book was full of sketches, careful rather than competent, of me and my brothers and sisters, at the dining table, reading, studying, fishing, playing tennis or board games. My mobile little paws turned page after page. In places the proportions of our arms and legs were off, and towards the end of the book the lines began to waver as my grandfather's palsied hands had struggled to hold the pencil still. As the pages turned we all grew up. The drawings didn't improve, but they were accurate enough for me to recognise certain occasions – birthdays, Christmas holidays, brought back with all the force of spontaneously up-welling memories.

Dreams have no prophetic power. If they did, I would have been torn to shreds by pitiless beasts many weeks ago (instead of which this process can take a lifetime). But I decided to call my father anyway.

"Why should there have been drawings? Did you ever see him drawing?" (He grows more like his own father, in spite of his careful efforts to the contrary.)

If not sketches, then what?

"Numbers," said my father. "Page after page of them. Numbers and nonsense. The perfect way to waste the last years of one's life. You do know he was mad. I assumed you were capable of working that out for yourself."

Did somebody still have the notebook?

"Notebooks. Note the plural. Hundreds of the damned things. He got them from a London stationers at a bulk discount."

It was not a pleasant surprise to learn that all of my grandfather's personal effects were in the possession of my eldest brother. On top of that there was something about my father's manner that made me disinclined to believe him about the "numbers and nonsense".

It was true, at the very least, that my brother was still holding onto the notebooks. His reply to my letter reminded me why we no longer speak. He thanked me for my interest. He had been named as the executor of my grandfather's will (a naked lie) and had been entrusted with what he referred to as my grandfather's "intellectual legacy". I would understand (would I?) if he were prevented by the trust placed in him from broadcasting my grandfather's writings to all and sundry.

I have instructed my solicitor to pursue the matter. The sundry are not ready to be so lightly dismissed.

Still the question nags me, and images from the dream recur when I am on my way to work and the tube train emerges suddenly into daylight and I close my eyes against the glare. Did my grandfather bequeath anything but contempt? I have dredged. I have stewed and I have mulled. There is time for it, now that it is so quiet and I am so often alone.

What remains of my childhood? Empty rooms where pillars of dust motes danced unobserved for hours together; the cry of a wounded animal carried through the crack of my bedroom window, but silent in the morning; a car idling in the courtyard, ready to take my sister away to a ball, or away to the picture-house, and finally simply away; the sound of the latch on the cellar door, unlike any other latch in the world; the taste of wet ashes from sucking my father's stale pipe. These are undimmed; the rest is a fog of facts and false memories. But I have caught a glimmer, down there in the depths. It may just be somebody else's trash, half-buried in the silt, but it will do.

Here it is: I am the last child to leave. The rest have escaped to boarding schools, jobs, marriages. The end of August, the night reluctant to arrive, though it is

long past my bedtime. I am hoping to have gone
unnoticed. But here comes my grandfather stumping
into the kitchen, and whatever he has to dish out, it
will be me on the receiving end. Chores? Homework?
Shoelaces? All are irreproachable, but if I have learnt
anything at all it is that there are no safeguards.

"Just you and me then, lad."

(My father is somewhere in the house with Sir
Gawain, my mother somewhere in Knightsbridge with
her analyst.)

I feel that nodding may be permitted, in the
circumstances. At the window, he snorts derisively at a
pink sunset.

"Come on then, boots on!"

Questions only exacerbate my grandfather (and
"why" is the worst of the bunch), so we march down
the darkening path in our wellingtons and our
respective silences. There is still a bit of blue not quite
drained out of the sky. The stars show no eagerness to
emerge. I can make out the tops of untrimmed
hedgerows. Skinny arms of new growth flounce forth
in the mild breeze. We are not wearing our coats.

"Get a move on," says my grandfather. "Not a bloody
Sunday school picnic."

We hear the whistles of night birds, sheep mourning
the end of the day, frogs broadcasting lonesomeness
from the ditches. My grandfather has never taken me
out before. (He never did again.) I know we're not on
our way to the next village. This farm track gives up at
a fence, and the fields beyond are someone else's
business – we were never farmers. But at that same
fence we seem to have reached our destination.

"Keep still, for God's sake, stop fidgeting."

The way we have come quickly sinks into the dark
distance. A patch of sky clears to make room for the
full moon. For a moment it shines unimpeded, is
wreathed in thick scarves, is encased by them, is

hidden altogether, but light continues to leak out, until the clouds fatten and it is lost. I turn, ready to go back to the house, but a hand clamps on my shoulder.

"Didn't I tell you to keep still?"

I bury my hands in my pockets. I cannot even see his face now. How will I tell if he has gone to sleep?

Then they come. The first is a flicker, a speck on the filmstrip. Then another, at the edge of vision, gone before eyes can dart after it. I keep my head perfectly still. Scraps of darkness tear themselves from the silhouettes of trees and swoop down to their prey. They are oblivious to us. They fly so close that I can hear their wing beats and feel the displaced air on my face. My grandfather breathes audibly as the black shapes flit around our heads.

The Morning of Seventeen Suns

The Two Husbands #1

Walt Brunston

The Two Husbands stare at the sky in disbelief. Seventeen suns in the sky! It is the brightest morning there has ever been on this blue-green planet of ours, the brightest morning there will ever be, at least until the far-off day when our sun goes supernova!

"What the hell is going on?" asks Husband One. "This is impossible!"

Husband Two nods, and frowns. "The heat of so many suns should burn us to a crisp."

"There is light but no heat."

They stand on the top of the Husband Headquarters, far above the panic that is kicking in on the streets below. As ever, the Two Husbands face the most difficult dilemma of them all: help the people in danger right now, or sort out the problem at the heart of the danger?

Husband Two looks at his digital cufflink. It is currently monitoring the heartrate of every person living in Pseudo City, letting him know from moment to moment how far the panic has spread.

"Not too bad yet," he says to Husband One, who looks at him with questioning eyes.

"Not everyone is awake yet," says Husband One.

"Call the Little Sisters. Get them out on the street, calming people down and lamping any looters. Too many suns isn't going to be the end of the world, not today, anyway."

All across the city young women are pulled from their everyday lives by the sound of the Husbands' call. Students, bakers, teachers, police officers, engineers, writers, fire fighters, card sharks, librarians, artists, builders, doctors and truck drivers, among many other occupations, they stop what they are doing and step into a quiet room to put on their outfits. The Little Sisters are on the case! Jeans, green lumberjack shirts, brown boots, and brown leather gloves are thrown on, with a red domino across the eyes.

As one the call goes up. "Little Sisters, to arms!"

They run out on to the streets, alerted via their own cufflinks to the closest spot of trouble.

Here, a man stares at the sky and screams! A Little Sister gives him a slap on the back to remind him he isn't dead yet.

Here, an elderly woman steps through a broken window with a shopping bag full of electronic tablets. A Little Sister gives her a stern look until she takes them back inside and neatly puts them away.

Here, a school bus resounds to the noise of two dozen wailing children, wishing they were still safely tucked away in their beds. A Little Sister steps on board and tells them the story of how she once fought three dragons without blinking. The children don't understand the story, but thinking about it calms them down.

Here, a man in his nightshirt fires an old service pistol at the suns, as if hoping to shoot them out of the sky. A Little Sister waits till he needs to reload and then slaps the gun out of his hand. "Buck up, soldier!" she shouts. "Who knows where those bullets will land?" He looks at her with anger, then becomes embarrassed at himself and goes back indoors to eat his breakfast.

Bit by bit, street by street, Pseudo City begins to calm down. That leaves the Two Husbands to do their job.

Husband One has poked a hole in a piece of cardboard fished from the recycling bin on the roof of the Husband Headquarters. He studies the seventeen dots of light cast through the hole onto the shadow at his feet, how quickly they move, relative to each other, and harrumphs loudly.

"There are not seventeen suns," he declares.

"Don't be a fool! I can see them!" shouts Husband Two.

There are a few moments of silence before Husband Two realises that he should apologise.

"I'm sorry. What have you discovered."

Husband One lets the silence continue for a moment longer, then points at the sky: "It's just one sun! Seventeen times!"

"I'll be damned," said Husband Two. And as anyone who knows him would tell you, that isn't just a figure of speech for him. He's never made a mistake for which he's forgiven himself. Each time he gets something wrong he damns himself to hell and beats himself up. Again, literally. He pummells his punching bag till it's had enough, then lets it pummell him back. He gave it robot arms.

Husband Two is a complicated guy.

Husband One: complicated also. But right now things are simple for him: "Time is being distorted over Pseudo City. We're seeing the sun from different times of day, that's why it's all over the sky. Peer a bit and you can see there are a whole bunch of moons up there too. We need to find the source of the temporal distortion."

"I agree!" shouts Husband Two. He likes to shout, so

get used to it. "To-do list for today. 1. Find the source of the temporal distortion. 2. End the temporal distortion. 3. Order a meat feast pizza."

"If we must," says Husband One. "But you must also... order garlic bread."

"Cheese or no cheese on it?" asks Husband Two.

Husband One gives him a sour look. "Do you not think there will be cheese enough on the pizza?"

"Look, I'm just finding out what you want. Not trying to kill you. You'd moan if I ordered the wrong thing."

"No cheese, alright? No cheese." He says it through gritted teeth. "If I wanted cheese, I'd have said garlic bread with cheese."

Husband Two clenches his fist to express his frustration. He knows Husband One can see it. He wouldn't do it otherwise. "Garlic bread, then. And a meat feast pizza. And some Coca Cola."

"Diet Coke," says Husband One, witheringly.

"See," says Husband Two. "That was a test, and you fell for it."

Don't make the mistake of thinking that the Two Husbands are arguing over these things while the world burns. During the course of this conversation they have been scribbling plans in Husband Two's squared paper moleskine notebook, plans for a device to let them find what is causing the distortion in time. Arguing about trivialities like pizza and garlic bread is a trick they have developed over years of working together, a way of getting their egos out of the way so their brains can work in perfect unison.

"What do you think?" says Husband One. "Will that do the trick?"

Husband Two traces a finger over the plans, following the routes of circuits and logic lines. He imagines it in operation, the clicks and buzzes and beeps and whirrs, his brain creating a four-dimensional working model. "I think it will!"

"Okay," says Husband One. "You go build it in the workshop, and I'll get the Husband Rider warmed up. We'll track this problem to its source before the suns go down."

"You don't think we'll need the Husband Flyer?" says Husband Two. "I like the Flyer."

"So do I," says Husband One, putting a hand on his shoulder. "So do I. All my favourite CDs are in there. But I don't think we'll need to be airborne for this. And time is short."

Husband Two nods, and runs to the door that leads back into the building. His hand print gets it to open. He goes to the workshop and starts to work, a blur of tools and goggles.

Husband One takes another look up at the sky, checks the horizon for any smoke from burning buildings, and slaps his digital cufflink three times before jumping off the roof. Onlookers scream and put their hands to their mouths, before remembering where they are and realising who he is.

It's hard to imagine how they could forget, the Husband Headquarters being so distinctive. Golden, it is thirty-six storeys high. From directly above it would look like two golden interlocking wedding rings, from the front two wide golden curves.

As Husband One falls, he enjoys the moment and waves to onlookers, to assure them that all is well. A great cheer goes up. Some are even tourists, cameras at the ready, there in hopes of seeing the Two Husbands go into action. With twenty storeys of his fall still to go, the garden that welcomes visitors to the Husband Headquarters throws up safety fences and separates cleanly in the middle, opening to allow the Husband Rider to emerge from its basement parking space.

Husband One immediately feels the waves of force

pulsing up from the ride, slowing his fall to the point where his landing upon its driver's seat is as gentle as a leaf saying farewell to a tree.

The Husband Rider is the oddest vehicle you will ever see on the road, no matter where you live or in what century. Its body resembles that of the land speed record holders of the twentieth century, but it has no wheels! It runs on two huge golden hoops, one on the left, one on the right. They give it an incredible manoeuverability and speed, as well as the ability to tip itself up and down as required.

Husband One looks through the CDs in the dashboard. There are none that he likes – or rather, none that he likes that Husband Two will not complain about. He turns the radio on to BBC Radio 426. Hyperspeech-acid-prog piped in from Rochdale. That will do for now.

Predictably, upon landing in the passenger seat, gerry-rigged gadget in hand, Husband Two begins to complain about the music.

"Give it a rest," says Husband One. "We have a temporal distortion to sort out."

The Husband Rider winds into action, speeding them through the streets of Pseudo City in reaction to the findings of the temporal distortion locator. Travelling at such speeds, Husband One's driving ability is stretched to the limit, but the work of the Little Sisters has done a great deal to keep the roads safe and clear.

Husband Two shouts his announcement: "It's here! That house there!"

They get out of the Husband Rider and knock on the door of a quiet semi-detached home with vines creeping up the walls.

A young girl, aged five or six, opens the door. "It's the Two Husbands!" she shouts with glee, then runs off to bring her mum and dad to the door.

"What's wrong?" asks the mum.

"It's the seventeen suns," says Husband Two. "They were caused by a temporal distortion, and we've tracked the source of the distortion to your home."

The girl looks sheepish.

"Have you been playing with Lego again?" asks the dad.

The girl nods, and leads everyone to her playroom. It is full from top to bottom of the most incredible construction, all strange geometries and abstract philosophies.

"Good work," says Husband One. "But it must be destroyed, before it destroys the world. What is your name?"

"Shell."

"(It's short for Rochelle,)" says the mum.

"Well then, Shell," says Husband One. "It must be destroyed, but why should I get all the fun. Breaking your own Lego buildings is the best bit!" He looks at his cufflinks. "But please do it quickly. There are just fifteen minutes before the end of the world."

Husband Two hands her a hammer.

Love at First Sight

A Dim Star Is Born, Part 1

Howard Phillips

Hello reader! Perhaps you expected me to be upset and downcast after the events of the last year? Perhaps you thought I'd be crawling into a hole, never again to show my face among poets and their ilk? Well, stuff that, my friends! For if I should be shamed, I, the writer of so much of the world's greatest poetry, the composer of so many of the world's greatest songs, the author of so many earth-shatteringly original novels, if I – I! – should be shamed, by mere dint of one excruciating, embarrassing, enervating year, then what about you? What have you done over the last year? I've been watching you, reading your idiotically grandstanding blog posts, laughing at the witless inanity of your Facebook updates, cringing at your leaden tweets and hamfisted efforts on Tumblr, and you have done nothing to put you in a position to pass judgment on me.

Yes, I have been a fool.

But better a fool who lives, than a sage who simply watches others live. And let's put "sage" in inverted commas, just in case you think I'm serious. I think you're an idiot. I've always thought that you're an idiot. And after the last year, you know that I am an idiot too.

So listen to my side of the story.

You don't have to. I don't care if you do. But you may find it interesting. You like to gossip. You've run out of ideas and like a parasite you need to feed on others to keep going.

It began last January. January 2014. My adventures had apparently run their course, and I was keeping myself to myself, writing during the day, reading at night, and passing among the people of London like a ghost in the times in between. I wandered where I would, and wondered when I could. I knew too much, they knew too little; what true friendship could there be between one who has looked into the universe's barren grey heart, and those who think happiness can be ordered from Amazon with one-day delivery?

As I walked down Regent Street one day, a Tuesday in fact, I saw the most peculiar thing: a man with a gun. To those United States of Americans reading this that may seem like nothing out of the ordinary! Over there, I know, you carry guns the way we Englishmen carry teabags, on our person at all times in case of emergency. But in England, in London, even to see a police officer with a gun is unusual, never mind a suspicious-looking civilian.

For that is what he was: a very suspicious-looking civilian. Hat pulled down low, collars of a long coat turn up, sunglasses covering half his face. The gun was in his right hand, hanging loosely by his side. Anyone else who saw him might have assumed it was a toy, or a lighter, or more likely not have noticed it at all, as the coat flapped about, but I am experienced in spotting such dangers.

For I am Howard Phillips. And I have fought, and died, and more often lived, by my wits. I have lived to the end of the universe, and beyond to the universe in which you now live yourself, this perfect replica of the world whence I came.

"Hey," I said quietly, walking in step beside him, and

digging one finger sharply into his elbow. The gun dropped to the ground and I kicked it into a drain. This was a move I had learned long ago, back during my training at the foot of the Ghastly Mountain, right at the beginning of my adventures. I kept him walking. "How are you doing?"

He tried to jerk away, looking with panic back towards the drain. My grip was firm.

"It's gone," I said. "I'm afraid you won't be killing anyone today."

He scowled at me, growled even, baring a set of ragged, jagged teeth.

"Are you okay?" I asked.

He narrowed his eyes, and renewed his attempts to shake me loose.

"I don't want to hurt you, man. Just relax, and let's go find somewhere nice to talk."

I steered him in the direction of a coffee shop, forced him into a cubicle, tied him discreetly to the table, and got us both a large cup of tea.

"Do you take sugar?" I asked, having brought enough sachets for both of us. He said nothing. Didn't even show me his teeth this time!

I reached over to push open his coat. He tried to bite my hand but I flicked him on the nose. "Cheeky! What do we have here?"

I pulled a photograph from his inner pocket.

Then everything stopped.

I had never seen anything so beautiful in my life. It was a man, younger than me, probably approaching thirty. His chin was brushed with a dust of blonde stubble. His eyes were green, like summer grass after a rainshower. He was visible from the waist up, and though the peach shirt he wore was loose-fitting, he was clearly slim and well-toned. The top three buttons of the shirt were undone. I would normally have condemned such scruffiness, but I found myself staring at the lightly-tanned skin thus revealed and wishing I could stroke it.

He looked at the camera with an insouciant smirk, like he didn't care whether it looked at him or not. It made him all the more irresistable.

So why had this man been sent to kill him?

It did not compute.

"Who is he?" I demanded, trying not to let my feelings show. "Who sent you to kill him?"

He gave me nothing except more growling. I offered him the tea, and withdrew it quickly when I realised he intended to headbutt it in my direction. I should have gone for a frescato with a straw. I sipped my tea, and thought, hard.

My first thought was that I had forgotten to add any sugar to my tea. I corrected my mistake, as slowly as I could, to aggravate my taciturn assassin. The tearing of the sugar sachet ripped through his senses – or so I told myself. You know my penchant for overdramatisation!

My second thought was that I was unlikely to get anywhere with this fellow. I couldn't even be sure that he was human, let alone a speaker of any language in which I was conversant. I finished off my tea and put my plan into action.

That is to say, I went to the toilet.

Or least that's what my new friend thought.

The second I had passed out of his sight I dropped down to the ground and inched back to a position where I could see him. Luckily the coffee shop was not busy, or more than one eyebrow would have been raised to see me lying there like a human snake!

Of course, he began to free himself immediately. I hadn't tied him too tightly – I'm no monster! – and he was soon heading for the door.

I smiled, got to my feet, dropped a couple of pounds into the tip bowl and set off after him.

Outside, back on the street, I was careful to stay at a safe distance. He now had no gun, and no photograph, but I wagered he had a notion of where to find his quarry, and would do his best to complete his mission of death. He seemed like a determined sort of fellow.

He moved into a doorway that I had never seen before, for all the time I had spent on that street. I allowed time for him to enter, then approached the doorway myself.

No wonder I had never noticed it before. It had not existed before. I'm not even sure it existed then! The door's edges glowed with a scarlet radiance, the peculiar brickwork around it settling into the wall of a department store like a bear in an armchair.

I tried the knob. It turned, but the door didn't give to pressure. I tried my shoulder, with no luck. I decided to knock.

The door swung open.

I stepped inside.

The door closed behind me.

Readers of my adventures will be aware that I am not traditionally sober. I like to drink, and I like to take drugs. I used to believe that such experimentation connected me to the universe, gave me a particular insight, formed the wellspring of my creativity. What balderdash! I drink to forget. The miseries of my childhood. The miseries of my adulthood.

However, I was not drunk that morning, nor was I high. I feel it is necessary to say as much, given what I must now describe.

The corridor in which I now found myself was covered in fractal images that burst and shrank before my very eyes, even though, when I looked at the walls up close, they appeared to be covered in ordinary, static, patterned wallpaper. Seventies swirls. I moved my head away, and it began to spin again.

Looking down the corridor, no doors were visible,

and no end to the corridor either. It looked, and I
know this will sound impossible – hence the
explanation of my psychological status in the
paragraphs above – as if the only thing that stopped
me seeing the end of the corridor was the curvature of
the planet.

The air itself was thick and angry, needing to be
pulled into my chest against its will. The skin on my
face prickled, stung by the air's foulness. My hands
gripped and flexed against my will. The tiled floor
grasped at my feet, as if it were steel and there were
magnets sewn into the hem of my trousers.

I had no intention of leaving, not without getting to
the bottom of this, but it is always wise to establish
whether one has a means of escape, so I tried the door.
It wouldn't budge.

Forward, then! What was the worst that could
happen?

Crystal Castle Crashers

Les aventures fantastique de Beatrice et Veronique

Antonella Coriander

The giant crystal pilot fish, for all its fury, couldn't get through the half-open door to pursue them, and neither its remaining fin nor its half-broken tongue could reach them.

Veronique took the opportunity to thumb her nose in its direction. "Don't mess with the best, because the best don't mess with the rest!"

Beatrice took a deep breath. "Our victory could have been more resounding. I'm going to miss that arm."

"If it can be built, it can be replaced," said Veronique. "We're not humans now, if we ever were."

"Speak for yourself," said Beatrice. "I'm human. I'm just a better kind of human."

"I suspect you always were," laughed Veronique. "Better than me, at least."

Beatrice raised an eyebrow. "Regretting your life of crime?"

"A bit. Not much. Regretting I didn't take more holidays. So much I never saw. The nine wonders of New Delhi in spring, the flying handkerchiefs of the

Edinburgh winter. The infinite recursion of Tobago in the autumn."

"And in summer?"

"Summer can only ever be for Paris, my dear. I did at least do that. Every year without fail. Reading Sartre in the New Pompidou. A glass of wine in the Underseine. Dining at the Trésflunch."

"Sounds nice." Beatrice couldn't remember her last holiday. There had been day trips with her mum, but a week away? Never. Time off from work had been the perfect time to catch up on paperwork, or research, or training.

"It was. Nothing like a summer in Paris to force one into relaxing. It was the ban on dogs that did it. Once they were phased out, and one could walk the streets again without staring at one's shoes, Paris became the paradise it had always hoped to be."

Beatrice quite liked dogs, but she knew Paris had been famous for its street mess. *Boue*. The mud mentioned in the great French historical novels, as written by the likes of Amandine-Aurore Dupin, was only mud in the euphemistic sense. Hence the apparently peculiar and slightly obsessive love of the typical French protagonist for a good carriage!

"Now," said Beatrice. "On to the mission."

"Stealth isn't going to work – the wizard must know we're here by now."

"Speed, I think," said Beatrice. "We don't need to take down every obstacle between here and there. We just need to get to the machinery and blow it up."

"I agree," said Veronique. "Even if every crystal butthead in the building is on our tail by then, it won't matter if we get the job done. For all we know it'll shut them all down and we'll be golden."

"Fingers crossed. Let's go for it."

And they did.

I could spend a hundred pages or more describing

in detail the progress of the two women through the wizard's crystal base. When you think about it, I could probably spend a hundred pages describing the patterns of debris in the smashed-up laboratory they had just left. It could be done, but it would be dull. Telling you everything there is to know about the battle through the castle wouldn't be dull, not at all, but there are other adventures to get to, and I've already lingered on this one far too long. The island portion of this adventure was originally planned to last several thousand words fewer!

You know our protagonists, or at least you think you do, and it's time for us to press on, just as Veronique and Beatrice are doing as I speak.

Every door presented new enemies, new traps, new ways to die, but the two women sprinted past, leapt over, ducked at the right times. If the opportunity to throw a crystal cuboid at a wall presented itself, they took it. If there was a crystal computer monitor that might be used to track them down, they smashed it. If there were crystal racks of equipment lining a corridor, they pulled them down behind themselves to slow down the pursuit.

But they didn't slow down, they didn't hesitate, they didn't speak. From Cornelia they knew roughly where to go – up! – and there was no need to hang around. They were lucky not to find themselves in too many dead ends – the few times they did, they bounced right off the walls and charged into their pursuers with all the force two articulated women could bring to bear. It wasn't hard to punch through. The crystal cuboids were well suited to night attacks on cornered, injured, defenceless prey. Less so to capturing two desperate, motivated, deadly robots. It seemed that the larger beasts were kept – perhaps wisely! – outside the wizard's base.

Beatrice and Veronique picked up a hundred small

burns and wounds from the crystal beams that zapped at them at every turn, but they shrugged them off. If their robot bodies could be repaired, these new wounds wouldn't matter. If their robot bodies could not be repaired, these new wounds would be the least of their problems.

At last they reached the uppermost level of the base. They came to it via a grandiose flight of stairs, up which they ran with a hundred crystal cuboids at their heels. They had not seen a single living human in the building, which made them wonder what the wizard would look like. Would she be made of crystal herself? Would she be a robot like them? Would they have the chance to find out before they were buried under a pile of cuboids?

"I can hear the machinery," said Veronique, still on the run. Cornelia had told them to listen out for a particular sound, a high-pitched beeping interpolated alternately by high and low pops. "Over here."

Beatrice turned for one moment to sweep the stairs with a fully extended leg, knocking dozens of the cuboids back. As they fell they continued to fire their beams, hitting their colleagues and knocking them in turn off the stairs. For a few seconds it was the most beautiful avalanche you can imagine, a torrent of glorious colour and light.

Not that Beatrice saw it. She was already off after Veronique, who was working to open a pair of grand double doors.

"I think they're barred from the inside," said Veronique.

Beatrice ran faster instead of slowing down and punched her hand through the door. It hurt like heck but she reached around on the other side, found the bar, and threw it up. Veronique pushed the doors open and they were in. The bar back down, and they were safe, for the moment, from pursuit.

It took a moment for their eyes to make sense of what they were seeing.

"What is it?" asked Veronique.

"Breakable," answered Beatrice. "I hope."

She ran into the room and began smashing everything she could see. Which was... How to put it? Imagine a jewel, falling from ten metres up in the air, drifting down as if it were a snowflake, then bouncing up from the ground and rising back up as if it were a tiny hot air balloon. Now imagine a hundred jewels, of different colours, different sizes, doing the same thing, at different speeds. Now imagine a million jewels doing that, on every side, and across the roof, and under your feet.

And imagine the jewels are looking at you, and wondering why you've disturbed their work.

"There should be someone here," said Veronique.

Beatrice frowned in puzzlement. "Why?"

"The door was barred. Who barred it?"

No one was visible. There was no time to think about it. They shrugged and got on with their work.

As Beatrice found, it wasn't really possible to smash the jewels themselves. Here and there she managed to crack them, but on the whole lashing out just pushed them out of position, and they soon drifted back. However, around the room there were immobile nodes through which the gems drifted. The gems faded slightly after exiting the nodes, while the nodes shone brighter, pulsing with a light that seemed to be channelled off through the walls to the rest of the building via hard crystal cables.

They had their targets.

Beatrice took one side, Veronique the other. They pummelled the nodes until they cracked, then wrapped their arms around the cables and snapped them off. With each broken node, a bank of gems fell to the floor and did not rise. A noisy business, but not quite loud enough to drown out the noise of hammering upon the double doors.

They were three quarters done when the bar gave way. A thin trail of smoke explained it: a jewel beam through Beatrice's hole had burnt it through. The hammering had been a distraction to stop the two women noticing.

The double doors swung open. Beyond it were a thousand crystal cuboids, who poured into the power room to surround the women and protect the nodes. They didn't fire. Not yet. They were waiting.

"They're good little girls, aren't they?" said a voice, startling Beatrice and Veronique. They turned to see who it was.

Stepping out of a concealed compartment to the rear of the room was the most striking woman either of them had ever seen. Raven black hair, eyebrows like razor cuts, eyes with irises as dark as her pupils. She stood six feet tall and carried it without awkwardness.

"I'm sorry for hiding from you like that," she said. "I didn't want you to kill me. So when I heard you trying the door I popped into my little panic cupboard and waited for help. Terribly rude of me, I know."

"We'll forgive you for that," said Beatrice. "We are here to destroy your base. No surprise you'd be wary of us."

"Yes, my base," said the wizard, walking around them as if viewing a pair of statues – at a safe distance. "My base indeed. Why have you come to destroy it?"

"You sent your crystal cuboids to kill us," said Veronique.

"Crystal cuboids? Hm, I like the name. We should make that official." The wizard waved a hand to dismiss what she had said. "An automatic defence mechanism, nothing more. You shouldn't have taken it personally."

"They attacked us in the night," said Beatrice. "We

want off this island, and if destroying your power is what it takes then that's what we'll do."

The wizard laughed. An eerie tinkling trill. It was echoed by her assembled minions. "Is that what you think?"

Beatrice and Veronique were silent.

"Who told you that?" the wizard asked, a frown of concern upon her forehead but a cruel smile upon her lips. Neither woman answered. "It's true, I suppose, destroying my base probably would get you off this island. Permanently so, I expect."

She seemed to tire of the game, and let her arched features relax. It made her look no less beautiful, but infinitely sadder.

"If there's been a misunderstanding," said Beatrice, "explain it to us. Let us go. We don't like to fight. We thought you were the villain here."

Veronique nodded with vigour. "We just got off on the wrong foot. We could be great chums. I love jewels, you love jewels..."

The wizard shook her head. "I'm sorry, my dears, but I cannot trust you, and should you betray me everything I have worked for would be destroyed. Too much risk for not enough reward."

"I am a really good friend," said Veronique. "Very helpful in a fix."

"I can vouch for that," said Beatrice. "If you won't let me live, at least give Veronique a chance. She'll join your side in an instant."

"Sorry," said the wizard.

She waved to her minions. Instantly a thousand crystal beams burned on Beatrice and Veronique. Then a thousand more, as the gems that lined the room (those still active) joined the attack, lent purpose by the presence of their more capable cousins. Beatrice crouched instinctively into a ball, and felt first her hair, then her clothes, then her flesh burn away. This was the end.

And yet, somehow, it wasn't. She kept on living.

The crystal beams kept coming, but past a certain point there was nothing left for them to burn. She didn't pass out. She didn't die. The agony ended, her pseudonerves incinerated, leaving nothing but numbness, an absence of feeling. Every human knows that sense of being a passenger in their own body. How strong that feeling was now in Beatrice!

She opened her eyes and saw a body of gleaming chrome, reflecting the beams as if designed for that very purpose. The crumpling around her waistband spoilt the look a little, but she could live with it. No choice, really.

She stood up, provoking shrieks of horror from the crystal cuboids. Beside her Veronique had come to the same realisation and was pulling herself out of a ball. She too was now a thing of metal, all illusion of humanity burned away.

"You look good," said Beatrice. Her own voice was unfamiliar, no longer shaped by lips, tongue and cheeks, a pure electronic emission.

"Aye, robot," said Veronique. Her voice was the same. Different, but the same.

The fire from the crystal cuboids began to peter out. It was a waste of good energy. With this room damaged they knew – at whatever level the crystal cuboids could be said to know anything – that it might be worth conserving their power. They began to back away from the two robots.

The wizard, however, showed no sign of fear. She twirled her long black hair in one long-fingered hand, and smiled like the tiger that got the cow.

"Very good," she said. "Very good. You really are a

terribly durable pair of women. You must tell me how you do it sometime."

Four of the wizard's fingers bore crystal rings, one for each of the main classes of jewel they had encountered on the island: ruby, emerald, topaz and sapphire. Did she use those rings to control the jewels?

"You tried to kill us," said Veronique.

"I couldn't kill you if I tried! And yes, I admit I did try. Which rather proves my point: I failed. Don't be sour, dear. One has to do these things in my line of work, you know. Maybe you don't know."

"What do you think we should do with you, Wizard Gloaning?"

"Wizard Gloaning? Oh yes, that's what the dear cuboids call me. I don't know why. What should you do with me? Oh, I don't know. Perhaps you could let me introduce myself properly? Perhaps we did get off to a bad start. I am the crystal wizard of these parts, and you have invaded my island without the slightest invitation, blown up my *Tyrannosaurus Reg*, shot many of my lovely little crystal friends to pieces, and stirred up that nasty mistake down in laboratory six. My true name" – she paused for dramatic effect – "is Antonella Brandybake Coriander."

"My commiserations," said Veronique, earning a scowl for her sympathy.

"Where are we?" asked Beatrice. "Why were we brought here? Did you turn us into robots? What is the game and what are the rules?"

Now Antonella laughed. "What a lot of silly questions. You're adorable, quite adorable, my dear."

Veronique thumped the floor in anger. "I should warn you that I am not yet used to this robot body of mine. I am still very clumsy. Do you understand?"

There was a flutter of crystal beams in her direction. They had no effect. The cuboids soon desisted. If it is possible for a jewel encased in a transparent box to look nervous, these ones did.

"I understand, Veronique," said the wizard, holding out her hands, mockingly, as if for handcuffs. "You need answers, you think I have them, and I am utterly in your power. Do your worst, whatever it is."

Beatrice spoke now. "We don't need to do anything with you. If this is your island, we're happy to leave you to it. But we have to finish our mission. Maybe it's not a good mission, maybe we've been tricked, but as a rule of thumb I tend to give my trust to people who don't try to kill me."

She strode to one of the unbroken nodes and began smashing away at it. The crystal cuboids were stirred into action, but there was little they could do to her now. They clambered over her body, and over Veronique's as she joined in, but it barely slowed either woman down. Soon just one node remained, and now Antonella's calm had cracked.

"Stop it," she screamed. "You don't know what you're doing!"

"Then tell us," said Beatrice, raising her arm over the last node. "We want to know. We're ready to listen."

The wizard took a deep breath, thought about her options. "Oh, fiddlesticks. Destroy the bloody base. I'm leaving. See you on the scrapheap."

She stepped swiftly back into her panic room, and before Beatrice could make a grab for her the door had slid shut. A rowdy grumbling shook the room and the door leapt into the air, taking half the wall with it. The window thus created offered them a marvellous view of the island's north coast, and yet Beatrice preferred to look up at the one-woman rocket now tracing an arc across the bright blue sky.

(Where was I going? One day I'll tell that story. For now let's stay with Beatrice and Veronique.)

"Let's do it," said Beatrice. She dropped her robot

hand upon the final node, and smashed it to smithereens.

The lights of every jewel and crystal cuboid went out. All dropped to the floor. Beatrice and Veronique now stood in a room that would have been drab and unremarkable, were it not for the riches littering its floor, and the fact its walls were made of crystal.

"All dead. So what now?" Veronique's face, stripped of its flesh, was no longer capable of expressing emotions. But her words carried a distinct tone of disappointment.

"I guess we wait. Something will happen."

"And if it doesn't?"

Beatrice shrugged. "We'll choose our own adventure. We could go after Antonella."

"Why?" said Veronique. "It's none of our business."

"Crime is my business," said Beatrice.

"If you still had eyebrows, would one of them have been arched when you said that?"

Beatrice did not respond. Antonella's rocket was now lost from view, and there were other things to look at. Birds were flying up out of the treeline and heading out to sea. Most seemed to be heading north-north-east. She made a mental note. If they found a boat, they would head in that direction. But why were the birds leaving?

The ocean was beginning to look angry.

The room around them began to shake. Cracks appeared in the floor beneath their feet. Cracks that were being mirrored across the island. The lines that had led out from the nodes were staining green and purple, corrupt like the giant crystal pilot fish they had battled below, and the stains were spreading.

"I didn't realise we were literally destroying the base," said Veronique. "I thought we would just shut it down."

"It looks like we've destroyed the entire island," said

Beatrice. "Antonella did warn us. The intelligence of the jewels seems to have been a technological trick, but there were living creatures down there. Maybe we should have listened."

"I doubt we'd have been any better off if we had," said Veronique. "I think the base *is* the island. That tunnel we came up mustn't have been the only one. This base is just the head. The nervous system riddles the island. Supported it too, I would bet."

In the power room, the cracks were deepening and spreading, and the crystal at the edges of the cracks was crumbling and dropping into the gaps. Crystal dust dropped onto their heads from the ceiling above, which was experiencing the same disintegration.

"This whole place is going to collapse. We should get out of here," said Beatrice.

The break in the wall was the only way out, and they were very high up, with only rocks below to break their fall. It still looked like their best option. They were robots. Perhaps they would survive. If not, at least the falling would be fun. Beatrice prepared to jump.

"Wait," said Veronique, putting a hand on her shoulder. "It's no better out there."

The beach went first, falling away, its foundations kicked out. For a second there was absence at the island's edge, then the ocean rushed in to fill it, rebounding and redoubling until there was a tidal wave smashing across the island, accelerating its destruction.

"Oops," said Veronique.

"It was a shipping hazard," said Beatrice. "I guess this is probably it, then."

"Maybe we'll float."

"Or maybe we're waterproof. There's so much we don't know about these new bodies. We might be able to walk across the ocean floor until we reach land."

Beatrice didn't have much confidence in her own words.

"The floor's going to go!" shouted Veronique, and she reached out to hold Beatrice's hand. Whatever happened, they'd be better off together.

They began to fall, their combined weight now too much for what remained of the crumbling floor. They fell through clouds of crystal dust, one metre, two metres, three metres, the whole base going up like dandelion seeds in a stiff breeze. Would they hit hard rock at the bottom? Or would the island be completely gone by the end of their fall, leaving them to land in the ocean?

"It's been fun," shouted Veronique, trying hard to smile.

"Nice to meet you," shouted Beatrice. "And now I arrest you in the name of—"

She wasn't quite done when they hit something solid. Solid, but not hard. She bounced up a couple of metres then came to a rest. All around them the crystal base continued to crumble.

"Hey ladies," said Cornelia Gilligan. "Good work, my brilliant idiots!"

Beatrice pushed herself into a sitting position. She and Veronique were resting in what would best be described as a breakfast bowl, albeit one big enough to seat five or six adults. Alternating red and white horizontal stripes lined its sides, with the bottom of the bowl entirely red – though it was rapidly filling with dust and debris.

Cornelia gave her a cheery wave from the steering apparatus – the only mechanical element visible on the bowl. "Brace yourself. Time to get out of here."

The bowl flew out of the rain of crystal base dust, taking them to a safe place to watch it all unfold. Within ten minutes there was nothing left to see. The island was gone, broken into a thousand pieces and buried under a billion tons of water. The ocean seemed much happier now, though the weather was quickly changing. The sky was much less blue, the sea developing a cast of maudlin grey. It began to rain.

Beatrice and Veronique barely spoke while the island sank. A few swear words of surprise from Veronique, and a few less explicit expostulations from Beatrice; that was about the sum of it.

Veronique was glad to survive, and felt little grief for an island that had given her no pleasure. She might have regretted the loss of all those jewels if she hadn't grabbed a handful the second the base began to crash.

Beatrice felt guilty. She had taken a mission from a random stranger, giving barely any thought to whether it was what she should really be doing, as if the fact of having a mission was more important than the morality of her actions. Maybe it was – to her. If she got out of this alive, she would do something about that.

When the island was all gone, Cornelia turned to look at them. That Beatrice was in a funk was immediately obvious, despite the lack of fleshy facial features. The tilt of her head. The looseness of her hand's grip upon the bowl's rim. The way her eyes reflected the cloudlight. (It looked and felt like they were properly back in the English Channel: calling it sunlight would have been an exaggeration.)

"Don't feel sad," said Cornelia. "That place wasn't meant to be. You did everyone a favour."

"Especially you," said Beatrice. There was more than a trace of accusation in her voice. "This was your job, wasn't it. You just found us here and used us, didn't you?"

Cornelia sighed, and scanned the horizon, looking for a hypothetical eavesdropper whose presence might give her an excuse not to speak. "Course not. I'm just here to help. This was your job."

"And the wizard, Antonella?" said Veronique. "She got away in a rocket. Is that a problem?"

"I saw that," Cornelia replied. "No, it isn't a problem. I'm sure we'll meet again, if she creates a situation that requires my attention. Her base is gone, the English Channel is back to normal, and the Queen can rest easy: no danger any more of that bloody egg hatching in the palace."

Beatrice's reply was lost in a roar from below, as if the sea itself had stubbed its toe. What new trouble was this? She'd thought that they were out of the worst of it.

"Oh, crap," said Cornelia, leaning out over the breakfast bowl's rim to see what was below. "Hold on tight, my friends, this could get rather toasty. Rather toasty indeed!"

Cornelia got back to the steering apparatus and pulled the bowl into a steep climb. Once again Beatrice had reason to be grateful for the strength of her robot body – no human would have been able to survive that g-force. Which made her wonder about Cornelia Gilligan...

Forget that, there were bigger fish to fry. She risked a look back to see what kind of fish it was this time.

"Oh. My. Gosh."

"Don't panic, Beatrice," said Cornelia. "There's plenty of life in my bowl yet. She'll get us out of here safely!"

The sea had opened up to disgorge the most gigantic structure Beatrice had ever seen in motion. Was it a living being? It was so big her brain was unable at first to make sense of it. As they pulled up into the sky it became easier. Ruby eyes the size of the centre circle on a football pitch. Emerald teeth like stalagmites and stalactites. A topaz tongue the length of Brighton Pier. No, longer, she realised, as it flicked up in their direction.

"Beatrice, could you take the guns, please?" shouted Cornelia. Or at least it began as a shout – by the time it reached Beatrice the rushing wind had reduced it to a whisper.

"What guns?" she shouted back, but there was no sign she had been heard.

Suddenly a pair of straps wrapped themselves over her feet and twisted her around to face rearwards. Or tonguewards, she thought. The thing seemed to move in slow motion, steadily creeping up on them, and she didn't think they were going to escape its reach.

"Drat! Sorry!" shouted Cornelia. "Weapons ahoy!"

A giant silver spoon whipped up from the outside bottom of the bowl to rest on the bowl's rim.

"I didn't think this looked like a breakfast bowl on purpose," Beatrice laughed. It felt darn good.

The spoon's ornate handle tucked softly into her hands. *Squeeze me*, it seemed to sing. She had no better ideas! Around the edge of the handle were a series of bumps, polished to perfection. She lined up her target, then chose one bump and gave it a squeeze.

The rim of the spoon's scooping bit (she didn't have time to think of a better word for it, given the situation) crackled with blue energy, which seemed to build as she kept squeezing.

"I think that'll be enough!" said Veronique beside her, and she was quite right – the tongue was about to reach them!

Beatrice released her hold and the energy coalesced in a sparking blue sphere at the spot which would, if the arc of the spoon had been part of a ovoid, have been its highest point. It made a weird angry sizzle of a noise and hurtled off in an arc towards the head of the immense being that was emerging from the ocean.

The energy ball grew so tiny and distant that she

couldn't tell if it hit or not, until the tongue began to flap and curl. The two great eyes blinked once.

"One lump or two?" shouted Veronique, shaking a metal fist at the behemoth.

"I think it wants another!" yelled Cornelia in reply. Her attention was mostly occupied by keeping the breakfast bowl out of reach of that tongue. "Keep firing, Beatrice. There's no shortage of ammo."

Beatrice fired off five quick shots in succession, then two slower, charged blasts. If it was hurting the creature it didn't show. Its gigantic head was now completely out of the water, and, though she couldn't know for sure from this perspective, it looked as though the head was still rising. It rested on a neck the width of Birmingham's Centenary Square.

"You should try the other buttons, Bea!" shouted Veronique. "Maybe something else will hurt it!"

Beatrice squeezed another knob and was gratified to see the spoon produce some short chunky laser blasts. Who knew if they would do any damage to this thing, but the kick was satisfyingly powerful. She blasted away at the tongue – which seemed to have an odd patch of white on its tip (poison?) – for all she was worth. Between the twisting of the tongue and Cornelia's evasive manoeuvres, it was hard getting on target. She hit it a few times. Pushed it back a bit. No apparent damage, though.

Seconds later, the tongue slapped down on the breakfast bowl, knocking it out of Cornelia's control and forcing Veronique to grab on to Beatrice for dear life. But that was it. The tongue didn't try to attack them, or destroy the bowl. Having reached them, it simply withdrew, leaving the white thing from its tip in a pool of steaming, sticky liquid.

"What's that white thing?" said Cornelia, whose glasses had been cracked in the attack. She wrestled to get the breakfast bowl's flight back under her control.

"Can you see what it is? Should I flip the bowl to get it out?"

Beatrice got back to shooting at the creature, though now she was shooting at the top of its head. Apparently, she thought, it no longer wishes to concern itself with us. Well, I'll make it think again.

So it was Veronique who approached the pool. If she had still had a toe to poke into the pool that's what she would have done. No choice, though – had to be her fingers! "It's a note," she told the others. The bowl had now levelled out and was hovering, so there was no longer any need to shout.

"Read it out, then," said Cornelia. "Don't leave us in suspenders!"

"It's from Antonella," said Veronique. "'If you are reading this you have destroyed my base. Well done. You are doubtlessly a credit to whatever tediously lawful organisation sent you my way. I do not hold it against you. Still, I'm afraid that I must take my revenge. If you play the game, you must be ready to raise the stakes! The beast upon which my island rested is now on its way to destroy your capital city, whatever it is. I do so hope it's London. I've never forgiven them for closing the British Library.'"

"London!" said Beatrice, shocked to the core. She kept shooting. "What have we done?"

Few are made of sterner stuff than the brave police officer Beatrice Gill, so don't take it as a knock on her courage when I tell you that she is about to go weak at the knees. From the corner of her eye she saw what looked like a mountain breaking through the waves, forging forward in parallel with the head, though the two were separated by at least half a kilometre. A moving mountain? On a crazed notion she looked in the opposite direction. Half a kilometre in that direction was a second mountain. A lightbulb went off. Not above her head, but right in the middle of it, frying her thoughts and shattering her senses. Those mountains were the tops of the behemoth's wings.

She let go of the spoon. What could it possibly do to this colossal ocean beast? What could anyone do? London was doomed.

"Right then," said Cornelia, having noticed Beatrice's despondency. "You've been a flipping brilliant help, ladies. You've done more than anyone could have expected of you. But that thing out there? That's my show."

"And us?" said Beatrice. "What happens to us now?"

Cornelia motioned to Beatrice's dusty chrome torso. "I think it's time to switch off these robot suits, don't you? Your part in this is done. You can get back to your own bodies. All limbs intact."

Beatrice and Veronique looked at each other, trying to fight the hope that suddenly exploded in their chests.

"She could be just switching us off," said Beatrice. "She's done with us. We've no guarantee that we'll wake up anywhere."

"Do you want to live like this?" asked Veronique. "I loved my body and I'd like to get back to it. I had the nicest legs. They took me everywhere without complaint."

I don't know what the two women would have decided, left to their devices. It didn't come down to that. Cornelia Gilligan made the decision for them. She took a small black device from her pocket, pointed it at each of them in turn, and then pushed the motionless robot bodies into the ocean.

"Nice girls," she said, setting the breakfast bowl in swift pursuit of the behemoth. "But I didn't have all day!"

Ask Theaker's!

Answers from Stephen Theaker, Douglas J. Ogurek, Howard Watts and Jacob Edwards

Are there any plans for TQF to become a paying publication?

Stephen Theaker: Fair enough question, but no. We have considered making a move in that direction at times, but it's just not what we're doing here. We give it away for free and don't take any paid advertising or anything for it. It's purely a hobby. It does seem to me that the tide is moving against this kind of publication, though, and of course I think it's quite reasonable for writers and artists to want to be paid for their work. I think what may eventually happen is that we take down our submissions page altogether and work only with existing contributors, or even go back to writing it all ourselves.

Can we define human creativity?

Stephen: It's what we do to distract ourselves from the crushing inevitability of the deaths of ourselves and everyone we love.

Have you thought of writing a story with your fellow editor?

Stephen: We wrote a round robin story together with Steven Gilligan back in the nineties which I think can still be found on our old yellow website. It was fun but frustrating too! One thing we once discussed was to plan each other's Nanowrimo novels and exchange plans on November 1. I hope we get around to doing that.

How many years have you done it?

Stephen: I began the magazine in October 2004, putting out issues 1, 2 and 3 all at once. Wow, that means we should just have celebrated our first decade of publication, but in all the excitement about our fiftieth issue we forgot.

If you could only eat one meal over and over again for the rest of your life, what would it be?

Douglas J. Ogurek: I'm a vegetarian, so it would have to be something with lots of vegetables, fruit, and a good source of protein. Maybe a "nutloaf" (like meatloaf, but made with nuts) with soy gravy, a vegetable conglomeration with tofu, and a salad with many veggies and some berries. Wash it down with a glass of water.

Howard Watts: A roast chicken dinner, roast potatoes and jersey royal new potatoes, onion mash with chantenay carrots, new season sprouts, bread sauce, stuffing (paxo) and gravy (bisto) with full fat Alpen and low fat milk, a bacon sandwich (four smoked slices thick cut with the fat removed and fried before the medallions) with tomato ketchup, my homemade beef chilli with white rice, garlic bread and a Gino's Al Capone pizza (the best pizza ever – look it up, I live in Seaford), fried cod, poached haddock, prawns, with a baked potato and baked beans, ham and egg salad, pasta cabonara, cottage pie with cabbage, tandoori chicken tikka (dry) with chicken korma, rice, sweet potato onion bhaji, garlic naan, chips, cheese and onion crisps, coke, Hophead ale, Maker's Mark whiskey, water, orange squash, gin and tonic ice and lemon. Obviously I'd pick and choose what and how much I'd eat and drink at any given time of the day, for the sake of variety. It's a lot I know, but it's a cheat day, okay?

Jacob Edwards: First of all, let's rule out Vonnegut's *Breakfast of Champions*. That almost finished me off the first time, and your question presumably is not intended to delve into death-wish fulfilment. Dr Seuss's *Green Eggs and Ham*, perhaps? Or is this not a literary discussion? Literally speaking (and assuming replication rather than regurgitation), I suppose "dinner" is the answer. But let's try a little harder. Proton energy pills have a certain appeal; Atomic Thunderbusters always looked like fun: but neither of these strikes me as being nutritionally viable beyond the short term. ("Who wants to live forever?" Queen asked in *Highlander*. Fair point, but equally, who wants to waste away within weeks?) I suspect, if pressed, I would have to choose a bevy of Al Capp's shmoos. I also like fruit nougat.

Stephen: Toast. I would never get sick of it.

If you have enjoyed a book, should you write to the author to let them know? What if you haven't enjoyed it?

Douglas: The reader should ask herself what her true goal in writing the author would be. This would take a great deal of self-awareness.

If the goal is a selfish one, don't write. If the goal truly is to compliment the writer or suggest improvement, then go for it. A good writer will like feedback, whether positive or negative.

Howard: Personally I wouldn't write to an author if I've enjoyed their book(s). Most of the authors I enjoy are dead anyway. If I do get the chance to attend a signing, I go along and tell them face to face and have done so with Harry Harrison, Brian Aldiss, James Herbert – obviously I don't do this to authors I don't like because A: It's a waste of time and money. B: I might get a telling off or a slap. C: There's too many of them – which kind of outweighs A & B. Certainly not Asimov's 3 laws, but sorta close.

Jacob: Reaching an author can be tricky business, so a nice review (either in *Theaker's* or elsewhere) should be considered as an alternative. I think most authors do like to receive letters of affirmation and to know their work is being read and enjoyed by actual, tangible, count-on-one-finger people. What you don't want to do, however, is saddle them with the burden of *correspondence* (which is just impractical), or even the vague guilty feeling that they should be writing back to you. Some might choose to do so, but don't ask them to! As for letting them know you *don't* like their book... Well, put it this way: authors are fragile people. By all means, review what you've read. Be honest. But don't go out of your way to ruin their day. That's like demonstrating to a fine china teapot just how much you don't approve of its inability to resist gravity.

Stephen: Probably not. Better to say online that you have enjoyed it. The author will see it at some point when googling themselves and will be delightfully surprised. But if you encounter them on social media by all means say how much you liked their work. I'm glad I told Lucius Shepard how much I liked his comic *Vermillion*. If you haven't enjoyed it, you should write to them not once but several times.

In the new year, can I be included on the contributors list? – Howard

Stephen: Is that Howard Phillips, miscreant poet? If you want to be included on the contributors list, contribute! But if that is Howard Watts, inestimable artist, and you're talking about the Amazon credits, I'm afraid cover artists aren't really supposed to be included in bibliographical listings!

Is it egotistical to fantasise about being a guest on Desert Island Discs? What if you entertain these fantasies on a daily basis?

Stephen: No, this is perfectly normal. But I suggest you spend a day alone with a bible and the complete works of Shakespeare, just to see if you would really enjoy it.

Is it true that reading *Theaker's Quarterly* regularly has been shown to extend life expectancy of the average adult by at least five years? – Sam

Stephen: Without any regular readers, there is no way of telling.

What are the three most important things for a happy and contented life? – Sam

Douglas: (1) God. (2) Love. (3) A passion for something with a benevolent intent.

Howard: Sight, hearing and speech. Otherwise? My wife, my children and my friends – some that I've never even met. Then there's a comfortable pair of shoes, a sharp razor and a good shirt. In a previous life – yes, I do remember it. A sharp sword, a warm fire and a poncho of sheepskin, seriously! Then there's my guitar, my love of solitude, the quiet night sky and ability to swear in a foreign language. Seriously, only three? Great question that I'm still pondering as the list goes on and on and...

Jacob: Curiosity; discernment; a healthy disregard for social media.

Stephen: Leaving aside the obvious things like home,

food and family, I would say: a good quality keyboard, at least one book you haven't yet read, and low expectations.

What is a failsafe strategy for winning at the board game *Carcassonne*?

Douglas: Never played it.

Howard: Carcassonne? Sorry, I've never played it, and probably won't get around to it anytime soon. Is it any good?

Jacob: In answering this, I would like to make reference to a cautionary tale from the chess world. It concerns world champion Alexander Alekhine (1892–1946), who late in life is said to have made a confession dating back to when he was a young man. A Russian peasant came to him one night at the St Petersburg tournament, claiming to have found a forced win with the white pieces. Alekhine knew this was impossible, but humoured him and set up the board... only to be beaten over and over, no matter what he tried. Aghast, Alekhine invited his good friend (the previous world champion) José Raúl Capablanca (1888–1942) to play against the peasant. Just like Alekhine, Capablanca lost game after game. Thus it was that in 1912 a Russian peasant uncovered a chess secret the likes of which you crave for *Carcassonne*. "What happened next?" Alekhine's confidant asked, no doubt curious as to why the Russian peasant did not himself then succeed Alekhine as world champion. To which Alekhine admitted, "Why, we killed him, of course."

The story is no doubt apocryphal, but please allow me to clarify my stance beyond any possible misunderstanding: I know nothing about *Carcassonne*. I've never played it and never will; and even if I did, Australia is a big country. You won't find me.

Stephen: Keep a worker in hand as long as you can. Make sure you have a nice road on the go. Encourage other players to make bad decisions under the guise of helping them.

What is your favourite time of day to write?

Douglas: 9.30 am until noon.

Howard: My favourite time of day to write is when I feel like it, and that's when everyone should. *Every* writer should carry a pen and notebook with them, as well as having them at your bedside – yes, turn the light on and write it down, you will not remember that idea in the morning, no matter how much you kid yourself. Something I mentioned in a BSFA article way back. Sorry, I'm rambling again – probably the morning after breakfast and coffee is my time. I'll write, then grab lunch, edit as I'm eating, then continue to write. I can knock out 4000 plus words a day this way, with an average of 3400 of them being any good. The best advice I was given is to write every day, *no matter* how you're feeling, *no matter* if you have nothing to say of any great relevance. Its product is far more useful to look back on the following day than nothing at all.

Jacob: I find time of day less important than general ambiance. The bloke across the road and two houses down (to cite an instance of how this works) has taken to welding for hours on end within a custom-built open platform that he's set up on his front driveway. He does this by day or night with no discernible pattern, and indeed with no apparent output or design other than to mess with my writing environment. Regardless of what the clock says, welding time is not my favourite Dali-melted hour of the day. I do like to write when the rain sets in.

Stephen: Between six and seven in the morning, and nine and twelve at night. But lately I've been writing on my iPod using the app Editorial, which has had me writing at all times of day, whenever I have a spare minute.

What is your favourite TQF story ever?

Stephen: Impossible to choose! I'm incredibly grateful to everyone who has ever let us publish one of their stories.

What was the best ever issue of Theaker's Quarterly and why?

Stephen: My favourites are always the one that just came out, and the one *after* the one I'm currently working on.

What would life be like if people who died didn't leave us, but just carried on hanging around the house like guests who have outstayed their welcome?

Stephen: It'd be okay. We'd get used to it. This is why I don't believe in ghosts. There would be so many of them around at all times that there couldn't possibly be any doubt about their existence.

What's the best book (or thing) you've ever reviewed for the magazine?

Douglas: *Paranormal Activity* (TQF31) – This happens to be the first of the films that I reviewed during my five years with the TQF team. *Paranormal Activity* turned the tables on a society that seeks films with explosions galore, constant action, huge soundtracks, and expensive special effects. So little really happens in this film, but director Oren Peli manages a tight, low-budget masterpiece that remains the scariest movie that I've seen.

I've heard people say that they're unimpressed with *Paranormal Activity* because "it doesn't show anything". I mourn their inability to suspend disbelief: often, the scariest things are those that we cannot see.

Howard: The best thing I've ever reviewed for the mag is *Borderlands 2* (which I'm still playing – all those DLC packs!).

Jacob: Surely this is evident from the reviews themselves? (What, you haven't read them all? Why not go panning for gold through the *Theaker's* back catalogue? Reviews don't have to be ephemeral creatures, you know, born of our insatiable need to know and our devilishly short attention spans. They have life beyond the here and now!) To be honest, I haven't reviewed all that many "things". I would like to set eyes on a *Hitchhiker's* towel (anyone?) or new Eric Frank Russell editions in which might be found all manner of allamagoosas and bopamagilvies. Or a recording of *The Twenty-First Century Show* (Graeme Garden and Bill Oddie's unaired Montreux entry from 1979). The problem is that people just don't submit these items for review. (Actually, they don't often send me books, either. I hear that *City of Death* is coming out in 2015. Anyone? Anyone?) Even the concert performance of *The Wall* I had to seek out myself; Roger Waters didn't bring it to my rumpus room and say, *Here, what do you think?* I have a soft spot for Infocom-style computer games if anyone's still making them.

Stephen: I don't think I've ever been in such raptures as I was when reading the Henghis Hapthorn trilogy by Matthew Hughes. It was like they were written just for me. *The Art of McSweeney's* was very special too.

What's the worst book you've ever reviewed for the magazine?

Douglas: *Red Riding Hood* – a bit of a rip-off of *Twilight* by the same director. Still, the film has its moments; I watched it twice, so it can't be that bad.

Howard: The worst thing I've reviewed is probably *Aliens: Colonial Marines*.

Jacob: So as not to rehash the previous answer, let's just say *Man of Steel* and be done with it. I did once converse with KITT, the car from *Knight Rider*, but that was before my reviewing days and strictly off the record.

Stephen: *A Game of Groans* by George R.R. Washington. I wouldn't have read the thing past the first few pages but I took it out with me to one of our monthly editorial meetings and got stuck waiting for a bus home. Execrable.

Which contributors were real and which were pseudonyms?

Stephen: I think only one of John's stories appeared in this magazine under a pseudonym, as Ben Chadwick. My work has appeared here under the names Howard Phillips, Antonella Coriander, Walt Brunston, Vicki Proserpine and William Higman. The original idea for the publication was for it to be all written by me, under various names, like a Badger Books anthology by Lionel Fanthorpe.

The draft contents list in my notebook lists me ("Rolnikov: Terrible Trio"), Dany Jones ("My Heart, the Wind"), Alec Abernathy ("Aardvark Attack"), Howard Phillips ("The Cartesian Conundrum"), B— M— ("Billy's Modification"), Lord Barnes ("Tractor Beam Failure Throb"), Walter Brunston ("The Bad News Came First"), Salston Vega ("The Return of the Grim

Thinker"), Charlton Silvers ("The Earth-Begotten") and X the Unknown ("Time/Space Shadows"). So if you ever see those names or titles in the magazine you'll know it's me.

Other real (so far as I know) people to have contributed include Jacob Edwards, David Tallerman, Charles Wilkinson, Douglas Ogurek, Douglas Thompson, Rafe McGregor, Mitchell Edgeworth, Ross Gresham, Michael Wyndham Thomas, my wife (Ranjna), and my daughter (Lorelei, credited as LCT, who reviewed a Pirates of the Caribbean film when she was a pre-schooler). I believe John Hall to have been a pseudonym, but I'm not sure who for.

Which famous people read Theaker's Quarterly?

Stephen: Not sure if any do, but I'm grateful to whoever indexes us for the ISFDB! Thanks! Mark Kermode, Reece Shearsmith and Elizabeth Bear have retweeted our reviews of their work. Our review of the Kermode book is quoted in the paperback edition.

Why are you so slow to read submissions?

Stephen: John began a demanding new job in 2014 so reading the subs has been mainly my job since then. I do most of my reading at bedtime and when reading submissions I like to be able to make notes I go along, which is tricky in bed. But it's tricky to find enough free time during the day to read a long submission. I do feel guilty when there's a submission in hand and I've read half a dozen comics, but it's because I read them in different slots. This year we've experimented with having a set reading period for each issue but I don't think it's entirely worked, and it's not as if we receive so many hundreds of submissions that we need to manage them. I think in 2015 I'm going to treat submissions like the proofreading jobs I get, booking them in as tasks and responding to them within a couple of days. I'm also experimenting on issue 51 with dividing the magazine into separate Quark files, to make it easier to process stories from start to finish individually. (The first story accepted for #51 was ready for publication before this issue was complete.)

Why don't you have a dedicated Twitter account for the magazine?

Stephen: Good question! It would make a lot of sense, but I don't want us to look like a proper magazine. We're a hobby zine thrown together by friends in their spare time, and so while we try to make it look as good as possible within those boundaries, we don't want to present ourselves in what might appear to be a professional way in the public sphere, because then people would expect more professionalism from us in other areas. Our paucity of female contributors is a great regret for us as a zine, but it would be unsupportable for a professional or semi-pro magazine, so it's good to be clear that we're not playing in that arena.

Will the new Star Wars film be any good? People seem to think so, but then they said that before the three prequels were released, didn't they?

Douglas: They did say that, and I liked the three prequels, minus Jar Jar Binks. The pressure is on director J.J. Abrams for this new film. He has $200 million to play with. You get what you pay for. It'll be fun!

Howard: The new Star Wars film will probably be rubbish. Full of little nods and winks to the fans (of which I'm a huge fan of the firs— sorry, fourth film) which will cause a few groans to say the least. I kinda like the idea of another film with the three main cast members, but there's a nagging feeling telling me it's going to cause a few giggles – and may be camped up a little. I don't know. I'm guessing Han Solo will die, probably sacrificing himself to save his children or child. I will write a review for TQF and plan on seeing the film with my son on the day of release. J.J. Abrams = not too sure... I could write an entire essay on this subject, but have wound my neck in for the sake of Stephen's exhaustive editorial duties for this landmark issue.

Jacob: Well, I for one said no such thing. But the definition of "good" (or "any good" or "carrying even the remotest semblance of goodness") probably depends very much on context. I suspect the people who didn't think much of the prequelogy were mostly those who grew up on the originals, so there was a healthy amount of nostalgic disapproval mixed in with the purely objective criticism and the unavoidable Jar Jar Binks-bashing. In terms of grand sweeping story arcs, I thought *Revenge of the Sith* could and should have been a masterpiece (rather than a soppy, stilted love story gone awry). Expectation is a terrible thing. But let's try to be objective. *The Force Awakens* has potential. It has John Williams; it has Lawrence Kasdan (who co-wrote *The Empire Strikes Back, Return of the Jedi* and *Raiders of the Lost Ark*); and, assuming that Harrison Ford, Carrie Fisher and Mark Hamill are limited to cameos, it has a relatively unknown cast, which suggests there may be a return to story- and ideas-focussed "newness", as it were, rather than a star-studded and grandiloquent attempt merely to mimic episodes IV–VI on a larger scale. (Because, what is the point of a sequel that offers nothing new? *Terminator*. Classic. *Terminator II*. Progression. *Terminators III, IV, V* ad infinitum... Cinematic midlife crisis, no more.) On the downside we have director J.J. Abrams, whose blockbusters occasionally hit the bullseye but for the most part seem to require the bull to turn around first.

And then there's the $200 million budget. The original *Star Wars* cost something like $11 million at a time when the technology was both ground-breaking and prohibitively expensive. Even allowing for inflation, that makes *The Force Awakens* almost five times as costly. That's a lot of money to recoup and, as we learned when Douglas Adams traded his magnificently sangfroid cow for the glitzy beans of Tinseltown, this can so easily translate into haemorrhaging compromise. Fingers crossed, then, but keep those expectations low. Personally, I'd be happy just to see a wookiee in an Hawaiian shirt. I've been on at George Lucas for years but he just won't listen.

Stephen: I think all the Star Wars films are okay, and this one will probably be okay too. The problem isn't really with the Stars Wars films – kids love them all – but with the fact that no one is making space adventure films for grown-ups to enjoy. *Guardians of the Galaxy* is the first one I can think of that comes close since *Chronicles of Riddick*.

Will TQF keep going?

Stephen: Yes, I think so, as long as my health and work situation are good. If I ever find myself unemployed I would probably put the magazine on hold and try my hand at more commercial writing. I had a wobble round about issue 44, where I began to wonder if I should spend my time writing more seriously, but the issues since then have flown by. We have a nice team of contributors and I love working with them. I think in 2015 we may go down to three issues a year, just to take the pressure off a bit, or we may make individual issues a bit shorter.

Would it even be theoretically possible for a computer to predict something complicated, like the weather or the stock market, by creating lots

of little programs that each make a fairly stupid informed guess, and then weighting their answers depending on their past performance, and coming up with an overall prediction, let's say about whether it will rain tomorrow, that takes all these stupid answers into account? Or would the computer do no better than a random guessing machine? I find myself thinking about this question rather a lot, I don't know why.

Stephen: That sounds like a story to me. Submissions for issue 51 are now open!

The Quarterly Review

Reviews by
Stephen Theaker,
Jacob Edwards,
Douglas J. Ogurek,
and Howard Watts

As Above, So Below

Review by Douglas J. Ogurek

Scooby Doo gone wild: no-frills subterranean archaeological horror offers deep scares despite shallow characters/storyline.

A group gets lost in a maze-like expanse and the threats escalate. Maybe some make it out, maybe none do. *The Blair Witch Project* (1999) employed the technique masterfully in a wooded setting. *The Descent* (2005) took the concept to an underground cave system inhabited by violent creatures. The less well-known but still impressive *Grave Encounters* (2011) used an abandoned asylum.

With **As Above, So Below**, director John Erick Dowdle takes to the catacombs beneath Paris to add another gem to the vault of lost in creepy places films. *As Above, So Below* mixes the treasure-hunting adventure of Indiana Jones with the underground exploration of *The Descent*.

Young Scarlett Marlowe – is that a *Heart of Darkness* reference? – is quite the archaeologist. She holds multiple degrees, speaks five languages, and approaches her goals with unflagging determination. Though she has all the introspection of a cave bat, she approaches her mission with, to put it bluntly, "balls of steel". Scarlett continues her father's driven-to-madness quest to find the Philosopher Stone that holds the key to alchemy and eternal youth. So the Brit bats her eyelashes, mentions hidden treasures, and talks, talks, talks to convince a group of American and French people to take to the Parisian catacombs, where she believes the stone is hidden.

During their expedition, the group will encounter an increasingly disturbing and dangerous menagerie of horrors. They will crawl over rat-infested bones and

attempt to squeeze through the tightest of openings. They will approach dark passages and descend through darker tunnels in which scares both cheap and exquisite await. In the most disturbing scenes, they will confront motionless figures. Are they alive? Will they move? An odd collection of sounds (e.g. female cult chanting, distant growling, even a telephone) augments the ominous tone that pervades this film.

These elements add up to make this one of the tensest films this reviewer has seen in a while.

Critics Don't Get It

Many critics have derided *As Above, So Below* as thin and rudimentary. Sure, the characters aren't fully developed and are driven by a Scooby Doo-like mentality, but we do know that Scarlett's archaeologist father was driven to suicide by his quest, and that (kind of) love interest George witnessed the drowning of his younger brother. Isn't that enough?

Besides, how much backstory and characterisation does a film like this need? We as viewers are, in a sense, accompanying these people (who we've just met) into the bowels of the earth. Perhaps we are less interested in getting to know characters and more interested in getting scared.

Several critics have commented on the senselessness behind this quest. Although the map viewing, clue accumulation, and especially the translation of ancient Arabic into rhymed verse that kick off the film are silly, there is also some historical information about the catacombs. Still, none of that really matters once the crew plunges into the depths. They could have been looking for a slice of pizza and it still would have been engaging.

Then there's the ongoing critical gripe about the overuse of the found footage filming technique. It's too shaky, they complain. There's no justification for using it. I can't tell what's going on. How about this: it makes the film seem real. In an age of selfies and home videos, found footage adds a sense of authenticity.

As Halloween approaches, many of us will line up at abandoned buildings temporarily converted into haunted houses. And if, while exploring the dark corridors and spooky chambers, our hearts are repeatedly jump-started, then we will consider that venue a success. Who says that a movie can't be judged by the same criteria? ★★★★☆

Borderlands the Pre-Sequel

Review by Howard Watts

Borderlands the Pre-Sequel sits chronologically between the original *Borderlands* game and *Borderlands 2*. The developers (2K Australia) have managed to write a fairly convincing partner to the first two games, even though their appointment caused some concern within the gaming community. Many players and journos alike feared the move from 2K's Texas outfit to 2K Australia was perhaps a cost cutting move that would impact quality and continuity. Others commented the Texans had perhaps farmed the pre-sequel out, as they didn't want to be associated with it, for whatever reason or reasons undisclosed, or had other projects to develop of more importance. Let's be fair, considering the huge sales generated by the first two games and their various DLC, it was all too obvious BTPS wouldn't sit on the virtual shelves of pre-order retailers.

I couldn't wait for its release, having watched a few trailers on YouTube. The thought of playing in a low gravity environment, blasting away at space-suited adversaries, was a huge attraction to me – not only from a gaming POV, but also from an *SF gaming perspective* in general. Lasers! They have laser guns! Sadly, eviscerating an opponent is not on the cards, slicing off limbs and or even halving opponents cannot be done. This was a little disappointing, as I really enjoyed corroding a shoulder joint to which a bot's gun arm was attached in *Borderlands 2*, a wonderful way of disarming (if you'll pardon the pun) bot combatants.

More of the game play and my expectations later. For now, a brief overview of the story.

BTPS shoehorns itself into the overall Borderlands mythos. A great deal of thought has gone into expanding the plot, character origins and motivations from the first game, working these up so they segue (almost) seamlessly into *Borderlands 2*. If you're a fan of the first two games, some of the explanations given here for various characters' behaviour and origins will make you smile, nod in recognition or gasp, "Oh, so that's why so and so did such and such, that makes sense now, brilliant!" For the most part, these explanations work, others are a little contrived and feel forced, as if the shoehorn doesn't match the size of the foot or the shape of the shoe. Yes, amid the frenetic combat there are moments of sheer brilliance as we play our way up towards the events of the superb B2, but sometimes it's impossible not to groan and wonder "WTF?" Furthermore, a few key characters from B1 and B2 are noticeably absent from this outta space outing, three or four of which I must admit are my favourites, and are sadly missed along with their backstories. There are instances mentioned in B2 that, at the time of playing the game, I wished I could witness, and that these are sadly not seen during BTPS is a drop the ball moment for 2K. This aside, there are many more new characters added to this saga, again, some effective, others cardboard walk-ons serving to

further your main and side quests, or simply get in the way.

Essentially, this is Jack's story, how he came to be handsome, and absolutely crazy. This is worked up perfectly, and we can feel Jack's determination to achieve his goals as he slowly grows into a psychotic madman before us. Voice acting is wonderful, you really can feel for the character as time and again he loses it in the face of stupidity. Familiar faces from B1 and B2 witness this, and you'll be surprised at the original relationships between these characters. But again, I cannot help feeling something is missing here. Perhaps it's all to do with the sheer number of characters from the previous games – impossible to cater for them all? I don't know, and I don't think 2K did either – obviously there's a point where you have to (as a developer) say "No more, enough is enough there's no more room." This is where the problem lies I think, there's just too much "story" to figure out from the previous outings, and then make it all work in such a short game. Okay, prequels seem to be in vogue at the moment, but releasing the second part of a (now) trilogy is a momentous task in any genre. BTPS has a lovely narrative from familiar voices, but be warned, playing the story missions only to complete the game will remove these comments and observations once the story is complete – leaving you with a gap in the soundscape as you play the side missions.

From a technical POV, the game looks identical to B2, all the inventory screen layouts exactly the same – so it's an easy task to just jump from playing B2 to BTPS. There have been a few tweaks – you can now order weapons by value which is cool when it comes to selling off unwanted items, but usually the rare items enjoy the highest value anyway. These games have always been about the millions of weapons, shields, grenades the game code generates, and this game is no different. In fact, it builds upon the first two games by adding freeze and laser weapons. The former can be great fun, freezing an enemy and them hitting them so they shatter into tiny pieces. But to be fair, this does become a little tiresome after a while as it's all about the guns. When you're running around the lunar surface you have to keep an eye on your oxygen level, but killing an adversary causes them to drop oxygen canisters, and this, along with patches of terrain that vent oxygen for you to replenish your tank, means this "threat" quickly becomes a "meh" moment of little consequence.

There's a neat new machine called the Grinder. It allows you (after much trial and error) to place three weapons into the machine and "grind" them together – essentially combining their attributes and receiving a new weapon of higher ability in exchange. This is great fun, and the same technique can be used for shields and grenades. However, nine times out of ten the machine informs you your three offered weapons cannot be ground together – it seems to be a bit hit and miss and frustrating. Couple this with the machine moaning at you to hurry up just as you scroll through your inventory for suitable objects to grind, and it all gets irritating quite rapidly. Bloody annoying #1. Unfortunately, the game is not without its playability problems. It feels a little "heavy" with the controller, not as smooth as B2, not as fluid. I have made numerous kills while in "Fight for your life" mode that have gone undetected, thus ending my life when it should have been saved. I've had a few collision detection problems where a shot has not registered even though it was clearly on target. On one occasion I stepped out of my vehicle to land beneath the actual floor level, unable to jump to another area – essentially "glitching out". There's also a noticeable lag to some places, the frame rate dropping off causing all kinds of combat problems – bloody annoying #2.

Saying this, the game is, well, a game – and it's a great deal of fun! Perhaps some missions and areas are a little too much fun rather than serious, considering the storyline, as it certainly has an Australian humorous edge or flavour. If you're familiar with Australian humour, you'll know exactly what I mean. *Strictly Ballroom* and *Bad Boy Bubba* spring to mind here as cinematic examples of how off the wall this humour can be – sometimes hitting the mark, other times way off target. At times the Australian influence is repetitive and irritating, as character after character fall into parody (even the oxygen canister's label, originally to be marked as "O2" is explained in the story as being printed badly, making the label appear to read "oZ" – ouch!). Sure, it was made in Australia – my wife's favourite country in the world, having lived and worked there for just over a year – yeah why shouldn't they introduce a little of their culture into the game? But even my wife raised a critical eyebrow at the Australian archetypes inhabiting Pandora's moon, Elpis. You have the drunk, talking gibberish about billabongs and fair dinkum, cobber, and you begin to believe that Elpis is somehow representing a NuAustralia, a kind of new world in space. Other characters are equally annoying, and this aspect distracts from the overall Borderlands experience we're so used to. There's the little cockney kid that speaks in cockney rhyming slang – although he doesn't, because after he's spoken the slang he drops in the actual word the slang refers to. *"Mind the apples and pears, stairs, mister."* I was expecting him to mention Mary Poppins at some stage. Pointless and bloody annoying #3. Another character points the finger at colonialism – the intrepid upper crust Englishman replete with handlebar moustache and monocle, staking a claim on Pandora's moon on behalf of the king. As the player, all you have to do is hoist the flag and protect him as he salutes it, humming along to a national anthem, and fetch a broom to support his arm as he grows tired saluting. A comment along the lines of *"Why do they all sound Australian?"* from one of the familiar narrator characters that pops into the soundscape now and again for a critical or amusing comment would have taken the edge of this – but hey, Mr Torgue still has a few amusing and bleeped out lines, and thank goodness for him.

From a visual standpoint the game's various environments are beautifully rendered. One level in particular took my breath – a huge space station partly completed. It was wonderful to jump around this place, assisted by jump pads – small illuminated chevrons that boost your jump height and distance from one area to another. Exteriors are extremely colourful and boast a plethora of interesting natural plants, objects and indigenous life forms. There are a few hidden areas that provide tough bosses – these are essential as they allow you to farm upgraded loot, again, essential to complete the entire story mission, but somehow the majority of these areas seem truncated compared to B2.

The game took me two weeks to complete – playing a couple of hours perhaps four or five days a week. I'm now on my second play through, but have capped my level out at 50, so completing the remaining missions will not afford any more experience points and therefore upgrades. I'm certain there will be a downloadable upgrade allowing you to play other areas and gain more XP, much in the same way B2 did some time ago, but for now – I find it pointless to continue playing. BTPS's length sits between its predecessors, being a little longer than B1, but much shorter than B2. So perhaps this is the issue for me, as replaying the

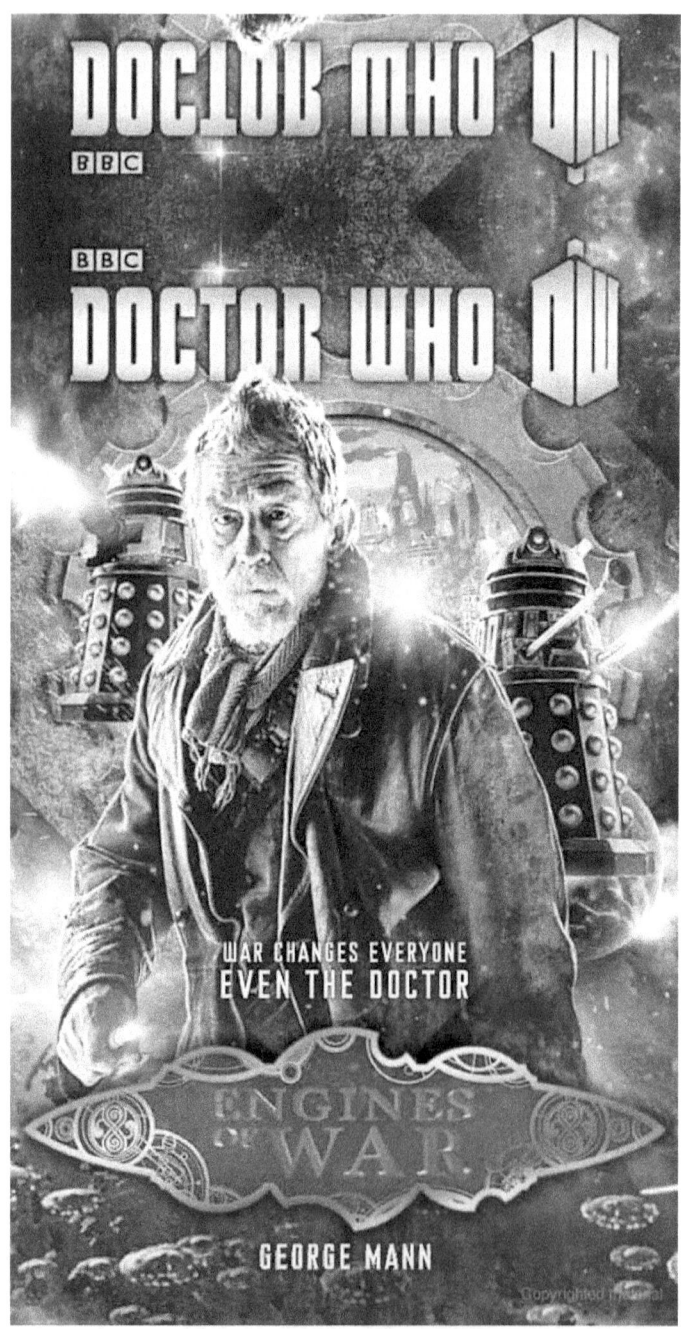

BBC

WAR CHANGES EVERYONE
EVEN THE DOCTOR

ENGINES OF WAR

GEORGE MANN

missions still so fresh in my memory and for no reward other than doing so seems somewhat pointless.

If you're a Borderlands vet, you'll have to play this – that's a given. But I think you'll soon tire of it during the second play though as it's very tough and unforgiving – glitches aside – although there are another three characters to play (four if you include the Handsome Jack add-on available for purchase) to keep you busy and feeling as though you have value for money. Today I found my mind wandering as I played, and loaded up B2. The difference between the two played back to back is startling.

If you're not familiar with the Borderlands games, then for heaven's sake buy number 1 first, then number 2, and when you've completed them and their add-ons, BTPS will probably be available for around a fiver, representing excellent value for money.

Doctor Who: Engines of War

Review by Stephen Theaker

For a long time people assumed that the eighth Doctor (played on television by Paul McGann) had fought in the Time War, that the Doctor we saw in "Rose" was freshly regenerated. However, the notes in the last of the four eighth Doctor collections from *Doctor Who Magazine* popped a hole in that idea, making it clear that (in Russell T Davies' head at least) it was the Doctor *after* McGann who had fought. Davies had been willing to let the magazine handle the regeneration, and have them send the ninth Doctor on his way, ready to fight the Time War.

On-screen events didn't work out too differently. The eighth Doctor did his best to stay out of the war, before regenerating into a Doctor who would fight. If Christopher Eccleston had signed up for "The Day of the Doctor", presumably that would have been him.

He'd have got hold of the Moment, and stepped into the Tardis at the end, about to forget that he didn't use it. As it was, we got the War Doctor instead, as played by John Hurt, who came between eight and nine and lived long enough to age from a young man to an elderly one.

Doctor Who: Engines of War by George Mann comes from the latter stages of his battle with the Daleks. This is what everyone wanted: the Time War! As it turns out, though we're told that it has consumed him, the Doctor's way of going about things during the Time War isn't all that different to how he went about things at other times. There are still no weapons on the Tardis, though he uses it as a battering ram. He kills Daleks, but then so do most of the other Doctors at one time or another. He is still the conscience of the Time Lords, still risking everything to do the right thing.

This particular adventure stems from the plans of the Time Lords, led by Rassilon, to destroy the Tantalus Eye, an area of "temporal murmurations" surrounded by conquered human colonies. It's where the Daleks are building a weapon that will wipe Gallifrey off the spatio-temporal map forever. So the Doctor has to stop the Daleks, he has to stop the Time Lords, and he has to do it all while keeping an eye on Cinder, a resistance fighter from the world of Moldox who joins him in the Tardis.

No book could ever live up to the Time War that lives in every fan's imagination, but this comes pretty close, with space/time battles between military Tardises and armadas of Dalek stealth ships, Dalek progenitors being seeded through the dark corners of history, and the Doctor having to admit he once had the chance to wipe the Daleks out and didn't do it. Strands from the programme's history are woven together, nicely intertwining the original and current runs of the show.

The serious tone is similar to Target adaptations like *Doctor Who and the Day of the Daleks* and *Doctor Who and the Planet of the Daleks* – the War Doctor is not too different from the third Doctor on a bad day. I often found myself wondering why he hadn't asked Ace to join him in battle, given her excellent Dalek-fighting skills, but it's made clear that this Doctor doesn't want companions, doesn't want to put them at risk, even if he misses having them along. He's still the same guy, really. Bit of a grump, heart of gold.

Russell Davies and Steven Moffat have both been generous in leaving spaces between their stories for new adventures to take place. The War Doctor is the best example yet – like the eighth Doctor, his life is wide open, and there are surely more adventures to come, more battles for him to fight. John Hurt's casting is a gift to anyone writing novels in this space – though he only appeared in two episodes, we know the actor well enough to imagine him saying the dialogue and striding over ruined Moldox. This novel harnesses that to a satisfying Dalek war story, which I would recommend to any fan.

My only criticism is that the Doctor felt too much like the Doctor, making you wonder why he gave up the name. I'm not sure any of the other Doctors would have acted all that differently in the course of these events, and some of them would have been surprised at his restraint. They may have forgotten what happened with the Moment, but if they remember adventures like this they would know that the War Doctor wasn't a bad sort at all. ★★★★☆

Gatchaman
Review by Jacob Edwards

The tokenism of casting a bat (and batted eyelids) amongst the pigeons.

Anime pioneer Tatsuo Yoshida's *Science Ninja Team Gatchaman* has gone through several permutations since the seminal television series of 1972, perhaps foremost of which is the fondly remembered English-language adaptation *Battle of the Planets* (1978). *Gatchaman / Battle of the Planets* centres around five orphans – Ken (Mark), Jun (Princess), Ryū (Tiny), Jinpei (Keyop) and Jō (Jason) – whose bird-themed ninja superpowers and techno-wizardry enable them to stand against the evil forces of Galactor (Spectra). Imagi Animation Studios (which released *Astro Boy* in 2009) began work on a *Gatchaman* feature film in 2004, but the project stalled, languished and eventually was cancelled in 2011. *Gatchaman* then rose again as a live action movie directed by Toya Sato and released by Nikkatsu Studios in 2013.

Back in 1978, cuts and voiceovers were used to make the American-tailored *Battle of the Planets* more children-orientated than the original serial, the main differences being less violence, fewer human casualties, no references to transgenderism, and the rather upbeat replacement of environmentally conscienceless corporate villains with a more SF-generic alien foe. Thirty-five years on, the live action incarnation of *Gatchaman* serves as something of a prequel, not only restoring much of what was lost to English translation (Berg Katse's hermaphroditic shifts, for instance) but also fleshing out the backstory of Ken and Jō's strained relationship. Oddly enough, given that *Battle of the Planets* twisted its reworking partly so as to cash in on the *Star Wars* phenomenon

of the late 1970s, *Gatchaman* also now genuflects to
George Lucas, postulating a yin-yang relationship
between Galactor's and Ninja Team Gatchaman's
powers, and even culminating in a fluorescent
pastiche of the lightsaber duel from *The Empire
Strikes Back*. Notwithstanding such concessions, much
of Yoshida's founding premise remains, albeit
somewhat revamped and elevated to the brash
absurdities of the big screen.

The Japanese film industry has a special term –
tokusatsu – for works that make extensive use of
special effects. Cultural nuance renders the word
closer to Hollywood's *blockbuster* than to the more
British *utter codswallop*, but anyone who's seen *Man of
Steel* (2013) will doubtless have suffered through the
gist. Clocking in at 110 minutes, *Gatchaman* has more
than enough bouncing-off-buildings and faster-than-
the-eye-can-follow fight sequences to tick off those
viewers who weigh their lives by number of hours
invested and pointlessly lost; yet, such is the speed
disparity between the movie's live action and animated
sequences, that the blur becomes at times quaintly
cartoonish, as if the feature film format were being
used not to break but rather to recreate the constraints
of its forerunner. Harking back to and elevating the
action components of 1972's *Science Ninja Team
Gatchaman* may seem at once questionable yet
strangely in keeping with the cinematic zeitgeist of the
21st century, but then again there can be little doubt
that 2013's *Gatchaman* has been realised at least in part
as a new-age kitsch homage.

Certainly, this is the case when we see the prototype
Phoenix (G-Force's distinctive supersonic plane)
launch belatedly upon its maiden flight, and then
again when it turns fiery, the dramatic pre-eminence
of these events clearly playing more to notions of
audience nostalgia than to their function within the

film. As per the television series, music is employed to rousing effect in underscoring such iconic themes, but Toya Sato and writer Yusuke Watanabe also use it to cheat their way out of attention to scripting, manipulating the audience so as to cover up (or indeed barefacedly create drama from) some conspicuously nude plot points. One brazen example of this is when Ken and Jun must infiltrate a high-security masquerade, Jinpei scrambling desperately to hack the computers and establish forged identities before they reach the checkpoint. It's undeniably a tense moment, but of course the timing is arbitrary and there was no reason for them to line up before Jinpei had finished his work. The sense of peril is entirely manufactured.

Although its plot is loose, its action cartoon-chaotic and its themes as vague as they are epic, *Gatchaman* 2013 does in one respect meaningfully elevate itself above the franchise's small-screen origins of forty years previous. Live action affords, if nothing else, the potential for stronger characterisation, and in the persons of Ken (Tori Matsuzaka) and Jō (Gō Ayano) – and to a lesser extent Ryū (Ryohei Suzuki) and Naomi/Berg Katse (Eriko Hatsune) – that opportunity has been capably seized. Matsuzaka has a real presence. Ayano positively smoulders. Whenever there is (inter)acting to do, rather than racing all about the place, fatuously martial-fartsing, we are given at last a fully rounded sense of what those teeth-grinding, angst-ridden expressions were all about back in the days of hand-drawn emotions. Watanabe's script, in truth, gives the actors precious little to work with, but Matsuzaka and Ayano nevertheless put in performances well worthy of both 1970s *Gatchaman* and the dark superhero genre's broader swathe. It's just unfortunate that Toya Sato's modernisation – to give a western comparison – proves rather closer to

Michael Bay's oeuvre of filmmaking than to
Christopher Nolan's.

Possibly the most damning evidence of *Gatchaman*'s
failure to better itself for the big screen and the new
millennium, is the mind-blowingly vapid
characterisation of Jun (Ayame Gouriki). Granted, the
animated Jun/Princess was never much more than a
wet handkerchief with which to dab the perspiring
foreheads of the male leads, but the Jun of 2013, far
from correcting this imbalance, has fallen into a
condescension machine and emerged, wide-eyed and
pouting, as a perverse archetype of bland, tittering,
puerile, hormonal brainlessness. Jinpei (Tatsuomi
Hamada) may be the least developed of Ninja Team
Gatchaman's quintet, but whereas he is merely
neglected by Sato and Watanabe, Jun has been actively
depicted (objectified? fantasised?) as recycled plastic.
She is to female dignity and empowerment what Elmo
has been to the Muppets, which is more than just a
shame; it's out-and-out shameful.

One advance trailer for the curtailed Imagi
Animation production of *Gatchaman* shows Ken, Jun,
Ryū, Jinpei and Jō leaping from a skyscraper and
swooping down towards an insectoid death mecha,
Jun's inane little giggle jarring badly with the urgent
musical score and the more determined exertions of
her fellow ninjas. In another piece of test footage she
winches (wenches?) up through a scene of explosions
and mayhem, waving coquettishly. Could it be that
some quirk of Japanese culture has doomed her
character to play the flighty swan and to candy all
those action scenes, no matter what form *Gatchaman*
takes? If such is true then it hints at a damning
shallowness of artistic vision, and we can only lament
that the courageous orphans of Science Ninja Team
Gatchaman – and those who shape their adventures –
have matured little across forty years. Some fans may

rejoice that a feature film treatment of *Gatchaman* even made it off the ground, but if the 2013 movie soars at all then, sadly, it is to heights not much greater than adolescent wish fulfilment.

"Bird, go!" has always been the command phrase for transforming the Gatchaman team into ninja mode, but in this instance somebody should most definitely have stood up to director Toya Sato and screamed instead, "Bird, no!"

Happy
Review by Stephen Theaker

With **Happy** (Image, pb, 112pp) it feels Grant Morrison has taken a step into Garth Ennis territory. It's a violent mini-series, collected here in a book. Nick Sax is an ex-cop now working as a hitman. Hired to kill the Fratelli brothers, he hires them to come and kill him, figuring it's the easiest way to get them all in a room together. Unfortunately an extra brother tags along and Nick is shot. Badly wounded, on his way to (he thinks) hospital, he starts having visions of a chatty blue flying donkey unicorn thing. It wants him out of hospital and off saving some kidnapped children.

Darick Robertson's artwork is good, reminding me here more than elsewhere of Phil Jimenez. By Grant Morrison's standards this is a quick and straightforward read, a fantasy-tinged adult thriller that'd make an ideal vehicle for Nic Cage at his demented best. It wasn't a bad book, but if it were in my power to pick Grant Morrison's next projects, a sequel to this would be a long way down my list, below *Kill Your Boyfriend* and just above *Skrull Kill Krew*.

★★★☆☆

The Hunger Games: Mockingjay – Part 1

Review by Douglas J. Ogurek

Games shift from arena to conference room as heroine juggles public persona with personal quandary.

Director Francis Lawrence had his work cut out for him with *The Hunger Games: Mockingjay – Part 1*, the first of the two-part conclusion to the Hunger Games series. He had to adapt the first (and more subdued) half of the final novel in Suzanne Collins's trilogy into a film that maintains the viewer's attention and builds tension without stealing the show from the finale.

Though the film's beginning suffers from an overindulgence in mourning war ruins, Lawrence pulls off what turns out to be a tense and emotionally stirring film more about psychological games than fights and explosions... but it still has some of the latter!

Protagonist Katniss Everdeen, having thrown a wrench (an arrow actually) into the most recent game, recovers in the underground headquarters of District 13, hitherto rumoured to be destroyed. Here Katniss discovers that although the arena games are over, she's still a contestant in a game whose stakes are much higher.

The districts of Panem, fuelled by Katniss's Hunger Games heroics, have grown more hostile toward the Capitol, their wealthy oppressor. District 13's scheming leadership wants to intensify this animosity to overthrow the Capitol. Their plan: convince Katniss to become the Mockingjay, a symbol of revolution that will stoke the fire building within the districts.

Sounds like a great plan. However, one huge obstacle deters Katniss from jumping into that role wholeheartedly: her two-time Hunger Games cohort and budding love interest Peeta Mellark has been captured by the Capitol.

When Action Wanes, Bring in the Big Shots

Because *Mockingjay – Part 1* has notably less action – I count two brief action scenes – than *The Hunger Games* and *The Hunger Games: Catching Fire*, it needs something beyond the reputation of its predecessors to keep the viewer engaged. The solution comes in an all-star cast.

The Hunger Games mainstays Haymitch Abernathy (Woody Harrelson) and Peeta (Josh Hutcherson) continue to offer strong performances. Particularly impressive is Hutcherson's portrayal of Peeta's mental deterioration, shown in a series of video interviews. Nevertheless, these two take a back seat, enabling other equally engaging characters to step forward.

The Manipulators

The buttons in *Mockingjay – Part 1* get pushed mostly by three conference room connivers intent on manipulating the public and duping their adversaries.

Philip Seymour Hoffman's post-mortem appearance as Plutarch Heavensbee shows what a loss the film world experienced. Heavensbee, a District 13 political puppeteer, seeks to unveil and capitalise on what makes Katniss so appealing to the public. He sees Katniss as a tool to overcome the Capitol. When Katniss gets angry, Hoffman/Heavensbee could just as well be an automobile enthusiast admiring the roar of a Maserati.

Julianne Moore slips rather than barges into the conflict as District 13 President Alma Coin, a less easily categorised complement to the other publicity-seeking (Heavensbee) and confrontational (Snow) power players. With her grey clothes, eyes, and hair, Moore portrays a tepid leader whose true intentions are hazy. Is she good? Is she bad? She's "in the grey". Flip a coin!

On the Capitol side, Donald Sutherland's President Snow is a case study in self-control, arrogance, and cunning. Snow, whose pristine white hair and suit belie his malicious intent, has a nearly omniscient view of district goings-on. His carefully prepared televised speech explains to the have-nots that the Capitol is the reason they are alive. "Your districts are the body," he says. "The Capitol is the beating heart." The implication: you can't survive without a heart. And don't you dare let him catch you giving the Mockingjay salute!

Katniss Everdeen: Pawn, Liberator, or a Bit of Both?

In popular films, there are still far too many beautiful numbskulls and female action heroes who do what a typical male action hero would do. Jennifer Lawrence's Katniss Everdeen, ranging from tentative warrior to distraught teenage girl, offers hope for the plight of female leads. Katniss uses guile and pluck rather than sexuality or boys' club bravado to achieve her objectives.

One example of Lawrence's talent is the contrast between Katniss's awkwardly delivered prepared speech and a rage-charged impromptu invective against President Snow. "If we burn, you burn with us!"

With all those power players tweaking the dials, what is Katniss's role? Is she merely a pawn, or does she influence the outcome? Here's something to think about: Katniss must find the balance between District 13's desire to fuel the uprising and her own desire to protect Peeta. Complicating matters, a psychologically off-kilter Peeta doesn't win any district friends when he encourages would-be Capitol enemies to lay down their arms.

Peeved with a Capitol President

With President Snow and the Capitol's privileged

inhabitants, *Mockingjay – Part 1* gives us "The Man". What makes this film (and the whole series) so compelling is the goal of "sticking it" to him.

And who does society rest its hopes on? Not on Thor or Jason Bourne. Not on James Bond or the Men in Black. Instead, the fate of Panem rests on a 17-year-old girl who can't stand seeing others in pain.

So we wait another year until the conclusion. Hopefully, it's faithful to the book.

In the Broken Birdcage of Kathleen Fair

Review by Stephen Theaker

In the Broken Birdcage of Kathleen Fair (The Alchemy Press, ebook, 784ll) is an interesting novella by Cate Gardner, but the tone is a bit hard to describe. There are horrific elements, but it isn't really horror. Comic horror fantasy, maybe? Weird fantasy? Kathleen Fair is in a room of objects that are too big for her – like a dressing table stool which comes up to her nose – but this isn't a new development. She's been here a while. What's new is a mirror, through which she sees "a bloodshot eye pressed against the glass, its lashes long and spider-like", before a man comes through: Frederick Schentenfreude III, who drains people of their scent in order to keep himself young. He will later decide that he wishes to marry Kathleen. She follows him out of the mirror, and sees the body of a boy, Bobby, that Schentenfreude has drained. She makes it her mission to restore him. I found it difficult to get a handle on this story; I'm not sure what it was aiming for, or whether it achieved it, which makes this rather a useless review. But I enjoyed reading it, and look forward to reading more from the same author.

★★★☆☆

Interstellar

Review by Jacob Edwards

A stellar cast, interred amidst the stars.

At almost three hours in length, Christopher Nolan's epic SF film Interstellar falls roughly into three acts: humanity clinging to life on a dust-ridden, dying Earth; a last-ditch mission to seek out habitable planets through a wormhole in spacetime; and the consequences (small- as much as large-scale) of that mission going awry. Such is the broad progression of plot. In a critical sense, what plays out on screen is a compellingly envisaged scenario that compromises itself in favour of the box office and then descends further still into the warm glow of metaphysics. For all its cinematic excellence, this is the equivalent of Albert Einstein and his conceptual twin brother playing four-dimensional *Monopoly* and each contriving to make need of a specially tailored get-out-of-jail-free card. It is an engrossing spectacle, to be sure, but a somewhat unsatisfying comedown from what might have been.

In terms of bringing the script to life, Matthew McConaughey leads an outstanding cast performance, the tone of which he sets in the first act alongside charismatic child actress Mackenzie Foy and an effortlessly world-weary John Lithgow. *Interstellar* is told through unaffected, very human characters, with Jessica Chastain and Casey Affleck adding a touch of despair to the grim faces of act two. Michael Caine does what he does, and Anne Hathaway is more Sandra Bullock than Barbarella in taking womankind into space. Even the NASA robots have real personality. The one blemish, it could be argued, is Matt Damon, whose name is to the cast list as the roiling, pestilent blight is to future Earth's crops,

hanging with Damoclean foreboding until his
appearance in the third act signals the onset of the
apocalypse. Damon is revived as the craven Dr Mann,
a minor role in which he can be seen thumbing his
nose at those who might question his acting range.
Mann's aura is intentionally jarring, his demeanour
scripted to arouse our suspicions; let it be noted, then,
that Damon can play an unconvincing character as
convincingly as he can a convincing character
unconvincingly. His injection into the storyline cuts
the hair by which our belief was suspended, and
triggers a cinematic cataclysm of untethered
action/drama.

Like *Gravity* before it, *Interstellar* strives for realism
but comes to rely on a manipulation as overt as it is
irreconcilable with the story being told. The state of
play is signposted at any given moment by Hans
Zimmer's score, the excellence of which is difficult to
judge because of its prescriptive and patronising,
heavy-handed use of **VOLUME**. Whoever mixed the
film has done Zimmer no favours; nor the actors, who
at times have their lines drowned out entirely so that
music may be used to prod the audience towards
whatever emotional shearing shed Nolan has
designated. This bombastic approach becomes more
prevalent as the film progresses. By the time the
supermassive black hole has selectively extended its
gravitational pull to reel in any ship lifting off from
Matt Damon's planet (bypassing the influence of the
sun around which that planet orbits), the soundtrack
has gone berserk. The effect is not unlike that of an
archetypal miscreant whistling in faux innocence to
cover up a petty larceny, only in *Interstellar*'s case this
has been amplified to decibels beyond the credulity
horizon.

Sometimes a writer will begin with a particular idea,
only later to find that the framework they construct to

present that notion comes to hold more interest than the premise itself. Given *Interstellar*'s unimpeachable first act and then the eyebrow-raising liberties taken by the second in reaching the incongruous fanfare of the third, it would be easy to assume this is what happened to Christopher Nolan. The truth, however, is somewhat less flattering. Nolan is credited as having co-written *Interstellar* with his brother Jonathan, but as it transpires their project was not a genuine collaboration. Jonathan in fact wrote an earlier script by himself, and it was the first third of this that was used as *Interstellar*'s opening, the remainder being binned so that Christopher had somewhere to affix his own, less grounded story idea. In filmmaking in general and Hollywood in particular, success and failure are relative terms, but whatever the perspective of verdict passed on *Interstellar* – glass one-third empty or one-third full – there should be little wonder that such a piecemeal, Frankensteinian approach has led to at least some measure of ruinous consequence.

There will be many viewers, of course, who take no issue with *Interstellar*'s storyline, and indeed who will point to the involvement of theoretical physicist Kip Thorne serving as both scientific consultant and executive producer on the film; instead of taking this legitimising presence with a grain of salt, such people will toss that salt over their shoulders and maintain that Christopher Nolan's physics are faultless. Well... Yes, clearly a lot of attention was paid to the *visual depiction* of wormholes, black holes and associated phenomena, but that's not altogether the same kettle of fish as declaring them scientifically accurate. Metaphysics aside – and the third act of *Interstellar* surely is no more scientific than *Flatliners* or *What Dreams May Come* – we still are left with some decidedly odd compressions of plot-space and plot-time, while the real life effects of time dilation, though soundly based in theory, are applied inconsistently and only when they serve Nolan's purposes. When they don't, they are ignored, and in this respect the so-called laws of physics are treated more in the sense of judicial laws than the universally immutable workings of cause and effect. Perhaps to some extent this is unavoidable, for a film without poetic license is liable to be a very dry film indeed. Yet, Christopher Nolan's two-thirds of the script compounds any affront by falling prey also to an unconscionable compression of characters' thinking time. Whether or not a story can withstand bad physics, metaphysics or consciously eschewed physics, it really is going beyond the pale to have the protagonists make decisions – choices that speak to the very survival of the species – in less time and with less discussion than most people would need in standing in the dairy section, deciding whether to buy low fat or regular. Drama there must be, but when the milk is spilt and Newton's apple turns pear-shaped, our heroes' calamities should move us to something greater than a sardonically muttered, "Whoops."

Interstellar is by no means a bad film; indeed, its positioning amidst the upper echelons of its cinematic peers might well suggest a manifest disproportion between criticism levelled and criticism warranted. But then again, with Christopher Nolan's having set his sights on the stars, *Interstellar* surely could have been a masterpiece (and for an hour or so looked like being just that). The fact that it so poignantly loses its way is in a sense far more distressing than the abject floundering exhibited by its happy-go-hapless Hollywood fellows. *Interstellar* tantalises, but falls short: not with the high-octane bluster of Evel Knievel but rather the down-to-earth tragedy of a Cape Canaveral launch that, for all its meticulous planning and having just made a successful lift-off, inexplicably then jettisons the wrong rocket segments... and if, further to this, such a mishap should come to form the crux of a closed time loop, then let it be noted that cosmic contrivances are not in all contexts as interesting as Christopher Nolan might have thought. When E.T. phoned home, was he unwittingly calling through time and summoning himself to the rescue? Indeed, no – and let us all join together in extending one long, bony finger at the prospect of a mashup remake in which Drew Barrymore plays her own mother – but with such doomsday scenarios in mind, could it be that Nolan injected *Interstellar* with a weak dose of glitzy goose so as to immunise it against a fully-fledged bout of Tinseltown turkey later in life? Stranger things have been known to make themselves happen.

Invincible, Vol. 17: What's Happening

Review by Stephen Theaker

Invincible, Vol. 17: What's Happening (Image, ebook) is written by Robert Kirkman, with pencils shared between Ryan Ottley and Cory Walker, who illustrate scenes depending on whether they take place on Earth or in the alternate, quick-time dimension from which the Flaxan Empire launches its regular invasions. The latter are flashbacks, showing us what happened when Monster Girl and Robot were stranded there, explaining their tense relationship and the way that she is now a full-grown woman. (Previous volumes had shown her slowly growing younger the more she used her power to transfer into a huge green monster.) The scenes on Earth show follow the old and new Invincibles. The original Invincible is having trouble with his powers on the blink, the consequences of which are demonstrated in the

brilliant shock ending to chapter one. The new Invincible, filling in to keep the Invincible business going, has to fight the alien invaders, though he's glad for the break from his visiting parents, forever comparing him to the brother whose failings they don't know. *Invincible* is always a reliable source of superhero adventure, and volume 17 was no exception. If it felt like a less than weighty read, that might be down to my last reading session on this comic having lasted for about 70 consecutive issues! There's so much to like here. A universe of heroes that may, for all I know, have their own comics, but if they do there's nothing here that forces me to read them. It isn't like DC or Marvel, where endless company-spanning crises leave almost every individual superhero title feeling like a badly cut jigsaw piece. If an infinite crisis or a civil war happens in Invincible's universe, it'll happen in his comic. ★★★☆☆

Megalex: The Complete Story

Review by Stephen Theaker

Megalex: The Complete Story (Humanoids), by Alejandro Jodorowsky and Fred Beltran, takes us to a world where the rich literally bathe in the blood of the hoi polloi, the clones who gather for their appointment with death at the age of forty. The children left behind are told to watch out for the magical food parcels that fall from the sky. The ruling family are an ancient wizened magican, his sorceress wife, and their vampire daughter. Only two parts of the world escape their dominion: the haunted forest and the deadly sea.

This bizarre world is of course ripe for disruption, and it comes in the gangly form of an overgrown clone soldier who escapes his routine termination and meets up with an improbably and presumably uncomfortably

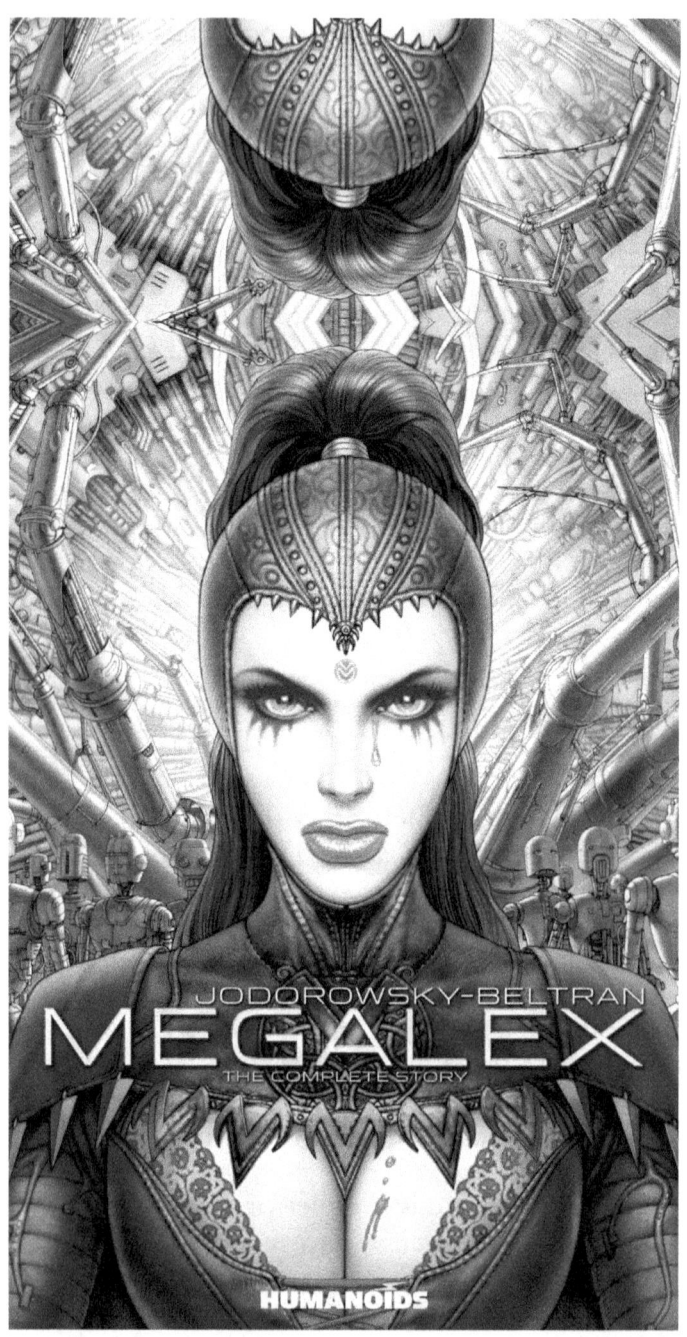

buxom member of the revolution. She'll take him to their leader, get him trained up, and maybe even give him a nice cuddle if he's a good boy.

The writer is Alexandro Jodorowsky, and it's as wild and woolly as anyone who has read *The Incal* or *The Metabarons* would expect. His work for French publishers is much more mystical than we're used to seeing in science fiction, his science fiction following the logic of dreams instead of the rules of physics. This collects all three volumes of the story, a fairly short run for a French graphic novel series, and there is definitely a sense of things being wrapped up swiftly in the latter third.

The art style changes too, moving from computer-generated to hand-drawn backgrounds and objects, though it's quite possible I wouldn't have noticed if the artist Fred Beltran hadn't brought it up in the introduction. ★★★☆☆

Tusk

Review by Douglas J. Ogurek

Juvenile premise spurs tour de force of eccentricity, turns contemporary horror film formula on its head.

As I walk out of a horror film, I'm typically thinking one of three things: great, so-so, or crap. However, every once in a while, there is another thought: did I like this film? Such was my initial reaction to director Kevin Smith's *Tusk* (2014), a film whose premise involves a madman who wants to physically and psychologically transform another man into a walrus. Yes. You read that correctly.

Obnoxious LA-based shock jock Wallace Bryton (Justin Long), stuck in the "frozen shithole" of Canada, wants to find a "weirdo" interviewee to ultimately make fun of in his popular Not-See Party podcast.

Wallace ends up on the doorstep of Howard Howe, a reclusive ex-seafarer who has a boatload of adventure tales, and a few skeletons (human and otherwise) in the closet. Howe seeks to rekindle the bond he once developed with a walrus he named Mr Tusk while stranded after a shipwreck. His strategy: make Wallace a walrus.

Directors of recent horror movies tend to manipulate their predominantly unmemorable characters through frightful settings (e.g. catacombs, haunted houses, etc). There's nothing wrong with that. However, Kevin Smith, the brains behind *Mallrats* (1995), *Dogma* (1999), and *Clerks* (1994), tends to create talk-heavy films with quirkier characters. *Tusk* follows this strategy and in so doing, departs from – or maybe I should say, in tusk lingo, protrudes discernibly from – the current body of horror films.

One is often hard-pressed to identify something original that characters say in horror movies. *Tusk*, with its extended scenes of two or three characters talking, offers a smorgasbord of quotable gems. "You want characters?" Smith seems to ask those who consistently blast horror film casts. "You got them!" In *Tusk*, there are three such characters: the self-involved victim, the astute madman, and the comically eccentric detective.

The Self-Involved Victim
Wallace Bryton, with his walrus-like name and moustache, is the type of guy who snaps at convenience store clerks and uses strangers' backs as desks. He looks down on Canadians ("I don't want to die in Canada") and cheats on his girlfriend. His growing fame has gone to his head. This is most apparent when he interviews Howe. Wallace, "not-seeing" the threat inherent in Howe's anti-human sentiments, examines the odd specimens Howe has

accumulated and expresses (loudly and tactlessly) his observations. "Who are you? Rudyard fucking Kipling?"

Typically, films are wise to shy away from obnoxious protagonists, but Wallace, with his crude comments and gestures, contrasted with the literary allusions and deviant philosophies of Howe, captivates the viewer.

Justin Long's performance as Darry in the film *Jeepers Creepers* (2001) revealed his strong talent for expressing shock and fear. It's a talent that he fully exploits in *Tusk*, whether he's in a drug-induced stupor and coming to terms with what's happening to him, making a hushed emergency phone call, or screaming as Howe taunts him.

The Astute Madman
It's difficult to portray a villain who's both off his rocker and intelligent. Michael Parks pulls it off admirably with Howard Howe. "I don't understand," he says. "Who in the hell would want to be human?"

One never knows what is coming from the misanthropic Howe. He might quote Tennyson or Hemingway, tell an adventure story, or mimic his victim's screams. He might laughingly sing a nursery rhyme, or he might growl. Howe, the sufferer of egregious childhood abuse, stifles laughter when a horrified Wallace discovers he's been severely mutilated.

In one of the film's most off-the-wall scenes (a flashback), Howe stands on a porch with detective Guy Lapointe (more on him later). Howe, pretending to be a dim-witted assistant children's hockey coach, tries to coax Lapointe inside ostensibly to *shoot* a brown recluse (spider), but more likely to try to turn Lapointe into a walrus.

Though it probably won't get credit due to the film's outlandishness, Parks's performance puts him in the company of Anthony Hopkins's Hannibal Lecter and Heath Ledger's Joker. Howe. What a perfect name for a film like this. *How* will this turn out? *How* could a man do something like this? "The walrus," he says, "is far more evolved than any man I've ever known." Howe indeed!

The Comically Eccentric Detective

The credits reveal that an unknown actor named Guy Lapointe plays himself, a French-Canadian alcoholic investigator on the trail of Howe. Though Lapointe's time in the film is limited, his crooked eye, stilted delivery, and odd mannerisms make a huge impression. Lapointe is ridiculous, but we can't look away.

Lapointe's main scene takes place in a restaurant in which he dominates a conversation with Wallace's girlfriend Ally and fellow podcaster Teddy. It may be a fast food place, but Lapointe's audience sits dumbfounded as he treats them to an idiosyncratic feast that's less about what he's saying, and more about what he's doing. He stands up and smashes down his burger, pours hard liquor into his milkshake, and engages in a slew of other fascinating behaviours all while describing his history with Howe.

People often comment on how many of today's films (and society in general) never slow down. Guy Lapointe does slow down. At one point, he actually breaks from his twisted monologue to suck from his spiked milkshake while his audience waits – he even comments on his shake's thickness – for him to continue. And the porch scene with Howe is legendary. Never has so much been communicated with so many words and so little actually said.

Lapointe even offers a bit of intrigue to the film. When the viewer looks closely, he or she might notice familiarity in the eyes, and the voice. That's because

Guy Lapointe is none other than Johnny Depp. It's as if Smith has transformed one of the most well-known actors into a sideshow act to reinforce what's happening in the film. Brilliant.

An Opinion Transformed

With *Tusk*, we get humour, we get gore, we get surprises, we get scares, and we get sadness. Kevin Smith stitches the surgical splatterpunk film like *The Human Centipede* (2009), the "find the bad guy before he kills his captive" film (think *The Silence of the Lambs* (1991)), and the dialogue of, well, a Kevin Smith film. *Tusk* both entertains and gives one an appreciation for the finer things in life, like his or her legs.

During your life, you might encounter a handful of people who are true characters. Some of these people are profound A-holes, some offer a twisted view of the world, and others are so quirky that they are worthy of a movie. *Tusk* treats us to all three in just over an hour-and-a-half.

Back to my initial question: did I like this film? My opinion on it has metamorphosed, slowly, from one of uncertainty to a walrus-sized yes.

The X-Files: Season 10, Vol. 1

Review by Stephen Theaker

The X-Files: Season 10, Vol. 1 by Joe Harris, Carlos Valenzuela and Michael Walsh (IDW, tpb, 138pp) tries to follow the example of *Buffy the Vampire Slayer: Season 8* in providing the comics continuation of a beloved and much-missed television series. Unlike Buffy, Mulder (as played by David Duchovny, until recently shedding his trousers twelve weeks a year on *Californication*) and Scully (Gillian Anderson, last seen on *Hannibal* and the BBC) had pretty much given up the fight by the time their series ended, their replacements Doggett (Robert Patrick) and Reyes (Annabeth Gish) taking the limelight up until the originals returned for the disappointingly low-key second feature film.

All four feature in this series, as do other favourites like Skinner, the [redacted] and the [redacted], but Mulder and Scully are the stars. They're still a couple, still retired from the FBI, but living under assumed names, Scully working as a doctor. The plot follows on from the final episodes of the TV series, which tried to link the cyborg assassin storyline of the later seasons with the alien invasion story that drove its glory days. A group of mysterious types with glowing eyes want to prepare the way for the alien colonisation of Earth to finally go ahead, and for that they need Mulder and Scully's magical baby William.

I wish I could say it's fantastic. I really wanted it to be, because I do miss these characters and at its best *The X-Files* could be magnificent. But this book's just okay, about on the level of the old Topps series. The sketchy artwork tells the story clearly and does a fair job of capturing likenesses without conveying the eerie atmosphere of the programme – Mulder and Scully fill the frame like superheroes. The story covers all the right territory, but not enough of it is new. If Mulder and Scully ever return to television, you'd be surprised if this story was considered canonical. Readable – for fans, anyway – without being essential. ★★★☆☆

Also Read

Notes by Stephen Theaker

I don't have time to review in full everything I read, much as I'd like to, especially when I plough through a pile of comics, and that leaves lots of review fragments and unreviewed books behind. Here then, as a special fiftieth issue "treat", and as a way of clearing the decks for next year, is a round-up of everything I read this year but didn't have time to review, plus ratings and notes on a handful of books from even longer ago that I kept meaning to review but never did. The credited writers and publishers here are mostly taken from Goodreads, and haven't been fully checked against the actual books, so apologies to anyone who is miscredited or missing.

Abe Sapien, Vol. 1: The Drowning (Dark Horse Books), by Mike Mignola, Mike Alexander and Jason Shawn. Moody and spooky story of Hellboy's aquatic chum. ★★★☆☆

Adventure Time, Vol. 1: Playing With Fire (KaBOOM!), by Danielle Corsetto. A black and white *Adventure Time* graphic novel featuring the Flame Princess. ★★★☆☆

Adventure Time, Vol. 2: Pixel Princesses (KaBOOM!), by Danielle Corsetto and Zack Sterling. Another black and white graphic novel, this time featuring several of the princesses as they get stuck inside their computer pal. Bought for the children (possibly by the children with their pocket money) but I enjoyed it too. ★★★☆☆

Afterlife with Archie, Vol. 1: Escape from Riverdale (Archie Comics), by Roberto Aguirre-Sacasa and Francesco Francavilla. Interesting alternative take on the gang. Shows real understanding of the characters. Doesn't have a proper ending. ★★★☆☆

Amazing Screw-On Head and Other Curious Objects (Dark Horse Comics), by Mike Mignola and Dave Stewart. Collecting weird tales by Hellboy creator Mike Mignola. The lead story is about a head who can screw himself into various bodies, and does so in order to help the President, Abraham Lincoln. ★★★★☆

Amelia Cole and the Hidden War (Monkeybrain Comics), by Adam P. Knave, D.J. Kirkbride and Nick Brokenshire. Book two. Amelia works as the city's magic sheriff while her predecessor fights in a magical war. ★★★☆☆

Amelia Cole and the Unknown World (Monkeybrain Comics), by Adam P. Knave, D.J. Kirkbride and Nick Brokenshire. Book one in a well-drawn and readable series about a young woman who can do magic. ★★★☆☆

American Elf 2009 (Top Shelf Productions), by James Kochalka. Kochalka's daily comics from 2009. ★★★☆☆

American Elf 2010 (Top Shelf Productions), by James Kochalka. Kochalka's daily comics from 2010. ★★★☆☆

American Elf 2011 (Top Shelf Productions), by James Kochalka. Kochalka's daily comics from 2011. ★★★★☆

American Elf 2012 (Top Shelf Productions), by James Kochalka. Conclusion of the wonderful autobiographical series. ★★★★★

Asterix and the Magic Carpet (Orion), by Albert Uderzo. Asterix goes to India, in theory. It seems more like Arabia. ★★★☆☆

Asterix in Corsica (Orion), by René Goscinny and Albert Uderzo. Not the best in the series. ★★★☆☆

Asterix in Switzerland (Orion), by René Goscinny and Albert Uderzo. Very funny. Reminded me why I loved Asterix so much as a youngster. ★★★★☆

Axe Cop, Vol 2: Bad Guy Earth (Dark Horse Comics), by Malachai Nicolle and Ethan Nicolle. Nothing could ever be quite as hilarious as *Axe Cop, Vol. 1*, which made me laugh so much the sides of my eyes were sore for days from wiping away the tears, and this isn't, but it comes pretty close. Axe Cop and friends have to battle two psychic bad guys who want to turn everyone on Earth into bad guys. Written by a little kid and drawn by his grown-up brother, this does a great job of harnessing the imaginative fireworks that go off whenever children start to rattle off stories. ★★★★☆

Batman: The Black Mirror (DC Comics), by Scott Snyder, Jock, Francesco Francavilla. Good story about Batman (Dick Grayson, who I think might be my favourite Batman) fighting a weird secret society. ★★★☆☆

The Beauty (Unsung Stories), by Aliya Whiteley. A very good novella. In a world without women, men embrace mushrooms. Reviewed in full for *Interzone* #254. ★★★★☆

Black and Brown Planets: The Politics of Race in Science Fiction (University Press of Mississippi), by Isiah Lavender III (ed.). Interesting book of essays. Two about one episode of *Star Trek: Deep Space 9* are maybe a bit much, and given the title it seems odd that it doesn't cover India, the country that might well come to lead the space race (the "Brown" section is more about South America), but I learnt a lot from it. Like any book of literary criticism, it can be dull, but that's outweighed by the issues, authors and stories it works so carefully to bring to our attention. A few essays make great claims without much evidence, but all provide much to think about; it opens up the conversation, rather than having the last word. Walter Mosley is quoted inside as saying: "The power of science fiction is that it can tear down the walls and windows, the artifice and laws by changing the logic, empowering the disenfranchised or simply by asking, What if?" *Black and Brown Planets* shows how writers and critics are doing just that. Reviewed in full for *Interzone* #255. ★★★★☆

Black Science, Vol. 1: How to Fall Forever (Image Comics), by Rick Remender, Matteo Scalera, Dean White. Begins with a pair of scientists dashing through a bizarre alien world, desperate to get back to the children who will die if they don't get back in time. As the story goes on, it begins to feel a bit like *Sliders* or *Primeval*, one of those shows where characters pitch up in a place and have to get out again. It's better than either of those so far, let's hope that continues. The art is spectacular. ★★★☆☆

Bone and Jewel Creatures (Subterranean Press), by Elizabeth Bear. A superb novella about an elderly woman who takes in a feral child and fits it with a new arm made from jewels and the remains of its own original arm, while facing the challenge of an evil necromancer. It's a Subterranean Press book, but the ebook was available at a very reasonable price via Weightless Books. ★★★★☆

The Book of Iod: Ten Cthulhu Stories (Diversion Books), by Henry Kuttner. Not much Cthulhu, and didn't feel much like Kuttner. ★★★☆☆

BPRD, Vol. 1: Hollow Earth and Other Stories (Dark Horse Comics), by Mike Mignola and friends. Collects one-shots and other stories about Abe Sapien

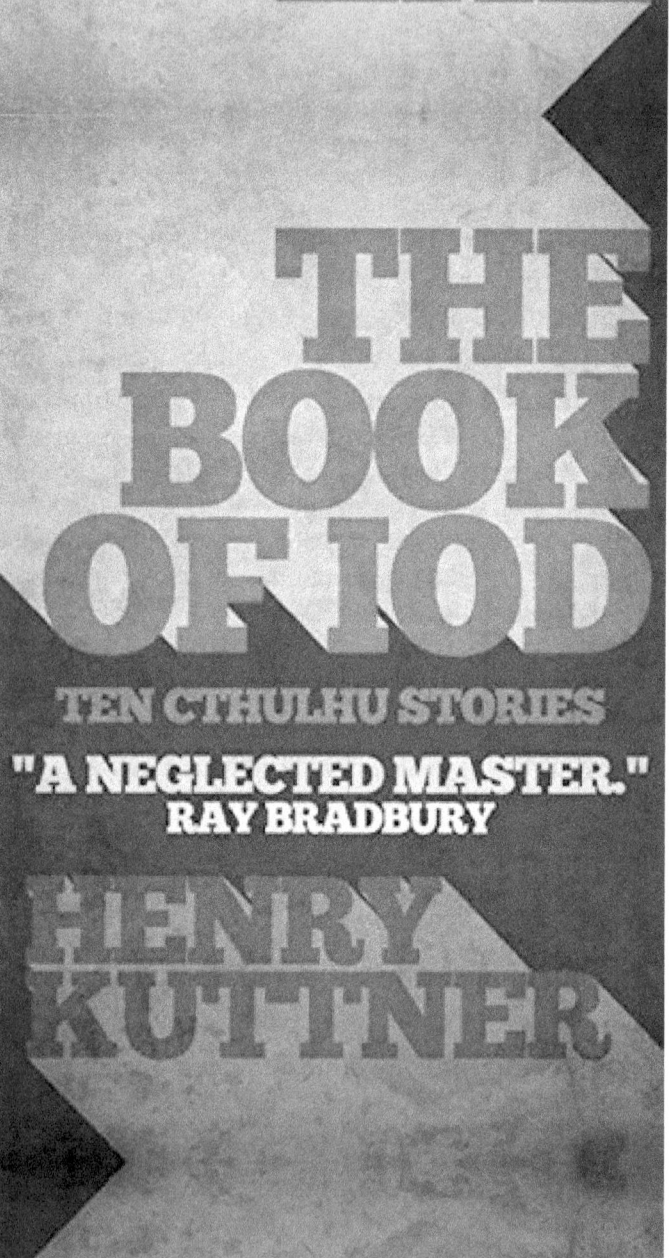

and the other members of the BPRD, the organisation Hellboy works for. ★★★☆☆

BPRD, Vol. 2: The Soul of Venice and Other Stories (Dark Horse Comics), by Mike Mignola, Scott Allie, Michael Avon Oeming, Guy Davis and friends. More great stories about Hellboy's friends and colleagues. ★★★★☆

BPRD, Vol. 3: Plague of Frogs (Dark Horse Comics), by Mike Mignola, Guy Davis and Dave Stewart. The first BPRD volume to collect a single mini-series, this spins out from events in the first Hellboy book. I'd forgotten how much I loved Guy Davis's art on *Sandman Mystery Theatre*; it's brilliant here. ★★★★☆

BPRD: Hell on Earth, Vol. 1: New World (Dark Horse Comics), by Mike Mignola, John Arcudi, Guy Davis and Dave Stewart. Some time after the events that began in *Plague of Frogs* reached their conclusion, the BPRD are working for the UN and investigating the matters the UN wants investigating. Abe Sapien heads off to the woods and encounters an old friend and a demon baby and its giant-sized twin. I enjoyed this a lot. I really like Abe, more even than Hellboy. ★★★★☆

BPRD: Vampire (Dark Horse Comics), by Mike Mignola and Scott Allie. A member of BPRD has had a pair of vampire souls trapped within him (I think) and he wants to find out more about the creatures. I wasn't entirely sure what was going on, but it looked terrific. I'll probably need to re-read all these Hellboy books and spin-offs in order once I have them all. ★★★☆☆

Bravest Warriors, Vol. 1 (KaBOOM!), by Joey Comeau, Mike Holmes, Pendleton Ward and Ryan Pequin. Based on the new science fiction cartoon from

the creator of *Adventure Time*, and just as much fun.
★★★★☆

Buffy the Vampire Slayer, Season 8, Vol. 6: Retreat
(Dark Horse Books), by Jane Espenson, Georges Jeanty
and Joss Whedon. I can't hate any Buffy comic, but
didn't enjoy this as much as hoped. ★★★☆☆

Buffy the Vampire Slayer, Season 8, Vol. 7: Twilight
(Dark Horse Books), by Brad Meltzer, Georges Jeanty
and Joss Whedon. The series gets a bit wobbly.
★★☆☆☆

**Buffy the Vampire Slayer, Season 8, Vol. 8: Last
Gleaming** (Dark Horse Books), by Joss Whedon,
Georges Jeanty and Scott Allie. A disappointing end to
a series that had begun so promisingly. ★★★☆☆

Buffy the Vampire Slayer, Season 9, Vol. 1: Freefall
(Dark Horse Books), by Joss Whedon, Andrew
Chambliss, Georges Jeanty and Karl Moline. An
improvement on Season 8, which by the end I'd gone
off so much that I would never have bought this if the
Kindle edition hadn't been on sale. ★★★☆☆

**Buffy the Vampire Slayer, Season 9, Vol. 2: On Your
Own** (Dark Horse Books), by Andrew Chambliss,
Scott Allie, Georges Jeanty and Cliff Richards. Feels
more like a continuation of the TV series. ★★★★☆

**Buffy the Vampire Slayer, Season 9, Vol. 3:
Guarded** (Dark Horse Books), by Andrew Chambliss,
Jane Espenson, Drew Z. Greenberg, Georges Jeanty,
Karl Moline and Joss Whedon. Buffy has a go at being
a bodyguard, but can she put work before her true
calling? Enjoyable but the emphasis on how easy the
zompires (zombie vampires, created after Buffy's
world was sealed off from magic) are to kill is making
them feel like a negligible threat. ★★★☆☆

Child of a Hidden Sea (Tor Books), by A.M.

Dellamonica. Liked the book, loved the protagonist. A young woman is whisked off to a fantasy world that has the same moon as Earth, where magic works and her birth mother was part of a family of elite couriers. What I liked best was the way she's keen to get photographs of the wildlife and things like that, and is careful to keep her camera charged. The idea of taking a solar powered charger to a fantasy world tickles me. Reviewed in full for *Interzone* #253. ★★★☆☆

Cloud Permutations (PS Publishing), by Lavie Tidhar. Terrific novella about a boy who wants to fly on a world where it isn't allowed. ★★★★☆

Criminal Macabre Omnibus, Vol. 1 (Dark Horse Books), by Steve Niles, Ben Templesmith and Kelley Jones. From the writer of *30 Days of Night*. Cal McDonald is the American equivalent of John Constantine. He is drunker, druggier, more screwed-up, and prefers his friends dead to begin with so that they can't get killed. Weird creatures seek him out and his job is usually to kill them. Stories involve ghouls, vampires, werewolves, a haunted car and a succubus. First half has impressionistic artwork by Ben Templesmith, and the second half has cartoonier art by Kelley Jones, which I think suits the OTT stories a bit better. ★★★☆☆

The Darkness: Accursed, Vol. 2 (Top Cow Productions), by Phil Hester and friends. A colossal improvement on the original run, but disappointing compared to some of the things Phil Hester has been involved in before. (I adored his run as an artist on *Swamp Thing*.) ★★★☆☆

The Darkness: Accursed, Vol. 3 (Top Cow Productions), by Phil Hester and friends. More murky shenanigans. ★★★☆☆

The Darkness: Accursed, Vol. 4 (Top Cow

Productions), by Phil Hester and friends. I should have read a Darkness book before buying so many in a sale. ★★★☆☆

The Delicate Prey (Penguin Books), by Paul Bowles. One of the scariest books I read all year. One creepy story ("The Circular Valley", about a haunted monastery) and two that are terrifying ("The Delicate Prey" and "A Distant Episode", about desert travellers and a foolish professor). ★★★★☆

Doctor Who: The Chains of Olympus (Panini UK Ltd), by Scott Gray, Mike Collins, Martin Geraghty, Dan McDaid. Eleventh Doctor adventures from *Doctor Who Magazine*. The Doctor meets the Greek gods. ★★★☆☆

Doctor Who: Hunters of the Burning Stone (Panini UK Ltd), by Scott Gray, Martin Geraghty, Mike Collins. Eleventh Doctor adventures from the pages of *Doctor Who Magazine*. Sees the return of Ian and Barbara. ★★★☆☆

Doctor Who: Into the Nowhere (BBC Digital), by Jenny Colgan. Novella by Jenny Colgan about the eleventh Doctor and Clara, who end up on a rather nasty planet where skeletons have a tendency to rise up from the ground. An enjoyable little book, perfect for a rainy afternoon. Colgan captures the relationship of Clara and the Doctor rather well. Steven Moffat deliberately built lots of tie-in friendly gaps into their television adventures, so there's plenty of scope for the two of them to travel together again. ★★★☆☆

Doctor Who: Lights Out (Puffin), by Holly Black. The twelfth Doctor is buying coffee for Clara when another person in the queue falls down dead. Somehow manages to have a good handle on Peter Capaldi's Doctor despite being written before his first full episodes were on. ★★★☆☆

Doctor Who: The Ripple Effect (Puffin), by Malorie Blackman. A nice little Doctor Who book. The seventh Doctor and Ace land on Skaro, centre of learning and peace, the Athens of space. Nice to read a Doctor Who book that is actually aimed at children. ★★★☆☆

Doctor Who: Something Borrowed (Puffin), by Richelle Mead. The sixth Doctor and Peri encounter an enemy, who is about to get married. Captures very well what came closest to being good about that period of the show. ★★★☆☆

Drunk with Blood – God's Killings in the Bible (SAB Books), by Steve Wells. Eye-opening account of how many people get killed in the Bible, often for the silliest of reasons. At times you'd think it was the Master or Lex Luthor messing with history. The stuff in here makes the Red Wedding look like a pleasant family gathering. ★★★★★

The Etymologicon: A Circular Stroll Through the Hidden Connections of the English Language (Icon Books), by Mark Forsyth. Fascinating wander through the nooks and crannies of English. Constantly amazing, which is why I liked reading it in bursts. You can only do so many double-takes a day before your neck gets tired. ★★★★★

Fatale, Vol. 1: Death Chases Me (Image Comics), by Ed Brubaker and Sean Phillips. Graphic novel written by Ed Brubaker and drawn by Sean Phillips, who previously collaborated on several well-regarded crime comics. It is the story of Jo, an ageless, beautiful femme fatale (on double duty as this book's McGuffin), and the men who enter her life. In the forties that was a US soldier, who has become by the fifties a corrupt, dying police officer who barely visits her any more, ashamed of his own ageing. Dominic Haines is a married journalist who meets her in the fifties. Nicolas Lash is Dominic's inheritor, who discovers among his godfather's papers an unpublished manuscript from 1957, "The Losing Side of Eternity". But before he can read it weird guys with bowler hats, round glasses and guns pull up outside. "And I realised *exactly* how far out in the woods I *actually* was. And how far away the police would be." Jo comes to the rescue (well, almost) and the convalescent Lash reads his godfather's story, of black magic, cultists and Lovecraftian gods. Dave Stewart (presumably not the one with spiky headphones) does a wonderful job on colours, finding exactly the right tone. ★★★★☆

Fear Itself (Marvel), by Matt Fraction and Stuart Immonen. An underwhelming crossover story. Odin has given up on Earth, but Thor and the Avengers think there is still hope. ★★★☆☆

G.I. Joe: Classics, Vol. 4 (IDW Publishing), by Larry Hama, Rod Whigham, Frank Springer, Mark Bright, Bob Camp and Rod Wigham. Collection of Marvel's attempt to create decent comics based on the daft soldier toys. ★★★☆☆

The Gifts of War (Penguin Books), by Margaret Drabble. Two excellent stories by Margaret Drabble, editor of the equally excellent *Oxford Companion to English Literature*. The first is "The Gifts of War", about a downtrodden mum who has been saving up to buy her child a special present, and a young anti-war protester who doesn't think toyshops should sell a particular kind of toy. Each has their own half of the story, but it's holding each in your mind at once that renders the story so devastating. The second story is "Hassan's Tower", about newlyweds having a terrible honeymoon in a hot country who climb the stairs of a random building. Like *The Delicate Prey*, the book is a Penguin Mini Modern. I'm grateful for how many wonderful writers that series has induced me to try for the first time. I bought the box set of them for myself as an expensive birthday present, and it was some of the best money I've ever spent. ★★★★★

The Glorkian Warrior Eats Adventure Pie (First: Second), by James Kochalka. Another fab adventure for the glorious idiot and his friends. Full review to follow next issue. ★★★★☆

God's War (Del Rey), by Kameron Hurley. Grimdark science fiction about an unlikeable mercenary and her gang. Nyx used to be a Bel Dame, sent by the government to take the heads of boys running away from the war, but now she's freelance. Her world is one of strong religion and what seems to us like magic, where insect life is the basis for technology and wombs can be dropped off at organ banks to avoid putting them in any danger. It's a bit of a grind, full of torture, misery, and characters who hate each other, but it was good. Reminded me of things like John Carpenter's *Escape from New York* and Roger Zelazny's *Damnation Alley*. A bit like *2000AD* if it were written by John Brunner instead of Pat Mills & co. ★★★☆☆

The Goon, Vol. 0: Rough Stuff (Dark Horse Comics), by Eric Powell. A mob enforcer is secretly also the mob boss, and his main rival is the leader of a zombie gang. These collect very early issues, from before Eric Powell was really happy with it, but it seemed pretty good to me. ★★★☆☆

The Goon, Vol. 1: Nothin' But Misery (Dark Horse Comics), by Eric Powell and Robin Powell. More adventures of the Goon. It's like a cartoonish, supernatural version of *Sin City*. ★★★☆☆

Gorel and the Pot-Bellied God (PS Publishing), by Lavie Tidhar. Not, as a previous issue of this magazine had it, Gorel and the Pot-Bellied Pig! This is, as its subtitle tells us, a guns and sorcery novella. Gorel was "cast out of Goliris", "exiled to the harsh lands of Lower Kidron", where he makes his way as a hired hand, riding an insectoid Graal, hoping always to return home to avenge his family and punish his betrayers. In this story he encounters the froggish falang and the god they worship. This novella dates back to 2011, and ever since this review has glared balefully at me, even while I've reviewed several of the author's other books. That was just because I read it quickly in amongst a bunch of other books, not because I didn't enjoy it enough to write a review. Far from it: I thought this was terrific, and began a run of Tidhar's books that have made him one of my favourite authors. It's an extremely interesting book, reminding me of Elric in the way it attacks the conventions of the genre. You read it assuming that Gorel is a Conan-type hero, but as he does bad things it's almost as if the author is saying, this is your hero? He's a drug addict, injecting himself with gods' dust, and he's still your hero? What about when he does this? Or this?! How bad can a badass hero get before the reader stops admiring them? ★★★★☆

Guardians of the Galaxy, Vol. 1: Legacy (Marvel), by Dan Abnett, Andy Lanning, Paul Pelletier. Inspiration for the film, with a similar spark. Here the new Guardians assemble in the aftermath of a galactic crisis. ★★★☆☆

Half a King (Audible), by Joe Abercrombie. Deposed boy king tries to survive on his wits. Good, especially in the way it reflects on whether fighting his way back to power benefits the country or just him. ★★★☆☆

Harley Quinn Vol. 1: Hot in the City (DC Comics), by Jimmy Palmiotti and Amanda Conner. Ropey comic about the Joker's girlfriend. Trying to be *Deadpool* or *Hitman* with added cheesecake, and doesn't work. At the time of writing it's only 50p or so on Kindle. I wouldn't pay much more than that for it. ★★☆☆☆

Hellblazer: City of Demons (Vertigo), by Si Spencer and Sean Murphy. Very good miniseries about John Constantine's half-demon blood being used to infect people in London. Excellent artwork. Would have loved a full run in this style. ★★★★☆

Hellboy in Hell, Vol. 1: The Descent (Dark Horse Books), by Mike Mignola. Hellboy has been killed and gone to hell, where he wanders around and meets various demons, including (maybe) his dad. Gorgeous art, but it's just the beginning of a story. ★★★☆☆

How to Write Everything (Oberon Books), by David Quantick. Okay, with some good advice, but a bit thin, given how much experience he has. For example he says he's written ten thousand reviews but only talks about it for half a page (and not all the advice is admirable: "If you are are going to make a review up, make it look convincing"). On interviewing, I got a lot more out of Jason Arnopp's *How to Interview Doctor Who, Ozzy Osbourne and Everyone Else.* ★★★☆☆

The Kosher Guide to Imaginary Animals (Cheeky Frawg Books), by Ann VanderMeer and Jeff VanderMeer. Brief but amusing book exploring whether various imaginary animals would be considered kosher or not, and how one might cook them. ★★★☆☆

Lagoon (Hodder & Stoughton), by Nnedi Okorafor. Aliens land in the ocean off Lagos, and one of them comes out and takes human form. The city isn't ready for them. Reviewed in full for *Interzone* #252. ★★★★☆

Lobster Johnson, Vol. 1: Iron Prometheus (Dark Horse Books), by Mike Mignola, Jason Armstrong and

Dave Stewart. A superhero fighting Nazi spies in a spin-off from Hellboy and the BPRD. ★★★☆☆

Magnus Robot Fighter Archive, Vol. 2 (Dark Horse Comics), by Russ Manning and Philip Simon. Collection of old comics about a guy with super-strength who battles robots who go bad, and when necessary the people who control them. Notable for Russ Manning's art and the way the bad robots shout "Squeee!" when he knocks off their heads. ★★★☆☆

The Many Adventures of Miranda Mercury: Time Runs Out (Archaia), by Brandon Thomas and Lee Ferguson. Space adventure. Enjoyable, but falls a bit short of its very high ambitions. ★★★☆☆

Nemo: The Roses of Berlin (Top Shelf Productions), by Alan Moore and Kevin O'Neill. These short Nemo books in the world of the League of Extraordinary Gentlemen are instant purchases for me. This one brings in characters from *Metropolis* and *The Great Dictator*. ★★★★☆

Of Whimsies & Noubles (PS Publishing), by Matthew Hughes. Another fabulous Luff Imbry novella. In this one he is apprehended and sent to a prison world. ★★★★☆

Planet of the Apes, Vol. 1: The Long War (BOOM! Studios), by Daryl Gregory. Set in the continuity (if you can call it that) of the original film series, this was okay but not much fun. ★★★☆☆

Rat Queens, Vol. 1: Sass & Sorcery (Image Comics), by Kurtis J. Wiebe and Roc Upchurch. Funny comic about a group of adventurers whose world is modelled after our world's roleplaying games. ★★★★☆

Rebel at the End of Time (PS Publishing), by Steve Aylett and Michael Moorcock. A short novel which throws Leo Del Toro, a 21st century Che Guevera, into

of
WHIMSIES
& NOUBLES

MATTHEW
HUGHES

the bewildering world of Michael Moorcock's brilliant Dancers at the End of Time trilogy, where he must battle his despair among people for whom action is meaningless, novelty everything. The difficulty of reading the story comes from the misunderstandings of the people of the future, which leads to surprises in every sentence. Aylett's story is a great addition to the End of Time, in that it shows us (or speculates on) how a different type of protagonist would handle it. The great man himself Michael Moorcock contributes a twenty-page story to the book, "Sumptuous Dress", which comes close to causing a meltdown in the space-time continuum by crossing the end of time with the equally confusing Second Ether, producing more bafflement than most readers will be able to bear in a single story ★★★★☆

Secret Lives (Cheeky Frawg Books), by Jeff VanderMeer. A series of stories written for and about the people who bought the special edition of one of the author's other books. Not at all as throwaway as their provenance might lead you to expect; some stories are downright excellent. ★★★☆☆

Sin City, Vol. 3: The Big Fat Kill (Dark Horse Comics), by Frank Miller. The last book I read by Frank Miller was so bad that I'd almost forgotten how good he can be. ★★★★☆

Sin City, Vol. 6: Booze, Broads & Bullets (Dark Horse Comics), by Frank Miller. Short stories collected from various *Sin City* one-shots. ★★★☆☆

Smiler's Fair (Hodder & Stoughton), by Rebecca Levene. Slightly disappointing and unimaginative fantasy. Reviewed in full for *Interzone* #254. ★★★☆☆

Star Trek: New Visions (IDW Publishing), by John Byrne. Photo-stories based on the original TV series.

Not as much fun as expected. Lots of recapping.
★★☆☆☆

Star Wars Tales, Vol. 1 (Dark Horse Books), by Jim Woodring and Dave Land. Entertaining anthology of non-canonical stories. ★★★☆☆

Steed and Mrs. Peel: The Golden Game (BOOM! Studios), by Grant Morrison, Anne Caulfield and Ian Gibson. Liked it, but a problem with the colour separations made it difficult to read. ★★★☆☆

Suddenly, Zombies (self-published), by Amanda C. Davis. Quirky pair of short stories, one about zombies on a spaceship, the other about giant zombie gorillas. Cheap and cheerful. ★★★☆☆

The Unquiet House (Jo Fletcher Books), by Alison Littlewood. A woman moves to a haunted house, and we travel back in time to find out who haunts it and why. Several terrifying scenes. Reviewed in full for *Black Static #43*. ★★★☆☆

Werewolves of Montpellier (Fantagraphics), by Jason. A thief who dresses as a werewolf on the job attracts the attention of the real thing. ★★★★☆

Willful Child (Tor Books), by Steven Erikson. *Star Trek* in the style of *Archer*. Reviewed in full for *Interzone* #256. ★★★☆☆

Winter Well: Speculative Novellas About Older Women (Crossed Genres), by Kay T. Holt (ed.). A decent book collecting four novellas, including "Copper" by Minerva Zimmerman, "The Other World" by Anna Caro, and "To the Edges" by M. Fenn, which begins with an older woman being fired from her job on the day of a terrorist atrocity. "The Second Wife" by Marissa James was for me the best story here. It's a fantasy or science fantasy story about a second wife whose husband is killed by a conqueror who marries

her for her magic. Before he can really set her to work, visitors come from the south, one of whom burns brightly in her mystical visions. Reminiscent in some ways of the Darkover series, but much better. The story has a mature approach to transgender issues.
★★★☆☆

X-Men: The Complete Age of Apocalypse Epic, Book 1 (Marvel), by Scott Lobdell, John Francis Moore, Howard Mackie, Brian K. Vaughan, Ralph Macchio, Terry Kavanagh and Judd Winick. A barely readable muddle set in an alternative X-Men universe.
★★☆☆☆

Yuki vs Panda, Vol. 1: Revenge. Lust. Karaoke (Duskleaf Media), by Graham Misiurak, Nick Dunec and A.L. Jones. Short and not very good graphic novel about a girl whose nemesis is a panda. ★★☆☆☆

Also Received, But Not Yet Reviewed

Notes by Stephen Theaker

Brown, Timothy, *Polaris* (PS Publishing)

Bursztynski, Sue (ed.), *Andromeda Spaceways Inflight Magazine #60*

Dunn, Robin Wyatt, *A Map of Kex's Face* (John Ott): "Kex is the administrator of the Eidon Academy, a college with an interdimensional porthole on campus, and the intellectual center of a recently seceded Southern California."

Edginton, Ian, and INJ Culbard, *Brass Sun* (Rebellion)

Elliott, Kate, *The Very Best of Kate Elliott* (Tachyon Publications)

Farrell, Kate, *My Name Is Mary Sutherland* (PS Publishing)

Gevers, Nick (ed.), *Far Voyager: Postscripts 32/33* (PS Publishing): includes stories by Andrew Hook, Thana Niveau and Alison Littlewood.

Joshi, S.T. (ed.), *Letters to Arkham: The Letters of Ramsey Campbell and August Derleth 1961–1971* (PS Publishing)

Magrs, Paul, *The Brenda and Effie Mysteries: The Woman in a Black Beehive* (Bafflegab Productions)

Morrison, Grant, and Steve Yeowell, *Zenith Phase One* (Rebellion)

Morrison, Grant, and Steve Yeowell, *Zenith Phase Two* (Rebellion)

Murphy, Mark, *Minology* (Netherworld Books)

Parks, Richard, *To Break the Demon Gate* (PS Publishing)

Pederson, Nate (ed.), *The Starry Wisdom Library* (PS Publishing)

Purser-Hallard, Philip, and others, *Tales of the Great Detectives: Sherlock Holmes in the City of the Saved* (Obverse Books)

Schweitzer, Darrell (ed.), *That Is Not Dead* (PS Publishing): subtitled *Tales of the Cthulhu Mythos Through the Centuries.*

Tidhar, Lavie, *Black Gods Kiss* (PS Publishing): book of stories about Gorel.

Unsworth, Simon Kurt, *Strange Gateways* (PS Publishing)

Wagner, John, Alan Grant and Ron Smith, *Judge Dredd: The Daily Dredds 1981–1986* (Rebellion)

Wagner, John, and friends, *Predator versus Judge Dredd versus Aliens* (2000 AD/Dark Horse)

Forthcoming Attractions

Expect **Theaker's Quarterly Fiction #51** in April as
we shift (probably) to a four-monthly schedule.
Deadline for submissions is **February 28**.

Most weeks begin with a new review on our blog:
www.theakersquarterly.blogspot.com

Stephen tweets every few days or so at:
www.twitter.com/Rolnikov

Our email address is:
theakersquarterlyfiction@gmail.com

www.ingramcontent.com/pod-product-compliance
Lightning Source LLC
Chambersburg PA
CBHW071240170626
46809CB00001B/30